50¢

SO-AAZ-814

Ransom

GARRANS
28.95

Con

Julie Garwood

Ransom

SS
FIC
GARWOOD, J.

WHEELER
PUBLISHING, INC.
ROCKLAND, MA

★ AN AMERICAN COMPANY ★

HUNTINGTON BEACH PUBLIC LIBRARY
7111 Talbert Avenue
Huntington Beach, CA 92648

M 41285080

Copyright © 1999 by Julie Garwood
All rights reserved.

Published in Large Print by arrangement with Pocket Books, a division of Simon & Schuster, Inc. in the United States and Canada.

Wheeler Large Print Book Series.

Set in 16 pt Plantin.

Library of Congress Cataloging-in-Publication Data

Garwood, Julie.
  Ransom / Julie Garwood.
    p. (large print) cm.(Wheeler large print book series)
  ISBN 1-56895-722-X (hardcover)
  1. Great Britain—History—John, 1199-1216—Fiction. 2. Scotland—History—1057-1603—Fiction. 3. Historical fiction. gsafd. 4. Historical fiction. gsafd. 5. Love stories. gsafd. 6. Large type books.
I. Title. II. Series
[PS3557.A8427R36 1999]
813'.54—dc21
                                                                        99-030864
                                                                              CIP

For Bryan Michael Garwood,
business and law graduate extraordinaire—

With your keen mind, your passionate soul,
and your merciful heart, there's no
stopping you.

As you embark on this most noble career,
remember: "Justice is a machine that, when
someone has given it a starting push, rolls
of itself."
Galsworthy, *Justice II*

Start pushing, Bryan

PROLOGUE

England, in the reign of King Richard I

Bad things always happen during the night. In the dark hours of the night Gillian's mother died struggling to bring a new life into the world, and a young, unthinking servant, wishing to be the first to impart the sorrowful news, awakened the two little girls to tell them their dear mama was dead. Two nights later, they were once again shaken awake to hear that their infant brother, Ranulf, named in honor of their father, had also passed on. His frail body hadn't been able to take the strain of being born a full two months early.

Gillian was afraid of the dark. She waited until the servant had left her bedroom, then slid down from the big bed on her stomach to the cold stone floor. Barefoot, she ran to the forbidden passage, a secret hallway that led to her sister's chamber and also to the steep steps that ended in the tunnels below the kitchens. She barely squeezed behind the chest her papa had placed in front of the narrow door in the wall to discourage his daughters from going back and forth. He had warned over and over again that it was a secret, for the love of God, only to be used under the most dire of circumstances, and certainly not for play. Why, even his loyal servants didn't know about the passageways built into

1

three of the bedchambers, and he was determined to keep it that way. He was also extremely concerned that his daughters would fall down the steps and break their pretty little necks, and he often threatened to paddle their backsides if he ever caught them there. It was dangerous, and it was forbidden.

But on that terrible night of loss and sorrow, Gillian didn't care if she got into trouble. She was scared, and whenever she got scared, she ran to her older sister, Christen, for comfort. Managing to get the door open only a crack, Gillian cried out for Christen and waited for her to come. Her sister reached in, latched onto Gillian's hand and pulled her through, then helped her climb up into her bed. The little girls clung to each other under the thick blankets and cried while their papa's tormented screams of anguish and desolation echoed throughout the halls. They could hear him shouting their mama's name over and over and over again. Death had entered their peaceful home and filled it with grief.

The family wasn't given time to heal, for the monsters of the night weren't through preying on them. It was in the dead of night that the infidels invaded their home and Gillian's family was destroyed.

Papa woke her up when he came rushing into her chamber carrying Christen in his arms. His faithful soldiers William—Gillian's favorite because he gave her honeyed treats when her papa wasn't watching—and Lawrence and Tom and Spencer followed behind him. Their expressions were grim. Gillian sat up in bed and rubbed her eyes with the backs of her hands as her father handed Christen to Lawrence and hurried to her. He placed the glowing candle on the chest next to her bed, then sat down beside her and with a trembling hand gently brushed her hair out of her eyes.

Her father looked terribly sad, and Gillian thought she knew the reason why.

"Did Mama die again, Papa?" she asked worriedly.

"For the love of... no, Gillian," he answered, his voice weary.

"Did she come back home, then?"

"Ah, my sweet lamb, we've been over this again and again. Your mama isn't ever going to come home. The dead can't come back. She's in heaven now. Try to understand."

"Yes, Papa," she whispered.

She heard the faint echo of shouts coming from the floor below and then noticed that her father was wearing his chain mail.

"Are you going to battle now, for the love of God, Papa?"

"Yes," he answered. "But first I must get you and your sister to safety."

He reached for the clothes Gillian's maid, Liese, had laid out for tomorrow and hastily dressed his daughter. William moved forward and knelt on one knee to put Gillian's shoes on her.

Her papa had never dressed her before, and she didn't know what to make of it. "Papa, I got to take my sleeping gown off

3

before I put my clothes on, and I got to let Liese brush my hair."

"We won't worry about your hair tonight."

"Papa, is it dark outside?" she asked as he slipped the bliaut over her head.

"Yes, Gillian, it's dark."

"Do I got to go outside in the dark?"

He could hear the fear in her voice and tried to calm her. "There will be torches to light the way and you won't be alone."

"Are you going with Christen and me?"

Her sister answered. "No, Gillian," she shouted from across the room. "'Cause Papa has to stay here and fight the battle, for the love of God," she said, repeating her father's often used expression. "Don't you, Papa?"

Lawrence told Christen to hush. "We don't want anyone to know you're leaving," he explained in a whisper. "Can you be real quiet now?"

Christen eagerly nodded. "I can," she whispered back. "I can be awful quiet when I got to, and when I..."

Lawrence put his hand over her mouth. "Hush, golden girl."

William lifted Gillian into his arms and carried her out of the chamber and down the dark hallway to her father's room. Spencer and Tom guided the way, carrying bright candles to light the corridor. Giant shadows danced along the stone walls keeping pace with them, the only sound the hard clicking of their boots against the cobbled floor. Gillian became fearful and put her arms around the

4

soldier's neck, then tucked her head under his chin.

"I don't like the shadows," she whimpered.

"They won't harm you," he soothed.

"I want my mama, William."

"I know you do, honey bear."

His silly nickname for her always made her smile, and she suddenly wasn't afraid any longer. She saw her papa rush past her to lead the way into his chamber, and she would have called out to him, but William put his finger to his lips, reminding her that she was to be quiet.

As soon as they were all inside the bedroom, Tom and Spencer began to slide a low chest along the wall so that they could open the secret door. The rusty hinges groaned and squealed like an angry boar whose mouth was being pried open.

Lawrence and William had to put the little girls down in order to soak and light the torches. The second their backs were turned, both Christen and Gillian ran to their father who was down on his knees leaning over another chest at the foot of the bed and sorting through his belongings. They flanked his sides and stretched up on tiptoes, their hands on the rim of the chest so they too could peer inside.

"What are you looking for, Papa?" Christen asked.

"This," he answered as he lifted the sparkling jeweled box.

"It's awful pretty, Papa," Christen said. "Can I have it?"

"Can I have it too?" Gillian chimed in.

"No," he answered. "The box belongs to Prince John, and I mean to see that he gets it back."

Still down on his knees, their father turned toward Christen and grabbed her arm, pulling her close as she tried to wiggle away.

"You're hurting me, Papa."

"I'm sorry, love," he said, immediately lessening his grip. "I didn't mean to hurt you, but I do need you to pay attention to what I'm going to tell you. Can you do that, Christen?"

"Yes, Papa, I can pay attention."

"That's good," he praised. "I want you to take this box with you when you leave. Lawrence will protect you from harm and take you to a safe place far away from here, and he'll help you hide this evil treasure until the time is right and I can come for you and take the box to Prince John. You mustn't tell anyone about this treasure, Christen."

Gillian ran around her father to stand next to Christen. "Can she tell me, Papa?"

Her father ignored her question and waited for Christen to answer.

"I won't tell," she promised.

"I won't tell no one neither." Gillian vehemently nodded to prove she meant what she said.

Their father continued to ignore his younger daughter for the moment because he was intent on making Christen understand the importance of what he was telling her. "No one must ever know you have the box, child. Now watch what I'm doing," he ordered. "I'm going to wrap the box in this tunic."

"So no one will see it?" Christen asked.

"That's right," he whispered. "So no one will see it."

"But I already seen it, Papa," Gillian blurted out.

"I know you did," he agreed. He looked up at Lawrence then. "She's too young... I'm asking too much of her. Dear God, how can I let my babies go?"

Lawrence stepped forward. "I'm going to protect Christen with my life, and I'll make certain no one sees the box."

William also rushed to offer his pledge. "No harm will come to Lady Gillian," he vowed. "I give you my word, Baron Ranulf. My life to keep her safe."

The vehemence in his voice was a comfort to the baron and he nodded to let both soldiers know that his trust in them was absolute.

Gillian tugged on her father's elbow to get his attention. She wasn't about to be left out. When her papa wrapped the pretty box in one of his tunics and gave it to Christen, Gillian clasped her hands together in anticipation, for she assumed that since her sister had been given a present, she would be getting one too. Even though Christen was the firstborn and three years older than Gillian, their father had never shown favoritism for one over the other.

It was difficult for her to be patient, but Gillian tried. She watched as her father pulled

Christen into his arms and kissed her forehead and hugged her tight. "Don't forget your papa," he whispered. "Don't forget me."

He reached for Gillian next. She threw herself into his arms and kissed him soundly on his whiskered cheek.

"Papa, don't you have a pretty box for me?"

"No, my sweet. You're going to go with William now. Take hold of his hand—"

"But Papa, I got to have a box too. Don't you have one for me to carry?"

"The box isn't a present, Gillian."

"But, Papa—"

"I love you," he said, blinking back the tears as he fiercely clasped her against the cold chain mail of his hauberk. "God keep you safe."

"You're squishing me, Papa. Can I have a turn holding the box? Please, Papa?"

Ector, her father's chief reeve, barged into the room. His shout so startled Christen she dropped the treasure. The box rolled out of the tunic onto the floor and clattered across the stones. In the firelight from the flaming torches, the rubies and sapphires and emeralds imbedded in the case came to life, glistening and twinkling brightly like sparkling stars that had fallen from the sky.

Ector stopped short, startled by the dazzling beauty that tumbled before him.

"What is it, Ector?" her father said.

Intent on giving his baron the urgent message from Bryant, the baron's commander in arms, Ector seemed barely to be paying attention to what he was doing as he scooped up the box and handed it to Lawrence. His focus returned to his leader. "Milord, Bryant bade me to come and tell you that young Alford the Red and his soldiers have breached the inner bailey."

"Was Baron Alford seen?" William blurted out the question. "Or does he continue to hide from us?"

Ector glanced back at the soldier. "I don't know," he confessed before turning to the baron once again. "Bryant also bade me tell you that your men are calling for you, milord."

"I shall go at once," the baron announced as he gained his feet. He motioned for Ector to leave the chamber, then followed him, pausing in the doorway to gaze upon his beautiful daughters one last time. Christen, with her golden curls and cherub cheeks, and little Gillian, with her mother's brilliant green eyes and pale skin, looked in jeopardy of bursting into tears.

"Go now, and God keep you safe," the baron ordered harshly.

And then he was gone. The soldiers hurried to the passage. Tom went ahead to unlatch the door at the end of the tunnel and make certain the area hadn't been breached by the enemy. Lawrence held Christen's hand and led the way into the dark corridor with his fiery torch. Gillian was right behind her sister, clinging to William's hand. Spencer followed them, then reached through the opening to drag the chest back before he closed the door.

9

"Papa didn't tell me he had a secret door," Gillian whispered to Christen.

"He didn't tell me neither," her sister whispered back. "Maybe he forgot."

Gillian tugged on William's hand to get his attention. "Me and Christen got a secret door too, but it's in our bedrooms. We can't tell nobody about it though 'cause it's a secret. Papa says he'll paddle us good if we tell. Did you know it was a secret, William?" The soldier didn't answer her, but she wasn't deterred by his silence. "You know where our passage goes? Papa says when we come out of our tunnel, we can see the fish in his pond. Is that where we're going?"

"No," William answered. "This tunnel will take us underneath the wine cellar. We're getting close to the steps now, and I want you to be real quiet."

Gillian kept a worried eye on the shadows following her along the wall. She moved closer to William and then turned her attention to her sister. Christen was clasping the jeweled box against her chest, but an edge of the tunic was dangling down below her elbow, and Gillian couldn't resist reaching for it.

"I got to have a turn holding the box. Papa said."

Christen was outraged. "No, he didn't say," she cried. She twisted toward Lawrence so Gillian couldn't get near the box, and then tattled on her. "Lawrence, Gillian told a lie. Papa said I was supposed to have the box, not her."

10

Gillian was determined. "But I got to have a turn," she told her sister as she once again tried to grab hold of the tunic. She pulled back when she thought she heard a sound behind her. She turned to look. The stairway was pitch-black, and she couldn't see anything, but she was certain that there were monsters lurking in the shadows waiting to grab her, maybe even a fiery dragon. Frightened, she held tight to the soldier's hand and squeezed up against his side.

"I don't like it here," she cried. "Carry me, William."

Just as the soldier bent down to lift her up with his free arm, one of the shadows against the wall leapt out at her. Gillian screamed in terror, stumbled, and fell into Christen.

Her sister shouted, "No, it's mine," and swung toward Gillian as the shadow barreled into William. The blow struck William behind his knees and threw him into Lawrence. The steps were slick with moisture dripping down from the walls, and the men were too close to the edge to brace themselves. They plunged headfirst into the black hole with the girls. Sparks from the torches flew about them as the fiery balls cascaded down the stairs ahead of them.

William desperately tried to enfold the child as their bodies plummeted down the jagged steps, but he couldn't shield her completely, and Gillian's chin struck the sharp stone.

Stunned by the blow, she slowly sat up and looked about her. Blood poured onto her gown, and when she saw the blood on her hands, she began to scream. Her sister lay beside her, facedown on the floor, not making a sound.

"Christen, help me," Gillian sobbed. "Wake up. I don't like it here. Wake up."

William struggled to his feet with the hysterical child and, holding her tight against his chest, ran through the tunnel. "Hush, child, hush," he whispered over and over again.

Lawrence followed with Christen. Blood trickled down from the cut high on her forehead.

"Lawrence, you and Tom take Christen on to the creek. Spencer and I will meet you there," William shouted.

"Come with us now," Lawrence urged over Gillian's screams.

"The child's in a bad way. She needs stitches," William called back. "Go now. We'll catch up with you. God's speed," he added as he rushed ahead.

"Christen," Gillian screamed. "Christen, don't leave me."

When they neared the door, William cupped his hand over Gillian's mouth and pleaded with her to be quiet. He and Spencer took her to the tanner's cottage on the edge of the outer bailey so that Maude, the tanner's wife, could sew the injury. The underside of Gillian's chin was completely flayed open.

Both soldiers held the child down while Maude worked on her. The battle raged dangerously close, and the noise became so deafening they had to shout to be heard.

12

"Finish with the child," William ordered the woman. "We must get her to safety before it's too late. Hurry," he shouted as he rushed outside to stand guard.

Maude tied a knot in the string, then clipped the threads. As quickly as she could manage, she wrapped a thick bandage around Gillian's neck and chin.

Spencer lifted the little girl and followed William outside. The enemy had set fire to the thatched roofs of several of the huts with their flaming arrows, and in the bright light, the three ran toward the hill where their mounts waited.

They were halfway up the incline when a troop of soldiers came swarming over the crest. More of the enemy cut off their retreat at the bottom. Escape was impossible, but the two valiant men still held steadfast to their duty. With Gillian on the ground between them, their legs the only barrier shielding her from the attack, they stood with their backs to each other, raised their swords high, and rendered their final battle cry. The two noble soldiers died as they had lived, with honor and courage protecting the innocent.

One of Alford's commanders, recognizing the child, carried her back to the great hall. Liese, Gillian's maid, spotted her when she came inside with the soldier and boldly broke away from the group of servants huddled together in the corner under the watchful eye of the enemy's guard. She pleaded with the soldier to let her take over the care of the little girl. Fortunately, the commander considered Gillian a nuisance and was happy to be rid of her. He ordered Liese to take Gillian upstairs and then ran back outside to join in the fight.

Gillian appeared to be in a stupor. Liese grabbed her and raced up the stairs and across the balcony toward the child's room to get away from the massacre. Panic seized her as she reached for the door latch. She was clawing at it and silently crying when a sudden crash made her jump. She turned just as the heavy oak doors leading to the great hall burst open and soldiers poured inside with their bloody battle axes raised and their swords drawn. Crazed with power, they swung their weapons against the weak and the defenseless. The unarmed men and women held their hands up as shields in a pitiful attempt to ward off the enemy's razor sharp swords. It was a needless slaughter. Horrified, Liese fell to her knees, closed her eyes, and covered her ears so she wouldn't see or hear her friends' desperate pleas for mercy.

Gillian stood passively next to Liese, but when she saw her father being dragged inside, she ran to the banister rail and knelt down. "Papa," she whispered, and then she saw a man in a gold cape raise his sword over her father. "Papa!" she screamed.

Those were the last words she spoke. From that moment, Gillian retreated into a world of numb silence.

Two weeks later, the young man who had

seized control of her father's holding, Baron Alford the Red of Lockmiere, called her before him to decide what was to be done with her, and without speaking a single word, she let him know what was in her mind and her heart.

Liese held Gillian's hand and walked into the great hall to meet the monster who had killed the child's father. Alford, barely old enough to be called a man, was an evil, power-hungry demon, and Liese was no fool. She knew that with the snap of his fingers or a wave of his hand, he could order both their deaths.

Gillian jerked away from Liese just inside the entrance and walked forward alone. She stopped when she reached the long table where Alford and his young companions dined. Without a hint of expression on her face, and with her hands hanging limply at her sides, she stood motionless, staring vacantly at the baron.

He had a pheasant leg in one hand and a wedge of black bread in the other. Specks of grease and meat clung to the red scraggy stubble on his chin. He ignored the child for several minutes while he devoured his food, and after he had tossed the bones over his shoulder, he turned to her.

"How old are you, Gillian?" Alford waited a full minute before trying again. "I asked you a question," he muttered, trying to control his rising temper.

"She cannot be more than four years old," one of his friends volunteered.

"I'd wager she's past five," his cohort suggested. "She's small, but she could even be six."

Alford raised his hand for silence while his eyes continued to bore into the little girl. "It's a simple question. Answer me, and while you're at it, tell me what you think I should do with you. My father's confessor believes you can't speak because the Devil has taken possession of your soul. He pleads the right to force the demon out, using very unpleasant methods. Would you like me to tell you exactly what he would do?" he asked. "No, I don't suppose you would," he added with a smirk. "Torture will be necessary, of course, for it's the only way to get the demons out, or so I'm told. Would you like to be strapped down to a table for hour upon hour while my confessor works on you? I have the power to order it done. Now answer my questions and be quick about it. Tell me your age," he demanded in a snarl.

Silence was her response. Chilling silence. Alford could see that his threats didn't faze her. He thought she might be too simpleminded to understand. She was her father's daughter after all, and what a naive, stupid fool he had been to believe that Alford was his friend.

"Perhaps she isn't answering you because she doesn't know how old she is," his friend suggested. "Get on with the important matter," he urged. "Ask her about the box."

Alford nodded agreement. "Now, Gillian," he began, his tone as sour as vinegar, "your father stole a very valuable box from Prince John, and I mean to get it back for him. There were pretty jewels on the top and sides of the case. If you saw it, you would remember it," he added. "Did you or your sister see this treasure? Answer me," he ordered, his voice shrill with his frustration. "Did you see your father hide the box? Did you?"

She didn't give any indication that she had heard a word he'd said. She simply continued to look at him. The young baron let out a sigh of vexation, then decided to stare her into timidity.

In the space of an indrawn breath, the child's expression changed from indifference to loathing. The hatred burning bright in her eyes quickly unnerved him and made the hair on the back of his neck stand up and the gooseflesh rise up on his forearms. It was unholy for a child of such tender years to show such intensity.

She frightened him. Infuriated by his own bizarre reaction to the girl who was little more than a baby, Alford resorted to cruelty once again. "You're a sickly looking child, aren't you, with your pale skin and drab brown hair? Your sister was the pretty one, wasn't she? Tell me, Gillian, were you jealous of her? Is that why you pushed her down the stairs? The woman who sewed you up told me you and Christen both went down the stairs, and one of the soldiers who was with you told the woman you pushed your sister. Christen's dead, you know, and it's all your fault." He leaned forward and pointed a long, bony finger in her face. "You're going to live with that black sin for the rest of your life, however short that might be. I've decided to send you to the end of the earth," he added offhandedly. "To the bitter, cold north of England where you will live with the heathens until the day comes that I have need for you again. Now get you out of my sight. You make my flesh crawl."

Trembling with fear, Liese stepped forward. "Milord, may I accompany the child north to look after her?"

Alford turned his attention to the maid cowering near the entrance and openly cringed at the sight of her scarred face. "One witch to look after another?" he scoffed. "I don't care if you go or stay. Do what you will, but get her out of here now so that my friends and I will not have to suffer her fetid stare a moment longer."

Hearing the tremor in his own voice sent Alford into a rage. He picked up a heavy wooden bowl from the table and hurled it at the child. It sailed past her head, narrowly missing her. Gillian neither flinched nor blinked. She simply continued to stand where she was, her green eyes glistening with hatred.

Was she looking at his soul? The thought sent a shiver down Alford's spine.

"Out," he screamed. "Get her out of here."

Liese dashed forward to get Gillian, and then ran out of the hall.

As soon as they were safely outside, she hugged the little girl to her bosom and whispered, "It's over now and soon we will leave this foul place and never look back. You'll never have to see your father's murderer again, and

18

I'll never have to look upon my husband, Ector. The two of us will make a new life together, and God willing, we'll find some peace and joy."

Liese was determined to get away before Baron Alford changed his mind. Permission to leave Dunhanshire liberated her, for it meant she could leave Ector behind as well. Her husband had gone over the edge of sanity during the attack on the castle and was too befuddled to go anywhere. After witnessing the slaughter of most of the soldiers and the household staff and narrowly escaping with his own life intact, his mind had snapped and he had turned as crazy as a rabid fox, roaming the hills of Dunhanshire during the days with his dirty knapsack filled with the rocks and clumps of dirt he called his treasures. Each night he made his bed in the southeast corner of the stables, where he was left alone to stew in his own nightmares. His eyes had a glassy, faraway look to them, and he constantly alternated between muttering to himself about how he was going to be a rich man, as rich as King Richard himself, and shouting obscenities because it was taking him so long to get his due. Even the infidels and their leader, Alford, who now claimed Dunhanshire for themselves in the absent king's name, were superstitious enough to give Ector a wide path. As long as the demented man left them alone, they ignored him. Some of the younger soldiers, it was observed, dropped to their knees and made the sign of the cross whenever Ector

19

passed by. The holy ritual was a talisman to ward off the possibility of catching the crazy loon's affliction. They didn't dare kill him, for they firmly believed that the demons controlling Ector's mind would leap into them and take control of their thoughts and actions.

Liese felt that God had granted her a dispensation from her marriage vows. In the seven years that they had lived as man and wife, Ector had never shown her as much as an ounce of affection or spoken a kind word to her. He believed that it was his duty as a husband to beat her into submission and humility so that she would be assured a place in heaven, and he took on his sacred responsibility with a gleeful vengeance. A hard, angry man who as a child had been coddled and shamefully spoiled by doting parents, Ector presumed that he could have anything he wanted. He was convinced that he should live the life of leisure, and he let greed control his every thought. Just three months before Gillian's father was killed, Ector had been promoted to the coveted position of chief reeve because of his clever way with figures. He then had access to the vast amount of money collected in rents from the tenants and knew exactly how much the baron was worth. Avarice took hold of his heart, and with it came a bitterness as rancid as bile because he hadn't been rewarded with what he believed was his share.

Ector was also a coward. During the attack, Liese witnessed her husband grab hold of Gerta, the household cook and Liese's dear friend, and use her as a shield against the arrows hailing down on them in the courtyard. When Gerta was killed, Ector had dragged her body over his and had pretended to be dead.

The shame was unspeakable, and Liese could no longer look at her husband without hatred. She knew she was in jeopardy of losing her own soul, for to despise another of God's creatures the way she despised Ector was surely sinful. She thanked God for giving her a second chance to redeem herself.

Concerned that Ector might take to the notion of following her, Liese, on the day she and Gillian were scheduled to leave, took the child with her to the stables to say goodbye. Clutching the little girl's hand in her own, she marched into the stall where her husband now made his home. She spotted his dung-and-blood-spattered knapsack hanging on the peg in the corner and turned her nose up in disgust. It smelled as foul as the man pacing about in front of her.

When she called out to him, he flinched, then ran to grab his knapsack and hide it behind his back. His eyes darted back and forth as he crouched down almost to his knees.

"You old fool," she muttered. "No one's going to steal your knapsack. I'm here to tell you I'm leaving Dunhanshire with Lady Gillian and I'll not ever see you again, praise the Lord. Do you hear what I'm saying to you? Stop your mumbling and look at me. I don't want you coming after me. Do you understand?"

Ector let out a low snicker. Gillian squeezed

closer to Liese and grabbed hold of her skirt. The woman immediately set about soothing her. "Don't you let him scare you," she whispered. "I won't let him do you any harm," she added before turning her attention and her repulsion to her husband again.

"I'm meaning what I say, Ector. Don't you dare try to follow me. I don't ever want to look upon you again. As far as I'm concerned, you're dead and buried."

He didn't appear to be paying any attention to her. "I'm getting my reward soon now... it's all going to be mine... a king's ransom," he boasted with a raucous snort. "Just like I deserve... his kingdom for a ransom. It's going to be mine... all mine..."

Liese tilted Gillian's head up so she would look at her. "Remember this moment, child. This is what cowardice does to a man."

Liese never looked back. Baron Alford refused to order his soldiers to escort the pair north. It amused him to think that the two witches would have to walk. The young brothers Hathaway came to their rescue, however. Waldo and Henry, tenants to the northwest, used their plowing horses and their cart to take them the distance. Both men were heavily armed, for there was also the threat of marauders lurking in the countryside waiting to pounce upon unsuspecting travelers.

Fortunately, the trip was uneventful, and they were both welcomed into the household of the reclusive Baron Morgan Chapman. The baron was Gillian's uncle by marriage, and though he was in good standing with the realm, he was considered an outsider and was therefore only infrequently invited to court. There was Highland blood running through his veins, and that made him untrustworthy and somewhat tainted.

He was also somewhat of a fright to look upon, for he was well over six feet two inches tall, had frizzy black hair, and wore what seemed to be a permanent scowl. Alford sent Gillian to this distant relative as punishment, but her exile to the end of England proved to be her salvation. Though her uncle was outwardly gruff and unapproachable, beneath the exterior beat the heart of a saint. He was a gentle, loving man who took one look at his pitiful little niece and knew that they were kindred spirits. He told Liese he wouldn't allow a child to disrupt his peaceful life, but immediately contradicted himself by devoting his full time to the duty of helping Gillian heal. He loved her as a father and made it his mission to get her to speak again. Morgan wanted to hear the child laugh, but worried that his hopes were too high.

Liese also made it her duty to help Gillian recover from the tragedy that had befallen her family. After months and months of patient coaxing and comforting without any results, the lady's maid was close to despair. She slept in the chamber with the little girl so she could soothe her and quiet her when the nightmares sent Gillian into fits of screaming.

Bits and pieces of that horrific night when

her father died were firmly locked inside the child's mind. Because of her tender years, it was difficult for her to separate truth from imagination, but she did remember fighting over the sparkling jeweled box and trying to grab it out of her sister's hands so she could have a turn holding it, then plunging down the stone steps that led to the tunnels underneath the castle. The jagged scar under her chin was proof she hadn't imagined it. She remembered Christen screaming. She also remembered the blood. In her hazy, confused memories, both she and Christen were covered in it. The nightmares that haunted her during the dark hours of the night were always the same. Faceless monsters with red glowing eyes and long, whiplike tails were chasing her and Christen down a dark tunnel, but in those terrifying dreams, she never killed her sister. The monsters did.

It was on one such night during a terrible thunderstorm that Gillian finally spoke. Liese awakened her from her nightmare, and then, as was her ritual, wrapped her in one of her uncle's soft Scottish plaid blankets and carried her across the room to sit by the fire.

The heavyset woman cuddled the little girl in her arms and crooned to her. "It ain't right the way you carry on, Gillian. You don't say a word during the day and then you howl like a lone wolf all night long. Is it because you've got the pain all stored up inside you and you need to get it out? Is that the way of it, my little angel? Talk to me, child. Tell me what's in your heart."

Liese didn't expect an answer and very nearly dropped the little girl on her head when she heard her whisper.

"What did you say?" she asked, a bit more sharply than she intended.

"I didn't mean to kill Christen. I didn't mean to."

Liese burst into tears. "Oh, Gillian, you didn't kill Christen. I've told you so over and over again. I heard what Baron Alford said to you. Don't you remember that, as soon as I carried you outside, I told you he was lying. Why won't you believe me? Baron Alford was just being cruel to you."

"She's dead."

"No, she isn't dead."

Gillian looked up at Liese to see from her expression if she was telling the truth or not. She desperately wanted, and needed, to believe her.

"Christen's alive," Liese insisted with a nod. "You listen to me. No matter how terrible the truth might be, I will never, ever lie to you."

"I remember the blood."

"In your nightmares?"

Gillian nodded. "I pushed Christen down the steps. Papa was holding my hand, but then he let go. Ector was there too."

"You've got it all mixed up inside your head. Neither your father nor Ector was there."

Gillian put her head down on Liese's shoulder. "Ector's daft."

"Aye, he is that," she agreed.

"Were you in the tunnel with me?" she asked.

"No, but I know what happened. While Maude was sewing you back together, one of the soldiers who was in the tunnel with you told her. You and your sister were awakened and carried to your father's chamber."

"William carried me."

"Yes."

"It was dark outside."

Liese felt Gillian shiver and hugged her. "Yes, it was the middle of the night, and Alford and his soldiers had already breached the inner walls."

"I remember the wall opened in Papa's room."

"The secret passage led to the steps down to the tunnel. There were four soldiers with your father, four men he trusted with your welfare. You know them, Gillian. Tom was there, and Spencer and Lawrence and William. Spencer's the one who told Maude what happened. They led the way down the secret corridor and carried torches to light the way."

"I'm not supposed to tell about my secret door."

Liese smiled. "I know you have one in your bedroom too," she said.

"How did you know? Did Christen tell you?"

"No, she didn't tell," she replied. "I would put you to bed in your room every night, but most mornings you were sleeping in Christen's room. I guessed there was a passageway because

I know you don't like going into dark places, and the hallway outside your bedroom door was very dark. You had to have found another way."

"Are you going to paddle me for telling?"

"Oh, heaven's no, Gillian. I'll never strike you."

"Papa would never paddle me neither, but he always said he would. He was just fooling me, wasn't he?"

"Yes," she answered.

"Did Papa hold my hand?"

"No, he didn't go with you into the passage. It wouldn't have been honorable for him to run away from the battle, and your father was an honorable man. He stayed with his soldiers."

"I pushed Christen down the steps and there was blood on her. She didn't cry. I killed her."

Liese sighed. "I know you're too young to understand, but I still want you to try. Christen did fall down the steps and so did you. Spencer told Maude he thought William lost his footing and slid into Lawrence. The stone floor was slippery, but William insisted someone had pushed him from behind."

"Maybe I pushed him," she worried out loud.

"You're too little to make a grown man lose his balance. You don't have the strength."

"But maybe..."

"You aren't responsible," Liese insisted. "It's a miracle none of you was killed. You needed stitches, however, and so Spencer and William took you to Maude. William stood guard outside the cottage until the battle came too close. Maude said he was desperate to get you to safety, but unfortunately, by the time she was done sewing you back together, Baron Alford's soldiers had surrounded the yard, and escape was no longer possible. You were captured and taken back to the castle."

"Did Christen get captured?"

"No, she was taken away before the tunnel was discovered."

"Where's Christen now?"

"I don't know," Liese admitted. "But perhaps your Uncle Morgan can tell you. He might know. Tomorrow you must go and ask him. He loves you like a daughter, Gillian, and I know he'll help you find your sister. I'm sure she misses you too."

"Maybe she's lost."

"No, she isn't lost."

"But if she's lost, she'll be scared."

"Child, she isn't lost. She's somewhere safe from Baron Alford's clutches. Do you believe me now? In your heart, do you believe your sister is alive?"

Gillian nodded. She began to twine Liese's hair around her finger. "I believe you," she whispered with a yawn. "When will Papa come and take me home?"

Liese's eyes filled with tears again. "Ah, love, your papa can't come for you. He's dead. Alford killed him."

"He put a knife in Papa's belly."

"Dear God, you saw it happen?"

"Papa didn't cry."

"Oh, my poor angel..."

"Maybe Maude can sew Papa up, and then he can come and take me home."

"No, he can't come for you. He's dead, and the dead can't come back to life."

Gillian let go of Liese's hair and closed her eyes. "Is Papa in heaven with Mama?"

"He surely is."

"I want to go to heaven too."

"It isn't your time to go. You have a long life to live first, Gillian, then you can go to heaven."

She squeezed her eyes shut so she wouldn't cry. "Papa got dead in the night."

"Yes, he did."

A long while passed in silence before Gillian spoke again. In a tiny whisper she said, "Bad things happen during the night."

CHAPTER ONE

Scotland, fourteen years later

The fate of the entire MacPherson clan rested in the hands of Laird Ramsey Sinclair. With the recent birth of Alan Doyle and the peaceful passing of Walter Flanders, there were exactly nine hundred and twenty-two MacPhersons, and the vast majority of those proud men and women desperately wanted and needed Ramsey's protection.

The MacPhersons were in a bad way. Their laird, a sad-eyed, mean-tempered old man named Lochlan, had died the year before, and by his own hand, God forgive him. His clansmen had been stunned and appalled by their laird's cowardly act and still could not talk openly about it. None of the younger men had successfully challenged for the right to lead the clan; though, in truth, most didn't want to fill Lochlan's shoes because they believed he had tainted the position by killing himself. He had to have been mad, they reasoned, because a sane man would never commit such a sin, knowing that he would spend eternity burning in hell for giving God such an insult.

The two elders who had stepped forward to temporarily lead the MacPherson clan, Brisbane Andrews and Otis MacPherson, were old and worn-out from more than twenty years of off-and-on fighting with the land-hungry clans to the east, south, and west of their holding. The fighting had intensified tenfold after the death of their laird, for their enemies knew their vulnerability with the lack of leadership. Desperate times called for cunning measures, however, and so Brisbane and Otis, with their clan's approval, decided to approach Laird Ramsey Sinclair during the annual spring festival. The social opportunity seemed the ideal time to present their petition, as it was an unspoken rule that all the clans leave their animosity at home and join together as one family for two full weeks of competition and goodwill. It was a time when old friendships were renewed, harmless grudges were stirred up, and most important, marriage contracts were sealed. Fathers of young daughters spent most of their days frantically trying to protect their offspring from unwanted suitors while at the same time trying to make the best possible match. Most of the men found it a thoroughly invigorating time.

Because the Sinclair land bordered the MacPherson holding on the southern edge, Ramsey assumed that the MacPherson leaders wanted to talk to him about a possible alliance, but as it turned out, the old men wanted much more. They were after a union—a marriage, so to speak—between the two clans and were willing to give up their name and become Sinclairs if the laird would give them his solemn word that every MacPherson would be treated as though he had been born a Sinclair. They wanted equality for every one of their nine hundred and twenty-two clansmen.

Ramsey Sinclair's tent was the size of a large cottage and spacious enough to accommodate the gathering. There was a small round table in the center with four chairs and several mats strewn around the ground for sleeping. Ramsey's commander in arms, Gideon, and two other seasoned Sinclair warriors, Anthony and Faudron, his trusted leaders, were present. Michael Sinclair, Ramsey's younger brother, fidgeted in the shadows while he waited for permission to rejoin the festivities. The child had already been rebuked for interrupting the meeting and kept his head bowed in embarrassment and shame.

Brisbane Andrews, a cantankerous old man with a piercing gaze and raspy voice, stepped forward to explain why the MacPhersons sought a merger.

"We have young soldiers, but they are poorly trained and cannot defend our women and children against our aggressors. We need your strength to keep the predators at bay so that we may live a peaceful life."

Otis MacPherson, a legend in the Highlands because of his remarkable though highly embellished feats as a young man, sat down in the chair Ramsey offered, clasped his hands on his knobby knees, and nodded toward Michael. "Perhaps, Laird, it would be best if you would listen to your brother's request and allow him to be on his way before we continue this discussion. Children often repeat secrets by accident, and I wouldn't like anyone to know about this... merger... until you have either accepted or denied us."

Ramsey agreed and turned to his brother. "What is it you want, Michael?"

The boy was still terribly timid around his older brother, for he barely knew him, having seen him only a couple of times in his short life. Ramsey had been living at the Maitland holding as an emissary after his mandatory years of training to become a fit warrior and had returned to his Sinclair home when their father had called for him on his deathbed. The brothers were nearly strangers to one another, but Ramsey, though somewhat inept at dealing with children, was determined to rectify that situation as soon as possible.

"I want to go fishing with my new friend," Michael stammered, his head still bowed low, "if it's all right with you, Laird."

"Look at me when you ask your question," Ramsey instructed.

Michael quickly did as he was ordered and repeated his request, adding the word "please" this time.

Ramsey could see the fear in his brother's eyes and wondered how long it was going to take for the boy to get used to having him around. The child still mourned their father, and Ramsey knew that Michael felt as though he had been abandoned. The boy didn't remember his mother—she had passed away when he was just a year old—but he had been extremely close to their father and still had not recovered from his death. Ramsey hoped that with time and patience Michael would learn to trust him and perhaps even remember how to smile again.

"You won't go near the falls, and you'll be back in this tent before sunset," he ordered quietly.

"I'll be back before sunset," Michael promised. "Can I leave now?"

"Yes," Ramsey answered, then watched in exasperation as his brother tripped over his own feet and knocked a chair over in his haste to join his friend.

"Michael," he called as his brother was rushing out the entrance, "haven't you forgotten something?"

The child looked puzzled until Ramsey nodded to the visitors. Michael immediately ran to the two men, bowed to his waist, and blurted out, "May I take your leave?"

Otis and Brisbane gave their permission, smiling as they watched the child bolt outside.

"The boy resembles you, Laird," Brisbane commented. "'Tis the truth he's your very image, for I well remember you as a lad. God willing, Michael will also grow into a fine warrior. A leader of men."

"Yes," Otis agreed, "with proper guidance, he could become a great leader, yet I couldn't help but notice that the child fears his brother. Why is that, Laird?"

Ramsey wasn't offended by the question, as

the old man spoke the truth and was simply making an observation. "I'm a stranger to the boy, but in time he'll learn to trust me."

"And trust that you won't leave him?" Otis asked.

"Yes," he answered, realizing how perceptive the old man was.

"I remember when your father decided to marry again," Brisbane remarked. "I thought Alisdair was too old and set in his ways to take another wife. Your mother had been dead over ten years, but he fooled me, and he seemed very content. Did you ever meet Glynnes, his second wife?"

"I attended their wedding," he said. "Because she was so much younger than my father, he was certain he would die first and he wanted to be sure she was well provided for," he explained.

"And he asked this of you?" Otis inquired, smiling.

"I am his son," Ramsey responded. "I would do whatever he asked."

Otis turned to his friend. "Laird Sinclair would never turn his back on anyone in need."

Ramsey had wasted enough time talking about personal matters and turned the discussion back to the primary subject. "You have said you want my protection, but could you not achieve this with a simple alliance?"

"Your soldiers would have to patrol our borders night and day," Otis said. "And in time they would grow weary of the duty, but if you owned the land..."

"Yes," Brisbane eagerly agreed. "If the Sinclairs owned the land, you would protect it at all cost. We have—" He suddenly stopped, for he was so stunned by the fact that Ramsey had moved forward to pour wine into their empty goblets, he lost his train of thought. "You are laird... yet you serve us as though you are our squire. Do you not know the power you hold?"

Ramsey smiled over their bewilderment. "I know that you are guests in my tent," he answered, "and my elders. It is therefore my duty to see to your comfort."

The men were honored by his words. "You have your father's heart," Otis praised. "It is good to see Alisdair lives on in his son."

The laird accepted the compliment with a nod and then gently led the men back to the topic he most wanted to discuss. "You were saying that I would protect your land at all costs if I owned it?"

"Aye," Otis agreed. "And we have much to offer in return for this union. Our land is rich with resources. Our lakes are glutted with fat fish, our soil is rich for planting, and our hills are filled with sheep."

"Which is why we are being constantly attacked on all our borders by the Campbells and the Hamiltons and the Boswells. They all want our land, our water and our women, but the rest of us can go to hell."

Ramsey didn't show any outward reaction to the passionate speech. He began to pace about the tent with his head bowed and his hands clasped behind his back.

"With your permission, Laird, I would ask a few questions," Gideon requested.

"As you wish," Ramsey told his commander.

Gideon turned to Otis. "How many soldiers do you count among the MacPhersons?"

"Nearly two hundred," he answered. "But as Brisbane explained, they have not been properly trained."

"And there are one hundred more of an age to begin training," Otis interjected. "You could make them invincible, Laird," he said. "As invincible as Laird Brodick Buchanan's Spartans. Aye, it's possible, for they already have the minds and hearts of warriors."

"You call Brodick's soldiers Spartans?" Gideon asked, smiling.

"We do, for that is what they are," Otis replied. "Haven't you heard the stories about the Spartans of times past from your fathers and grandfathers as we have?"

Gideon nodded. "Most of the stories have been exaggerated."

"Nay, most are true," Otis replied. "The stories were written down by the holy monks and retold countless times. They were a barbaric tribe," he added with a frown. "Sinfully proud but extremely brave. It was said they would rather die by the blade than lose an argument. 'Tis my opinion they were a stubborn lot."

"We wouldn't want our soldiers to be as ruthless as the Buchanan warriors," Brisbane hastily interjected.

Ramsey laughed. "Aye, Brodick's soldiers

are ruthless." His smile faded as he added, "Know this, gentlemen. Though we are often at odds, I count Brodick as one of my closest friends. He is like a brother to me. However, I will not take exception to what you have said about him, for I know Brodick would be pleased to know that you think him ruthless."

"The man rules with passion," Otis said.

"Yes, he does," Ramsey agreed. "But he is also fair to a fault."

"You were both trained by Iain Maitland, weren't you?" Brisbane asked.

"We were."

"Laird Maitland rules his clan with wisdom."

Ramsey concurred. "I also count Iain as my friend and brother."

Otis smiled. "Brodick rules with passion, Iain with wisdom, and you, Laird Ramsey, rule with an iron hand of justice. We all know you to be a compassionate man. Show us your mercy now," he pleaded.

"How can you know what kind of leader I am?" he asked. "You call me compassionate, but I've only been laird for six months and I've yet to be tested."

"Look at your commanders," Brisbane said with a nod. "Gideon and Anthony and Faudron led and controlled the Sinclair clan when your father was ill, and after he died and you became laird, you didn't do what others in your position would have done."

"And what would they have done?"

"Replace the commanders with men you know would be loyal to you."

"We are loyal to our laird," Gideon blustered. "You dare to suggest otherwise?"

"Nay," Brisbane countered. "I'm merely saying that other lairds would be less ... confident... and would rid themselves of any competitors. That is all. Laird, you showed compassion by allowing them to stay in their important positions."

Ramsey didn't agree or disagree with the old man's judgment. "As I just mentioned, I've been laird for a very short time, and there are problems I must solve within the Sinclair clan. I'm not certain that now is the time to—"

"We can't wait any longer, Laird. The Boswells have declared war and there's talk that they'll align themselves with the Hamiltons. If that happens, the MacPhersons will all be destroyed."

"Would your soldiers willingly pledge themselves to Ramsey?" Gideon asked.

"Aye, they would," Otis insisted.

"All of them?" the Sinclair commander persisted. "There are no dissenters?"

Otis and Brisbane glanced at one another before Otis answered. "There are but a few against this union. Before we came to you with our proposal, we put it to a vote four months ago. Everyone, man and woman, was included."

"You let your women vote?" Gideon asked, incredulous.

Otis smiled. "Aye, we did, for we wanted it to be fair, and our women will also be affected by the union. We wouldn't have thought to include them if Meggan MacPherson, granddaughter of our past laird, hadn't insisted on it."

"She is a most outspoken woman," Brisbane added, though the glint in his eye indicated he didn't see that as a flaw.

"If you voted four months ago, why are you just now making this request to Ramsey?" Gideon asked.

"We've actually voted twice now," Otis explained. "Four months ago we put the vote to the clan and then allowed a period for everyone to consider the matter again. The first vote went in favor of the union, but by a smaller margin."

"We didn't want it to be said that we rushed such an important issue," Brisbane added. "So we gave them time to consider all the ramifications. Then we voted again."

"Yes," Otis said. "Many who were at first against the union changed their minds and voted in favor."

"We shouldn't have waited so long to come to you, Laird, because now our situation has become critical."

"What was the result of the second vote?" Ramsey asked. "How many of your soldiers are still against the union?"

"Sixty-two are still against, and all of them are young, very young," Otis said.

"Pride has colored their judgment," Brisbane volunteered.

"They're led by a stubborn-headed rebel

named Proster, but all the others were in favor of the union, and the majority rules."

"Will the dissenters go along with the decision?" Ramsey asked.

"Yes, but grudgingly," Otis admitted. "If Proster can be won over, the others will come with him. There is a simple way to gain their loyalty... a very simple way."

"And what might that be?"

"Marry Meggan MacPherson," Brisbane blurted out. "And unite us by marriage."

"Men have married for far less than what we offer you," Otis interjected.

"And if I choose not to marry Meggan?"

"I would still plead with you if that is what it will take to get your agreement to let our clan unite with yours. Marriage to a MacPherson would only make the union stronger. My clan... my children... need your protection. Just two weeks ago, David and Lucy Douglas were murdered, and their only sin was that they ventured too close to the border. They were newly wed."

"We cannot lose any more of our good people, and if you do not take us in, one by one we will be hunted down. What will happen to our children?" Brisbane asked. "We have boys your brother's age," he added in an attempt to sway the laird.

Ramsey couldn't turn his back on their cry for help. He knew the lengths the Boswells would go to in order to claim more land. None of their soldiers would think twice about killing a child.

"The Boswells are jackals," he muttered.

Gideon knew his laird well and had already guessed what his answer was going to be. "Ramsey, will you put this matter to our clan before you give these men your decision?"

"I will not," he answered. "The matter isn't open for discussion."

Gideon held his frustration. "But will you think about this before you decide?"

Knowing his commander was trying to caution him to wait and was wanting a private discussion before any commitment was made, Ramsey gave Gideon a brisk nod before addressing the MacPhersons again.

"Gentlemen, you will have my answer in three hours' time. Does that suit you?"

Otis nodded as he stood. "With your permission, we will return then to hear your answer."

Brisbane latched onto his friend's arm. "You've forgotten to tell him about the competition," he whispered loudly.

"What competition?" Gideon asked.

Otis visibly colored. "We thought... to save our soldiers' pride, that you would agree to compete in a series of games. We can't possibly win, but it would be easier to give up our name and take the Sinclair name if we were soundly beaten in games of strength."

Gideon stepped forward. "And if you should win?"

"But we wouldn't," Otis insisted.

"But if you did?"

"Then the Sinclairs give up their name. You

would still rule as laird, Ramsey, but you would become a MacPherson, and the man who bested you would become your first in command."

Gideon was outraged, but Ramsey had the opposite reaction. So absurd was the request, he felt like laughing. He forced himself to maintain his stern expression as he said, "I have a commander and am well pleased with him."

"But, Laird, we thought only—" Otis began.

Ramsey cut him off. "My commander stands before you, gentlemen, and you insult him mightily with your proposal."

"What if you were to put the question to your clan?" Brisbane asked. "The games have only just started and there are still two full weeks. You could compete at the end of the games."

"Then I, like you, would want every man and woman to have a say, and since most are not attending the festival, I assure you it would take months before everyone had voted. We would have to wait until next year to compete."

"But we cannot wait that long for a decision," Otis said.

"I will be completely honest with you and tell you I wouldn't give the matter to my clan to decide anyway. The mere suggestion is obscene. The Sinclair name is sacred. However, since you say you wish only to save your soldiers' pride, if I decide on this union, then I will also suggest they compete for positions within my ranks under my commander. Those MacPherson soldiers who show strength and courage against my soldiers will be personally trained by Gideon."

43

Otis nodded. "We'll return then in three hours to hear your answer," he said.

"God guide you in making this momentous decision," Brisbane added as he followed his friend outside.

Ramsey laughed softly. "We've just been led down a crooked path," he remarked. "Otis believes the MacPherson soldiers could beat us and then he would have it all. Our protection and his name."

Gideon wasn't amused. "They come to you with hat in hand, begging, but then they have the audacity to put conditions on you at the same time. They are outrageous."

"What say you, Anthony?" he asked Gideon's second in command.

"I'm against this union," the yellow-haired soldier muttered. "Any man who would willingly give up his name disgusts me."

"I feel the same," Faudron interjected, his hawk-like face red with anger. "Brisbane and Otis are despicable."

"Nay, they're simply cunning old men who want the best for their clan. I've known for some time now that they were going to come to me, and I've had time to contemplate the matter. Tell me, Gideon, are you in favor of such a union?"

"I know you are," he replied. "Your heart is too soft, Laird. It's a troubling flaw, that. I see the problems involved in such a union."

"So do I," Ramsey said. "But Otis is right; they have much to offer in return. More important is their cry for help, Gideon. Can you turn your back on them?"

His commander shook his head. "Nay, the Boswells would slaughter them. However, I'm most concerned about Proster and the other dissenters."

"They've had time to come to terms with this union," Ramsey reminded him. "You heard what Otis said. They first voted four months ago. Besides, we'll keep a close eye on them."

"Your mind's made up, isn't it?"

"Yes, I'll welcome them into our clan."

"There'll be problems with our soldiers..."

Ramsey slapped Gideon's shoulder. "Then we'll deal with them," he said. "Don't look so bleak. Let's put the matter aside for now and join the festivities. Iain and Judith Maitland have been here since yesterday afternoon and I've still not spoken to them. Let's hunt them down."

"There is one more pressing matter you must attend to first," he said.

Ramsey dismissed Anthony and Faudron and then said to Gideon, "I can see from your grin the matter isn't serious."

"To your faithful soldier, Dunstan Forbes, the matter is very serious. You might as well sit down, Laird, for Dunstan has requested permission to marry Bridgid KirkConnell."

Ramsey was suddenly weary. "How many does this make now?"

Gideon laughed. "Including me, I count seven proposals in all, but Douglas swears there have been eight."

Ramsey sat down and stretched his long

legs out in front of him. "Does Bridgid know about this latest suitor?"

"Not yet," he answered. "But I have taken the liberty of sending for her. She's waiting outside, and you will at last meet the thorn in your side." After making the comment, he burst into laughter.

Ramsey shook his head. "Do you know, Gideon, all this time I believed that when I challenged you for the position of laird, I beat you fairly."

Gideon instantly sobered. "But you did beat me fairly."

"Are you certain you didn't let me win just so you wouldn't have to deal with Bridgid KirkConnell?"

Gideon laughed again. "Perhaps," he said. "I'll admit I like being in her presence, for she's a beautiful woman and a true delight to observe. She has a spirit few other women possess. She's quite... passionate... but alas, she's also as stubborn as a Buchanan. I'm glad now she turned me down, for I have no wish to marry such a difficult woman."

"How is it that I have had to deny three proposals on this woman's behalf while I have been laird but I have yet to meet her?"

"She sent her refusals from her uncle's home in Carnwath. I specifically remember telling you that I had given her permission to help her aunt with the new bairn. They, too, are here at the festival."

"If you told me, I've forgotten," he said. "I do remember her rejections though. She always sent back the same message."

"I've a feeling she'll say those very words today and Dunstan will join the rapidly growing ranks of the brokenhearted."

"My father is to blame for this nuisance duty I'm now saddled with because he was the one who gave his promise to Bridgid's father that she could choose her husband. It's unthinkable to me that she alone will decide her future."

"You don't have a choice in the matter," Gideon said. "You must honor your father's word. Bridgid's father was a noble warrior, and he was on his deathbed when he forged this promise. I wonder if he knew how stubborn his daughter was going to be."

Ramsey stood and then suggested Gideon call Bridgid inside. "And stop grinning," he ordered. "This is an important matter to Dunstan, and we shall treat it as such. Who knows? She may say yes to his proposal."

"Aye, and it might rain pigs this afternoon," Gideon drawled as he folded back the flap of the tent. He hesitated, turned back to his laird, and in a soft voice asked, "Have you ever had your head turned by a lady?"

The question exasperated Ramsey. "No, I haven't."

"Then I'd brace myself if I were you. I swear your head's going to spin."

A moment later, Gideon's prediction almost came true, as Bridgid KirkConnell walked into the tent and literally knocked the wind out of her laird. She was an astonishingly pretty young lady, with fair skin, sparkling eyes, and sinfully curly, long honey-colored hair that floated beyond her shoulders. Her gentle curves were in all the right places, and Ramsey was surprised that there had been only eight proposals.

She made a curtsy, smiled ever so sweetly up at him, and said, "Good day to you, Laird Ramsey."

He bowed. "So we meet at last, Bridgid KirkConnell. I've had to break the hearts of several suitors on your behalf without benefit of knowing why those good men were so anxious to wed such an obstinate woman. Now I understand the reason my soldiers are so persistent."

Her smile vanished. "But we have met before."

He shook his head. "I assure you that if I had met you, I would not have forgotten."

"But it's true, we did meet," she insisted. "And I remember our encounter as though it had taken place just yesterday. You had come home for your cousin's wedding. While my parents were attending the celebration, I decided to go swimming in the lake beyond the glen. You fished me out."

He clasped his hands behind his back and tried to concentrate on what she was telling him. Gideon hadn't exaggerated. She was an extraordinary woman.

"And why did I fish you out?"

"I was drowning."

"Didn't you know how to swim, lass?" Gideon asked.

"Much to my surprise, I didn't."

She smiled again, and Ramsey's heartbeat began to race. He was stunned by his own reaction to the woman, for he couldn't seem to get past the fact that she was so damned pretty. It wasn't like him to behave like this—he wasn't a boy and he had certainly been in the presence of comely women before. It was her smile, he decided then. It was really quite infectious.

He wondered if Gideon was experiencing a similar response to the lass, and just as soon as he could find the discipline to stop gawking at her, he'd look at his commander.

"If you didn't know how to swim, why did you go in the lake?" Gideon asked, trying to make sense out of such an illogical act.

She shrugged. "Swimming didn't look difficult, and I was sure I could figure it out, but alas, I was mistaken."

"You were a bold lass," Gideon commented.

"Nay, I was stupid."

"You were young," Ramsey offered.

"You must have turned your parents' hair white," Gideon said.

"I was accused of doing just that on several occasions," she replied before turning her attention to Ramsey again. "I understand why you don't remember. I've changed in my appearance and it has been a long while. I'm grown up now, but I'm not obstinate, Laird. Truly I'm not."

"You should have married by now," Ramsey said. "And it would seem to me that you are

49

being difficult. All of the men who have proposed marriage are fine and worthy soldiers."

"Yes, I'm certain they are good men," she agreed.

Ramsey took a step toward her. She took a step back, for she knew what was coming and wanted to be close to the opening of the tent so she could make a quick exit.

Ramsey noticed her glancing over her shoulder and thought she might be judging the distance to freedom. He maintained his serious demeanor, but it was difficult. Her panic made him want to laugh. Was marriage that repulsive to her?

"Now another soldier has stepped forward to ask for your hand in marriage," he said. "His name is Dunstan. Do you know him?"

She shook her head. "No, I don't."

"He's a good man, Bridgid, and he would certainly treat you well."

"Why?" she asked.

"Why what?" he countered.

"Why does he want to marry me? Did he give you a reason?"

Since Ramsey hadn't spoken to Dunstan personally, he turned to Gideon. "Did he give you a reason?"

The commander nodded. "He wants you."

Ramsey could tell from the hesitation in Gideon's voice that he wasn't telling her the full story. "Give her his exact words," he ordered.

Gideon's face colored. "Surely the lass doesn't wish to hear every word, Laird."

50

"I think she does," Ramsey countered. "And Dunstan expects us to speak for him."

The commander scowled to cover his embarrassment. "Very well then. Bridgid Kirk-Connell, Dunstan swears his love for you. He treasures your beauty and worships the very ground you... float upon.... As God is my witness, those were his very words."

Ramsey smiled, but Bridgid wasn't the least bit amused. Insulted by the declaration, she tried to hide her feelings, knowing that her laird wouldn't understand. How could he? He was a man and, therefore, couldn't possibly know what was in her heart.

"How can this be?" she asked. "I have not even met this man, yet he declares his love for me?"

"Dunstan is a good man," Gideon told her. "And I believe he means what he says."

"He's clearly infatuated with you," Ramsey added. "Would you like time to consider his proposal? Perhaps if you were to sit down with him and discuss this matter—"

"No," she blurted out. "I don't want to sit down with him, and I don't need time to consider his proposal. I would like to give my answer now. Would you please tell Dunstan that I thank him for his proposal, but..."

"But what?" Gideon asked.

"I won't have him."

Those were the identical words she had used to deny eight other men.

"Why not?" Ramsey demanded, his irritation obvious.

"I don't love him."

"What does love have to do with a marriage proposal? You could learn to love this man."

"I will love the man I marry or I won't marry at all." After making her vehement statement, she took another step back.

"How do I reason with such an absurd belief?" Ramsey asked Gideon.

"I don't know," he replied. "Where could she have gotten such notions?"

Their rudeness in openly discussing her as though she weren't even there angered and frustrated her, but she tried to control her temper because Ramsey was her laird and she should respect his position.

"You won't change your mind about Dunstan?" Ramsey asked.

She shook her head. "I won't have him," she repeated.

"Ah, Bridgid, you are a stubborn lass to be sure."

Being criticized a third time stung her pride, and she found it impossible to keep silent any longer.

"I have been in your presence less than ten minutes, but in that short while you have called me obstinate, difficult, and stubborn. If you are through insulting me, I would like to join my aunt and uncle."

Ramsey was astonished by her burst of anger. She was the first woman ever to speak to him in such a tone. Her behavior bordered on insolence, yet he couldn't fault her because he had said those very words to her, and they were insulting.

"You will not speak to your laird with such disrespect," Gideon commanded. "Your father would turn in his grave if he could hear you now."

She lowered her head, but Ramsey saw the tears in her eyes. "Let's leave her father out of this," he said.

"But, Laird, at the very least she should apologize."

"Why? I insulted her, though not deliberately, and for that I apologize."

Her head snapped up. "You apologize to me?"

"Yes."

Her smile was radiant. "Then I must tell you I'm sorry for being so contrary." She bowed, then turned and ran outside.

Gideon frowned after her. "She's a difficult woman," he remarked. "I pity the man who does marry her, for he will have a fine battle on his hands."

Ramsey laughed. "But what an invigorating battle it would be."

Gideon was surprised by the comment. "And would you be interested in pursuing a—"

A shout stopped his question and he turned to the entrance just as a young soldier came running inside the tent. He was Emmet MacPherson's son, Alan, and he looked as though he had just seen the ghost of his father.

"Laird, come quickly. There's been a terrible accident... terrible... at the falls," he stammered, panting for breath. "Your brother... oh, God, your little brother..."

Ramsey was already running outside when Alan's next words hit him.

"Michael's dead."

CHAPTER TWO

England, in the reign of King John

He was hanging by a thread. In his desperation to hide from his enemy, the little boy had wrapped the old discarded rope he'd found in the corner of the stables around and around the jagged boulder, then tied a tight triple knot the way his Uncle Ennis had taught him to do, and quickly, before he became plagued with second thoughts, slithered over the lip of the canyon on his belly with the rope twined around his left arm. Too late, he remembered he should have looped the rope around his waist and used his feet to brace himself the way he'd seen the seasoned warriors do when they worked their way down Huntley Cliffs to their favored fishing spot.

The boy was in too much of a hurry to climb back up and start all over again. The rocks were as sharp as needles against his tender skin, and his chest and stomach were soon scraped raw and bleeding. He was sure that he would end up with scars, which would make him a real warrior, and while he thought that was a very good thing for a boy of his age to accomplish, he wished it didn't have to hurt so much.

He wouldn't cry though, no matter how fierce the sting became. He could see speckles of bright red blood dotting the rocks he'd already squirmed over, and that scared him almost as much as his precarious position. If his papa could see him now, he'd surely ask him if he'd gone and lost his senses, and he might even shake his head in disappointment, but he'd also be hauling him up and making everything all right and safe too, and... *oh, Papa, I wish you were here now.* Tears came into his eyes then, and he knew he was going to forget his own promise and cry like a baby.

He wanted to go home and sit on his mama's lap and let her muss his hair and hold him close and make a fuss over him. She'd help him find his senses too—whatever those were—and then Papa wouldn't get upset.

Thinking about his parents made him so homesick he began to whimper. His fingers dug into the rope until they, too, were raw and bleeding, making his grip less sure. His arm ached, his fingers throbbed, and his belly burned, but he tried to ignore the pain, for panic had taken hold and all he could think about was getting away before the devil discovered he was missing.

Lowering himself into the gorge was much more difficult than he'd supposed it would be, but he continued on, not daring to look into the yawning mouth of the abyss that was surely as deep as purgatory. He tried to pretend he was climbing down from one of the big old trees back home, because he was a good, nimble tree climber, even better than his older brother. His papa had told him so.

Exhausted, he stopped to rest. He looked up and was surprised at how far he'd come, and for an instant he felt pride over his achievement. But then his lifeline began to unravel. His pride turned to terror and he burst into tears. He was certain that he would never see his mama and papa again.

By the time Lady Gillian caught up with the boy, her chest felt as though it were on fire, and she could barely catch her breath. She had followed his trail through the thick forest, running as fast as her legs would carry her, and when at last she reached the cliffs and heard the child crying, she collapsed to her knees in acute relief. The little boy was still alive, thank God.

Her joy was short-lived however, for when she reached for his rope to pull him up to safety, she saw how threadbare it was and knew it was only a matter of minutes before the unraveling threads completely disintegrated. She was afraid even to touch the rope. If she dared pull on it, the threads would rub against the rocks and shred more quickly.

Shouting the order for him to stay completely

still, she stretched out on her stomach and forced herself to look over the edge. Heights terrified her and she felt a wave of nausea as she looked down into the chasm below. How in God's name was she going to get him? It would take too long to retrace her steps to fetch a good sturdy rope, and her chances of being spotted by one of Alford's soldiers were too great to risk. There were jagged stones jutting out from the rock, and she knew that a more experienced man or woman might be able to climb down.

But she wasn't experienced—or nimble. Looking down made her dizzy, but, dear God, she couldn't leave him, and time was critical. The rope would soon snap, and the child would plunge to his death.

There wasn't any choice, and so she said a frantic prayer to God to give her courage. *Don't look down,* she silently chanted as she turned and cautiously scooted over the edge on her stomach. *Don't look down.*

Gillian cried out with joy each time her foot touched one of the protruding stones. Just like stairs, she pretended. When at last she was level with the boy, she leaned her forehead against the cold rock, closed her eyes, and thanked God for letting her get this far without breaking her neck.

She slowly turned toward the child. He couldn't be more than five or six years old, and he was desperately trying to be brave and bold at the same time. He had been clinging to the rope for several minutes now, holding tight with one hand and clutching a dagger—her dagger—in his other hand. His eyes were wide with terror, but she could see the tears there as well, and, oh, how her heart ached for him.

She was his only hope for survival, but he was stubbornly afraid to trust her. Defiant, foolishly so, he would neither speak to her nor look at her, and each time she tried to grab hold of him, he thrust the dagger, slicing her arm with each jab. She wouldn't give up though, even if it meant she died trying.

"Stop this nonsense and let me help you," she demanded. "I swear to heaven, you don't have any sense at all. Can't you see your rope is tearing?"

The sharpness in her tone jarred the boy, and he was able to shake himself out of his terror. He stared at the blood dripping down her fingertips, suddenly realized what he had done to her, and threw the dagger away.

"I'm sorry, lady," he cried out in Gaelic. "I'm sorry. I'm not supposed to hurt ladies, not ever."

He'd spoken so quickly and his words were so garbled with his brogue, she barely caught what he said.

"Will you let me help you?" She hoped he understood her but wasn't sure if she'd used the correct words, for she only had a rudimentary knowledge of Gaelic.

Before he could answer, she cried out, "Don't wiggle like that, the rope will snap. Let me reach for you."

"Hurry, lady," he whispered, though this time he spoke her language.

Gillian edged close, held on to the indentation in the rock above her head with one hand to balance herself, and then reached out for him. She had just wrapped her bloody arm around his waist and was pulling him onto the ledge with her when the rope snapped.

If the child hadn't already had one foot securely on the rock ledge, they both would have fallen backward. She squeezed him against her and let out a loud sigh of relief.

"You were just in time," he told her as he uncoiled the rope from his wrist and tossed it down into the chasm. He wanted to watch it land, but when he tried to turn around, she tightened her hold and ordered him to stay perfectly still.

"We've made it this far," she said so weakly she doubted he heard her. "Now for the difficult part."

He heard the shiver in her voice. "Are you scared, lady?" he asked.

"Oh, yes, I'm scared. I'm going to let go of you now. Lean against the rock and don't move. I'm going to start climbing back up and..."

"But we got to go down, not up."

"Please don't shout," she said. "We can't possibly climb all the way down. There aren't enough footholds. Can't you see the rock is sheared smooth?"

"Maybe if you went and got a good rope, we could—"

She cut him off. "It's out of the question."

Both of her hands gripped the edge of the

tiny crevice above her head and she searched for a way to lift herself. The strength seemed to have gone out of her and, though she gave it a valiant try, she couldn't climb back up.

"You know what, lady?"

"Hush," she whispered as she said a silent prayer for strength and made another attempt.

"But you know what?"

"No, what?" she asked as she rested against the rock and tried to calm her racing heartbeat.

"There's a real big ledge down under us. I saw it. We could jump down. Look down, lady, and you can see for yourself. It isn't far."

"I don't want to look down."

"But you got to look so you can see where it is. Then maybe we can crawl along—"

"No!" she shouted as she again tried to raise herself to the next foothold. If she could only accomplish that little feat, she could surely figure out a way to reach down and pull the little boy up too.

The child watched her struggle. "Are you too puny to climb back up?"

"I suppose I am."

"Can I help?"

"No, just stand perfectly still."

Once again she tried to climb, but it was a futile effort at best. She was in such a panic inside, she could barely draw a decent breath. Dear Lord, she didn't think she had ever been this afraid in all her life.

"You know what, lady?"

The little boy was relentless, and she gave up trying to quiet him. "No, what?"

"We got to go down, not up."

"We're going up."

"Then how come we aren't moving?"

"Try to be patient," she ordered. "I can't seem to get a proper hold. Give me a minute and I'll try again."

"You can't climb up 'cause I hurt you. You got blood all over your clothes. I cut you bad. I'm awful sorry, lady, but I got scared."

He sounded on the verge of tears. She quickly tried to calm him. "Don't fret about it," she said as she made one more attempt. With a groan of frustration, she finally gave up. "I think you're right. We're going to have to go down."

Ever so slowly she turned around on the narrow ledge, and with her back pressed against the rock, she sat down. The child watched her, then spun around and plopped down beside her.

The quickness in his action nearly gave her heart palpitations, and she grabbed hold of his arm.

"Can we jump now?" he asked eagerly.

The boy really didn't have a lick of sense. "No, we aren't going to jump. We're going to ease our way down. Take hold of my hand and hold tight."

"But you got blood on your hand."

She quickly wiped the blood on her skirt, then took hold of his hand. Together they peered over the side. Gillian had to look to make certain the ledge was wide enough. She had to say a prayer too, and after she was fin-

61

ished, she held her breath and scooted off the ledge.

The distance wasn't all that far, but still, the impact jarred her. The little boy lost his balance as they landed, and she jerked him back just in time. He threw himself into her arms, pitching her hard against the rock wall, then buried his face in her shoulder and trembled violently.

"I almost kept going."

"Yes, you did," she agreed. "But we're safe now."

"Aren't we going to go down more?"

"No. We're going to stay here."

They huddled together for several minutes on the rock plate that protruded from the canyon wall before the boy was able to let go of her. He recovered from his near brush with death quickly, though, and after another minute or two, he crawled away from her side to reach the wider section of rock that had been hidden by a thick overhang.

Looking as pleased as could be, he folded his legs underneath him and motioned for her to come forward.

She shook her head. "I'm fine where I am."

"It's gonna rain and you'll get all wet. It isn't hard. Just don't look down."

As if to underscore his prediction, a clap of thunder rumbled in the distance.

Ever so slowly she scooted toward him. Her heart was pounding like a drum, and she was so scared she thought she might throw up. The child, it seemed, had more courage than she did.

"How come you don't like looking down?" he asked as he crawled forward to peer into the chasm.

He was dangerously close to the edge, and she frantically grabbed hold of his ankles and pulled him back. "Don't do that."

"But I want to spit down and see where it lands."

"Sit beside me and be quiet for a moment. I have to think what to do."

"But how come you don't like looking down?"

"I just don't."

"Maybe it makes you sick. Your face got real green. Were you gonna puke?"

"No," she answered wearily.

"Does it scare you to look down?"

He was relentless. "Why do you ask so many questions?"

He lifted his shoulders in an exaggerated shrug. "I don't know; I just do."

"And I don't know why it scares me to look down; it just does. I don't even like looking out of my bedroom window because it's up so high. It makes me dizzy."

"Are all English ladies like you?"

"No, I don't suppose they are."

"Most are puny," he announced authoritatively. "My Uncle Ennis told me so."

"Your uncle's wrong. Most ladies are not puny. They can do anything a man can do."

The child must have thought her remark was hilarious because he laughed so forcefully his shoulders shook. She found herself wondering how in heaven's name a boy so young could be so arrogant.

He turned her attention with yet another question. "What's your name, lady?"

"Gillian."

He waited for her to ask him his name, and when she didn't, he nudged her. "Don't you want to know my name?"

"I already know your name. I heard the soldiers talking about you. You're Michael and you belong to a clan led by a man named Laird Ramsey. You're his brother."

The boy was vehemently shaking his head. "No, Michael isn't my real name," he said. He cuddled up next to her and took hold of her hand. "We were playing a trick when the men came and grabbed me. They put me in a wheat sack."

"That must have been very frightening for you," she said. "What kind of a trick were you playing?" Before he could answer her, she asked, "Why didn't you wait for me in the stables? It could have been so easy to get away if you had only done what I told you to do. And why did you stab my arm? You knew I was your friend. I unlocked the door for you, didn't I? If only you had trusted me..."

"I'm not supposed to trust the English. Everyone knows that."

"Did your Uncle Ennis tell you that?"

"No, my Uncle Brodick did," he explained. "But I already knew."

"Do you trust me?"

"Maybe I do," he answered. "I didn't mean to cut you. Does it hurt fierce?"

It hurt like hell, but she wasn't going to admit it because of the anxiety she saw in his eyes. The little boy had enough worries on his mind, and she wasn't going to add to them.

"It'll be fine," she insisted. "I suppose I should do something about the bleeding though."

While he watched, she tore a strip from her underskirt and wrapped it around and around her arm. The boy tied the knot for her at her wrist. Then she tugged her torn, bloody sleeve back down over the bandage.

"There, I'm as fit as new."

"You know what?"

She let out a sigh. "No, what?"

"I hurt my fingers." He sounded as if he were boasting of an incredible feat and smiled when he held his hand up for her to see. "Now I can't do nothing to help us, 'cause my fingers burn."

"I imagine they do."

His face lit up. He was a beautiful little boy, with dark curls and the most beguiling gray eyes she'd ever seen. His nose and cheeks were covered with freckles.

He scooted away from her and pulled his tunic up so she could see his chest and stomach. "I'm gonna get scars."

"No, I don't think you will," she began, but then she noticed his crestfallen expression. "Then again, I do suppose you'll have some. You do want them, don't you?"

He nodded. "Yes."

"Why?"

"All warriors have scars. They're marks of valor."

He was so serious she didn't dare laugh. "Do you know what valor is?"

He shook his head. "I know it's good."

"Yes," she agreed. "Valor is courage, and that is very good indeed. I imagine those cuts sting," she added as she leaned forward to pull his tunic down over his belly. "When we're taken back to the holding, I'll ask one of the servants to put some salve on your fingers and chest and stomach, and then you'll feel much better. Some of the older women remember me," she added. "They'll help us."

"But we can't go back," he cried out.

The change in him was so abrupt it startled her. "Try to understand," she said. "We're trapped here. This ledge doesn't go any-where."

"I could crawl to the end and see if—"

"No," she interrupted. "The rock might not be sturdy enough to hold your weight. Can't you see how it thins out near the curve?"

"But I could—"

"I cannot let you take such a chance."

Tears came into his eyes. "I don't want to go back. I want to go home."

She nodded in sympathy. "I know you do and I want to help you get back home. I'll find a way," she promised. "I give you my word." He didn't seem convinced. He relaxed against her and yawned loudly. "Do you know what

66

my Uncle Ennis says? If an Englishman gives you his word, you'll come away with nothing."

"I really must meet this uncle of yours one day and set him straight about a few matters."

He snorted. "He wouldn't talk to you," he said. "Leastways I don't think he would. Gillian?" he asked then. "I know I was supposed to wait in the stables for you, but then that man came inside and I got scared and ran."

"Do you mean the baron went into the stables?"

"The ugly man with the red beard."

"That's the baron," she said. "Did he see you?"

"No, I don't think so. When I was hiding in the trees, I seen him leave with two other men. Maybe they won't ever come back."

"Oh, they'll come back all right," she said, for she didn't want to give the boy false hope. "If not tomorrow, then the day after."

The child's wrinkled brow made him seem too wise for his young years, and that saddened her. Little boys should be outside running and laughing and playing silly tricks with their friends. This little one had been plucked away from his family to be used as a pawn in Baron Alford's scheme. The child had to feel as though he'd been dropped into the middle of a nightmare.

"Are you still afraid, Gillian?"

"No."

"I never get afraid," he boasted.

"You don't?"

"Almost never," he corrected.

"How old are you?"

"Almost seven."

"Almost?"

"I will be pretty soon."

"You're a very brave boy."

"I know," he said very matter-of-factly. "How come those men stole me away from the festival? It was the first one I ever got to go to, and I was having a fine time. Was it because me and my friend was playing a trick on our families?"

"No," she assured him. "That wasn't the reason why."

"Did I do something... bad?"

"Oh, no, you didn't do anything bad. None of this is your fault. You've just been caught in the middle, that's all. The baron wants something from me, but he hasn't told me what it is yet, and you're somehow involved."

"I know what it is," he boasted. "And you know what? The baron's gonna go to hell 'cause my papa will send him there. I miss my mama and papa," he admitted forlornly, his voice cracking on a sob.

"Yes, of course you do. They must be frantic, searching for you."

"No, they aren't, 'cause you know why? They think I'm dead."

"Why would they think such a thing?"

"I heard the baron talking to his friends."

"Then you do know what the baron's plans are?" she asked sharply.

"Maybe I do," he said. "The men who took

me made it look like I hit my head on the rocks and fell in the falls and drowned. That's what I heard them saying. I'll bet my mama's crying all the time."

"That poor woman..."

"She's missing me fierce."

"Of course she is. But think how overjoyed she'll be to have you back home again. Now tell me, please, what else you heard the baron say to his friends," she asked, trying to sound as though the question wasn't terribly important so that he wouldn't become fretful.

"I heard everything they said 'cause you know why? I played a trick. The baron didn't know I understood 'cause I didn't talk, not even Gaelic, in front of him or the others."

"That was very clever of you." She could tell her praise pleased him. He grinned up at her while he laced his fingers through hers. "Tell me everything you heard, and please take your time so you won't leave anything out."

"The baron lost a box a long time ago, but now he thinks he knows where it is. A man told him."

"What man? Did the baron say his name?"

"No, but the man was dying when he told him. The box had a funny name too, but I can't remember it now."

She suddenly felt sick to her stomach. She understood now why Alford had forced her back to Dunhanshire, and as the ramifications struck her full force, her eyes stung with tears.

"Arianna," she whispered. "He called it Arianna's box, didn't he?"

"Yes," he said excitedly. "How come you knew the name?"

She didn't answer him. Her mind was racing with questions. Oh, God, had Alford found Christen?

"How come you speak Gaelic?"

"What?" she asked sharply, startled by the abrupt change in topics.

He repeated the question. "Are you mad at me 'cause I asked?"

She could see the anxiety in his eyes. "No, no, I'm not mad," she assured him. "I learned to speak Gaelic because my sister, Christen, lives in the Highlands and I—"

He interrupted her. "Where in the Highlands?"

"I'm not exactly sure—"

"But—"

She wouldn't let him interrupt her again. "When I find out exactly where she is, I'm going to go see her and I want to be able to speak to her in Gaelic."

"How come she's got a clan and gets to live in the Highlands and you don't?"

"Because I got caught," she answered. "A long time ago, when I was just a little girl, the baron and his soldiers seized Dunhanshire. My father tried to get my sister and me to safety, but in the chaos, Christen and I were separated."

"Is your sister lost?"

"No, she isn't lost. She was taken north into the Lowlands by one of my father's loyal men. My Uncle Morgan went to great lengths

70

to find out exactly where she was, but she had vanished into the Highlands. I'm not sure where she is now, but I hope one day I will find her."

"Do you miss her?"

"Yes, I do. I haven't seen Christen in a long time though. I don't think I'll even recognize her. Uncle Morgan told me the family who took her might have changed her name to keep her safe."

"From the baron?"

"Yes," she replied. "Still, she'll remember me."

"But what if she doesn't?"

"She will," she insisted.

A long peaceful minute passed in silence before he spoke again. "You know what?"

"What?"

"I can speak your language real good 'cause my mama taught me how to talk to the English even though Papa didn't want her to and my papa only talks Gaelic to me. I don't even remember learning how. I just did."

"You're a very smart boy."

"That's what my mama says. Some Gaelic's hard to talk," he continued, "'cause clans got their own way of saying things and it takes a long time to learn all the different words. When Uncle Brodick talks to me, he has to talk my Gaelic or I wouldn't know what he was saying, but it wouldn't matter if you could understand what they were saying 'cause you know why? They wouldn't talk to you unless my uncle told them to."

"Why wouldn't they talk to me?"

He gave her a look that suggested she was just plain stupid. He was such an adorable little boy she had to fight the urge to hug him.

"'Cause you're English," he explained in exasperation. "It's gonna get dark," he worried out loud. "Are you gonna be afraid of the dark the way you were afraid of looking down?"

"No, I won't be afraid."

He was trying to get her to put her arm around his shoulders but she wasn't taking the hint, and in frustration, he finally grabbed hold of her hand and did it for her.

"You smell like my mama."

"And how's that?"

"Good."

His voice cracked on the word, and she surmised he was getting homesick again.

"Maybe the baron won't find us."

"His soldiers will see the rope tied around the boulder," she gently reminded him.

"I don't want to go back."

He burst into tears. She leaned over him and brushed his curls out of his eyes and kissed his forehead. "Hush now, it's going to be all right. I promise you, I'm going to find a way to get you back home."

"But you're just a lady," he wailed.

She tried to think of something to ease his mind and give him hope. His sobs were breaking her heart, and in desperation, she blurted out, "You know what a protector is, don't you?"

He hiccuped while he answered. "It's the

same as a champion." He sat up and mopped the tears away from his cheeks with his fists. "I had me a protector, and then I got another one. The day I was born I got one 'cause every bairn born in our clan gets to have one. He's supposed to look out for the boy or girl all his life long to make sure nothing bad ever happens to him. Angus used to be my champion, but then he died."

"I'm sorry to hear that," she said. "I'm sure Angus was a fine protector."

She was getting weary, and it was difficult to keep up with the idle chatter. Her arm was throbbing and felt as though it had been held over a flaming torch. As exhausted as she was from the long trip back to Dunhanshire, she still was determined to keep the boy occupied with conversation until he became too sleepy to worry.

"I just got me a new champion," he told her. "Papa had to ponder it a long time 'cause he wanted to make sure he picked the right one for me. He told me he wanted me to have a champion as strong and fierce as Graham's."

"Who is Graham?" she asked.

"My brother," he answered.

"And who did your father choose for you?"

"His friend," he answered. "He's a fierce warrior, an important laird too, and you know what?"

She smiled. "What?"

"He's awful mean. That's the best part. Papa says he'll make a fine champion."

"Because he's mean?"

73

"And 'cause he's strong," he explained. "He can split a tree in half just by glaring at it. Uncle Ennis told me so. He's only mean when he's got to be."

"Your champion isn't your Uncle Ennis, is he?"

"No," he answered. "Uncle Ennis wouldn't do. He's too nice."

She laughed. "And it wouldn't do to have a nice protector?" She could tell he thought she'd asked a stupid question.

"No, you got to be mean to your enemies, not nice. That's why Papa asked Uncle Brodick. He's my new champion, and he's not ever nice. You know what?"

Those three words were beginning to drive her to distraction. "No, what?" she asked.

"Brodick's probably spitting fire now 'cause he told Papa not to let me go to the festival, but Mama had her way, and Papa gave in."

"Did your Uncle Brodick attend the festival?"

"No, he'd never go to one 'cause there's too many Englishmen there. I'll bet he doesn't think I'm dead. He's the new laird over all the Buchanans, and everyone knows how stubborn the Buchanans are. Now that he's my protector, I get to call him Uncle. Maybe he's gonna come here and find me before my papa does."

"Maybe he will," she agreed to placate him. "Why don't you put your head down in my lap and close your eyes. Rest for a little while."

"You won't leave while I'm sleeping, will you?"

"Where would I go?"

He smiled when he realized how foolish his worry was. "I'm gonna be scared when you have to go away. I heard the baron tell his friends you got to go get your sister. He's gonna be mad when he finds out you lost her."

"Why didn't you tell me this before?"

"I forgot."

"What else did he say?" she implored. "I need to know everything."

"I remember he said your king's looking for the box too, but the baron's got to find it first. I don't know why. I don't remember anything else," he ended on a wail. "I want my papa to come and get me now."

"Please don't cry," she pleaded. She hugged him close. "A boy who has three protectors should be smiling, not crying."

"I don't have three. I only got one."

"Yes, you do too have three. Your father's one, Brodick is two, and I'm your third protector. I'll be your champion until the day I get you safely home."

"But ladies can't be champions."

"Of course they can."

He puzzled over the possibility a long minute and then nodded. "All right," he agreed. "But you got to give me something then."

"I do?"

He nodded again. "A protector always gives something important to the boy or girl he's supposed to watch out for," he explained. "You got to give me something of yours."

"Did your Uncle Brodick give you something important?"

"Yes," he answered. "He gave Papa his best dagger to give to me. It has his crest on the hilt. Papa made a leather sheath for it, and he let me take it to the festival. Now it's gone."

"What happened to it?"

"One of the baron's soldiers grabbed it from me. I saw him throw it on the chest in the great hall."

"We'll find a way to get it back," she promised.

"But what are you gonna give me?" he asked again.

She held up her hand. "Do you see this ring I'm wearing? I treasure it above all things."

In the dying light it was difficult to see the ring clearly. He pulled her hand toward him and squinted down at it. "It's pretty."

"It belonged to my grandmother. My uncle Morgan gave it to me on my last birthday. I'll loop it through my ribbon and tie it around your neck. You'll wear it under your tunic so the baron won't see it."

"Can I keep it forever?"

"No, you can't," she said. "After I've kept my promise to you and gotten you safely home, you'll give the ring back to me. Now close your eyes and try to sleep. Why don't you think about how happy your parents are going to be when they see you again."

"Mama will cry 'cause she'll be so happy, and

Papa will be happy too, but he won't cry 'cause warriors never cry. He won't be happy very long, though, 'cause I'm gonna have to tell him I disobeyed him."

"How did you disobey him?"

"He told me not to go near the waterfall. He said it was too dangerous for a boy to play there 'cause the rocks were slippery, but I went anyway with my friend, and when I tell Papa, he's gonna be mad at me."

"Are you afraid of your father?"

He snickered. "I could never be afraid of my papa."

"Then why are you so worried?"

"'Cause he'll make me take a walk with him, that's why, and then he'll make me think about what I did and tell him why it was wrong, and then he'll punish me."

"What will he do?"

"He maybe won't let me go riding with him for a spell... that would be the worst punishment 'cause I really like to ride on his lap. Papa lets me hold the reins."

She rubbed his back and suggested he not worry about it now.

He wasn't through confessing his sins. "But that's not all I got to tell him," he said. "I got to tell him what me and Michael did."

"Your friend's name is also Michael?"

"My friend *is* Michael," he said. "I told you, we were playing a trick."

"Don't fret about it now. Your father isn't going to care about a game you and your friend were playing."

"But..."

"Sleep," she ordered.

He quieted down and was silent for several minutes. She thought he'd finally fallen asleep, and she turned her thoughts to more urgent matters.

"You know what?"

She sighed. "No, what?"

"I like you, but I don't like most of the English. Uncle Ennis hates them all. He told me so. He says if you shake an Englishman's hand, you'll come away without your fingers, but that isn't true, is it?"

"No, that isn't true."

"Are you sorry you have to be English?"

"No, I'm just sorry Alford is."

"He's ignorant. You know why?"

She had the feeling he wouldn't let up until he had told her what was on his mind. "No, why?" she dutifully asked.

"'Cause he thinks I'm Michael."

She stopped rubbing his back and went completely still. "You aren't Michael?"

He rolled onto his back and then sat up to face her. "No, my friend's Michael. That's what I've been trying to tell you. The stupid baron thinks I'm Laird Ramsey's brother, but I'm not. Michael is. That's the trick we were playing. We changed plaids, and we were gonna see how long it took for anyone to notice. When it got dark, I was gonna go to Michael's tent and he was gonna go to mine."

"Oh, dear God," she whispered, so stunned she could barely catch her breath. The innocent little boy didn't have any idea of the significance of what he had just told her, and all he was worried about was his father's reaction when he found out about a silly game his son was playing with his friend. It was only a matter of time before Alford would discover the truth, and when he did, this child's fate would be doomed.

She grabbed hold of his shoulders and pulled him close. "Listen to me," she whispered urgently. "You must never tell anyone what you've just told me. Promise me."

"I promise."

There were only a few flashes of distant lightning to illuminate the gray stones of the canyon, and it was difficult for her to see his face clearly. She pulled him close, searching his eyes, and whispered, "Who are you?"

"Alec."

Her hands dropped into her lap and she leaned back against the wall. "You're Alec," she repeated. She couldn't get over her surprise, but the boy didn't seem to notice her stunned reaction.

He grinned at her and said, "Do you see? The baron *is too* ignorant 'cause he captured the wrong boy."

"Yes, I see. Alec, did your friend see Alford's men take you away from the festival?"

He held his lower lip between his teeth while he thought about what had happened. "No," he answered. "Michael went back to his tent to get his bow and arrows 'cause we wanted to shoot them over the falls, and that's when the men came and grabbed me. You know what? I don't think the men were the baron's soldiers 'cause they were wearing plaids."

"How many were there?"

"I don't know... maybe three."

"If they're Highlanders, they're traitors then in league with the baron," she muttered as she threaded her fingers through her hair in agitation. "What a mess this is."

"But what if the baron finds out I'm not Michael? He's gonna be mad, isn't he? Maybe he'll make the traitors go and get my friend then. I hope they don't put Michael in a wheat sack. It's scary."

"We're going to have to find a way to warn Michael's family of the danger."

Her mind was racing from one thought to another as she tried to understand the twisted game Alford was playing.

"Alec, if you both changed clothes and Michael was wearing your plaid, wouldn't his clan notice? Surely he'd tell one of them about the trick you were playing."

"Maybe he'd be too scared to tell."

"How old is Michael?"

"I don't know," he answered. "Maybe he's almost my age. You know what? Maybe he took my plaid off is what he did. That's what I'd do if I got real scared, and he'd be afraid to make his brother mad 'cause he doesn't know his brother very good at all since he only just came back home to be laird. Michael was kind of scared to play the trick too 'cause he didn't want to get in trouble. It's my fault," he cried out, "'cause I made him do it."

"I want you to stop worrying that you did anything wrong. No one's going to blame you. You were just playing a harmless game, that's all. Why don't you put your head down in my lap and be real quiet for a few minutes so I can think."

She closed her eyes then to discourage him from asking any more questions.

He wasn't going to cooperate. "You know what?" When she didn't answer him, he began to tug on her sleeve. "You know what?"

She gave up. "What?"

"My tooth is loose." To prove he was telling the truth, he grabbed her hand and made her touch one of his front teeth with the tip of her finger. "See how it wiggles back and forth when you touch it? Maybe it'll come out tomorrow."

The eagerness in his voice as he told her his important news was a jolting reminder of how very young he was. Losing his tooth obviously thrilled him.

"Papa was gonna pull it out for me, but then he said I had to wait until it got good and loose."

With a loud yawn, he put his head in her lap and patiently waited for her to rub his back again.

"I was gonna ask Papa to pull my tooth out at the festival 'cause Michael wanted to watch. Michael belongs to Ramsey," he added just in case she'd forgotten.

"And who do you belong to, Alec?"

He puffed up with importance. "I'm Iain Maitland's son."

CHAPTER THREE

Alford liked to play games. He was especially partial to any game that involved cruelty.

He was having a fine time now, though in fact his day hadn't started out well at all. He'd returned to Dunhanshire at midday on Sunday soaked through and chilled to the bone because of an unexpected and torrential downpour that had caught him unaware en route, and feeling quite miserable, he certainly wasn't in the mood to hear that Lady Gillian had tried to help the boy escape. Before he could work himself up into a good rage—he'd already killed the soldier who had imparted the unpleasant news—Gillian and the boy were located and brought back to the castle, and they now stood before him, waiting to hear their punishment.

Anticipation heightened Alford's pleasure. He wanted them to wallow in their own fears, and making them guess what torture he had in mind for them was all part of Alford's game. The boy, the simpleton brother of Laird Ramsey, was too stupid to understand or speak, but Alford could tell he was frightened because of the way he kept trying to edge closer to Gillian. She, on the other hand, was proving to be quite a disappointment, and if he hadn't known better, he would have thought she was deliberately trying to ruin his fun. She didn't appear to be the least bit concerned about her fate. He couldn't discern any fear at all in her.

The bitch still had the power to spook him, and he silently cursed himself for his own cowardice because he couldn't hold her gaze long. *Save me from the righteous,* he thought to himself. Going into battle against a league of soldiers was far less intimidating than this mere slip of a girl, and although he reminded himself that he was the one with the power and that he could order her death by simply uttering a quick command, in his mind she still had the upper hand. He'd never forgotten how she had looked at him when he'd ordered her brought before him after the massacre. She had been a little girl then, but the memory still made him inwardly flinch. He knew she had seen him kill her father, but he'd believed that in time the memory would fade from her mind. Now he wasn't so certain. What else did she remember? Had she heard him confessing his sins to her father before he gutted him? The question brought chills to Alford's spine. Gillian's hatred frightened him, weakened him, made his skin crawl.

His hand shook as he reached for his goblet of wine, and he diligently tried to shrug off his fears and get down to the business at hand.

He knew that his mind wasn't sharp now, but dull and muddled. It was unusual for him to become this inebriated in front of his friends. He'd been a heavy drinker for years because the memories wouldn't let him rest. But he'd always been careful to drink when he was alone. Today he'd made an exception to his own rule because the wine helped ease his anger. He didn't want to do anything he might later regret, and though he had considered waiting until tomorrow to deal with Gillian's defiance, he decided that he was still clearheaded enough to get the chore over and done with so he and his companions could continue their celebration.

Alford stared at Gillian through bleary, bloodshot eyes. He sat at the center of the long table and was flanked by his constant companions, Baron Hugh of Barlowe and Baron Edwin the Bald. He rarely went anywhere without his friends, as they were his most appreciative audience. They so enjoyed his games that they often begged to join in, and Alford never had to worry that either one of them would ever betray him, for they were just as culpable in their past transgressions as he was.

Gillian and the boy hadn't eaten since early morning the day before, and Alford assumed both would be ravenous by now, so he forced them to watch while he and his friends dined on a feast worthy of kings and discussed various punishments. The table was heavily laden with pheasant, rabbit, peacock and pigeon, yellow wedges of cheese, chunks of coarse black bread with jam and honey, and sweet blackberry tarts. Servants rushed back and forth with widemouthed jugs of dark red wine and additional breaded trenchers piled high with more offerings to tempt their gluttonous appetites.

There was enough food on the table to feed an army. Watching the three of them eat was such a disgusting sight to Gillian that her hunger pains quickly vanished. She couldn't make up her mind which one was the most foul. Hugh, with his big protruding ears and pointed chin, kept making grunting noises while he ate, and Edwin, with his triple chins and beady red eyes, had worked himself into a sweat as he frantically shoved fistfuls of greasy meat into his mouth. He acted as though he thought the food would disappear before he could fill his enormous belly, and by the time he paused for air, his face glistened with beads of oily perspiration.

All three of them were drunk. While she stood there watching, they downed the contents of six jugs of wine and were now waiting while the servant poured more.

They were like pigs at the trough, but Alford, she decided, was by far the worst offender. Strands of pigeon skin dangled from his lips, and when he shoved a full, plump tart into his cavernous mouth, blackberry juice squirted down on both sides of his chin, staining his red beard black. Too drunk to care about his manners or appearance, he eagerly reached for another.

Alec stood on her left, near the hearth, watching the spectacle without making a sound. Every now and then his hand would touch hers. As much as she longed to comfort him, she didn't dare even look at him because Alford was watching her closely. If she showed any concern or affection for the little boy, he'd have a weapon to use against her.

She had tried to prepare Alec as best she could by warning him that it would get worse before it was over, and she had also made him promise that no matter what happened, he would remain silent. As long as Alford believed the child didn't understand what he was saying, he would hopefully continue to speak freely in front of him and perhaps say something that would explain his purpose in stealing the boy.

When she couldn't stomach watching the animals eat any longer, she turned toward the entrance. She knew she must have played in this hall when she was a little girl, but she didn't have any memories at all. There was an old chest against the wall near the steps, and she wondered if it had belonged to her parents or if Alford had brought it with him. The top of the chest was cluttered with maps and rolls of parchment, but near the edge was a dagger. Alec had told her the soldier had taken one from him and tossed it on the chest. It was still there. She could see the unusual, intricate design on the handle and was strangely comforted by it. The dagger had been a gift from Alec's protector, Brodick.

Alford drew her attention when he let out a loud belch. She watched him wipe his face on the sleeve of his velvet tunic, then lean back in his chair. He seemed to be having difficulty keeping his eyes open, and his voice was heavily slurred when he spoke to her.

"What am I going to do with you, Gillian? You've resisted me at every turn. Don't you realize I only have your best interests at heart?"

Edwin burst into raucous laughter. Hugh chuckled as he reached for his goblet again.

"You've been quite a nuisance," Alford continued. "I've been very accommodating to you. Didn't I leave you alone all the while you were growing up? I'll admit I was shocked to see what a beautiful woman you've become. You were such a homely, unappealing child, the transformation is really quite amazing. You have value now, my dear. I could sell you to the highest bidder and make a pretty fortune. Does that possibility frighten you?"

"She's looking bored, not frightened," Edwin remarked.

Alford shrugged indifference. "Are you aware, Gillian, that it took a full unit of soldiers to pry you away from your sainted relative? I heard that your Uncle Morgan put up quite a fight, which I find quite amusing considering the fact that he's such an old, feeble man. Do you know I believe it would be an act of mercy on my part to put him out of his misery. I'm sure he'd appreciate a quick death in lieu of lingering on and on."

"My uncle is neither old nor feeble," she told him.

Edwin laughed. Gillian fought the almost irresistible urge to strike him. Dear God, how she wished she were stronger. She hated feeling so powerless and afraid.

"You will leave my uncle alone, Alford," she demanded. "He cannot hurt you."

He acted as though she hadn't spoken. "He's become a doting parent, hasn't he? Morgan wouldn't have fought so to keep you if he didn't love you like a father. Aye, he was defiant on your behalf, damn his hide," he added with a sneer. "I was also displeased to hear about your defiance. It was embarrassing, really. I expected you to immediately obey my summons. I am your guardian, after all, and you should have come running to me. I simply don't understand your resistance. No, I don't," he said. He paused to shake his head before resuming. "This is your home, is it not? I would think you would be eager to return. King John has decreed Dunhanshire will remain yours until you're wed. Then, of course, your husband will rule on your behalf."

"As it should be," Hugh interjected.

"You haven't weasled Dunhanshire away from the king yet?" Gillian couldn't keep the surprise out of her voice.

"I haven't asked for it," he muttered. "Why should I? It belongs to me all the same, for I am your guardian and therefore control all that is yours."

"Did John appoint you my guardian?" She

asked the question to irritate him, for she knew the king had not granted Alford that right.

Alford's face turned red with anger, and he scowled at her while he adjusted his ill-fitted tunic and took another drink of wine. "You're so unimportant to our king that he's all but forgotten about you. I have said that I am your guardian, and that makes it so."

"No, it does not make it so."

"Alford is our king's most trusted confidant," Edwin shouted. "How dare you speak to him in such an insolent tone."

"She is insolent, isn't she?" Alford remarked. "Like it or not, Gillian, I am your guardian and your fate is in my hands. I shall personally choose your husband. As to that, I might wed you myself," he added offhandedly.

She wouldn't allow herself to think about such a repulsive possibility and continued to stare at Alford without reacting to his threat.

"You've promised her to your cousin," Hugh reminded him. "I've heard that Clifford is already making grand plans."

"Yes, I know what I promised, but when have you ever known me to keep my word?" Alford asked with a grin.

Hugh and Edwin laughed until tears streamed down their faces. Alford finally demanded silence with a wave of his hand.

"You've made me lose track of what I was saying."

"You were telling Gillian how displeased you were with her defiance," Edwin reminded him.

"Yes, so I was," he said. "It simply cannot go on, Gillian. I'm a forgiving man—a flaw really—and I can't help pitying the less fortunate, so I let your uncle's outrageous behavior go unpunished. I also forgave you your resistance to my summons to come home."

He took another long swallow from his goblet before continuing. "And how do you repay me for my kindness? You try to help the little savage escape. As your guardian, I simply cannot allow your disobedience to go unpunished. It's time for you and the boy to learn a lesson in humility."

"If you beat her, Alford, she'll need time to recover before she goes on your important quest," Edwin cautioned.

Alford drained the rest of the wine, then motioned for the servant to refill his goblet. "I'm aware of that possibility," he said. "Have you noticed, Edwin, how the boy has attached himself to Gillian? He must foolishly believe she'll protect him from harm. Shall we prove to him how mistaken he is? Hugh, since you so enjoy your work, you can beat the boy."

"You will not touch him." Gillian made the statement very softly. It was far more effective than shouting, and she could tell from Alford's puzzled expression that she had caught him off guard.

"I won't?"

"No, you won't."

He drummed his fingertips on the table. "Pain will convince the boy how futile it is to try to escape. Besides, you have both inconvenienced me and I really can't disappoint Hugh. He so wants to hurt one of you." Alford turned to his friend. "Try not to kill the boy. If Gillian fails me, I'll have need of him."

"You will not touch the child," Gillian said again, though this time her voice was hard, emphatic.

"Are you willing to take his beating?" Alford asked.

"Yes."

Alford was stunned by her quick agreement and infuriated because she didn't look at all frightened. Courage was a foreign concept, and he had never been able to figure out why some men and women exhibited this strange phenomenon, while others did not. The trait had eluded him, and though he had certainly never felt the need to try to be courageous, those who did enraged him. What he lacked in his own character he detested in others.

"I will do whatever pleases me, Gillian, and you cannot stop me. I just might decide to kill you."

She shrugged. "Yes, you're right. You could kill me and I couldn't stop you."

He raised an eyebrow and studied her. It was difficult to concentrate, for the wine had made him quite sleepy and all he wanted to do was close his eyes for a few minutes. He took another drink instead.

"You're up to something," he said. "What is it, Gillian? What game do you dare play with the master?"

"No games," she answered. "Kill me if that is your inclination. I'm sure you'll come up with an adequate explanation to give our king. However, as you have just said, you have left me alone all these many years and then suddenly you force me to come back here. You obviously want something from me, and if you kill me—"

"Yes," he interrupted, "I do want something from you." He straightened up in his chair and looked triumphant when he continued, "I have joyous news. After years of searching, I have finally found your sister. I know where Christen hides from me." He watched Gillian closely and was disappointed because she didn't respond to his announcement. Rolling the goblet between his fingertips, he smirked. "I even know the name of the clan protecting her. It's MacPherson, but I don't know the name she uses now. One sister will surely recognize another, and that is why I want you to go and fetch her for me."

"Why don't you send your soldiers to get her?" she asked.

"I cannot send my troops into the thick of the Highlands, and that is where she hides from me. Those savages would slaughter my men. I could, of course, gain King John's blessing for this undertaking, and I'm certain he would give me additional soldiers, but I don't want to involve him in a family matter. Besides, I have you to do this errand for me."

"The soldiers wouldn't know which woman she is, and the heathens certainly wouldn't tell.

They protect their own at all costs," Hugh inter-jected.

"And if I refuse to go?" she asked.

"Someone else can bring Christen to me," he bluffed. "It would just be less compli-cated if you were to fetch her."

"And would this someone else be able to rec-ognize her?"

"The Highlander who gave us this infor-mation knows the name Christen uses," Edwin reminded Alford. "You could force him to tell you."

"For all we know the Highlander could be bringing Christen with him tomorrow," Hugh said. "The message he sent indicated there was a problem—"

"An urgent problem," Edwin interjected. "And it isn't for certain that he will arrive tomorrow. It could be the day after."

"I don't doubt the problem is urgent." Hugh leaned forward in his chair so he could see around Alford. "The traitor wouldn't take the chance of coming all this way if it weren't an urgent matter. He stands the risk of being seen."

Edwin rubbed his triple chins. "If you beat the boy, Hugh, the Highlander might be dis-pleased and demand his gold back."

Hugh laughed. "He wants the boy killed, you old fool. You were too drunk at the time to pay attention to the conversation. Suffice it to say that a bargain was struck between the Highlander and Alford. As you know, every so often a new rumor surfaces that the golden box has been seen, and every time King John hears of it, he sends troops to scour the kingdom. His desire to find the culprit who killed his Arianna and get his treasure back has not dampened over the years."

"Some say his fervor has increased tenfold," Edwin remarked. "The king has even sent troops into the Lowlands looking for information."

Hugh nodded. "And while John searches for his treasure, Alford searches for Christen because he believes she knows where the box is hidden. He means to prove her father stole it. Alford has also sent inquiries over the years to all the clans asking about Christen..."

"But none of his inquiries were ever answered."

"That is true," Hugh agreed. "No one would admit he knew anything about her... until the Highlander arrived."

"But what of the bargain struck between this traitor and our Alford?"

Hugh looked at the baron, waiting for him to answer the question, but Alford's eyes were closed and his head drooped down on his chest. He appeared to be dozing.

"I've never seen the baron so drunk," Hugh whispered loudly to his friend. "Look how the wine has lulled him to sleep."

Edwin shrugged. "And the bargain?" he nagged.

"The baron agreed to hold the boy captive to draw out his brother, Laird Ramsey Sinclair, so that the Highlander could kill him. The child's simply a pawn, and when the game is over and Ramsey is killed..."

"The boy no longer serves any purpose."

"Exactly," Hugh agreed. "So you see, beating him will not concern the Highlander at all."

"What did the baron get out of this bargain?"

"The Highlander gave him gold and something more," he said. "I will leave that for Alford to explain. If he wants you to know, he'll tell you."

Edwin was incensed to be left out. He shoved his elbow hard into Alford's side. The baron jerked upright and muttered a blasphemy.

Edwin then demanded to know the particulars of the bargain. Alford took a drink before answering.

"The traitor gave me information more important than gold."

"What could be more important?" Edwin asked.

Alford smiled. "I told you he gave me the name of the clan Christen hides in, and when he has gotten what he wants, he vows to tell me the name she uses now. So you see, if Gillian should fail me, the Highlander will come to my aid."

"Why won't he tell you now? It would make it so much easier if you knew..."

"He doesn't trust our baron," Hugh chuckled. "This Ramsey must die first. Then he swears he'll give us her name."

Gillian couldn't believe the three of them were talking so freely in front of her. They were all too drunk to be cautious, and she doubted that any of them would remember a word he said come tomorrow morning.

Edwin and Hugh seemed to think Alford was going to be given a reward by the king, and they were now discussing what he would do with it. She was blessedly thankful for their inattention, for when she had heard that the Highlander would soon arrive at Dunhanshire, she felt as though the floor had just dropped away. Inwardly reeling, her stomach lurched with her panic and she swayed on her feet. Fortunately, Alford appeared oblivious to her distress.

She knew why the traitor was coming, of course. He was going to tell Alford that the wrong boy had been taken, and God help Alec then. Time was about to run out.

Alford yawned loudly and squinted at her. "Ah, Gillian, I forgot you were standing there. Now what were we discussing? Oh, yes," he said as he turned to Hugh. "Since Gillian has so graciously offered to take the boy's beating for him, you may accommodate her. Don't touch her face," he warned. "I've learned from experience that the bones in the face take much longer to heal, and I do so want to send her on my errand as soon as possible."

"And the boy?" Hugh asked.

Alford sneered at Gillian when he answered. "I want him beaten too."

She pushed Alec behind her. "You'll have to kill me first, Alford. I'm not going to let you touch him."

"But I don't want to kill you, Gillian. I want you to bring your sister to me."

The mockery in his voice was deliberate, for he wanted her to know he was laughing at her pitiful attempts to protect the child. Did she really believe her wants mattered to him? And how dare she give him orders, telling him what he could and could not do. He would get his way, of course, but also teach her a valuable lesson at the same time. She would learn once and for all how insignificant she was.

"I swear to you, if you harm the boy, I won't bring Christen to you."

"Yes, yes, I know." Alford sounded bored. "You've already made that empty threat."

Hugh pushed his chair back and struggled to stand. Gillian frantically tried to think of something she could do or say that would stop the atrocity.

"You don't really want Christen back, do you?"

Alford tilted his head toward Gillian. "Of course I want her back. I have grand plans for her."

Deliberately trying to incite his wrath to take his attention away from the child, she laughed. "Oh, I know all about your grand plans. You want King John's precious box, and you think Christen has it, don't you? That's what you really want, and you think that if she's forced back here, she'll bring the treasure with her. You want to prove that my father murdered the king's lover and stole the box. Then you think you'll win the prize and Dunhanshire land. Isn't that your grand plan?"

Alford reacted as though she had just thrown boiling oil in his face. Howling in rage, he leapt to his feet. His chair flew backward, crashing into the wall.

"You do remember the box," he bellowed as he rushed around the corner of the table toward her, shoving Hugh out of his path. "And you know where it's hidden."

"Of course I know," she lied.

Another unearthly howl filled the hall as Alford ran to her. "Tell me where it is," he demanded. "Christen does have it, doesn't she? I knew... I knew she had taken it... that crazy Ector told me her father gave it to her. Your sister stole it from me, and you've known... all this time that I've been out of my mind searching... you knew... all this time you knew."

His temper exploded and he slammed his fist into her jaw, knocking her to the floor.

He was beyond reason now. His leather boot slammed into her tender skin. He viciously kicked her again and again, determined to make her scream in agony, to make her sorry that she had dared to keep the truth hidden from him. She had known all this time that the box could destroy her father's name and win Dunhanshire and the King's reward. All these years the bitch had deliberately tormented him.

98

"I will give the box to the king... and I alone," he railed, panting from exertion. "The reward will be mine... mine... mine."

Reeling from the blow to her face, Gillian was too dazed to fight back. Yet she had enough presence of mind to roll to her side and try to protect her head with her arms. Her back and legs took most of the pounding, but ironically the pain wasn't as terrible as Alford wanted it to be, for in her nearly unconscious state, she barely felt the blows from his booted foot.

She became fully alert when Alec threw himself on top of her. Hysterical, he screamed at the top of his lungs as she pushed him away from Alford. She threw her arms around him, hugging him tight, trying to shield him, and then she grabbed hold of his hand and squeezed, hoping he would understand she wanted him to be silent. Alford's rage was fully directed on her now, and she was terrified that the boy's interference would draw his wrath.

Spittle ran down the sides of Alford's face with each obscenity he shouted as he continued to inflict his punishment. Quickly exhausted, he lost his balance and staggered backward. The sight so amused Hugh, he was overcome with laughter. Edwin didn't want the entertainment to stop and shouted encouragement to spur Alford on. Gillian's ears rang from the deafening noise, and the room swirled around her in a hazy blur, but she desperately tried to focus on the terrified little boy.

"Hush," she whispered. "Hush now."

As though someone had cupped a hand over his mouth to silence him, Alec stopped screaming in mid wail. Only inches away from her face, his eyes wide with fear, he gave her a quick nod to let her know he would be quiet. She was so pleased with him, she forced a weak smile.

"Get hold of yourself, Alford," Hugh shouted between gales of laughter. He brushed the tears away from his cheeks before adding, "She won't be able to go anywhere if you kill her."

Alford stumbled back against the table. "Yes, yes," he panted. "I must control myself."

He wiped the sweat from his brow, shoved the boy away from Gillian, and jerked her to her feet. Blood trickled down the side of her mouth, and he smugly nodded in satisfaction, for he could see the glazed look in her eyes and knew he had caused her considerable pain.

"You dare to make me lose my temper," he muttered. "You have no one to blame but yourself for your pain. I'll allow you two days' time to recover, and then you will leave Dunhanshire and go to that godforsaken land called the Highlands. Your sister hides with the clan MacPherson. Find her," he ordered, "and bring her and the box to me."

He adjusted his tunic as he staggered back to the table, angrily motioning for the servant to pick up his chair. Once he had resumed his seat, he mopped his brow with his sleeve and downed a full goblet of wine.

"If you fail me, Gillian, the man you hold

so dear will suffer the consequences. Your uncle will die a slow, agonizing death. I swear to you that I will make him beg me to put him out of his misery. The boy should also be killed," he added almost as an afterthought. "But when you bring Christen and the box to me, I give you my word I will let the child live in spite of my promise to the Highland traitor."

"But what if she can only bring one back and not the other?" Hugh asked.

Edwin had also considered the question. "Which is more important to you, Baron, Christen or the king's box?"

"The box, of course," Alford answered. "But I want both, and if Gillian brings only one, her uncle dies."

Hugh swaggered around the table to face Gillian. The lust she saw in his eyes made her inwardly cringe.

He kept his gaze on her when he spoke to Alford. "You and I have been friends a long time," he reminded the baron. "And I have never asked for anything... until now. Give me Gillian."

Alford was surprised and amused by Hugh's request. "You would take a witch to your bed?"

"She's a lioness, and I would tame her," he boasted, obscenely licking his lips over the fantasy.

"She would cut your throat while you slept," Edwin called out.

Hugh snorted. "With Gillian in my bed, I assure you I wouldn't be sleeping."

He reached out to stroke her, but she shoved his hand away and took a step back. Hugh glanced down at the boy clinging to Gillian. She quickly forced him to look at her again and forget about the child when she said, "You are most foul, Hugh, and such a weakling, I almost pity you."

Shocked by the venom in her voice, he slapped her with the back of his hand.

She retaliated by smiling.

"Leave her be," Alford demanded impatiently when Hugh raised his hand to strike her again.

He leered at her for several seconds, then leaned forward and whispered, "I will have you, bitch." He turned around then and went back to his place at the table. "Give her to me," he nagged Alford. "I can teach her to be obedient."

Alford smiled. "I shall consider your request," he promised.

Edwin wasn't about to be left out. "If you give Gillian to him, then I must have Christen."

"She has already been promised," Alford said.

"You want her for yourself," Edwin accused.

"I don't want her, but I have promised her to another."

"Who did you promise?" Edwin asked.

Hugh laughed. "Does it matter, Edwin? Alford has never kept his word."

"Never," Alford snickered. "But there is always a first time."

Edwin grinned, for he was placated now and foolishly believed he still had a chance of winning Christen's hand. "If she is half as beautiful as Gillian, then I will be well-served."

"How long will you give Gillian to complete her errand?" Hugh asked.

"She must return to me before the celebration of the harvest begins."

"But that is not nearly long enough," Edwin protested. "Why, it will take her a full week, maybe two, just to get to her destination, and if there are any problems along the way or if she cannot find Christen..."

Alford raised his hand for silence. "Your prattle of worries on the bitch's behalf make my head spin. Hold your tongue while I explain the details to my ward. Gillian? Should you think to find sympathetic Highlanders to help you save your dear uncle, know this. A full contingent of my soldiers have surrounded his home, and if so much as one Highland warrior steps foot into the holding, Morgan will be killed. I will hold him ransom until you return. Do I make myself clear?"

"What if she tells Ramsey that his brother didn't drown and that you have him?" Hugh asked.

"She will not tell," Alford replied. "She holds the boy's life with her silence. Enough of your questions," he added. "I wish to talk about more amusing matters now, such as how I will spend the king's reward when I give the box to him. I have already suggested more than once that it was Gillian and Christen's father who stole the box and killed Arianna, and when the King finds out that Christen has had the treasure all this time, he will be convinced."

He motioned to the two sentries at the entrance to come forward. "The dear lady can barely stand up. See how she sways on her feet? Take her and the boy upstairs. Put her in her old room. See how thoughtful I can be, Gillian? I'm going to let you sleep in your own bed."

"And the boy, milord?" one of the soldiers inquired.

"Put him in the room next to hers," he said. "He can listen to her weep during the night."

The soldiers rushed forward to do their lord's bidding. One took hold of Alec's arm and the other reached for Gillian. She jerked away, steadied herself, and slowly, painfully, straightened up. Head erect, she held on to the edge of the table until she gained the strength in her legs, then took careful, measured steps. When she was close to the doors, she swayed and collapsed against the chest.

The soldier pulled her upright and dragged her the rest of the way to the stairs. Gillian folded her arms across her battered ribs and hunched over, and Alec held on to her skirt as they started up the steps. She stumbled twice before her legs gave out on her altogether. Making a tisking sound, the soldier lifted her into his arms and carried her the rest of the way.

The pain in her back became excruciating, and she fainted before they reached her door. The soldier dropped her on the bed and turned to grab hold of the boy, but Alec refused to leave. He bit and scratched and kicked the man who was trying to pry him away from Gillian.

"Leave him be," his friend suggested. "If we keep the two of them in the same room, we'll only have to post a guard in front of one door tonight. The boy can sleep on the floor."

The two men left the chamber then, locking the door behind them. Alec climbed up on the bed next to Gillian and held on to her. Terrified that she would die and leave him all alone, he sobbed uncontrollably.

A long while passed before she finally awakened. The pain pulsating through her body was so intense, tears flooded into her eyes. She waited until the room stopped spinning, then tried to sit up, but the pain was unbearable, and she collapsed against the bedcovers, feeling helpless and defeated.

Alec whispered her name.

"It's all right now. The worst is over, Alec. Please don't cry."

"But you're crying."

"I'll stop," she promised.

"Are you going to die?" he asked worriedly.

"No," she whispered.

"Do you hurt real bad?"

"I'm already feeling much better," she lied. "And at least we're safe now."

"No, we're not," he argued. "Tomorrow is gonna be—"

"Much better," she interrupted. "It's dark in here, isn't it? Why don't you tie the tapestry back from the window so we can have some light."

"The light's almost gone," he told her as he jumped off the bed and ran to the window to do as she had requested.

Golden ribbons of sunlight streamed into the room and, like silken banners, floated in the gentle summer breeze. They danced along the stone floor. She could see particles of dust in the air, could smell the musty scent of mildew in the bedcovers, and wondered how long the room had been closed. Had she been the last to sleep in this bed? It was unlikely. Alford liked to entertain, and he had surely had a multitude of guests at Dunhanshire since she had been banished.

Alec climbed back in bed with her and took hold of her hand. "The sun's going down. You slept an awful long time, and I couldn't get you to wake up. I got scared," he admitted. "And you know what?"

"No, what?"

"It *is too* gonna get worse 'cause I heard what the baron said. The Highlander's coming here."

"Yes, I heard what he said." She put her hand to her forehead and closed her eyes. She said a quick prayer that God would help her get her strength back—and soon—for time was critical.

"The Highlander will be here tomorrow or the day after." Alec became agitated. "If he sees me, he's gonna know I'm not Michael. Then maybe he'll tell on me."

While she once again struggled to sit up, she addressed his worry. "I'm sure he already knows you're not Michael. That's probably the urgent news he wishes to tell the baron."

He frowned intently, until the freckles on his nose blended together. "Maybe he wants to tell him something else."

"I don't think so."

"I don't want you to leave me."

"I'm not going to leave you," she promised.

"But the baron's gonna send you away."

"Yes," she agreed. "But I'm going to take you with me." He didn't look as if he believed her. She patted his hand and forced a smile. "It doesn't matter to us if the Highlander comes here or not, though in truth I would like to get a good look at him."

"'Cause he's a traitor?"

"Yes."

"And then you can tell my papa and Brodick and even Ramsey what the traitor looks like?"

Alec was looking happy now, and so she quickly agreed. "Yes, that's exactly right. I would tell your father what he looks like."

"And Brodick and even Ramsey too?"

"Yes."

"Then you know what would happen? They'd make him sorry he was a traitor."

"Yes, I'm sure they would."

"How come we don't care if the Highlander comes here or not?"

"We don't care because we're leaving tonight."

His eyes widened in surprise. "In the dark?"

"In the dark. Hopefully the moon will guide us."

His eagerness was almost uncontainable, and he bounced on the bed. "But how are we going to do that? I heard the soldier lock the door when he left, and I think maybe there's a guard outside in the hall. That's how come I'm whispering 'cause I don't want him to hear me."

"We're still going to leave," she said.

"But how?"

She pointed to the opposite end of the room. "You and I are going to walk right through that wall."

His smile vanished. "I don't think we can do that."

He sounded so forlorn she felt like laughing. She realized then that in spite of her pain, she was actually feeling euphoric because she wasn't going to have to leave the little boy in Alford's lair. It had been a wonderful piece of luck that Alford hadn't hidden the child away from her, and she planned to take full advantage of his error in judgment.

She couldn't resist pulling Alec into her arms and hugging him. "Oh, Alec, God is surely watching over us."

He let her kiss his forehead and brush his hair out of his eyes before he squirmed out of her embrace. "How come you think God's watching out for us?" He was too impatient to wait for her answer. "Is God gonna help us walk through the wall?"

"Yes," she replied.

He shook his head. "I think maybe the baron made you daft when he hit you."

"No, he didn't make me daft. He made me angry, very, very angry."

"But, Gillian, people can't walk through walls."

"We're going to open a secret door. This used to be my bedroom when I was a little girl," she told him. "My sister's room was right next to mine, and whenever I got scared or lonely, I would open the passageway and run into her room. My father would become very upset with me."

"How come?"

"Because the passage was only to be used in dire circumstances, and he didn't want anyone to know about it, not even his faithful servants. My lady's maid, Liese, knew about the doorway though, and she used to tell me that most mornings she would find my bed empty. Liese figured out there had to be a hidden door because she knew I was afraid of the dark and wouldn't have ventured out into the hall during the night. Do you see that chest in front of the wall? My father put it there to discourage me. He knew the chest was too heavy for me to move, but Liese told me that I used to squeeze behind it to get to the door."

His eyes grew wide. "You disobeyed your papa."

"It seems I did," she answered.

He found her admission extremely funny and laughed until tears came into his eyes. Concerned the guard would hear the noise, she put her finger over her mouth as a sign for him to quiet down.

"But if the door goes to your sister's room," he whispered loudly, "how will we get out of there?"

"The passage also leads to the staircase that goes down into the tunnels below the castle. If it hasn't been sealed, it will take us outside the walls."

"Then can we leave now? Please?" he asked.

She shook her head. "We must wait until the baron has gone to bed. He's had so much wine to drink he'll pass out soon. Besides, he might send one of the servants to check on us before nightfall, and if we aren't here, she'll sound the alarm."

He slipped his fingers through hers and held tight, all the while staring at the wall, trying to figure out where the door was. When he turned back to Gillian, he was frowning again. "What if the baron sealed it?"

"Then we'll figure out another way to leave."

"But how?"

She didn't have the faintest idea, but she did know that she had to get Alec out of Dunhanshire before the Highlander arrived. "We could trick the guard into coming inside—"

In his excitement he interrupted her. "And I could hit him on his head and knock him down," he said, acting out his plan by pounding the bed with his fists. "I'd make him bleed," he assured her. "And if I stood on top of the chest, I could maybe even grab his sword, and then you know what? I could slice him up and make him cry something fierce. I'm very strong," he ended with a boast.

She had to resist the urge to hug him again, and she didn't dare smile because he might think she was laughing at him. "Yes, I can see how strong you are," she said.

He grinned with pleasure over her compliment and lifted his shoulders as he nodded.

Were all little boys as bloodthirsty in their fantasies as this one? she wondered. One minute he was crying and clinging to her and the next he was gleefully planning gruesome revenge. She didn't have any experience with children—Alec was the first she had been around for any length of time—and she felt thoroughly inadequate, yet at the same time, she also felt tremendously protective. She was all the little boy had separating him from disaster, and in her mind that meant Alec was still in danger.

"Does it hurt?"

She blinked. "Does what hurt?"

"Your face," he answered as he reached up to touch the side of her cheek. "It's swelling."

"It stings a little, that's all."

"How come you got a scar under your chin?"

"I fell down the steps. It happened a long time ago."

She patted the bed beside her and said, "Why don't you stretch out beside me and try to get some sleep."

"But it isn't night yet."

"Yes, I know, but we're going to be up all night walking," she explained. "You should try to rest now."

He scooted up close to her and put his head down on her shoulder. "You know what?"

"What?"

"I'm hungry."

"We'll find something to eat later."

"Will we have to steal food?"

From his exuberance she assumed he was looking forward to the possibility. "Stealing is a sin."

"That's what my mama says."

"And she's right. We won't steal anything. We'll just borrow what we need."

"Can we borrow horses?"

"If we're lucky enough to find a sturdy one and no one's around to stop us, then yes, we'll borrow a horse."

"You could get yourself hanged for stealing a horse."

"That's the least of my worries," she said as she shifted in the bed. Every inch of her body throbbed, and there simply was no comfortable position. She moved her bandaged arm down to her side and felt a prick, and only then remembered the surprise she had for Alec.

"I have something for you," she said. "Close your eyes tight."

He bolted upright onto his knees and squeezed his eyes shut. "What is it?"

She held up the dagger. She didn't have to tell him to look, for he was already peeking. The joy in his eyes made her feel like weeping.

"Brodick's dagger," he whispered in awe. "How did you find it?"

"You told me where it was," she reminded him. "I grabbed it from the chest on the way out of the hall. Keep it inside the leather sheath so you won't accidentally cut yourself."

He was so happy to have his treasure back, he threw his arms around her neck and kissed her swollen cheek. "I love you, Gillian."

"I love you too, Alec."

"Now I can protect you 'cause I got my knife back."

She smiled. "Are you going to be my champion, then?"

"No," he giggled, drawing out the word.

"Why not?"

He pulled back and told her what he thought should have been obvious. "'Cause I'm just a little boy. But you know what?"

"No, what?"

"We got to find you one."

"A champion?"

He nodded solemnly.

She shook her head. "I don't need a protector," she assured him.

"But you got to have one. Maybe we can ask Brodick."

"The mean one?" she teased.

He nodded again.

She laughed softly. "I don't think..."

"We'll ask Brodick," he said, sounding very grown up. "'Cause you know why?"

"No, why?"

"You need him."

CHAPTER FOUR

They didn't like the message. Four of Laird Buchanan's elite guard surrounded the young MacDonald soldier, towering over him like avenging gargoyles as he stammered out his important information while quaking in his boots. Three of the warriors were rendered speechless by the announcement. Aaron, Robert, and Liam were outraged by what they immediately surmised was trickery on Laird MacDonald's part. Everyone in the Buchanan clan knew the messenger's laird to be a sneaky, lying, son of a bitch, and therefore refused to believe a word he said. The fourth Buchanan warrior, Dylan, had the opposite reaction to the news. Though he also believed Laird MacDonald to be a sneaky, lying, son of a bitch, he was so amused and intrigued by the message he was eager to hear the details.

Aaron, the most outspoken of the Buchanan group, shook his head in denial and moved forward with the demand that the messenger repeat every word.

"'Tis as I said before," the young Mac-Donald soldier insisted.

"Then say it again," Aaron commanded, deliberately moving close so that the man would have to crane his head back in order to look him in the eyes. "Word for word I would hear this foul message again."

The MacDonald soldier felt like a trapped rabbit. Robert stood behind him, Dylan faced him, and Aaron and Liam pressed in against his sides. All the Buchanan warriors were at least two heads above him in height, and they could easily crush him with their weight alone.

He turned to the warrior who had made the demand, then tried to step back so that he could put a little breathing distance between them. "There is a young lady who insists that your laird come to her at once. She waits inside the boarded up church near the crossroads below the Len holding. She claims... to be..."

The dark look on the warrior's face so terrified the soldier he couldn't go on. He turned to Dylan, then stepped back in an attempt to get away from his scorching glare and bumped into the warrior named Black Robert.

"My message is for Brodick and Brodick alone," he protested.

"He is *Laird* Buchanan to you, pup," Liam growled.

"Yes... yes, Laird Buchanan," the soldier hastily acknowledged. "I overstep myself."

"Aye, you do," Robert muttered from behind.

Dylan stepped forward to question the messenger. Brodick had already been summoned to the great hall but had not yet arrived, and so the commander over the elite guard of Buchanan warriors decided to take charge of the questioning. He knew the MacDonald soldier was scared, and so he clasped his hands behind his back as a signal that he wouldn't harm him and impatiently waited for him to regain his composure.

"Continue with your message," Dylan demanded.

"The lady, she claims to be his bride," the frightened young man blurted out. "And she demands that your laird escort her to his home so that she may take up residence."

Robert nudged the soldier to get his attention and accidentally sent him lunging forward. He bumped into Dylan, who didn't budge an inch, quickly righted himself, and whirled around to face the warrior. "I do not lie," he insisted. "I repeat only what I was bid to say."

"What is your name?" Robert asked. He thought his question a mild one and therefore was surprised by the messenger's reaction. The young man actually paled like a frightened woman.

"Henley," he blurted out with a sigh, thankful he'd been able to remember it. "My name is Henley."

Dylan demanded Henley's attention by prodding him to turn around again. The soldier quickly obeyed the order, dizzy now from twirling about in the center of the giants. He tried to concentrate only on the Buchanan commander, but it was difficult, for the other three were deliberately pressing in on him.

"Why did the MacDonald send a boy to give us this message?" Dylan asked contemptuously.

Henley's Adam's apple bulged and wobbled

116

as he swallowed. He didn't dare contradict the commander by arguing that he was a man, not a boy, and so he said, "My laird felt that a younger man would have a better chance of surviving your laird's temper. We have all witnessed your laird in battle and know of his remarkable strength. Many have claimed that they have seen him fell his enemy with but a flick of his wrist. We have also all heard that it is... unwise... to displease him. Laird Mac-Donald is not ashamed to admit that he respectfully fears your laird."

Dylan smiled. "Respectfully fears?"

Henley nodded. "My laird also said that Brodick..."

Liam shoved the messenger hard, sending him crashing into Robert. The warrior didn't flinch, but Henley felt as though he'd just run into a stone wall. He turned to Liam then, wishing with all his heart he had the nerve to suggest that if the warrior wanted to gain his attention, he simply say his name.

"Brodick is Laird Buchanan to you," Liam reminded him.

"Yes, Laird Buchanan," Henley quickly agreed.

"You were saying?" Aaron prodded.

Henley turned to his left to answer. "My laird said that Laird Buchanan is an honorable man and that he would not prey upon an unarmed man. I do not carry a weapon."

Henley was forced to whirl to the right when Dylan asked, "And does your laird also tell you that Brodick is reasonable?"

Henley knew that if he lied, the warriors would know it. "Nay, he said just the opposite," he admitted.

Dylan laughed. "Your honesty protects your hide."

Aaron spoke then, forcing the messenger to turn completely around.

"We don't kill messengers," he said.

"Unless, of course, we dislike the message." Robert grinned.

Henley turned back to address their leader once again. "There is more," he said. "I fear the rest will truly displease your laird." The quicker he got his message delivered, the quicker he could get out of their trap, and if God proved merciful, he would be well on his way home before Brodick arrived.

The laird had been summoned from the training fields below the holding and was irritated by the interruption, but when he heard that there was an urgent message, his heart leapt with hope that the news was from Iain Maitland, telling him that his son, Alec, had been found.

Gawain, another one of his trusted guards, dashed Brodick's hopes when he told him that the plaid the messenger wore was from the clan MacDonald.

The disappointment frustrated and angered him. He turned to Gawain and said, "Tomorrow we go back to the falls and search once again. Do you argue with me this time, Gawain?"

The soldier shook his head. "Nay, I know

that it's futile to argue with you, Laird. Until you believe in your heart that the boy is dead, I'll continue to search as diligently as you."

"Do you believe Alec drowned?"

Gawain's sigh was weary. "'Tis the truth I do."

Brodick couldn't fault his friend for his honesty. He continued up the hill with Gawain at his side.

"His father taught Alec how to swim," he remarked.

"But if Alec hit his head on the rocks as the blood indicated, he would have been unconscious when he hit the water. Besides, even a grown man would have difficulty surviving the pounding falls."

"Neither Iain nor I believe Alec is dead."

"Laird Maitland mourns his son," Gawain said. "In time he will accept his death."

"No," Brodick argued. "Until there is a body to bury, neither one of us will accept."

"You were just appointed his champion," Gawain said. "Perhaps that is yet another reason you cannot accept. As his new protector..."

"A protector who failed," Brodick interrupted harshly. "I should have gone to the festival. I should have watched out for him. I don't even know if Iain gave Alec my dagger and if the boy knew..." He shook his head and forced himself to think about the present. "Go and take over the training. I'll join you as soon as I've heard what the MacDonald soldier has to say."

A draft blew into the great hall when the doors to the courtyard were thrown open. Henley heard the sound of Brodick's boots pounding against the stone floor and closed his eyes. His panic nearly made him faintheaded and it took a supreme act of courage to stand still and not try to run.

"The message damned well better be urgent. Where's the MacDonald soldier?" Brodick demanded as he strode into the hall.

Dylan nodded to the guards surrounding the messenger. "Move back so our laird may hear this important message," he ordered. He tried to sound serious, but knew he'd failed in that endeavor.

Brodick stood next to Dylan to face the messenger. Henley felt his shivers increase tenfold, for the two warriors were extremely daunting. The Buchanan laird was even taller than his commander. Brodick was a giant of a man, with thick bulging muscles in his shoulders and upper arms and thighs, indicating his raw, superior strength. His skin was richly bronzed, his long hair golden. His eyes bore into Henley with a gaze so intense and probing, the young soldier felt as though he were staring into the eyes of a lion who was about to have him for his supper.

Aye, he was in the lion's den, and heaven help him when he gave the rest of his message.

Dylan had terrified Henley before, but now that the commander stood next to his laird, he didn't seem quite as intimidating. In coloring, Dylan was the antithesis of Brodick, for he was as dark as the night. In size and bulk he was equal, but his manner was less threatening.

"I would hear this urgent message," Brodick commanded.

Henley flinched. He found it impossible to hold the laird's stare, and so he cowardly looked at the tops of his boots while he repeated word for word what he had memorized.

"The lady... she bids you to come to her at the church of Saint Thomas at the crossroads below the Len holding, and the lady, she... demands... yes, demands that you escort her to your home."

Henley darted a quick glance up to judge Brodick's reaction and wished with all his heart he hadn't been so curious. The scowl on the laird's face made the blood rush to his temples, and he feared he might disgrace the MacDonald name by passing out.

"She?" Brodick asked quietly.

"Tell him," Dylan ordered.

"Your bride," Henley blurted out. "The lady, she's your bride."

"This woman claims to be my bride?"

Henley nodded. "'Tis true."

"The hell it is," Dylan replied.

"Nay, I meant to say only that she claims... She told me to say those very words. Laird, does my message displease you?" He held his breath while he waited for an answer. He firmly believed the gossip about Brodick and therefore thought his fate rested in the laird's reaction.

"It would depend upon the woman," Aaron said. "Know you if she is comely?"

Not only did Henley dare to contradict the warrior, but he also let a flash of anger appear in his expression and his voice while he was at it. "She is not a mere woman. She is a lady, a gentle lady."

"And what is this gentle lady's name?" Robert asked.

"Buchanan," Henley answered. "She calls herself Lady Buchanan." He took a deep breath and then said, "She must be your laird's wife, for she is most fitting. I believed her to be very sincere."

"She has obviously turned your head," Aaron interjected. "But then, you are a boy, and boys are easily influenced."

Henley ignored the criticism, his attention on the laird now. "May I speak my thoughts freely and tell you all that transpired?"

Brodick granted him permission, but Dylan qualified his laird's agreement. "As long as you speak only the truth."

"Yes, only the truth," Henley promised. "I was on my way home from the Lowlands when I was intercepted by a man I took to be a farmer. His voice was that of an Englishman. I was surprised, because it is unheard of for an Englishman to walk on Highland ground without it being known and permission granted. I thought the man was most impertinent, but I soon forgave him his transgression when I heard about his noble undertaking."

"What was his noble undertaking?" Aaron asked.

"He and his brother protected the lady."

"Only two men to protect such a treasure?" Robert mocked.

Henley ignored the comment and steeled himself against the laird's temper when he told him what he considered to be the worst of the news.

"Laird, your bride is English."

Liam, the quiet one of the group, let out a roar that so startled Henley he jumped. Robert muttered a dark curse, Aaron shook his head in disgust, and Dylan couldn't quite hide his grimace. Brodick seemed to be the only one unaffected by the announcement. He raised his hand for silence and calmly bid the messenger to continue.

"I didn't know about the lady at first," Henley explained. "The Englishman told me his name was Waldo, and he invited me to share his meager supper. He explained that he had been given permission to cross the Len holding by the old laird himself and that his wife's family was distantly related to the clan. I took his explanation as truth for I couldn't think of any reason why he would lie, and because I was both weary and hungry, I accepted his invitation. He seemed a likable sort—for an Englishman. After we ate, he told me he was very curious about the clans in the north. He knew of many of them and asked me to show him in the dirt with a stick where certain clans lived."

"Which clans in particular was he interested in?" Brodick's voice had turned hard.

"He was interested in the Sinclairs and the MacPhersons," Henley said. "But he was most interested in finding out where the Maitland clan was located and also where your clan resided, Laird. Aye, he was extremely curious about the Buchanans. 'Twas peculiar now that I think about it, but the farmer seemed disappointed to see how far north the Maitland clan lived. He smiled, though, when I showed him that your holding bordered the Sinclairs' and that it was the Sinclair holding that touched a corner of Maitland land. I should have asked him why he was so happy about this information, but I didn't."

"Did you think to ask him why he was interested in the clans?" Dylan asked.

Henley twitched over the anger in the warrior's tone. "Yes, I did ask," he answered. "Waldo told me he wanted to know who would give him permission to cross their land and who wouldn't. I told him he should turn around and go back home because none of the clans he had asked about would ever let him step on their ground."

"When did he tell you about the woman?" Aaron asked.

Henley dared to correct the warrior once again. "She is a lady."

Aaron rolled his eyes heavenward. "So you say," he replied. "I have yet to judge her so."

"Continue with this tale of yours," Dylan ordered.

"After I had drawn the map of the clans for Waldo, he asked me if I knew a warrior named Brodick."

"He is *Laird* to you," Liam snapped.

Henley quickly nodded. "I am only repeating the farmer's words to me," he rushed out. "He called your laird Brodick. I told him I did indeed know who he was asking about, and I also explained that he is called Laird Buchanan now. He asked many questions about you, Laird, but he was most interested in knowing, for a certainty, that you were... honorable. I told him that you were most honorable, and that was when he confessed his true reason for being in the Highlands. He said he was escorting your bride."

"Is that when her father's soldiers presented themselves?"

"Nay," Henley answered. "There were but two traveling with the lady, no less, no more, brothers they were, and much too old for such a duty. I searched for others, but there were none."

"What kind of father sends his daughter with but two old men to guard her?" Aaron asked.

"There were no others," Henley insisted. "Aye, they were old men, in their forties, but they were able to get her all the way to the Len holding, and that is quite a distance inside the Highlands. The brothers were very protective toward her. They wouldn't let me see her, but told me that she was inside the church. They gave me a message to relate to you, Laird, and then tried to send me on my way with the promise that you would richly reward me. I want nothing from you, though," he hastened to add, "for I have already been given my reward."

"And what was that?" Robert asked.

"I saw the lady and spoke to her. No gift could ever equal that moment."

Liam openly scoffed, but Henley ignored him. "Laugh if you wish, but you have not seen her yet, and you cannot understand."

"Tell us about her," Aaron commanded.

"She called out to me through the open window when I was leaving. I had agreed to gain permission from my laird to come to you, though in all honesty, I hoped Laird MacDonald would give the errand to another, because I had great trepidation about coming here."

"Get to the point," Dylan ordered.

The commander was curious over Brodick's reaction, for his laird hadn't said much of anything at all since the questioning had begun. He appeared to be somewhat bored by the news that an Englishwoman was claiming to be his bride.

Henley cleared his throat before continuing. "The lady, she called out to me and I leapt from my horse and rushed to the window before Waldo and his brother could stop me, as I was most curious to see her and hear what she had to say."

The messenger paused as he remembered the vivid details of that enchanting moment.

His entire demeanor changed in the blink of an eye from fearful to that of a man besotted, and his voice became as smooth as honey as he recounted the meeting.

"I saw her clearly and stood close enough to touch her hand."

"And did you touch her?" Brodick asked the question in a soft, chilling tone.

Henley frantically shook his head. "Nay, I would never dare such audacity," he insisted. "Your bride has been sorely mistreated, Laird," he added. "One side of her face was bruised, her skin the color of saffron with purple marks along her jaw and cheekbone. There was still some swelling evident, and I noticed other bruises on her hands and her right arm. Her left arm was bandaged from elbow to wrist, and there were bloodstains on the white linen. I wanted to ask the gentle lady how she had come by her injuries, but the words got trapped in my throat, and I found it impossible to speak a word. I could see the pain and weariness in her eyes, her glorious green eyes so like the color of our hills in spring, and I couldn't take my gaze away from her," he admitted with a blush. "I believed in that moment that I was seeing an angel."

Henley turned to address Aaron. "You asked me if she was comely, but that word does not do Laird Buchanan's bride justice." His face turned as red as fire as he added, "The lady... she is very beautiful... aye, she must be an angel, for I swear to you she is perfection."

Brodick hid his exasperation over the soldier's enthralled description of the Englishwoman. Angel, indeed, he thought to himself. An angel who blatantly lied.

"Did you describe the lady's perfection to your laird or any others in your clan?" Brodick asked.

"I did," Henley admitted. "But I didn't overly embellish."

"Why not?" Robert wanted to know.

Henley knew better than to turn his back on Laird Buchanan. It would be perceived as an insult, and for that reason he didn't look at Robert when he answered him. "I knew they would go and claim her for their own if they knew the full impression she had made upon me. I told my laird the truth, that two Englishmen asked me to relay a message to your laird. I told him the brothers wished to let you know that the time had come for you to go and fetch your bride. My laird was content with that much information and bid me come to you... but his commander wanted more details."

"Balcher questioned you?" Dylan asked.

"Yes," Henley answered.

"And what did you tell him?" Robert asked.

"He asked me directly if the lady was in the Highlands now, and I couldn't, and wouldn't, ever lie to him. I answered that she was. I wasn't specific, though," he admitted. "I had given my word to the lady that I would tell only you, Laird, of her exact whereabouts."

"Then you lied to Balcher?" Dylan questioned.

128

Henley shook his head. "No, I didn't. I told my commander that the lady was near the Len holding. I didn't mention the church."

"So even now Balcher could be on his way to steal Brodick's woman," Aaron muttered.

"I was not sworn to secrecy, and so I can tell you that without a doubt Balcher will scour the Len holding looking for the lady. Everyone in the Highlands knows how much he would like to best you, Laird, and if he can steal your bride..."

"He dares to take what belongs to us," Liam interjected, outraged by the possibility.

"If even one of the MacDonalds touches her, they will all die." Robert voiced what the others were thinking. "Is that not true?"

"Aye, it is," Liam agreed.

"I do not think you understand," Henley said. "If my clansmen see her, they will not care about your laird's wrath. They will become too besotted to think clearly."

Aaron shoved the messenger. "As you were besotted?" he asked.

"'Tis the truth I was."

"But you didn't touch her?" Dylan asked.

"I have just told your laird that I did not touch her, and I value my life too much to lie to any of you. Besides, even if she were not your laird's bride, I wouldn't have dishonored her by trying to touch her. She is the most gentle of ladies."

"Balcher won't care about honor," Robert muttered.

Dylan was annoyed. Robert and Aaron and

Liam had suddenly turned into the lady's champions. "Not five minutes ago you were outraged by this message," he reminded them. "What has caused this change in attitude?"

"The MacDonalds," Robert answered.

"Specifically Balcher," Aaron interjected.

"The lady belongs to Brodick and no other shall have her," Robert decreed.

So ludicrous had the conversation become, Brodick couldn't hold back his smile. "I have not claimed her," he reminded the warriors.

"But she has claimed you, Laird," Liam argued.

"And that makes it so?" Dylan asked.

Before anyone could answer, Brodick held up his hand for silence. "I would ask one last question of this messenger, and I would like to be able to hear his answer."

"Yes, Laird?" Henley asked, shivering anew.

"You have told me that she called you to the window to speak to you, but you haven't told me what she said."

"She sent an additional message to you."

"A request?" Aaron asked.

Henley found his first smile. "Nay, 'twas not a request but an order."

"She gives *me* an order?" Brodick was astounded by the woman's temerity.

Henley took a deep breath, hoping it wasn't going to be his last, and then blurted out, "She commands you to hurry."

CHAPTER FIVE

Gillian was having second thoughts about her rash plan. She and Alec had waited in the abandoned church for almost twenty-four hours now, and that was surely long enough for the laird to reach her, if he had been so inclined.

She felt ill and knew that if she sat down she probably wouldn't have enough strength to get back up again, and so she paced up and down the main aisle while she thought about their circumstances.

"We're going to have to leave soon," she told the little boy. "We simply cannot continue to wait."

Alec sat on a chair with his legs folded under him watching her.

"You don't look so good, Gillian. Are you sick?"

"No," she lied. "I'm just weary."

"I'm hungry."

"You just ate."

"But then I threw up."

"Yes, because you ate too fast," she replied.

She went to the back of the church, where she'd placed her cloth satchel and the basket of food her dear friends the Hathaway brothers had stolen for her. She glanced out the window and saw Henry pacing about the clearing.

"What are you staring at?" Alec asked.

"The Hathaways," she answered. "I don't know what we would have done without them. Years ago they helped me get to my uncle's home. They were very courageous. Neither one of them thought twice about helping me again. I must find a way to repay them," she added.

She handed Alec a wedge of cheese and a thick square of bread. "Please eat slowly this time."

He took a bite of the cheese and then asked, "Uncle Brodick will be here soon, won't he?"

"Remember your manners, Alec. It isn't polite to talk with a mouth full of food."

"You know what?" he asked, ignoring her criticism.

"No, what?"

"We can't leave 'cause then Uncle Brodick will be mad when he gets here and can't find us. We got to wait for him."

She sat down next to him on the chair. "We'll give him one more hour, but that's all. All right?"

He nodded. "I hate waiting."

"I do too," she admitted.

"Gillian? What are you gonna do if you can't find your sister?"

"I will find her," she countered. "I must."

"You got to find that box too," he said. "I heard the baron tell you so."

"I don't know. The box disappeared years ago."

"But you told the baron you knew where it was."

"I lied," she said. "It was all I could think

of at the time to get him to leave you alone. My father gave the box to my sister to take with her. There was an accident..."

"But how come the baron wants the old box, anyway?"

"It's extremely valuable, and it's also the key to a mystery that happened a long time ago. Would you like to hear the story?"

"Is it scary?"

"A little. Do you still want to hear it?"

He eagerly nodded. "I like scary stories."

She smiled. "All right then, I'll tell you. It seems that before John was King—"

"He was a prince."

"Yes, he was, and he was madly in love with a young lady named Arianna. She was said to be very beautiful—"

"As beautiful as you?"

The question took her aback. "You think me beautiful?"

He nodded.

"Thank you, but Arianna was far more beautiful than any other lady in the kingdom. She had golden hair that shimmered in the sunlight—"

"Did she get sick and die?"

"No, she didn't get sick, but she did die."

"Did she just up and keel over the way Angus did?"

"No, she—"

"Then what happened to her?"

She laughed. "I'll get this story told much quicker if you stop interrupting me. Now then, where was I? Oh, yes, as I was saying,

Prince John was smitten with the beautiful woman—"

"What does 'smitten' mean?"

"It means he was taken with her. He liked her." She rushed on when she saw he was about to interrupt her again. "She was his first true love, and he wanted to marry her. Have you ever heard of Saint Columba's box?"

He shook his head. "What is it?"

"A jeweled case that belongs to the Scots," she explained. "A long, long time ago, the sacred remains of Saint Columba were put inside the case—"

"What are 'remains'?"

"Fragments of bones," she answered. "Now, as I was saying, the remains were placed inside the box, and the Scots carried it into battle with them."

"How come they wanted to carry bones into battle?"

"They believed that having the case with them would bring them victory over their enemies."

"Did it?"

"I suppose so," she said. "The practice of carrying the box into battle is still going on. They don't take the box into every single battle, just some," she added.

"How come you know about the box?"

"My Uncle Morgan told me about it."

"I'll bet it's the Lowlanders who carry the box, not the Highlanders."

"Why do you say that?"

"'Cause Highlanders don't need a box when

they fight. They always win 'cause they're stronger and meaner. You know what my Uncle Ennis says?"

"No, but I'm guessing he said something outrageous."

"He says when English soldiers see more than three Highlanders riding toward them, they drop their swords and run away like scared rabbits."

"Not all Englishmen are like the baron. Most are quite courageous," she insisted.

He wasn't interested in her defense of the English. "Aren't you going to tell me what happened to the pretty lady and King John?" After asking the question, he turned and spit on the ground.

She ignored his crude behavior and continued on with the tale. "John took a fancy to the story of the Scottish jeweled box and decided to create a legend of his own. He commissioned his artisan—"

"What does 'commissioned' mean?"

"He ordered his artisan," she qualified, "to make a beautiful jeweled box for him. John has always loved being clever and cunning, and so he also decreed that he would be the only one who knew how to open the box. The artisan took over a year to complete the design and build the box, and when it was finally finished, it was said to be quite grand. It was impossible to tell which was the top and which was the bottom, though, because there were no visible latches or keyholes. The entire exterior was covered in a series of gold strips that crisscrossed, with sapphires as blue as the sky on a sunny day and emeralds as green as—"

"Your eyes?" he eagerly guessed.

"And there were rubies too, bright red rubies—"

"As red as blood?"

"Perhaps," she allowed. "All the precious jewels were set between the golden criss-crosses. Only John knew where to press to get the box to open."

"That's not true. The man who made the box knows how to open it."

"That's exactly what John realized," she said. "And so he did a terrible thing. He ordered the artisan's death."

"Did King John"—he paused to spit again before continuing his question—"kill the pretty lady and put her bones in his box?"

"Oh, no, the box was much too small," she explained. "Besides, John only wanted a lock of Arianna's hair because he was certain she would bring him good fortune when he went into battle. He opened the box, put his jeweled dagger inside, and then ordered his squire to take the box to Lady Arianna's chamber with specific orders that she put a lock of her golden hair into his golden box."

"Then what happened?"

"Lady Arianna received the open box and the dagger from the squire. He went into her chamber and placed it on the table, then took his leave. He later told the prince that she was the only person inside the room. Not even her lady's maid was present."

"I know what happened next. She stole the box and the jeweled dagger, didn't she?"

Gillian smiled over the child's enthusiasm. "No, she didn't steal the box. According to the story, when John's squire left her chamber, he heard her lock the door. He returned later to get the box for the prince, but Lady Arianna wouldn't answer his summons. John then went to her chamber."

"Did she let him in?"

"No."

"Did she tell him to go away?"

"No," she answered. "Not a sound could be heard from the room. John has always been known for his impatience. It didn't take long for him to become very angry because she refused to answer him, and so he ordered his soldiers to break the door down. They used their hatchets. John went rushing inside and he was the one who found her. Poor Lady Arianna was lying in a pool of blood on the floor. Someone had stabbed her."

"Then did John put her bones in his box?"

"No, he didn't. Remember I told you the box was far too small to hold her bones. Besides, neither the box nor the dagger was there. They had disappeared."

"Where'd they go?"

"Ah, that's the mystery."

"Who killed the pretty lady?"

"No one knows. John ordered his soldiers to search the kingdom for the box, but it had vanished into thin air. He believes that whoever stole the box murdered his own true love. Uncle Morgan told me that every couple of years a rumor surfaces that Arianna's box has been seen, and John renews his efforts to find it. The reward he's offered is staggeringly high, but to this day it hasn't been claimed."

"You know what?"

"Yes?"

"The lady's better off dead than married to King John." After making his comment, he once again turned away from her and spit on the floor.

"Why *are* you doing that?"

"I got to," he replied. "Whenever we say his name, we got to spit. It's a sign of how we feel."

She was both appalled and amused at the same time. "Do you mean to tell me that everyone in the Highlands spits each time one of them says King John's name?"

"Some curse, but Mama won't let me."

"I should hope not."

"Brodick curses when he's got to say your king's name. Are you gonna tell him to stop?" After asking the question, he began to giggle.

The sound proved infectious, and she lightly tapped him on the bridge of his nose. "You are the dearest little boy," she whispered. "But you do ask the most bizarre questions."

"But will you tell Brodick to stop?" he prodded.

She rolled her eyes heavenward. "Should he ever happen to say King John's name and then curse—or spit," she added, "I would, of course, order him to stop."

He burst into laughter. "You're gonna be

sorry if you try to tell him what to do. He won't like it," he said. "I wish he'd hurry up and get here."

"I do too."

"Maybe you should have sent the dagger like you were going to," he said. "How come you changed your mind?"

"If I sent Brodick the dagger he gave you, he would know the reason I wanted to see him had something to do with you, but then I worried that someone else might see the dagger, and it was simply too risky. I don't know who to trust."

"But you saw the traitor riding down the path," he reminded her. "You said you watched him from the hilltop while I was sleeping."

"Yes, I did see him, but remember what I told you? We aren't going to let anyone know about that."

"Not even Brodick?"

"No, not even Brodick."

"How much longer do we have to wait?"

She patted his hand. "I think we've waited as long as we can. He isn't going to come for us, but I don't want you to worry. We'll find another way to get you home."

"'Cause you promised, right?"

"Yes, because I promised. What was I thinking? It was a foolish idea to tell that MacDonald soldier I was Brodick's bride."

"But maybe Brodick needs a bride. He might come for us."

"I should have offered him gold."

Alec snorted. "Brodick doesn't care about gold."

She smiled. "It's just as well because I don't have any."

His eyes widened. "You would lie to Uncle Brodick?"

"I lied about being his bride."

"He's gonna be angry when he gets here, but I won't let him shout at you."

"Thank you. You aren't still angry with me, are you?"

"I was," he admitted. "But now I'm not."

"You needed a bath. You were rank."

"Brodick's gonna think you're pretty, but you know what?"

"No, what?"

"He won't tell you so. Do you want him to think you're pretty?"

"Not particularly," she answered, her mind clearly on more important matters. "We can't wait any longer, Alec. We're going to have to go on alone. Finish your food, and then we'll leave."

"But if you don't want Brodick to think you're pretty, how come you put on your pretty green clothes?"

She sighed. Alec asked the most outrageous questions. Inconsequential matters seemed to be extremely important to him, and he wouldn't let up until she gave him what he considered an adequate answer.

"I put on these clothes because my other gown was dirty."

He took another bite of bread while he thought about her answer, and then said, "You know what?"

She held on to her patience. "No, what?"

"You're gonna be afraid of Brodick."

"Why do you say that?"

"'Cause ladies are always afraid of him."

"Well, I won't be afraid," she insisted. "Stop talking now and finish your food."

A knock sounded on the door, and Gillian stood up just as Waldo, the older Hathaway, rushed inside.

"We've got trouble, milady," he blurted out. "The MacDonald soldier... the one I gave the message to..."

"Henley?"

He frantically nodded. "He must have told the other MacDonalds you were here, because there's over thirty of them coming across the meadow below. They're all wearing the same colors as Henley, but I didn't see him among the soldiers."

"I don't understand," she replied. "I didn't tell Henley about Alec. Why would his clan come here?"

"I'm thinking they're here to claim you, milady."

She was startled by the suggestion and shook her head. "But they can't claim me."

Waldo looked bleak and weary. "They do things different in these parts," he told her. "If they want something, they take it."

She grabbed Alec's hand and pulled him to his feet. "We're leaving now. Waldo, get your brother and meet us at the horses. Hurry."

"But, milady," Waldo protested. "There's more to the telling. There's another clan on the opposite side of the meadow riding hard toward the MacDonalds. I don't know for certain who they are, but I'm thinking they must be the Buchanans you sent for. There's nine of them."

"If it's Brodick and his soldiers, then they're pitifully outnumbered."

"Nay, milady, it's the MacDonalds I pity. I ain't never seen the like of these warriors. They're ferocious looking, and I could see by the way the MacDonalds were backing away, they fear them. If there's blood shed this day, I don't think it's going to be a Buchanan doing the bleeding. Are you certain you want to put yourself and the boy in the hands of such savages?"

She didn't know what to think, and she was in such a panic inside, her heart felt as if it might stop. "I hope it is Brodick and his men," she whispered.

Alec was struggling to get away from her so he could go outside and watch the fight, but she tightened her hold on him and wouldn't let go.

"Waldo, you and Henry should leave now before they get here. I thank you for all you've done for Alec and me. Hurry now, before you're seen."

Waldo shook his head. "My brother and I will not leave until we are assured you will fare well, milady. We'll stand guard at the door. The soldiers will have to kill us before they can get to you."

She couldn't dissuade him from what he considered a noble undertaking. As soon as he went back outside, she turned to Alec.

"Tell me what Brodick looks like," she demanded.

"He looks like Brodick," he answered.

"But what exactly does he look like?"

He shrugged. "He's big," he whispered. Then he smiled because he'd thought of something else he could add. "And old."

"Old?"

He nodded. "Terrible old," he explained.

She didn't believe him. "What color is his hair?"

"White."

"You're sure?"

He nodded. "And you know what?"

Her heart had sunk to her stomach. "No, what?"

"He doesn't hear too good."

She had to sit down. "Why didn't you tell me Brodick was an old man before I sent the message that I was his bride? The shock could have sent him to his grave." She jumped back up and pulled Alec along. "We're leaving."

"But what about the Buchanans?"

"It's apparent the other clan in the meadow isn't Brodick's. Waldo would have told me if any of the warriors had been old."

"I want to go look. I can tell you if it's the Buchanans."

Waldo opened the door and shouted, "The MacDonalds have taken off, milady, and the other clan is coming this way."

Gillian grabbed Alec by the shoulders and

forced him to look at her. "I want you to hide behind that stone font until I find out who these men are. I don't want you to say a word, Alec. Promise me... please."

"But..."

"Promise me," she demanded.

"Can I come out if it's Brodick?"

"Not until I've talked to him and gained his promise that he'll help both of us."

"All right," he said. "I promise I'll be quiet."

She was so pleased to get his cooperation she kissed him on his cheek. He immediately wiped it away with the back of his hand and squirmed when she hugged him.

"You're always kissing me," he complained with a wide grin that told her he really didn't mind. "Just like my mama."

"Go hide," she said as she led him to the back of the church.

He took hold of her left arm, and she grimaced in reaction. The injury from the knife wounds still hadn't healed, and from the way it was throbbing, she knew it was infected.

Alec had seen her flinch. "You need my mama's medicine," he whispered. "Then you'd feel better."

"I'm sure I would," she replied. "Now, Alec, not one word," she cautioned. "No matter what happens, you stay put and don't make a sound. May I have the dagger Brodick gave you?"

"But it's mine."

"I know it's yours. I would just like to borrow it," she assured him.

He handed the dagger to her, but as she turned to walk away, he whispered, "It's awful dark here."

"I'm here with you, so there isn't any need to be afraid."

"I hear them coming."

"I do too," she whispered back.

"Gillian, are you scared?"

"Yes. Now, be quiet."

She rushed down the center aisle and stood in front of the altar to wait. A moment later she heard Waldo shouting the order to halt. The command was obviously ignored because a second later the door flew open, and there in the center of the arch stood the most intimidating warrior she had ever seen. He was a towering figure with long, flaxen hair and deeply tanned skin. Barely covered, he wore only a muted plaid that didn't quite reach the tops of his knees. A wide strip of the cloth angled over his massive and scarred chest and draped down over his left shoulder. A dirk protruded from one of his deerskin boots, but he didn't carry a sword.

The man hadn't even stepped inside the church yet, but she was already quaking in her shoes. The sheer size of him blocked out most of the sun, though streaks of golden light shone all around him, making him appear almost ethereal. She gripped the dagger behind her back, and after slipping it into the sleeve of her gown, she slowly brought her hands forward and folded them in an attempt to fool him into believing she was thoroughly composed.

The warrior stood immobile for several seconds, his gaze searching for any threat that might be lurking in the corners, and when he was convinced she was all alone, he ducked under the doorframe, stepped inside, and slammed the door shut behind him.

CHAPTER SIX

Brodick strode down the aisle, shaking the rafters of the little church with each hard step as specks of dust rained down from the ceiling. Gillian valiantly held her ground.

Blessedly, when he was just a couple of feet away, he stopped, then clasped his hands behind his back and insolently studied her, his gaze moving from the top of her head to her feet and then back again. He took his sweet time, and after he had finished his rude inspection, he kept his eyes locked on hers and waited for her to speak.

She had planned for this moment and had rehearsed exactly what she would say to him. She would begin by introducing herself because that was the polite thing to do, and then she would ask him his name. He would tell her he was Brodick, but she wouldn't believe him until he had proven his identity by answering several questions she had cleverly come up with, a test, actually, to determine that she could trust him.

Aye, she was going to be clever with her questioning, and just as soon as she could calm down, she would begin. The way he was looking at her was unnerving, and she was having difficulty coming up with a single thought.

He quickly grew impatient. "Are you the woman claiming to be my bride?"

The anger in his voice heated her face. She felt herself blush with mortification. "Yes, I am."

He was surprised by her honesty. "Why?"

"I lied."

"Obviously."

"I don't usually..."

"Usually what?" he asked, wondering why she was so nervous. His stance was relaxed, his hands were clasped behind his back, and he had given Dylan his sword before coming into the church. Surely she realized he wasn't going to do her any harm.

"I don't usually lie," she explained, thrilled that she could remember what she was talking about. Staring at his chin helped, for his eyes were too intense. "You aren't old." She blurted out the thought and then smiled. "I was told you were very old," she whispered, "... with white hair."

And then she laughed, convincing Brodick she was out of her mind.

"I believe I should start all over. My name is Lady Gillian, and I really am sorry I lied, but claiming to be your bride was the only way I could think of to get you to travel such a long distance."

147

He shrugged. "The distance wasn't great."

"It wasn't?" she asked in surprise. "Then, pray tell, why did it take you so long to get here? We've been waiting in this church for a very long time."

"We?" he asked quietly.

"Yes, we," she replied. "The Hathaway brothers... the two guards outside the door... and I have been waiting all that time."

"Why were you so certain I'd show up at all?"

"Curiosity," she answered. "And I was right, wasn't I? That's why you came."

A hint of a smile softened his expression. "Yes," he agreed. "I wanted to meet the woman who dared such audacity."

"You are Brodick... I mean to say, you are Laird Buchanan, aren't you?"

"I am."

Her face lit up with relief. Damn, but she was pretty. The messenger hadn't lied about her appeal, Brodick thought. If anything, Henley had understated her beauty.

"I was going to test you to make certain you really were Brodick, but one look at you convinces me. I was told, you see, that your glare could part a tree trunk, and from the way you're scowling at me, I do believe you could do it. You're quite intimidating, but you know that, don't you?"

He didn't show any reaction to her remarks. "What is it you want from me?"

"I want... no, I need," she qualified, "your help. I have a very valuable treasure with me and I need assistance getting it home."

148

"Aren't there any Englishmen who could come to your aid?"

"It's complicated, Laird."

"Start at the beginning," he suggested, surprised by his own willingness to extend this meeting. Her voice appealed to him; it was soft, lyrical, yet husky and sensual, as sensual as the woman herself.

Brodick was conditioned to keeping his thoughts hidden, and for that reason he was certain she didn't have any idea of the effect she was having on him. Her wonderful scent was a clear distraction. It was very feminine and smelled faintly of flowers, which he found both alluring and arousing. He had to fight the urge to move closer to her.

"This should explain everything you need to know," she said as she slowly removed the dagger and sheath from her sleeve and held it up for him to see.

He reacted with lightning speed. Before she could even guess his intent, he'd snatched the dagger out of her hand, grabbed hold of her injured arm, and jerked her forcefully toward him. Towering over her, he demanded, "Where did you get this?"

"I will explain," she cried out. "But please let go of me. You're hurting me."

The tears in her eyes confirmed her words. Brodick immediately let go of her and stepped back. "Now explain," he demanded again.

"I borrowed the dagger," she said, and then she turned and called out, "Alec, you may come out now."

Brodick had never been so close to losing his composure. When the Maitland boy came running toward him, he felt his knees buckle and his heart lodge in his throat. He was too stunned to say a word, and then Alec threw himself into his arms. Brodick's hands shook as he lifted him up and clasped him to his chest.

The little boy wrapped his arms around his protector's neck and hugged him. "I knew you would come. I told Gillian you would help us."

"You are well, Alec?" he asked, his voice trembling with emotion. He turned to Gillian questioning her with his eyes, but she was watching Alec with a soft, motherly smile on her face.

"Answer him, Alec," she instructed.

The child leaned back in Brodick's arms and nodded. "I'm very well, Uncle. The lady, she took good care of me. She gave me her food to eat and went hungry when there wasn't enough for both of us, and you know what? She wouldn't let nobody hurt me, not even when the man wanted to."

Brodick stared at Gillian while Alec chattered away, but nodded when the little boy had finished his explanation.

"You will tell me exactly what happened," he told Gillian. It wasn't a question but a statement of fact.

"Yes," she agreed. "I'll tell you everything."

"Uncle, you know what?"

150

Brodick turned to Alec. "No, what?"

"I didn't drown."

Brodick was still too shaken to laugh over the ridiculous understatement. "I can see you didn't," he answered dryly.

"But did you think I did? I told Gillian you wouldn't believe it, 'cause you're stubborn, but did you?"

"No, I didn't believe you drowned."

Alec leaned around Brodick so he could see Gillian. "I told you so," he boasted before turning his attention to his uncle once again. "They put me in a wheat sack, and I got real scared."

"Who put you in a sack?" he demanded, trying to keep the anger out of his voice so he wouldn't frighten the child.

"The men who took me. I maybe even cried." He sounded as though he were confessing a terrible sin. "I wasn't brave, Uncle, but you know what? Gillian said I was."

"Who were these men who put you in a sack?"

His abruptness worried the boy, and he looked down when he answered forlornly, "I don't know. I didn't see their faces."

"Alec, he isn't angry with you. Why don't you go and collect our things while I speak in private to your uncle."

Brodick gently lowered Alec and watched him run to the front of the church.

"Will you help me get him home to his parents?" she asked.

He turned to her. "I'll make certain he gets home."

"And so will I," she insisted. "I made Alec a promise, and I mean to keep it, but I must also speak to his father. The matter is extremely urgent. Besides," she added, "I trust you, Laird Buchanan, but I don't trust anyone else. I was told eight men ride with you today. Is that true?"

"Yes."

"I would like to see every one of them before Alec steps outside."

"You want to look at them?" he asked, puzzled by the bizarre request. "They're Buchanans," he added, "and that's all you need to know."

Alec came running down the aisle just as Gillian made her demand once again. "I will see them first."

"'Cause you know why, Uncle?"

Brodick looked at the little boy. "Why?"

"She saw the traitor," he blurted out, wanting to be the first to explain. "I fell asleep, but Gillian saw him good. She told me so. She made us hide a long time just so she could see him. He's a Highlander," he thought to add.

"Oh, Alec, you weren't supposed to tell anyone—"

"I forgot," he interrupted. "But Brodick won't tell nobody if you ask him not to."

"The man I saw is probably just now on his way back to the Highlands," she said. "I don't know how long he was going to stay in England, but I'm not taking any chances. It's better to be safe."

"And you want to see my soldiers just to make certain one of them isn't the man you saw?" he asked, his outrage clearly evident.

She was suddenly feeling so weary she needed to sit down, and she certainly wasn't in the mood to be diplomatic and come up with a suitable reply that would placate the laird. "Yes, that's exactly what I'm wanting to do, Laird Buchanan."

"You have said that you trust me."

"Yes," she agreed, and then quickly qualified her answer. "But only because I have to trust someone, and you are Alec's protector, but I'm not going to trust anyone else. Alec told me he thought that there were three Highlanders who took him from the festival, but there could be more besides the man who planned the kidnapping, so you see, Alec is still in danger, and I'm going to continue to guard him until I get him safely home."

Before he could respond to her argument, a whistle sounded outside, drawing his attention. "We must leave now," he announced. "My men grow impatient, and it's only a matter of time before the MacDonalds gather more soldiers and come back here."

"Are you feuding with the MacDonalds?" Alec asked.

"We weren't," Brodick answered. "But now it seems we are."

"Why?" Gillian asked, puzzled by his half-given explanation to Alec. "The MacDonald I met was a very pleasant gentleman, and he obviously was also a man of his word because

153

he kept his promise and took my message to you."

Brodick nodded. "Aye, Henley was his name, and he did give me your message, but only after he had told his laird and pricked the curiosity of his clan."

"And they came here to fight you?" she asked, trying to understand.

He smiled. "Nay, lass, they came to steal you, and that, you see, is an insult I cannot allow."

She was astounded. "Steal me?" she whispered. "Why in heaven's name would they want to do that?"

He shook his head to let her know he wasn't willing to go into further explanation. "As much as I would like to kill a few MacDonalds, I will have to wait until after I have gotten you and Alec to the Maitlands. We're leaving now."

Alec would have run to the door if Gillian hadn't grabbed hold of his hand and forced him to stay by her side. "You will wait until I'm convinced that it's safe for you to go outside."

"But I don't want to wait."

"And I don't want to hear any argument, young man. You'll do as you're told. Do you understand me?"

Alec immediately looked to Brodick for help. "I keep telling her my papa's a laird and she's not supposed to tell me what to do all the time, but she won't listen. She isn't afraid of Papa at all. Maybe you should tell her."

Brodick hid his amusement. "Tell her what?"

"To let me have my way."

"The lady wants to do what's best for you, Alec."

"But tell her about Papa," he pleaded.

Brodick conceded. "Iain Maitland is a powerful man in the Highlands," he said. "Many fear his wrath."

She smiled sweetly. "Is that right?"

"Many would also guard what they say to his son."

Alec was nodding his agreement when Gillian looked at him. "I am more interested in keeping you alive than in winning your father's approval by spoiling you and perhaps getting you killed."

"Let me see your arm," Brodick demanded.

She blinked. "Why?"

He didn't answer her or wait for her to comply with his command but took hold of her hand and pushed the sleeve up past her elbow. A thick bandage covered her skin, but he could see from the swelling and the redness at her wrist that the injury was infected.

"How did this happen?"

Alec squeezed closer to her side. "Are you gonna tell on me?" he whispered worriedly.

Brodick pretended he hadn't heard the boy's question. He had his answer; Alec was somehow responsible for Gillian's injury, and later, when he and Alec were alone, he would get the particulars. For now he would let the matter rest.

Gillian and the boy were clearly exhausted, for both had dark circles under their eyes. Her complexion was flushed, and Brodick was pretty certain she was feverish. He knew that if the wound wasn't taken care of soon, she would be in real trouble.

"It isn't important how I hurt myself, Laird."

"You will call me Brodick," he said.

"As you wish," she replied, wondering why his voice had softened and the scowl had left his face.

Before she realized what he was doing, he grabbed hold of her chin and tilted her head to one side so he could see the faint marks on her cheeks. "How did you come by this bruise?"

"The man, he hit her with his fist," Alec blurted out, thankful his uncle's attention had turned away from Gillian's arm. He was ashamed that he had cut her and hoped that his uncle would never find out. "And, Uncle Brodick, you know what?" he rushed on.

Brodick was frowning at Gillian when he answered. "What?"

"Her back is all black and blue too. It used to be, anyway, and maybe it still is."

"Alec, do be quiet."

"But it's the truth. I saw the bruises when you got out of the lake."

"You were supposed to be sleeping," she said before pushing Brodick's hand away from her face. "May I see your soldiers now?"

"Yes," he replied.

She had intended to leave Alec inside while

she stepped out on the step to look at the soldiers, but Brodick had other ideas. He whistled, loud and shrill, causing Alec to giggle and cover his ears with his hands. The door flew wide and eight men immediately rushed inside the church. Gillian noticed that every single one of them had to duck under the doorframe. Were all the Buchanans giants?

The second the door had opened, she had shoved Alec behind her back, thinking to protect him, which really was laughable considering the sheer size and obvious strength of the warriors coming toward her. Brodick saw how she shielded the boy and tried not to take offense over the insult she was giving him and his soldiers. Though considered ruthless against their enemies, the Buchanans would never raise a hand against a woman or a child. Everyone who lived in the Highlands knew them to be honorable, but Gillian was from England, and he therefore excused her behavior because she didn't know any better.

Dylan tossed his laird's sword to him as he strode forward, and Brodick slipped the weapon into the sheath at his side, inwardly smiling over the stunned soldiers' faces. They were obviously taken with the beautiful lady, for they couldn't take their eyes off her.

His amusement quickly turned to irritation, however, and he found he didn't like them openly staring at Gillian after all. It was one thing to look, and quite another to gawk. Hadn't they ever seen a pretty woman before?

157

Alec peeked out from behind Gillian, spotted Dylan, and waved to him. The commander's step faltered, and he bumped into Robert, who promptly shoved him back.

Gillian studied each man while Brodick kept his attention focused on her. "You are convinced now?" he asked calmly after she had finished scrutinizing each one of his soldiers.

"Yes, I am convinced."

"Is that a Maitland hiding behind a woman's skirts?" Dylan asked, his composure still not completely recovered. "I swear to God, the brat looks like Alec Maitland."

Alec immediately ran to Dylan and laughed with delight when the soldier lifted him high up over his head. "She made me hide. I didn't want to, but she made me."

"We thought you drowned, boy," Liam whispered, his voice as raspy as dried leaves.

Dylan lowered Alec and settled him against his shoulder. The child immediately put his arms around the warrior's neck and then leaned to the side so he could see the others. "I didn't drown," he announced.

The eight soldiers surrounded Alec, but several continued to stare at Gillian. Broderick took a possessive step closer to her and scowled his displeasure at Liam and Robert, the worst offenders, so that they would know their laird was angered by their behavior.

"Is the Maitland holding a great distance from here?"

"No," he answered. "Robert, get her satchel and tie it behind your mount," he ordered as

158

he took hold of Gillian's hand and started for the door. "Alec will ride with you, Dylan," he added, and as he marched past Robert, he muttered, "Have you never seen a pretty woman before?"

"Never one as pretty as this," Robert replied.

Dylan shifted Alec to one side and stepped forward to boldly block his laird's path. "Aren't you going to introduce us to your bride, Laird?"

"She's Lady Gillian," he said. He then introduced his soldiers to her, but he said their names so quickly and in such a thick brogue, she only caught one or two.

She would have made a curtsy, but Brodick continued to hold her hand, and so she bowed her head instead. "It is a pleasure to meet you," she said slowly, speaking in Gaelic for the first time since she had met Brodick, and she thought she had done an adequate job until they all smiled at her. Were they pleased with her attempt at their language or were they laughing at her because she'd failed miserably? Her speech became more halting with her growing lack of confidence when she continued, "And I would thank you now for your assistance in helping me get Alec back to his parents."

She was thrilled when all of them nodded.

Robert stepped forward. "Are you his bride?" he asked, blunt as always.

"No," she answered, blushing slightly.

"But you claimed to be his bride," Aaron reminded her.

She smiled. "Yes, I did, but you see, it was

just a lie to make your laird curious so that he would come here."

"A claim's a claim," Liam said. The others immediately concurred.

"What does that mean?" she asked the warrior.

Dylan smiled. "It means, lass, that you're his bride."

"But I lied," she argued, thoroughly confused by the conversation. Her explanation seemed simple to understand, yet these soldiers were acting perplexed.

"You have said it is so," a soldier said. She remembered his name was Stephen.

"Now isn't the time for this discussion," Brodick announced.

He led the way outside, pulling Gillian along in his wake, and barely paid any attention to the two Englishmen waiting by the side of the steps. The horses were tethered near the line of trees.

"You'll ride with me," Brodick told her.

She pulled away from him. "I must say goodbye to my friends."

Before he could stop her, she hurried over to Waldo and Henry. Both men bowed their heads and smiled when she spoke to them. Brodick couldn't hear what she was saying, but he could tell from the men's faces that they were pleased.

When he saw her take hold of their hands, he went back to her side. "We've wasted enough time."

She ignored him. "Laird, I would like you

to meet Waldo and Henry Hathaway," she said. "If it were not for these courageous men, Alec and I would never have made it this far."

He didn't speak, but he did bow his head slightly to the two brothers.

"Waldo, will you please return the horse I borrowed," she requested.

"But you stole the horse, milady," Henry blurted out.

"No," she countered. "I borrowed the mount without permission. Please promise me, too, that you will both hide until this is finished. If he finds out you helped me, he'll kill you."

"Aye, milady," Waldo said. "We know what the blackheart is capable of, and we will both hide until you return. God protect you on your quest."

Tears came into her eyes. "Twice now you have come to my aid and saved me from disaster."

"We've come a long way together," Waldo said. "You were such a little girl when we first met. You didn't speak then."

"I remember what my dear friend Liese told me. You came forward to offer your escort on that black day. And now you once again have come to my aid. I will forever be in your debt, and I don't know how I will ever be able to repay you."

"It was an honor for us to help you," Henry stammered.

Brodick took hold of her arm and pulled her

back so she would have to let go of the older brother's hand. "We must leave now," he demanded, though this time his voice was much more forceful.

"Yes," she agreed.

She turned, spotted Alec in Dylan's arms, and motioned to the Hathaway brothers to wait. Then she pushed Brodick's hand away and rushed across the clearing.

"Alec, you will want to say thank you to Waldo and Henry for helping us."

He shook his head. "No, I won't," he said. "They're English, so I don't have to say thank you. Highlanders don't like the English," he added arrogantly.

She held her temper. "Dylan, would you please give Alec and me a moment of privacy?"

"As you wish, milady."

As soon as he put Alec down, Gillian latched onto his arm and dragged him toward the trees. Then she leaned down and whispered in his ear while the child squirmed to get away.

Dylan turned to Brodick. "What's she doing?" he asked.

Brodick smiled. "Reminding the boy of his manners," he answered. He glanced at the two brothers once again, then let out a sigh. "It seems I have also been reminded."

Before Dylan could ask him to explain his odd remark, his laird turned toward Waldo and Henry. The brothers were obviously afraid, for both backed away from him until he commanded them to stand still.

Dylan couldn't hear what Brodick was saying to the men, but he saw him reach down and pull his jeweled dirk from the top of his boot and hand it to Waldo. The stunned expression on the Englishman's face mirrored Dylan's. He watched as Waldo tried to refuse the gift, but Brodick won the argument.

Gillian also saw what was happening and smiled as she continued to instruct Alec in his duty.

A moment later, Alec, deliberately dragging his feet, made his way across the clearing to speak to the Englishmen. Gillian gave him a little push between the shoulder blades to get him to quicken his step.

Alec lowered his chin to his chest and stood next to Brodick when he addressed Waldo and Henry. "I thank you, 'cause you both watched out for me," he said.

"And?" Gillian prodded.

"And 'cause you didn't have to but you did anyway."

Exasperated, she said, "Alec means to say that he is sorry he was a bother, Waldo and Henry. He also knows that the two of you put your lives at risk for him. Isn't that right, Alec?"

The child nodded and then took hold of Gillian's hand as he watched Waldo and Henry take their leave.

"Did I say it right?"

"Yes, you did just fine."

Dylan lifted Alec onto his mount and then

turned to his laird. "Has she told you what happened or how she and Alec ended up together?"

Brodick swung up onto his stallion's back before answering. "No, she hasn't told me anything yet, but she will. Be patient, Dylan. Right now it's more important to get her and the boy away from the MacDonalds. Once I know they're safe, and I don't have to keep looking over my shoulder, I'll get her explanation. Tell Liam to take the lead," he commanded. "We're going to Kevin Drummond's cottage before we head north. Robert will take the rear to watch our backs."

"The Drummonds are several hours out of our way," Dylan said. "It'll be sunset before we get there."

"I know where the man lives," he countered. "But Kevin's wife is well known for her healing ways, and Gillian's arm needs attention."

Gillian stood in the center of the clearing, shivering from the cold while she patiently waited for the men to finish discussing her. It was apparent she was their topic, for they both frowned at her while they conversed with one another. The summer sun beat down on her face, but she was getting more chilled by the minute, and every muscle in her body ached. She knew it wasn't just fatigue, and, dear God, there wasn't time now for her to get sick. She needed every minute of every day before the fall festival to search for her sister. Oh, it all seemed so hopeless. She shouldn't have lied to Alford by telling him that her sister had King John's precious box. How was she ever going to find it when every soldier in the kingdom had searched for the treasure at one time or another over the past fifteen years? Could Christen still have it with her? Alford seemed to think she did, and Gillian had fueled his belief because at the time Alec had been in terrible danger. In her heart she knew the box was gone forever, and now she felt she was weighed down in a quagmire and sinking rapidly.

She did have a fragment of a plan. Once she got Alec home, she was going to plead with his father for assistance in getting her to the MacPherson holding, where Christen was reported to be living. And then what? she thought. Her mind was filled with unanswerable questions, and she prayed she would be able to sort it all out when she was feeling better.

Rubbing her arms to ward off her chills, she forced herself to think about the present. Brodick nudged his mount toward her. He didn't slow the stallion's gait as he approached. He leaned to the side and, with little effort, wrapped his arm around her waist and swept her onto his lap.

She adjusted her skirts to cover her knees and tried to sit straight so her back wouldn't touch his chest, but Brodick wouldn't let her maintain any formality. He tightened his hold and hauled her up against him.

In truth, she was thankful for his warmth, and his masculine scent appealed to her. He smelled like the outdoors. She wanted to close her eyes and rest for just a few minutes and maybe even pretend this nightmare was all over. She didn't dare give in to the foolish fantasy though, because she needed to keep a watchful eye on Alec.

She turned in Brodick's arms and looked up at him. He was really quite handsome, she thought, forgetting for the moment what she wanted to say to him. She had heard stories about the Viking warriors who roamed England centuries before and thought Brodick was surely a descendant, for he was as huge as the Vikings were reputed to be. His bone structure was well-defined from his high cheekbones to his gently squared chin. Aye, he was handsome all right and had surely caused many a lady to lose her heart. That thought led to another. Alec had told her Brodick wasn't married, but did the laird have a sweetheart at home waiting for him to return?

"Is something wrong, lass?"

"Could Alec ride with us? We could make room for him."

"No."

She waited a full minute for him to explain why he had denied her request, then realized he had said all he was going to say. His manner was distant, but she tried not to take offense. Her Uncle Morgan had often told her that the Highlanders were a different breed of men and danced to what he called their own strange tune, and she therefore assumed that Brodick wasn't actually trying to be rude.

His abruptness was simply part of who he was.

She leaned back against him and tried to relax, but every so often, she looked behind him to make certain Alec was all right.

"We're almost there," Brodick said. "You're going to get a stiff neck if you keep looking back every other minute. Alec's fine," he insisted. "Dylan isn't going to let anything happen to him." With that, he shoved her head down on his shoulder. "Rest," he ordered.

And so she did just that.

CHAPTER SEVEN

Brodick shook Gillian awake when they reached their destination.

She pulled herself from her slumber and rubbed the stiffness in her neck. It took some effort, but she finally forced her eyes to focus, and for a brief moment she thought she was still dreaming. Where was she? What was this place? Lush green hills surrounded her. A narrow stream gently meandered down the slope and in the center of the green valley sat a gray stone cottage with a thatched roof. The yard on either side was ablaze with wildflowers of every color in the rainbow, their perfumed scent floating around her. Birch trees flanked the clear-water stream that flowed on the west side of the cottage, and to the east was a broad meadow blanketed in a thick carpet of grass. A flock of sheep, ready for shearing, clustered together at the far end of the field, bleating at one another like gossiping women, while a rather regal-looking guard dog sat on his haunches with his head held high, eyes ever watchful as he surveyed his charges. Smoke gently curled up into the cloudless blue sky from the cottage chimney. A faint breeze touched Gillian's cheek. This was a paradise.

A shout shook her from her musings. A tall, thin-faced man stood on the front step of the cottage and was smiling and calling to the approaching soldiers. As she watched the men disappear through the doorway, everything that had happened in the last few days flooded back to her memory.

Dylan had Alec on his shoulders and was bending down to go inside. Brodick had already dismounted but was waiting to assist Gillian. When at last she turned to him, he reached for her and she slid into his arms. For a fleeting moment their eyes met, and she studied the face of this man she hardly knew and yet trusted with her life. His piercing eyes made her think he knew all her secrets. She tried to shake herself out of such foolish thoughts. He was just a man, nothing more—and he needed to shave. His cheeks and jaw were covered with golden brown whiskers, and she had the insane urge to find out what it would feel like to run her fingers down the side of his face.

"Why are you staring at me?" she asked.

"The same reason you're staring at me, lass."

From the sparkle in his eyes, she guessed he had a bit of the Devil in him and she simply wasn't up to the task of being clever or flirtatious. She wasn't even sure she knew how.

She pushed his hands away from her waist and stepped back. "Why have we stopped here? And who was that man in the doorway? Alec shouldn't have gone inside until I—"

He cut her off. "This is the last time I'm going to tell you that Alec is safe with Dylan. He would be highly insulted to know you don't trust him."

"But I don't trust him," she whispered so the other soldiers wouldn't overhear. "I don't know him."

"You don't know me either," he pointed out. "But you've decided to trust me, and you therefore have to believe that what I tell you is true. My soldiers will protect Alec with their lives." The briskness in his voice indicated he was finished discussing the subject.

"I'm too weary to argue."

"Then don't. It's pointless to argue with a Buchanan," he added. "You can't possibly win, lass. We Buchanans never lose."

She thought he might be jesting, but she couldn't be absolutely sure, and so she didn't laugh. Either he had a very strange sense of humor or he was sinfully arrogant.

"Come along. We're wasting time," he said as he caught hold of her hand and started up the stone path.

"Are we going to spend the night here?"

He didn't bother to turn around when he answered. "No, we'll move on after Annie tends to your arm."

"I don't want to be a bother."

"She'll be honored to serve you."

"Why?"

"She thinks you're my bride," he explained.

"Why would she think that? I only told the lie to one MacDonald soldier."

He laughed. "News travels fast, and everyone knows the MacDonalds can't keep secrets."

"Oh, dear, I've caused you considerable trouble, haven't I?"

"No," he answered.

When they reached the doorway, he stepped back to let her go inside first. She moved close to him and asked in a whisper, "Do you trust these people?"

He shrugged. "As much as I trust anyone who isn't a Buchanan," he answered. "Kevin Drummond's sister is married to one of my soldiers, so he's considered kin of a sort. Anything you say in front of them will be held in confidence."

Dylan introduced her to the couple. Annie Drummond stood near the hearth and bowed low to Gillian. She was about her age and was heavy with child. Kevin Drummond also bowed and welcomed her into his home. Both of them, Gillian thought, appeared to be extremely nervous.

Their cottage was small and smelled of freshly baked bread. An oblong table took up a good deal of space in the center of the room and from the number of chairs, six in all, Gilliam assumed the Drummonds were used to entertaining visitors. It was a home, warm and comfortable and inviting, the kind of place Gillian dreamed of when she allowed herself to fantasize about falling in love and having a family. Such a foolish notion, she thought to herself. Her life was consumed with worry now, and there wasn't room for such yearnings.

"It's a privilege to have you in our home," Kevin told her, but his eyes, she noticed, were fully directed on Brodick.

After formally greeting the laird, Annie suggested Gillian take a seat at the table and let her have a look at her injury. She pulled a chair out on the opposite side and waited for Gillian to get comfortable. Then she spread a cloth on the tabletop while Gillian pushed up her sleeve and unwrapped the bandage.

"I would appreciate any medicine you have," she said. "It isn't a serious injury, but I believe it's become a bit inflamed."

Gillian didn't think her arm looked all that bad, but Annie visibly blanched when she saw it.

"Ah, lass, you must be in terrible pain."

Brodick and his men moved forward to look at the injury. Alec ran to Gillian and pressed against her. He looked scared.

"How in heaven's name did this happen?" Dylan asked.

171

"I cut myself."

"It's got to be opened and drained," Annie whispered. "Laird, you're going to have to stay with us a couple of days at the least while I tend to this. She's a lady," she added, "and I must therefore use the slow method of curing her."

"No, I cannot stay that long," Gillian protested.

"If she were a man? What would you do then?" Brodick asked.

Thinking he'd asked the question out of simple curiosity, Annie replied, "I'd open the skin and drain the infection, but then I would pour mother's fire on the open wound, and though the special brew has cured everything I've ever used it on, it causes terrible pain."

"I've seen warriors shout during Annie's treatment with her mother's fire," Kevin said.

Brodick waited for Gillian to decide which method would be used.

She believed the Drummonds were exaggerating the treatment, but it really didn't matter. She couldn't afford to lose so much time just to avoid a little pain. Brodick seemed to be reading her mind.

"Do these warriors you've treated with this mother's fire of yours stay for days or do they leave?" he asked.

"Oh, they leave once I've put the healing salve on the wounds," Annie answered.

"The ones who can stand leave," Kevin interjected.

Brodick caught Gillian's barely perceptible nod and then said, "You will use this warrior's treatment on Gillian, and she will not make a sound while you're tending her. She's a Buchanan." He added the last as though that explained everything.

"I will not utter a sound, Laird?" she asked, her voice laced with amusement over his galling arrogance.

He was serious when he answered. "Nay, you will not."

She had a sudden urge to start screaming like a wild woman before Annie even touched her just to irritate the pompous man, but she didn't give in to the desire because the kind woman and little Alec would both become upset. When she was alone with Brodick, however, she was going to remind him that she wasn't a Buchanan, and she might also add that she was going to thank God for that fact, because the Buchanans were a little too full of themselves. She had noticed that when Brodick announced that she wouldn't make a sound, every one of his soldiers had nodded.

Oh, yes, she certainly wanted to scream all right.

Annie had turned as pale as milk after Brodick chose the treatment to be used. She leaned against her husband and whispered into his ear. Because she spoke so rapidly, Gillian only caught a word or two, but it was quite enough for her to figure out that Annie was asking Kevin for permission to give Gillian a sleeping draft.

Kevin put the request to Brodick while Annie rushed about the cottage gathering her supplies. Before Brodick could answer, Gillian spoke up. "I don't wish to be drugged. I appreciate your concerns, but I must insist on remaining clearheaded so that we may continue on our journey."

Brodick nodded, but Gillian wasn't certain if he was agreeing with Kevin's request or with her denial. "I mean what I say," she pressed. "I don't want to be drugged."

Alec demanded her attention then by tugging on her sleeve. As she leaned down to him, out of the corner of her eye she saw Annie sprinkle brown powder into a goblet and then add wine.

"What is it?" she asked Alec.

"Are you gonna tell on me?" he whispered.

"About the cuts on my arm?" He bumped her chin when he nodded. "No, I'm not going to tell, and I want you to stop worrying that I will."

"All right," he said. "I'm hungry."

"We'll get you something to eat in a little while."

"With your permission, Laird, I would like to toast you and your bride," Kevin announced as he carried a tray of goblets to the table.

"Oh, but I'm not—" Gillian began.

Brodick interrupted her. "You have my permission."

She frowned at him, puzzled as to why he hadn't corrected Kevin's misconception, but decided to wait until later to ask him to explain.

Kevin put Gillian's drink in front of her. He

174

then placed the other goblets a good distance away, no doubt so that the drugged wine wouldn't get mixed up with the others. The toast was but a clever ploy, and though she knew Kevin's intentions were good-hearted, it still rankled her that he had ignored her wishes. After the toast was given, she would have to take a drink, for otherwise she would be considered rude. That left her only one choice.

"May I call your other soldiers inside to share this toast?" Kevin asked.

In answer Brodick went to the door and whistled. The sound echoed through the cottage. Less than a minute later, the rest of his soldiers filed inside to take a goblet. Gillian helped by handing one to each man.

When everyone held a drink, Kevin stepped forward and raised his goblet high.

"To a long happy life filled with love and laughter and healthy sons and daughters."

"Here, here," Aaron agreed.

Everyone waited until Gillian had taken a drink before they downed their wine. Brodick nodded to Annie, pulled out a chair, and straddled it to face Gillian. He motioned for her to put her arm out again, and then put his hand down on top of hers.

She didn't have to ask him why he was holding on to her. He was making sure she didn't pull away during Annie's treatment.

Dylan came around the table and placed one hand on her shoulder. "Robert, take the boy outside," he ordered.

Alec frantically clutched Gillian's arm. "I

want to stay with you," he whispered anxiously.

"Then put your request to Dylan," she instructed. "And perhaps he will reconsider, but be polite when you ask him, Alec."

The boy hesitantly looked up at the soldier, craning his neck back as far as it would go. "Can I stay... please?"

"Milady?" Dylan asked.

"I would be happy for his company."

"Then you may stay inside for a little while, Alec, but you mustn't interfere. Can you promise me that you won't?"

Alec nodded. "I promise," he said, then leaned into Gillian.

Annie stood beside her, watching her closely. She was ready to begin, yet continued to wait. "Are you feeling a bit sleepy, milady?" she inquired casually.

"Not overly," she replied.

Annie glanced at the laird. "Perhaps I should wait another minute or two."

Gillian looked up at the men surrounding her and noticed that Annie's husband was yawning every other minute, but then the soldier named Robert also yawned, and she couldn't decide which one was actually getting drowsy. Then Kevin began to sway.

"Annie, would you please ask your husband to sit down?"

Kevin heard her request and, blinking furiously, tried to make sense of it. "Why would I want to be sitting down, lass?" he asked.

"So you won't have so far to fall."

No one understood her suggestion until Kevin suddenly pitched forward. Fortunately, one of Brodick's soldiers was quick on his feet and caught him before his head struck the edge of the table.

"Ah, lass, you switched goblets, didn't you?" a soldier asked.

"She drugged Kevin?" another soldier asked, grinning.

Gillian could feel her face burning and concentrated intently on the tabletop while she tried to think of a proper apology to give Kevin's wife.

Startled by such trickery, Annie turned to the laird. Brodick shook his head as though in disappointment, but there was a definite sparkle in his eyes and voice when he said, "It seems Kevin drugged himself. Toss him on the bed, Aaron, and let's get this done. Annie, we need to be on our way."

She nodded, and with trembling hand she put her knife to Gillian's arm. Brodick tightened his hold on Gillian's wrist just before she felt the first prick of the blade cutting through her tender skin. At first Gillian let him know she thought he was overreacting, yet once Annie began to probe the wounds, she was glad for his anchor. The need to flinch was instinctive, but Brodick's grip wouldn't allow any movement at all.

The treatment wasn't nearly as awful as she had anticipated. Her arm had been throbbing from the pressure of the infection swelling beneath the surface of her inflamed skin, but once the wounds were opened, she felt immediate relief.

Alec squeezed under her right arm and clung to her. Frightened, he whispered, "Does it hurt bad?"

"No," she answered quietly.

When he saw how calm she was, the tension eased out of him. Curious, he asked, "Does it hurt as bad as when that man punched you in the face?"

"Hush, Alec."

"But does it?" he pestered.

She sighed. "No."

Annie had been cleaning the wounds with clean strips of cloth, but paused when Alec asked the question. "Someone struck you, milady?" she asked. The sweet woman looked so appalled, Gillian immediately tried to reassure her.

"It was nothing, really," she insisted. "Please don't concern yourself."

"This man... who was he?" Annie asked.

The room grew deadly quiet while everyone waited to hear her response. She shook her head. "It isn't important."

"Oh, but it is important," Dylan said to a chorus of grumbled agreements.

"He was an Englishman," Alec blurted out.

Nodding to indicate she didn't doubt the child's statement, Annie picked up another cloth and resumed her task of cleaning the wounds. Gillian winced from the discomfort, unaware that she was now gripping Brodick's hand.

"I knew he had to be English," Annie grumbled. "I don't know of any Highlander who would raise his hand against a woman. Nay, I don't."

Several soldiers nodded their agreement. Desperate to change the subject, Gillian latched onto the first thought that came into her mind. "It's a fine day today, isn't it? The sun is bright and the wind is mild—"

Alec interrupted her. "The man was drunk, terrible drunk."

"Alec, no one wants to hear the particulars—"

"Ah, but we do want to hear," Brodick drawled out, his mild voice belying what he was truly feeling. He tried to be patient, but his need to hear the full story from start to finish was driving him to distraction. What kind of a madman would prey on such a gentle lady and a little boy? Alec had already painted a dark picture of the horror he'd survived and had let them all see a glimmer of the courage Gillian had shown. Aye, he wanted all the details, and he decided that he would hear the full tale before nightfall.

"He was drunk, wasn't he, Gillian?" Alec pestered.

She didn't answer him, but the boy wasn't deterred. Since she hadn't actually forbidden him to talk about the beating, he decided to tell everything he knew.

"Uncle Brodick, you know what?"

"No, what?"

"The man, he hit her with his fist and knocked

her clear off her feet to the ground, and then you know what he did? He kicked her and kicked her and kicked her. I got real scared, and I tried to make him stop, but he wouldn't."

"How did you try to make him stop?" Dylan asked.

Alec lifted his shoulders. "I don't know," he admitted. "Maybe I cried."

"Annie, are you almost finished?" Gillian asked.

"Just about," the woman answered.

"And then you know what? I threw myself on top of Gillian, but she pushed me away, and then you know what she did? She rolled on top of me and put her hands on my head so I wouldn't get kicked none."

"What happened then, Alec?" Liam asked.

"She patted me and told me to hush 'cause she said it was going to be all right. She wouldn't let nobody hurt me. She didn't neither," he added. "I never once got kicked."

Gillian wanted to put her hand over Alec's mouth. The men looked horrified by what the child was telling them, but their gazes were locked on her. She felt ashamed and embarrassed by what had happened.

"Was it just one Englishman who touched Lady Gillian?" Robert asked. "Or were there others?"

"Another man hit her," Alec said.

"Alec, I wish you wouldn't—" Gillian began.

"But he did hit you, don't you remember? The man kicked you, and then the other man hit you. How come you don't remember?"

She bowed her head. "I remember, Alec. I just don't want to talk about it."

The boy turned to Brodick. "You know what she did after he hit her? She smiled just to make him mad."

Annie gathered up her cloths and put them aside on one of the stools, then spread a thick towel under Gillian's arm. "Laird, I'm finished cleaning out the infection."

Brodick nodded. "The boy's hungry. He would appreciate a piece of your bread if that isn't too much trouble."

"Maybe with honey on it," Alec suggested.

Annie smiled. "Of course with honey."

"You must eat it outside," Brodick ordered. "Robert will go with you and see you don't get into mischief."

"But, Uncle Brodick, I want to stay with Gillian. She needs me, and she might get lonely."

"I'll keep her company," he promised. "Robert?"

The soldier moved forward. Alec saw him coming around the table and pressed closer to Gillian. She leaned down and whispered, "I'll call out to you if I need you."

She had to promise on her mother's heart before Alec was convinced that she wouldn't disappear if he left her for a few minutes. Then he snatched the bread from Annie's hand and ran out the doorway, forgetting in his haste to thank her properly.

"He'll remember his manners later and then thank you," Gillian said. "I appreciate your patience with him. He's just a little boy and he's been through a very difficult time."

"But you got him through it unharmed." Dylan made the comment from behind her and once again put his hands on her shoulders. She wasn't sure if he was offering her praise and comfort or making sure she didn't try to escape.

Annie appeared a moment later with an oblong pan of foul-smelling brew she'd heated over the fire. She held the pan with a thick rag she'd wound around the iron handle and tested the warmth of the liquid with the tip of her finger.

"It isn't too hot, milady, but it's going to hurt something fierce. If you need to scream..."

"She will not make a sound." Brodick repeated the comment in a firm, no nonsense voice.

The arrogant man sounded as though he were stating a fact, and she couldn't help but be a little perturbed with his high-handed manners. She should be the one to decide if she were going to be brave or not. Why did he think it was his decision to make?

Annie continued to hover, looking frightened and unsure. Gillian glanced up. "Why is your treatment called mother's fire?"

She asked the question a scant second before Brodick nodded to the woman and she poured the liquid over Gillian's open wounds. The pain was instantaneous, horrific, consuming. Her arm felt as though it had been flayed and then dipped in lye. Her skin was on fire, the flames shooting down to her bone. Her response was just as instantaneous. Her stomach lurched, her head spun, and her vision blurred. She would have leapt out of the chair if Dylan and Brodick hadn't been holding her down. Dear God, the excruciating agony wouldn't let up. After the first spasm of wrenching pain, her skin began to throb and pulsate, and her arm felt as though hot embers were embedded in her wounds. Arching her back against Dylan, she took deep, gasping breaths, squeezed her eyes shut to hold her tears back, clenched her jaw tight so she wouldn't scream out loud, and gripped Brodick's hand with all her might.

Had he shown her a glimmer of sympathy, she would have broken down and sobbed like a baby, but when she looked at him for help and saw his calm, dispassionate expression, she was able to regain her control.

Realizing she was pressing against Dylan, she forced herself to sit forward in the chair. But she couldn't stop squeezing Brodick's hand, though God knows she tried. Just when she was certain she couldn't take another second of the torture, it began to ease.

"The worst is over, lass," Annie whispered in a voice that sounded as though she, too, wanted to have a good cry. "Now I'm going to put some soothing salve on your skin and wrap it up tight in a nice bandage. Is the pain easing yet?"

Gillian tried, but she found it impossible to speak just yet, and so she stiffly nodded. She stared beyond Brodick's shoulder, focusing on a splinter of wood in the far wall, and prayed she wouldn't pass out.

Annie worked quickly, and within minutes Gillian's arm was covered in a thick white ointment and then wrapped from elbow to wrist. It was awkward work, for Gillian still refused to let go of Brodick's hand. Now that the pain was bearable, she realized he was rubbing her palm with his thumb. His countenance hadn't changed, but the little caress had a powerful effect. She felt as though he had taken her into his arms and was holding her.

After Annie tied the ends of the bandage at her wrist, Gillian took one last calming breath and finally pulled her hand away from Brodick's.

"There, it's done," Annie whispered. "You'll be as fit as ever tomorrow. Please try not to get the injury wet for a couple of days."

Gillian nodded again. Her voice was hoarse when she thanked the woman for her help.

"If you'll excuse me for a moment," she began as she slowly stood up. Dylan took hold of her elbow and helped her. She sagged against him, slowly righted herself, and then inclined her head to Annie before she left the cottage. The soldiers bowed as she passed them.

Gillian was certain they watched her from the doorway, and so she didn't give in to the urge to run to the cover of the trees. Alec was skipping barefoot in the stream while Robert stood guard. Fortunately, the child didn't notice her when she hurried in the opposite direction or hear her when the first sob escaped.

Liam frowned with concern as he watched her leave, then turned back to Annie. "Is there any of that mother's fire left?"

"Aye, a few drops," she answered.

Liam went to the table, pulled out his dirk, and made a small cut above his wrist. All of his friends knew what he was going to do, and none of them was the least bit surprised, for Liam was known as the doubting Thomas of the group and also the most curious.

Wanting to know exactly what the liquid felt like against a raw cut, he put his arm out over the cloth Annie had left on the table and ordered, "Pour some of the liquid on this nick. I would know how it feels."

If Annie thought the request was insane, she was smart enough not to remark on it. She felt as though she were in a cave with a family of bears. The men were the most ferocious warriors in the Highlands. Easily insulted and quick to react, they made frightening enemies. Yet at the same time, they were the best of allies. Annie counted herself fortunate to be related to the Buchanans, because that meant she and her husband would never by preyed upon by other more civilized clans.

She stepped forward to do as he ordered. "Your cut is paltry compared to milady's," she remarked. "So the sting won't be near as bad."

After making the comment, she tipped the

pan and let the liquid pour into the cut. Liam didn't react. His curiosity assuaged, he nodded to Annie and then turned and strode outside. Brodick and the others followed. Surrounding him, they patiently waited for him to give his report. Aaron smiled when Liam finally spoke because his voice sounded very like the croak of a drowning frog.

"It hurt like a son of a bitch," he whispered. "I don't know how the lass stood it."

Robert joined them, carrying Alec like a sack of wheat over his shoulder. The child squealed with delight until he noticed that Gillian wasn't there. A look of stark terror crossed his face as he scrambled to the ground and screamed Gillian's name at the top of his lungs. Robert clapped his hand over the boy's mouth to quiet him.

"She's just beyond the trees, Alec. She'll be right back. Calm yourself."

Tears poured down the child's face as he ran to his uncle. Brodick picked him up and roughly patted his back. "I forgot how very young you are, lad," he said gruffly. "Gillian didn't leave you."

Ashamed that he had panicked, Alec hid his face in the crook of Brodick's neck. "I thought maybe she did," he admitted.

"Since you've known her, has she ever left you?"

"No... but sometimes... I get scared," he whispered. "I didn't used to, but now I do."

"It's all right," Brodick said, and with a sigh he added, "You're safe now. I'm not going to let anything happen to you."

"That's what Gillian said," he remembered. "She's not gonna let anyone hurt me, not ever." He lifted his head and stared into Brodick's eyes. "You got to take care of her too 'cause she's just a puny lady."

Brodick laughed. "I haven't noticed anything puny about her."

"But she is. She cries sometimes when she thinks I'm sleeping. I told her she needed you. I don't want nobody to hurt her any more."

"I'm not going to let anyone hurt her," he assured the child. "Now stop worrying and go with Robert to fetch his horse. We'll leave as soon as Gillian returns from her walk."

Gillian didn't return to the clearing for another ten minutes, and it was evident from her red eyes that she'd been crying. Brodick waited by his stallion while she said her thank-you to Annie, and when she hurried over to him, he lifted her up into the saddle, then swung up behind her. She was so exhausted from her ordeal, she collapsed against him.

Brodick was suddenly overwhelmed with the need to protect and comfort her. He tried to be gentle as he settled her on his lap, then wrapped his arm around her and held her close. Within minutes she was sound asleep. He nudged his mount forward and gently settled Gillian in the crook of his arm, her long curls brushing his thigh. She had the most angelic face, and with the back of his hand he brushed her cheek tenderly. He finally gave in to the desire that had been plaguing him since the moment he'd laid eyes on her. He leaned down and kissed her soft lips, smiling when she wrinkled her nose and sighed.

His mind kept telling him to be reasonable. She was English, and God only knew, he couldn't abide anyone or anything English. He had learned his lesson well on his one foray into that hateful country when he was young and foolish. He'd wanted to find a bride as fitting as Iain Maitland's wife, Judith, but the quest had been futile, for Iain had found the only treasure England had to offer.

Or so Brodick had believed until he met Gillian. Now he wasn't so certain.

"You're a courageous lass," he whispered. And with a nod, he added, "I'll give you that."

But no more.

CHAPTER EIGHT

Alec's needs came first. As impatient as Brodick was to get some answers, he decided to wait until after the boy had been fed to question Gillian. It was late, well past sunset, and the moon shone brightly. The woman and the child were tired. They made camp at the base of Carnith Ridge in a narrow, secluded tract of land buffered on three sides by towering pines. The clearing eased down to the grassy bank of Beech Lake, a clear, stone-bottomed basin filled with speckled trout.

Aaron placed a plaid on the ground near the small campfire Liam had built after noticing Gillian was shivering. She thanked him with a smile that caused the soldier to blush like a little boy.

Gillian sat with her legs tucked under her on the edge of the woolen cloth while Alec sprawled like a lazy Roman statesman beside her. Brodick thought his angel looked as though she had just been to battle. Her complexion was gray; her lips were pinched, and her eyes were bright with fever, yet she didn't utter a word of complaint. She didn't want any of the food Robert offered, but she made certain that Alec filled his seemingly hollow stomach. He wanted to gulp his food down and would have done just that if she hadn't given him only small portions at a time. In a whisper, she kept reminding him to eat slowly so he wouldn't get sick again and she showed amazing endurance by listening to his nonstop chatter without losing her patience.

The little boy was in good cheer until she suggested he bathe. He scrambled to his feet and ran to his uncle shouting, "I don't need a bath."

Gillian was the only one who wasn't surprised by the child's outburst. "You'll feel better after," she promised.

Alec vehemently shook his head. "No, I won't," he shouted. "You can't make me."

"Alec, you will not speak to the lady in

such a tone," Brodick ordered. "And stop hiding behind me. A Maitland doesn't cower."

From the boy's puzzled expression Brodick surmised he didn't know what the word "cower" meant, but he must have guessed it wasn't good because he immediately stepped out to stand next to his uncle. His shoulder pressed against Brodick's thigh.

"I don't want to have a bath," he muttered.

"Why not?"

He pointed to Gillian. "She'll make me use her soap, and then I'll..."

"You'll what?" Brodick prodded.

"I'll smell like a girl."

"I doubt that, Alec."

"I went to considerable trouble borrowing this soap," she called out.

"You stole it."

"No, Alec, I borrowed it," she corrected before glancing at Brodick. "The soap has rose petals in it, and Alec seems to think that because I use it..."

The child finished her explanation for her. "It makes me smell like a girl," he insisted as he took a step back and warily watched her out of the corner of his eye.

Robert came up behind Alec, hooked his arm around him, and carried him to the lake. Liam asked her for the soap and then followed.

Gillian heard Robert promise Alec that although they would surely smell like roses after they had bathed, the sweet scent would in no way turn them into females.

Alec was laughing a minute later, and the

crisis, it seemed, was over. She decided to stand up and stretch her legs and had made it to her knees when Aaron and Stephen rushed forward to offer their assistance. Without asking, they each grabbed an elbow and pulled her up.

"Thank you, gentlemen."

"You may call me Stephen," the dark skinned soldier said.

"I doubt you have all our names straight in your mind," Aaron remarked.

"I know most of you. Robert took Alec to the lake, Liam went with him, and I know you're Aaron, but I don't know the other names yet."

"My name's Fingal," a redheaded soldier announced as he pressed forward.

"I'm Ossian," another called out as he, too, moved close. He was tall and so thick through the shoulders his neck disappeared.

Gillian suddenly felt as though she were enclosed by a six-foot male wall. The men were all staring down at her as if they considered her an oddity that had dropped from the sky to land at their feet. Had they never encountered a woman from England before? And why were they acting so peculiar now? She'd been in their company a full day, and that was surely time enough for them to get past their curiosity.

She stepped to the left so she could see between two soldiers and spotted Brodick leaning against a tree with his arms folded across his chest. He, too, was watching her, but unlike his soldiers, he wasn't smiling. She tilted her head ever so slightly toward the men pressing into her, fully expecting Brodick to catch her subtle hint and order his soldiers to give her breathing room. He didn't seem inclined to come to her assistance, however.

"You didn't eat much supper, milady," Ossian said. "Are you feeling poorly?"

"I'm feeling quite well, thank you," she replied.

"You don't have to be brave in front of us," Stephen commented.

"But you see, sir..."

"Please call me Stephen." Before she could agree, he added, "I meant what I said. You don't have to be brave in front of us."

Yet another soldier joined the wall. He was going to be the easiest to remember, because he had a scar that crossed the left side of his face and the most handsome brown eyes.

"My name's Keith," he reminded her. "And you may always speak freely in front of us. We're your laird's guard."

"But he isn't my laird."

Dylan joined the conversation in time to hear her comment. He noticed none of the men contradicted her, but they were all grinning like idiots.

"Milady, Annie Drummond gave Liam a pouch of medicine powder. You're to take half tonight, mixed with water, and the rest tomorrow night."

Liam had returned from the lake and thrust a cup of liquid into her hand. "I tasted it, milady," he said. "It's bitter, so you might want to gulp it down quick. It smells vile too."

She studied his blue eyes for several seconds and then asked suspiciously, "Are you thinking to drug me to sleep, Liam?"

He laughed. "Nay, milady, we learned our lesson with Kevin Drummond. The potion will help rid you of your fever."

She decided to believe him and drank the liquid as quickly as she could. The urge to gag was overpowering, but taking deep, gasping breaths helped. Blanching, she said, "The cure is worse than the illness."

"Does your arm hurt?" Stephen asked.

"No," she answered. "If you'll excuse me, gentlemen, I would like to sit on that boulder next to your laird so that I may speak to him."

Fingal and Ossian moved out of her way so she could get past them, while Keith grabbed the plaid from the ground and hurried ahead to put the woolen cloth on the flat surface of the rock for her to sit on.

She thanked him for his consideration as she took her seat.

"Is there anything else we may do for you, milady?" Fingal asked.

"No, thank you," she replied. "You have all been very kind and gracious to me," she added.

"You need not thank us for doing our duty, milady," Ossian told her.

"Please call me Gillian."

He appeared scandalized by her suggestion. "I cannot, milady."

"No, he cannot," Brodick announced as he walked over to stand in front of her. "Leave us now," he ordered quietly.

One by one the soldiers bowed to Gillian before heading to the lake. She watched them until they disappeared from view, all the while gathering her thoughts because she knew the time had come for her to give a detailed explanation of what had transpired. Lord, reliving the past was exhausting to even think about.

Straightening her shoulders, she folded her hands in her lap and waited for Brodick to tell her to begin. Dylan remained by her side with his arms folded across his chest.

"How did you and Alec end up together?" Brodick asked.

"I'm not certain where to start."

"At the beginning," he ordered.

She nodded. "The obsession started a long time ago."

"Obsession?" Dylan asked.

"Let her explain without interruption," Brodick suggested. "Then we will both ask questions."

"I have a sister," Gillian said. "Her name is Christen, and when we were little girls, our home was invaded and our father was killed."

The rising wind whistled through the pine trees, the sound eerily melancholy. Gillian gripped her hands as she described the black night in vivid detail, though in truth she wasn't certain if she actually remembered what had happened or if Liese had given her the memory. The story of Arianna's treasure and the king's obsession to find the man who had murdered his love intrigued Brodick, but he didn't bother her now with questions. He merely nodded when she hesitated, urging her to continue.

"If the baron finds the treasure before anyone else, he will receive a great reward. He's motivated purely by greed," she explained. "Still, I don't think he knew for certain that Christen was given the box when she left England or he surely would have intensified his search for her."

Brodick interrupted her concentration when he lifted her plaid and wrapped it around her shoulders. "You're shivering," he said gruffly.

Surprised by his thoughtfulness, she stammered her thank-you.

"Continue," he ordered, shrugging off the gratitude as inconsequential.

"The baron has learned that Christen does indeed hide in the Highlands."

"And where did he get this information?"

"From the Highlander who came to him with a proposal. Remember," she hastily added, "over the years the baron has sent inquiries to all the clans, but none responded until about a month ago, when the Highlander arrived. He told the baron he knew where Christen was and that he could give the baron the information he needed if in return he would do something for him."

"And what did this Highlander want done?" Brodick asked.

"He wanted Laird Ramsey's brother taken from the festival to draw Ramsey out so he could kill him. He wants both of them dead."

Dylan couldn't keep silent. "But the Maitland boy was taken."

"Yes, they stole the wrong child."

Their questions began, one following another until her head throbbed. The sound of Alec's laughter carried from the lake. The soldiers were keeping him occupied, she knew, so he wouldn't interfere with Brodick's inquisition.

"Where do you fit in this puzzle, Gillian?" Brodick asked.

"I was told to find my sister and the treasure and bring both back to the baron before our fall festival begins."

"And if you fail?"

"My Uncle Morgan will be killed." Her voice broke on a sob that took her by complete surprise. Exhaustion was making her emotional, she decided, and she willed herself to calm down. "He is the dearest man. He took me into his home and raised me as his daughter. I love him and I will protect him at all cost."

"The baron isn't related to you?"

"No, he isn't. Are you almost finished questioning me? I would like to get Alec settled for the night. It's late."

"I'm almost finished," he replied. "Give me the name of this Highlander who made the pact with the baron."

" I cannot give you the name, for I never heard it."

"Are you telling me the truth? Surely the baron or one of his friends said the man's name," he said, his frustration palpable in the sudden stillness.

"Why would I lie? To protect a traitor?"

"But you did see him, didn't you?" Brodick pressed. "Alec told me you saw the Highlander from the hill."

"Yes."

"And you would recognize him if you saw him again?" Dylan asked.

"Yes," she answered. "Alec and I were well hidden on a knoll with a path just below. I saw him clearly as he rode toward me. He isn't the only traitor involved, though," she added. "Alec said there were two... maybe three... who took him from the festival." So weary now she could barely hold her head up, she whispered, "You do know why the Highlander was returning to Dunhanshire, don't you?"

"To inform the baron he'd taken the wrong boy," Dylan answered. "And then Alec would have been killed. Isn't that right?"

"Yes."

"Milady, why were you beaten? Did the bastard give you a reason?" Dylan asked.

"A man who strikes a woman is a coward, Dylan, and cowards don't need reasons to justify their actions." Brodick's voice radiated anger.

Gillian pulled the plaid close. "Our first attempt to escape failed, and the baron wanted to punish Alec and me."

"The boy said you threw yourself on top of him to protect him," Dylan said. "It was a brave act, milady."

She disagreed. "I wasn't brave; I was terrified they would kill him. I don't think I've ever been so scared. I had just heard the Highlander was on his way, and I knew why, and I was in such a panic to get Alec away before—" She stopped suddenly and took a deep breath. "So many things could have gone wrong. They could have separated us or hidden Alec away from me, and every time I think what could have happened, I become terrified all over again. Brave? I think not."

Brodick and Dylan shared a look before Brodick continued. "Who specifically inflicted the punishment? Was it the baron or one of his soldiers?"

"Why do you want to know?"

"Answer me."

"The baron."

"Alec said that another man struck you. Is that true?" Brodick's voice was low and frightfully menacing.

"I don't remember."

"Yes, you do," he snapped. "Tell me."

Startled by his curt tone, she stiffened her spine. "As a matter of fact, one of his friends struck me. I don't understand why you need to know about it, though. It's over and done with."

"Nay, lass," he said softly. "It's only just begun."

CHAPTER NINE

Beneath the steely exterior of a warrior beat the heart of a true gentleman. The revelation was both surprising and amusing, for though Brodick obviously wanted to be solicitous, it quickly became apparent he didn't have the faintest idea how. When he finally called a halt to the questioning, she hastily stood up before he could change his mind. She turned to leave, but her feet got tangled up in the plaid, and she stumbled forward into his arms instead. He grabbed her by her shoulders to steady her, which was a very thoughtful thing to do, of course, but he didn't stop there. Once he had her, he decided to keep her. As though he had every right to do so, he threw his arm around her shoulders, his staggering weight all but knocking her to the ground, and hauled her up against him. She tried to delicately shrug him away, but that didn't work, and so she looked up at him to tell him to let go. He was waiting for her, and, Lord, the impact of those dark penetrating eyes, filled with such compassion and tenderness, made her heart quicken and her knees tremble.

Did he have any idea of the effect he had on her? The warmth of his skin made her wish she could snuggle closer to him. His heat felt better than ten blankets piled on top of her. And his voice, too, so rich and gruff, was wonderfully sensual. Why, even the way he walked, with such unbridled arrogance, as though he believed he owned the world, his hips moving with easy grace, and those muscular thighs of his...

She blocked the unseemly thought. She shouldn't be noticing such things. 'Twas the truth she'd never known any man like him, though, or felt this kind of reaction. All she wanted to do was put her head down on his shoulder for a few minutes and close her eyes. When she was with him, she didn't feel so vulnerable and unsure of herself. Brodick seemed to be the kind of man who wasn't afraid of anything. Did he think he was invincible? And did thinking it make it true? Where had his arrogance and confidence come from, she wondered, and, oh, how she wished she could borrow a little of both.

Exhaustion was surely taking its toll. She glanced up at him and smiled. Odd that she'd known him for less than a full day, yet she felt as though she'd been with him for years. They walked to the lake leaning into one another like old friends, comfortable with the closeness and the silence, but also like lovers, she imagined, who were breathless in anticipation for what might come.

Aye, his effect on her was quite strange. He made her believe she wasn't alone. Would he help her slay the monsters? No, she immediately decided. She couldn't, and wouldn't, involve him in her battles. She understood her responsibility. She would fight the dragon alone, and if she failed...

"Are you cold, Gillian?"

"No."

"You're shivering."

"I was thinking about my uncle. I worry about him."

"Is he worth your worry?"

"Oh, yes, he is."

He leaned close to her ear. "Can you do anything about your uncle tonight?"

"No," she answered, trying to ignore the caress of his warm sweet breath against her sensitive skin.

"Then let it go for now. Worrying won't help him."

"That's easier said than accomplished."

"Perhaps," he allowed.

Alec ran past them, dragging a stick behind him. The child was barefoot and bare-chested and obviously having a fine time. His laughter echoed through the trees.

"He's too excited to sleep."

"He'll sleep soundly," he predicted.

He didn't let go of her until they reached the water's edge. Then he asked, "Can you manage on your own or do you need help?"

"I can manage, thank you."

"Don't get your arm wet," he reminded her as he started back to camp.

"Wait."

He turned back to her. "Yes?"

"You..."

She suddenly stopped. Wondering why she hesitated, he took a step toward her. She bowed her head and folded her hands together

201

as though in prayer. She looked terribly vulnerable now... and sweet... he thought.

"Yes?" he repeated.

"You make me feel safe. I thank you for that."

He didn't know how to respond. He finally managed a quick nod, then walked away.

Even though Gillian could tell she'd startled him, she was still glad she'd told him how she felt. She knew she could have been more eloquent, but it was too late now to start over.

Her arm still hurt, though not nearly as much as it had earlier in the day, and she was hopeful her fever would ease soon. By morning she would either be as right as rain or dead, and at the moment she had trouble deciding which would be better. Fatigue was pressing down on her like a vise. Perhaps a bath would make her feel better, she decided. The water didn't look deep near the bank, the stone bottom appeared smooth, and she would be careful, of course, not to get her bandage wet.

She got trapped in her tunic when she tried to pull it over her head, then she bumped her arm. It was all suddenly too much, and she burst into tears and collapsed.

But before she could fall to the ground, she felt strong arms lifting her up to her feet. She couldn't see; the tunic was pressed against her face, yet she knew Brodick had come to her rescue.

"Are you wanting this off or on?" he asked gruffly.

She nodded. It wasn't a proper answer,

and so he made the decision for her and pulled the tunic over her head. Tossing it on the grass, he tilted her chin up, saw the tears, and wrapped his arms around her. "You can cry all you want. No one's here to bother you."

She wiped the tears away with his plaid. "You're here," she whispered, sounding pitiful.

His chin dropped to the top of her head, and he continued to hold her until she grew calm. Allowing her to pull back, he asked, "Better now?"

"Yes, thank you."

She couldn't believe what she did then. Before she could stop herself, she leaned up on tiptoes, put her arms around his neck, and kissed him on the mouth. Her lips brushed over his for the barest of seconds, but it was still a kiss, and when she came to her senses and dared to pull away and look at him, he had the most curious expression on his face.

Brodick knew she regretted her spontaneity, but as he stared into her brilliant green eyes, he also knew, with a certainty that shook him to the core, that his life had just been irrevocably changed by this mere slip of a woman.

Dazed by her own boldness, she slowly stepped back. "I don't know what came over me," she whispered.

"When this is over..."

"Yes, Brodick?"

He shook his head, unwilling for the moment to say another word, and then turned abruptly and walked away.

What had he been about to say? She longed to go after him and demand that he explain, and then immediately changed her mind. When Brodick wanted her to know what he was thinking, he would tell her. Besides, she was pretty certain she knew exactly what it was. Soon she would return to England and it was therefore foolish to become attached.

Why in God's name had she kissed him? Was she out of her mind or just plain stupid? She didn't need a complication like this now, not with all the trouble she was in. She thought about going after him then to explain that she really hadn't meant to kiss him—it had just happened—a spontaneous act nurtured by his kindness and her curiosity. Perhaps she should just pretend it hadn't happened, she thought as she touched her mouth with her fingertips and let out a long sigh of regret.

A bath, she decided, was out of the question, for in her bemused state, she would probably drown. She washed as thoroughly as she could, then took her time dressing as she summoned the courage to go back to camp and face Brodick.

All of the Buchanans were sitting together on the far side of the clearing, talking to one another until they spotted her coming toward them. The sudden silence unnerved her and she didn't dare look at Brodick for fear she'd blush and cause the other soldiers to wonder why. She kept her head down while she prepared her bed on the opposite side of the clearing, but she could feel all of them watching her. Alec was drawing circles in the dirt with his stick.

"Are you ready for bed, Alec?" she called out.

"I'm gonna sleep with the men. All right?"

"Yes," she answered. "Good night, then."

She lay down on her side facing the woods, her back to the soldiers, fully convinced she wouldn't get a moment's rest with an audience observing her every move, but exhaustion won out and she was asleep minutes later.

So that they wouldn't disturb her, the men continued their conversation in low whispers. Brodick couldn't stop watching her, worrying about foolish matters such as whether she had enough blankets. The wind had picked up and heavy rain clouds moved in, covering the moonlight. The sound of thunder rumbled in the distance, and the air became thick and heavy.

The darker it got, the more agitated Alec became. Robert doused the fire, and the camp became nearly pitch-black. Grabbing his blanket, the child scrambled to his feet and blurted out, "I've got to sleep with Gillian."

"Why?" Brodick asked, wondering if the boy would admit he was afraid of the dark.

"'Cause she gets scared in the night." Without waiting for permission, he dragged his blanket across the clearing and placed it next to Gillian. Carefully putting his stick within grabbing distance, he yawned and then curled up against her back.

Brodick watched him struggle to keep his

eyes open, then heard him whisper, "Uncle?"

"What is it, Alec?"

"You won't leave... will you?"

"No, I won't leave. Go to sleep."

Gillian was awakened from a deep sleep during the night by a howling scream like the sound of a tortured animal. She was very familiar with the unearthly sound. Alec was trapped in another nightmare. She quickly rolled to her side and took the little boy into her arms to soothe him.

"Hush," she whispered as she stroked his brow. "It's all right now. You're safe."

The screams turned to whimpers, and his terror abated. She continued to stroke him until she felt him relax and heard his breathing calm.

The heart-stopping howling started all over again an hour later, and she repeated the ritual a second time. During the predawn hour, she awakened yet again, but this time for an altogether different reason. She was on her back with her left arm stretched wide. It was pinned down and throbbing painfully. She turned her head and saw that Alec was using her bandage as a pillow. Ever so slowly, so as not to disturb him, she eased her arm out from under him. She was bringing her hand down to her side when she noticed something resting on her stomach. It was a hand; it was heavy, and it didn't belong to her. Stupefied, she squinted at it for several seconds while she tried to clear her mind, and then she slowly followed the path from the hand up the muscular arm to the broad shoulder. She blinked. Good Lord, she was sleeping with Brodick. She slowly sat up and looked around her and realized she was in the center of a cocoon. Surrounding her in a circle were all of Brodick's soldiers. She couldn't comprehend how they had gotten there, or how she had ended up in Brodick's arms. She tried to think about it, but she was so sleepy she couldn't keep her eyes open long enough to make sense out of anything, and so she lay back down, put her head on Brodick's shoulder, her hand on his chest, and went back to sleep.

For the first time in a long, long time, she felt protected. Blessedly, her nightmares left her alone.

CHAPTER TEN

Brodick shook her awake an hour after dawn. The poor lass looked all wrung out and he hated to interrupt her sleep, for she'd had precious little of it but time was wasting away, and they had a hard ride through hostile territory ahead of them.

"We have to get going, Gillian."

"I'll only be a minute," she promised as she hurried to the lake with her satchel tucked under her arm. She washed quickly, then brushed her hair and dug through her bag for a ribbon.

Because of the bandage, her left hand was useless and she couldn't get her hair braided. After trying unsuccessfully to bind it behind her neck with the ribbon, she gave up.

They were waiting for her when she returned to camp. Liam took her satchel and tossed it to Robert.

"You must eat, milady," Liam said as he thrust what looked like a fried triangle of mush into her hand.

"I'm not hungry, Liam, but I thank you …"

He wouldn't take the food back. "You must eat, milady," he insisted.

She didn't want to be difficult, and so she forced herself to swallow the bland-tasting food.

"Liam, would you please tie my hair back with this ribbon? I can't seem to…" Her voice trailed away when she saw his appalled expression. "It wouldn't be proper?" she asked.

"Nay, milady, it wouldn't. Your laird should be the only man to touch your hair."

Her laird indeed. How could she argue with such an absurd idea? The Buchanans, she'd already learned, were an obstinate lot, and when they got a notion into their hard heads, nothing could prod it loose.

They were also good and honorable men who were now protecting Alec and her, and nothing any of them did would cause her to lose her patience.

"All right then," she agreed.

Brodick was leading his horse toward her when she ran to him and asked his assistance. He also looked startled, but he did accept the ribbon. She turned around, swung her hair over her shoulder, and lifted it up with one hand. He pushed her hand away, pulled on her hair as though he were grooming his horse's tail, and roughly tied the ribbon into a hard knot.

The man was as delicate as a bull. She thought he might have pulled her hair on purpose because she'd asked him to do a woman's chore, but she held her smile and thanked him profusely.

"Will we reach Laird Ramsey Sinclair's holding before nightfall?"

"No," he answered curtly. He grabbed her by her waist and lifted her onto his stallion's back, then swung up behind her and took the reins. "We're going to the Maitlands'."

She bumped his chin when she turned to him. "We must go to Ramsey first and warn him of the danger to him and his brother before we take Alec home."

"No."

"Yes."

He was astonished that she had the gumption to contradict him. No woman had ever dared argue with him before, and he wasn't quite certain how to proceed. Didn't she realize his position of power?

"You're English," he said. "And I will therefore make certain allowances for you. I realize you don't understand you shouldn't argue with me, and so I'll explain it to you. Don't argue with me."

Incredulous, she said, "That's it? 'Don't argue

with me' is your explanation as to why I shouldn't argue with you?"

"Are you trying to irritate me?"

"No, of course not."

Presuming she now understood he wasn't going to waste valuable time debating his decisions with her, he turned to call out to Dylan, but she regained his full attention when she put her hand on his chest. Her voice was low, insistent. "I must warn Laird Sinclair."

He tilted his head ever so slightly as he studied her. "Do you know him?" he asked softly. "Have you seen Ramsey?"

She couldn't understand why he had suddenly become so tense and irritable. His behavior was most puzzling, but she decided not to remark on it now because she was more interested in making him be reasonable.

"No, I've never met the man, but I know a good deal about him."

He raised an eyebrow. "Tell me what you know."

Ignoring his gruff tone, she answered, "I know he rules the Sinclair clan and that he's their new laird. Isn't that true?"

"It is," he answered.

Her fingertips were slowly trailing a path down his chest, her touch damned distracting. He wondered if she realized what she was doing or if it was a deliberate ploy to gain his cooperation. Did the woman actually believe that a kind word and a gentle caress would sway him? It was laughable, really. Anyone who knew him well understood that once he had made up his mind, he never changed it.

"And I have made certain assumptions about him," she continued. "A man doesn't become laird unless he's a very fit warrior. I imagine he's... almost... as strong as you are."

The tension eased out of him. "Almost," he arrogantly allowed.

She didn't smile, but the urge was nearly overwhelming. "I also know that Ramsey has a brother as young as Alec. He's a child, and it's therefore your duty, and mine, to watch out for him. Every child should be protected from harm, and Michael's no exception."

Her argument was sound. Brodick had thought first to get her and Alec to Iain Maitland, with whom they would be safe, and then go to Ramsey to warn him.

He reevaluated his decision now. "Your primary concern is for the boy, isn't it?"

"Yes," she replied.

"I'll send Dylan and two others to warn Ramsey, but the rest of us will go to the Maitlands'. Does that satisfy you?"

"Yes, thank you."

He grabbed her hand to get her to stop stroking him and said, "In future, you will not argue with me."

It wasn't a request but a statement of fact, and Gillian decided to let him think she agreed. "As you wish."

After receiving his instructions, Dylan left with Ossian and Fingal to go to the Sinclair holding. Alec rode with Robert, and Liam took the lead as they continued toward their destination. When they stopped to rest the horses at the nooning hour, Keith and Stephen split from the group. The soldiers caught up with the procession again an hour later, looking as smug as could be, and leading a feisty gray mare.

Gillian took to the animal right away. She was pleased they had borrowed the horse until she found out they didn't plan to ever give her back. Appalled, she refused to ride the horse unless they promised her that when they reached the Maitlands', they would return the mare to her rightful owner, but the soldiers were as stubborn as their laird and wouldn't agree to any such thing. Keith tried to be clever by changing the subject while Stephen tried to convince her that the man who owned the horse felt honored because a Buchanan had chosen his mare to steal.

"Do you want us to insult the man?" Stephen asked.

"No, of course I don't, but—"

"It would shame him," Keith told her.

"If you think I'm going to believe—"

"It's time to go." Brodick gave the order as he lifted her onto the mare. His hand rested on her thigh. "You do know how to ride, don't you?"

She began to push his hand away, but he merely tightened his grip while he patiently waited for her to answer his question.

She decided to give him a dose of his own arrogance. "Better than you, Laird."

He shook his head at her and tried to ignore the sweet smile she gave him with her outrageous boast. "I don't like arrogant women."

"Then you aren't going to like me at all," she replied cheerfully. "I'm horribly arrogant. Just ask my uncle Morgan. He tells me it's my greatest flaw."

"No, arrogance isn't your greatest flaw."

Before she realized what he was going to do, his hand cupped the back of her neck and he roughly pulled her toward him. He'd moved so quickly, she didn't even have time to blink, and she was still smiling at him when his mouth settled possessively on hers.

He kissed the breath right out of her. The heat of his mouth against hers sent a jolt of excitement surging through her body. The kiss was exhilarating, and then it got better. His tongue stroked hers, and the pleasure was so intense, she was certain it had to be a sin, but she couldn't make herself care. All she wanted to do was kiss him back as passionately as he was kissing her.

She wanted to get closer to him, to throw her arms around his neck, hold him close, and never let go. She tried to do just that, and when he ended the kiss, she very nearly toppled to the ground. Fortunately, he wasn't as addle-brained as she was—'twas a fact he didn't look at all affected by the searing kiss—and he was able to catch her before she disgraced herself.

She could hear Alec making gagging sounds of disgust in between his giggles, but didn't turn to look at any of the soldiers, knowing that her face was burning with embarrassment.

"You mustn't ever kiss me again, Brodick," she whispered hoarsely.

He laughed as he swung up onto his mount and took the lead. She nudged her horse into a trot to catch up with him.

"I mean it," she whispered.

He acted as though he hadn't heard her, and she decided to let the matter go.

They rode hard that day, stopping only once more to rest the horses and let Alec stretch his legs. Gillian stayed behind Brodick as they rode through rough, untamed, but breathtakingly beautiful land.

When they stopped for the night, she went to the nearby stream and washed, all the while thinking about the comment Brodick had made but hadn't explained, and the longer she thought about it the more curious she became. He'd told her that arrogance wasn't her greatest flaw, indicating he believed there was another more serious imperfection.

She was dying to ask him to explain himself, but determined not to, and though it was frustrating, she was able to control her curiosity for a while. She and Alec were so worn out from the long day, they went to bed directly after supper. Both of them slept like the dead, and if Alec had nightmares, she didn't remember soothing him. She awakened a little before dawn and found herself cuddled in Brodick's strong arms again. Content, she closed her eyes and went back to sleep.

So that Alec could catch up on his sleep, they got a late start the following day and didn't stop until the middle of the afternoon. Alec was more relaxed now, but he still wouldn't let her out of his sight. She had to order him to sit with Keith when she needed a few minutes of privacy, and as soon as she returned, he ran to her and latched onto her hand.

The poor innocent looked relieved to see her again.

"I'm not going to disappear on you, Alec."

"Uncle Brodick says we're close to my home now."

"Does this valley look familiar to you?"

"No," he admitted. Then he tugged on her hand. "Gillian?" he whispered.

She leaned down. "Yes?" she asked, wondering what he was worrying about now.

"Can I ride with you?"

"Don't you like riding with Robert?"

"He won't let me talk, not even when it's safe."

"You can ride with me."

"But you got to ask Uncle Brodick."

"I will," she agreed. "Finish eating, and I'll go ask right now."

Brodick was walking back from the forest and appeared to be preoccupied when she approached him.

"Brodick, how much farther is it to Alec's home?"

"A couple of hours."

"Would it be all right if Alec rode with me for a little while?"

"He'll ride with Robert."

"But Robert won't talk to him."

Exasperated, he said, "My soldier has more important matters on his mind."

"The child doesn't understand that."

With a sigh, he said, "All right. He can ride with you. We're on safe land now."

He started toward his horse, then stopped. "Do all boys his age talk as much as he does?"

"I don't know. Alec's the first child I've ever been around."

"You're good with him," he said abruptly. "You have a kind heart, Gillian."

She watched him walk away. The sun seemed to be following him. Beams of light shone down on his head and shoulders as he crossed the glen, and in the golden glow, her bronzed warrior looked as though he'd been sculpted by God in the archangel Michael's image so that he, too, could fight the demons roaming the world. It was at that moment that she became aware of him in a way she never had before. Now she reacted as a woman, and she was consumed with a yearning so intense tears came into her eyes. Annie and Kevin Drummond's charming home suddenly came into her mind. She pictured their pretty little cottage, but in her fantasy, Kevin wasn't standing in the doorway, Brodick was, and he was beckoning her.

Daydreams were dangerous because they made her wish for things she could never have.

"Milady, is something wrong?" Liam asked.

At the sound of his voice she jumped. "No, nothing's wrong."

Before he could question her further, she picked up her skirts and hurried to her horse. She couldn't get a proper grip with her left hand, and after trying twice without success, she gave up and called Brodick for assistance.

He nudged his mount close, leaned down, and all but tossed her onto her mare's back. Robert lifted Alec into her lap and went to fetch his horse.

"Brodick?" she whispered so the others wouldn't overhear.

"Yes?"

"You told me that arrogance wasn't my greatest flaw. You had another imperfection in mind?"

He'd wondered how long it would take her to get around to asking him that question and had to force himself not to laugh. "You have many flaws," he announced. He swore he saw a spark of fire ignite in her emerald eyes as she straightened her shoulders. The lass had a temper, and he found that flaw quite pleasing. "But there was one flaw that made all the other imperfections pale in comparison."

"Was?" she asked. "I don't have this flaw any longer?"

"No, you don't."

"Pray tell," she muttered in exasperation, "what was this terrible flaw?"

He grinned. "You used to be English."

CHAPTER ELEVEN

Gillian felt as though she'd entered another world. Even the sunset seemed different in the Highlands. The sky had turned into a brilliant canvas filled with broad, sweeping strokes of gold and splashes of orange. The center of the sun was a bold red, unlike any color Gillian had ever seen before, and she knew tomorrow the palette would be just as magnificent. God, she thought, surely favored this land.

"Gillian, you know what? I'm almost home."

"We must be close," she replied. "We've climbed almost to the top of the mountain."

Alec yawned loudly. "Tell me the story again when you scared your uncle Morgan and made him scream," he pleaded.

"I've told you that story at least five times now."

"But I want to hear it again. Please?"

"You close your eyes and rest and I'll tell you the story again."

Alec cuddled up against her chest and yawned once more. "I'm ready now."

"When I was a little girl—"

"You didn't talk for a whole long year."

The little boy obviously had memorized the story. "Yes, that's right. I didn't speak for almost a full year."

Brodick slowed his mount and waited until Gillian was even with him. He'd heard what she'd said to Alec and was curious to know the rest of the story.

"And you went to live with your Uncle Morgan, remember?"

She smiled. "I remember."

"But you got to tell it."

"One night I had a terrible nightmare—"

"Like the nightmares I sometimes have."

"Yes," she agreed. "My lady's maid, Liese, woke me up so I'd stop screaming, and as was her habit, she held me in her lap and rocked me."

"And then she almost dropped you on top of your head 'cause you finally talked to her."

"That's right, Alec."

"And the bad man who told you you killed your sister lied 'cause Liese said you didn't kill her. He was being mean, but you know what?"

"No, what?"

"Uncle Brodick will make him sorry he was mean."

Embarrassed because she knew Brodick could hear what the child was saying, she hastily continued the story.

"I was very happy to learn that Christen was alive, but then I also worried that she might be lost. Liese told me not to fret about my sister because she was certain my Uncle Morgan would help me find her. She said that all I needed to do was ask him. She meant for me to wait until morning, but I surprised her when I jumped off her lap and went running to my uncle's chamber."

"'Cause it was the middle of the night, right?"

"Right," she answered.

Alec started giggling because he knew what was coming and he could hardly contain himself. His shoulders shook as he covered his mouth with one hand and eagerly waited, his eyes twinkling with anticipation.

"Liese tried to stop me, but she wasn't fast enough, and she couldn't chase me into my uncle's private chamber. I ran to the side of his bed, climbed up on the platform, and poked him in the ribs to get him to wake up. He was in such a deep sleep, he was snoring, and no matter how hard I poked and prodded, I couldn't get him to open his eyes."

The story captured Brodick's attention, but he wasn't sure if it was because of the way she told the tale or if it was Alec's reaction that so amused him. The child could hardly sit still in her lap.

"And then what did you do?" Alec demanded.

"You know very well what I did. I've told you this story so many times you know it better than I do."

"But you got to tell it."

"I shouted at the poor man and gave him quite a fright."

Alec burst into raucous laughter. "And then he screamed, right?"

"Oh, my, yes, he screamed all right."

"And then you screamed, didn't you?"

She laughed. "Yes, I did. Poor Uncle was so startled, he leapt up and grabbed his sword, but his feet got all tangled up in the covers, and he fell out of bed and rolled all the way down the platform. And that's the end of the story."

"But you got to tell how you followed him around everywhere he went, talking and talking and talking all the day long."

"You just told it," she said. "Uncle told me that for the year I didn't speak he would pray every night that I would one day say his name—"

"But when you started talking and you wouldn't stop, that's when he started praying for a little peace and quiet?"

"Yes," she answered. "You know, Alec, when you get home, there's going to be quite a lot of excitement, and I doubt you'll get to bed early tonight. Why don't you close your eyes and rest?"

Yawning, he wrapped his arms around her waist. "Gillian?" he whispered.

"Yes?"

"I love you."

"I love you too, honey bear."

The little boy was clearly worn out and fell asleep minutes later. It was blissfully silent as they continued the steep climb up the side of the mountain. Every once in a while, Brodick would turn back and look at her, a puzzled expression on his face, as though he were trying to work something out in his mind.

The wind picked up, a brittle cold wind that felt as if it were slicing through her bones. She felt Alec shiver and wrapped the plaid around him.

The weight of the child against her left arm

soon became unbearable, and she finally asked Brodick for help. Alec was so exhausted he didn't wake up as he was transferred onto his uncle's lap. The tenderness in Brodick's eyes as he carefully placed the child's head against his chest made her think of her uncle Morgan and how he used to hold her on his lap while he told her bedtime stories, and she was suddenly so homesick and scared she wanted to weep.

Brodick caught her watching him. "Alec will get an ache in his ear if you don't cover his head," she blurted to cover her embarrassment.

He pulled the plaid over Alec's head but kept his attention centered on Gillian.

"What has you so worried, lass?"

"Nothing," she lied. "I was thinking..."

"Thinking about what?" he prodded.

He'd moved so close, his leg rubbed against hers. She pretended not to notice.

"Answer me," he demanded.

She sighed. "I was thinking that when you marry and have children, you will make a fine father."

"What makes you think I don't already have children?"

Her eyes widened. "But you're not married."

He laughed. "A man need not be married to father children."

"I realize that," she replied, trying her best to sound worldly. "I'm not completely ignorant."

"But you are completely innocent, aren't you?"

"That, sir, is none of your affair."

Her cheeks had turned bright pink with embarrassment. She was a delight to observe, he thought, and a sure temptress.

"Do you?" she whispered.

"Do I what?"

"Have children."

"No."

"Then you were teasing me."

She seemed to require an answer to her statement, and so he gave her a quick nod before he nudged his mount and took over the lead.

A few minutes later she heard the sound of thunder and the ground began to tremble. Stephen, Aaron, Liam and Robert all moved forward to circle her.

"Protect Alec and your laird," she ordered.

"Milady, we're on Maitland land now. There isn't any danger," Stephen explained.

"Then why are the four of you pressing in on me?"

Robert grinned. "We're just letting the Maitlands know."

"Know what, Robert?"

He wasn't inclined to explain. The Maitland soldiers crashed through the trees then and surrounded them. The noise startled Gillian's mare. Before she could calm the horse, Liam grabbed hold of the reins and forced the mare's head down.

They were encircled by warriors, and their closeness became oppressive. They were at least forty in number, and every one of them looked grim.

One soldier broke through the line and rode forward to speak to Brodick. There was something vaguely familiar about the man.

She asked Liam, "Is that soldier angry with your laird?"

"No, milady," he answered. "His name is Winslow, and he always frowns."

"Winslow is Iain Maitland's commander in arms," Stephen told her. "He's also Brodick's brother."

No wonder he seemed so familiar to her, for now she could see the resemblance in the brother's coloring and piercing eyes. Winslow even frowned like Brodick, she thought, when the Maitland commander turned toward her, narrowed his eyes, and said something to his brother.

Stephen deliberately nudged his mount closer to Gillian on one side and Liam squeezed closer on her other side.

"Winslow wants to know who you are, milady," Robert whispered from behind.

She watched Brodick shrug as though she were so unimportant to him he couldn't remember who she was.

And that's the way it should be, she thought to herself. She wasn't important to him; she was simply a means to an end. For a short time, she and Brodick had a united goal of getting an innocent child back to his family. But now they were on Maitland land, and soon their duty would be over. Alec would be with his parents again, Brodick would no doubt go home, and she would begin her search for her sister. Her mind understood that their time together was over, yet her heart ached with regret. It was logical that Brodick would return to his duties as laird over the Buchanans... and it was right. Why, then, did she feel so alone? Gillian didn't need him, or any other man... except her uncle, of course. Uncle Morgan was her family, and when her quest was over, if she succeeded, she would return to him.

But she would never forget Brodick... or the spontaneous kiss he'd given her that had meant nothing to him and everything to her.

Winslow caught her attention when he once again glanced her way and frowned with obvious displeasure. She heard him say the word "English" and assumed he was angry because Brodick had brought an outsider to the Maitlands.

Brodick's response was severe, but he spoke so rapidly, Gillian couldn't catch a single word. Whatever he said seemed to placate his brother, though, because he backed down and reluctantly nodded. Then Brodick lifted the blanket away from Alec's face. Winslow was so stunned he let out a shout. Alec immediately woke up, pushed the plaid down, and sat up straight, smiling as the Maitland soldiers moved forward.

All of the men began to hoot and holler, making such a ruckus Gillian's ears rang.

Alec loved the attention. He gleefully waved to his father's soldiers, then turned in Brodick's lap to look back at Gillian. Alec's joy was wonderful to see, and she knew that she would never forget this wonderful moment. *Thank you, God,* she prayed, *for getting this child home.*

Gillian's radiant expression took Brodick's breath away, and when she looked at him and smiled, she made him feel invincible. How could one woman have such an impact on him in such a short time? He felt as though his world had been changed forever, and, honest to God, he didn't know if he liked that one bit. Gillian was a disruption—

"Iain's on his way back from the training fields," Winslow said, breaking into his brother's thoughts.

"You should prepare him," Brodick said. "It's bound to be a shock having a son return from the dead."

Winslow laughed. "A joyous shock," he remarked before leaving.

The Maitland soldiers tried to press in on Gillian, which the Buchanan soldiers took immediate exception to, and had Brodick not put an end to the budding hostility, Gillian was certain a real fight would have broken out. Angry words and hard shoves were exchanged, but no real damage was done.

Brodick led the procession up the last steep hill. There were cottages of every shape and size nestled in the side of the mountain, some stark, others adorned with brightly colored doors. As they rode past, men and women poured out of their homes to follow them. They all looked as though they were witnessing a miracle, and several, Gillian noticed, made the sign of the cross and bowed their heads in prayer. Others mopped at their eyes to stem their joyful tears.

The Maitland home was at the top of the crest on a wide, flat plane. The gray stone structure was quite forbidding, as there was a wide black cloth draped over the double doors. The windows were also covered.

Brodick dismounted with Alec in his arm, motioned to Robert to assist Gillian, and then put the boy down. Running to Gillian, Alec latched onto her hand, and started pulling her to the steps.

The crowd silently pressed forward. Brodick clasped Gillian's other hand, giving it a little squeeze when he noticed how uncomfortable she was with the sea of curious strangers gawking at her. He stopped at the entrance, reached up, and ripped the black cloth from the doors. The cheer that followed was earth-shaking. He pulled the door open and stepped back so Gillian could enter, but she shook her head and moved close so he could hear her above the shouting.

"Alec's homecoming should be private. I'll be happy to wait here."

He grinned. "I'll be happier to have you inside," he replied as he gently shoved her ahead of him. She decided she would wait by the door until Alec had had a few minutes alone with his parents and no amount of prodding or pushing was going to change her mind.

The stone entry was poorly lit with a single

candle flickering light on a low chest next to the staircase leading to the second level. On Gillian's left were three steps leading down to the great hall. A fire blazed on the hearth, and across the rectangular room was a long wooden table. A lady sat at one end sewing by the light of two candles. Her head was bent to her task, and Gillian couldn't see her face, but she was certain she was watching Alec's mother. The woman didn't look up, though surely she had heard the door open. She seemed completely impervious to the noise the crowd was making outside.

Gillian heard Laird Maitland's voice before she saw him.

"Who in God's name is making all that noise?" Iain demanded.

The voice came from the back hallway. Alec's father entered the great hall from the buttery, spotted Brodick, and demanded to know why everyone was shouting.

Alec had started up the steps to his parents' chamber, but when he heard his father's voice, he turned around and ran back down. He raced across the stone floor, jumped down the steps to the great hall, and threw his arms wide.

"Mama... Papa... I'm home."

CHAPTER TWELVE

The shock very nearly did his parents in. For the first time in his life, Iain Maitland was completely undone. As though he'd just run headfirst into a stone wall, he staggered back shaking his head in disbelief. His dark eyes misted. "Alec?" he whispered hoarsely. And then he roared, "Alec!"

Judith Maitland leapt to her feet and let out a joyful cry, her forgotten sewing basket spilling to the floor. Her hand flew to her heart. She took a shaky step toward her son and then fainted dead away. Unfortunately, Brodick was too far from her to catch her before she hit the floor, and her husband was still too shaken to do more than watch her collapse.

Alec almost knocked his father off his feet when he threw himself at his legs. Iain tried to shake himself out of his stupor. Trembling, the mighty warrior dropped to his knees and, with head bowed and eyes closed, wrapped his son in his strong arms.

The little boy put his head down on his father's shoulder and worriedly watched his mother. "Shouldn't you pick Mama up, Papa?" he asked.

Iain stood but couldn't make himself let go of his son, and so he ordered Brodick to do something about his wife.

Brodick slipped his hand under her shoulders and gently lifted her into his arms. Her face was white, and no amount of shaking was going to get her to wake up until she was ready.

"You've given your mother quite a surprise, Alec," Brodick remarked. "She had you dead and buried."

Iain shook his head. "No, she still had hope in her heart."

Judith opened her eyes and found herself in Brodick's arms. "Why are you..."

"Mama, you're awake."

Brodick slowly lowered Judith to the floor but held her about the waist in the event she felt like passing out again. Suddenly overcome by the tide of emotions engulfing her, she began to sob uncontrollably. Iain reached for her and held her while Alec watched and fretted.

"You're not supposed to cry, Mama. I'm not dead. I'm home. Papa, tell her not to cry."

Iain laughed. "She's happy to have you home. Give her a minute and she'll tell you so."

Judith touched Alec's face with her quivering hand. "I prayed that you..."

Brodick slowly backed away. He wanted to give the Maitlands a few minutes alone, and he also wanted to find Gillian. He had thought that she was with him when he'd entered the great hall, but now he realized she'd stayed behind. He found her sitting on a bench near the stairs. Her hands were folded in her lap and her eyes were downcast.

"What are you doing?" he asked, frowning.

"I'm waiting for the Maitlands to finish their reunion. I felt it would be intrusive for me to watch. They should have a few minutes alone."

Brodick sat down next to her and swallowed up all the space the bench allowed. She found herself squeezed up against him. She had likened him to a bear before, and now the image seemed all the more real.

He took hold of her hand and gently pushed up the sleeve of her gown. "You'll need to take this bandage off before you go to bed tonight."

"I will."

He didn't let go of her hand, and she didn't pull away. "Brodick?"

"Yes?"

She stared into his eyes a long minute before she spoke again. "I want to thank you for your help. Without you, Alec would never have made it back to his parents."

He disagreed. "I didn't get him home, Gillian. You did. I merely helped," he added. "But if I hadn't, you still would have found a way."

Iain called out to him, but she gripped his hand to get him to look at her again.

"Yes?"

"After you speak to Alec's parents... will you be going home?"

He stood up and pulled her to her feet. They were just inches apart, his head bent down toward her, her face upturned to his, like lovers about to come together. Damn, but

231

he suddenly wanted to kiss her. A long, hot kiss that would lead to another and another and another...

The way he was looking at her sent shivers down her arms. "Will you?" she whispered.

"What are you asking me?" he demanded impatiently.

Startled by the sharpness in his tone, she stepped back, the back of her knees bumping into the bench.

"After you speak to the Maitlands, will you be going home?" She stared down at her hands as she added, "You are a laird, after all. You must have many pressing duties."

"There's much that needs to be done," he agreed.

"Yes," she said, trying to keep her disappointment out of her voice. "I must thank you, Brodick, for all you've done for Alec, and me, but your duty is finished now that he's safely home. I don't know what I would have... done... without you..." She knew she was rambling, but she couldn't seem to make herself stop. "Of course you must go home. I just thought..."

"Yes?"

She lifted her shoulders in a delicate shrug. "I thought perhaps you would wish to see your good friend Ramsey Sinclair again."

He nudged her chin up with his thumb. "I'll see him before I leave the Maitlands. He should be here soon."

"What makes you think—"

He didn't let her finish her question. "I sent Dylan to warn him, remember?"

"Yes, but—"

"Ramsey will want to talk to you as soon as possible. He'll come here," he predicted once again.

"But will you go home then?" she asked.

"As I explained, I have many pressing duties."

Frustrated, she cried out, "Can you not give me a simple answer?"

Iain shouted Brodick's name.

"Come along, Gillian. Iain will want to meet you. He's had enough time to get over his surprise."

"And his wife?"

"It's going to take her a good week to get past her shock. I doubt she'll let Alec out of her sight for all that while."

Gillian brushed the dust from her gown. "I look a fright."

"Aye, you do."

She picked up her skirt to go down the stairs, but Brodick stopped her by taking hold of her arm. In a low voice he said, "You asked me if I would give you a straight answer. Now I'm wondering why you can't ask me a straight question."

"What in heaven's name is that supposed to mean? What is it you think I should ask you?"

"What you want to ask," he said.

"You're an exasperating man."

"So I've been told," he said. "I'm impatient too," he added. "But in this instance, I'm willing to wait."

"There she is, Mama. That's Gillian." Alec's shout echoed throughout the hall.

Gillian pulled away from Brodick, smiling as she watched the little boy run toward her. He grabbed her hand and started pulling. "Don't be afraid of Papa. Most ladies are, but maybe you won't be because you're not like most," he said.

She wasn't as confident as Alec assumed she was, for Iain Maitland was an imposing figure. He was a tall, muscular man with penetrating gray eyes. His dark hair was given to curl and seemed to soften the blistering scowl on his face. Had he not been so imposing, she would have thought he was almost as handsome as Brodick.

Judith Maitland's smile helped assuage her husband's frightening manner. She was a beautiful woman, but it was the color of her eyes that captivated. They were the color of violets. She was a little bit of a thing, yet had such a regal bearing about her Gillian felt as though she were in the presence of a queen.

Desperately in need of a bath and clean clothes, Gillian thought she must look like a lowly peasant.

As soon as Brodick made the introductions, Judith rushed forward to clasp Gillian's hand. Her voice trembled when she said, "You found our son and brought him home to us. I don't know how we will ever repay you."

Gillian darted a quick look at Brodick. The Maitlands obviously believed that Alec had been lost, and Lord help her, how was she ever going to explain what really happened?

"Come and sit at the table," Judith urged.

"You must be thirsty and hungry from your long journey. Alec told us you came here all the way from England," she remarked as she led Gillian to a chair near the end of the table.

"Yes, I came here from England."

"I, too, am English," Judith told her.

"No, Judith," her husband corrected. "You used to be English."

His wife smiled. "The men here change history when it's convenient."

"You're a Maitland," Iain countered. "And that is all anyone need know. Brodick, pour yourself some wine and sit down. I want to hear every detail of what transpired before I open the doors to family and friends. Alec, come and sit with your father." He added the command with a good deal of affection in his voice.

The little boy ran around the table and pulled a stool close to his father's chair. Gillian noticed Iain's hand shook when he touched his son's shoulder. Alec smiled up at him and sat down, but was promptly lifted back to his feet and reminded to wait until the ladies had taken their seats.

The Maitland commander, Winslow, came striding into the hall then, bowed to his laird and lady, and then announced, "Ramsey Sinclair has just crossed our border and should be here within the hour."

"Has he already heard of our good fortune?" Iain asked.

"I sent Dylan to him," Brodick explained before turning to his brother.

"Gillian, I would like you to meet my brother. Winslow, this is Lady Gillian."

Winslow bowed. "Lady Gillian, you are from England?" he asked, frowning.

"Yes, I am from England. 'Tis the truth I cannot and would not change that fact, sir. Does it displease you?"

Winslow surprised her with a quick smile. "It would depend, milady."

"Depend on what?"

"My brother." Without further explanation he dismissed the topic altogether and turned to Brodick. "You'll see my wife and my boys before you leave? They will be disappointed if you don't."

"Of course I'll see them."

"Bring them here, Winslow," Iain ordered. "We must celebrate tonight. The children will stay up late."

"Winslow, do you happen to know if Ramsey's brother, Michael, rides with the laird?" Gillian asked.

If the soldier thought the inquiry was peculiar, he didn't comment on it. "I don't know, milady, but we will soon find out." He bowed once again and left the hall.

Judith personally saw to the task of fetching a pitcher of water for her guests.

"Papa, where's Graham?" Alec asked.

"Your brother's with your Uncle Patrick, but he'll be home soon. He's going to be very happy to see you."

"'Cause he missed me?" he asked eagerly.

Iain smiled. "We all missed you, Alec."

236

"Mama missed me the most. She's still shaking something fierce 'cause I surprised her. Look, Papa. She can't even pour the water. Is she gonna cry again?"

Iain laughed. "Probably," he answered. "It's going to take your mother... and me," he added, "time to get over this joyous surprise."

Alec hadn't exaggerated Judith's condition. She had already spilled a good deal of water on the tabletop and thus far hadn't managed to get a single drop into the cup. Her hands were shaking violently and every time she looked at her son, her eyes brimmed with fresh tears.

Iain put his hand on top of his wife's. "Sit down, love," he quietly suggested.

She moved her chair close to her husband, collapsed in the seat, and leaned into his side. Iain poured the water for Gillian, but as she reached for the goblet, she noticed how dirty her hands were and quickly hid them in her lap.

Iain put his arm around his wife and hugged her. His attention, however, was centered on Gillian. "Start at the beginning and tell me how and when you found my son. I want to hear every detail," he ordered. He paused to pat Alec before adding, "It's a miracle a five-year-old could survive the falls."

"Alec's only five years old?" Gillian asked.

"But I'm gonna be seven."

"Your brother's seven," Iain reminded him.

"But I'm gonna be seven too."

Alec scooted off the stool and ran around the table to Gillian. Without asking permission, he climbed onto her lap, pulled her arms around him, and grinned at her.

"You and Alec have become close friends," Judith remarked, smiling.

"Iain, perhaps you could wait until Alec has gone to bed to hear the details," Brodick suggested.

"But I get to stay up late 'cause Papa said we have to celebrate," Alec blurted. "Didn't you say so, Papa?"

"Yes," his father agreed.

"You know what, Gillian?" Alec whispered loudly.

She leaned down. "No, what?"

"When I go to bed, Mama's gonna sit with me until I fall asleep, and my brother sleeps in the same room with me, so maybe I won't have bad dreams and I won't get scared."

"Perhaps you won't dream at all tonight."

"But you got to have someone to sleep with too, so you won't get scared 'cause I won't be there."

"I'll be just fine," she assured him.

Alec wasn't convinced. "But what if you do get scared? You got to have someone to wake you up. Maybe you could ask Brodick to sleep with you again like he did before."

She clapped her hand over his mouth to get him to hush and felt her face burn with mortification. She knew Brodick was watching her, but she didn't dare look at him.

Judith laughed. "Alec, sweetheart, you're embarrassing Gillian."

"Mama, you know what Gillian calls me?"

"No, what?"

Giggling, the little boy said, "Honey bear."

Iain's gaze went back and forth between Gillian and Brodick. "Father Laggan's back," he remarked. "And there's another, younger priest named Stevens with him."

"Why are you telling me this?" Brodick asked.

"I just wanted you to know there are two priests available," Iain explained with a meaningful glance at Gillian.

"I didn't sleep with Brodick," she blurted out. "I have no need for a priest."

"Yes, you did too."

"Alec, it isn't polite to contradict your elders."

"But, Mama..."

"Hush, sweetheart."

Gillian glared at Brodick. He could easily correct this horrid misunderstanding if he would only offer a quick explanation.

He wasn't inclined. He winked at her. "I didn't know a face could get that red," he remarked.

"Do explain," she demanded.

"Explain what?" he asked, feigning innocence.

She turned to Judith. "We were camping... and it isn't what it sounds like... I did sleep, and when I awakened... they were all there..."

"They?" Iain asked.

"His soldiers."

"You slept with his soldiers too?"

She didn't understand that Iain was teasing

her. "No... that is to say, we... slept. That's all that happened, Laird."

"Stop tormenting her," Judith ordered. "Can you not see how distressing this is for her? Gillian doesn't understand the Highlanders' humor. What happened to your arm?" Judith asked then, thinking to turn the subject to a less delicate one. "I noticed the bandage, and I was curious—"

Alec interrupted his mother. Jumping off Gillian's lap, he cried out, "Papa, we got to take a walk."

"Now?"

"Yes, Papa, now."

"Alec, I want to talk to Brodick and Gillian. I'm anxious to hear how they found you."

"But, Papa, I got to tell you what I did, and then you're gonna be mad at me. We got to take a walk so I can think about it."

"Come here, son," his father ordered, concerned by the anxiety he saw in Alec's eyes.

The little boy dragged his feet and kept his head down as he went to his father. Iain laid his hands on his shoulders and leaned forward.

Alec promptly burst into tears. "I got real scared, Papa, and I cut Gillian's arm, and then it got all swollen, and Annie had to fix it, and it's all my fault 'cause I hurt a lady, and I'm not ever supposed to hurt ladies, but I got real scared. I didn't like England and I wanted to come home." Alec threw his arms around his father's neck and began to sob in earnest.

"Alec has been very worried that he would disappoint you, Laird," Gillian explained. "He didn't understand that I was trying to help him. He had climbed down with a rope into a gorge, but it was an old rope, and it began to unravel, and he..." She looked to Brodick for help. The task of explaining suddenly became overwhelming and she was so weary she didn't know where to start.

"My son isn't making much sense," Iain said. "He says he was in England?"

Gillian braced herself for the ordeal ahead and quietly said, "He speaks the truth. Alec was in England."

"I told you so, Papa."

Iain nodded but kept his attention on Gillian. "How did my son get to England?"

"Alec didn't go into the falls. He was taken from the festival and imprisoned in a castle in England. That is where I met him."

The expression on Iain's face changed. He put Alec in Judith's lap, and stood. For his son's sake, he tried to keep his voice mild when in fact he wanted to shout.

"Who took him?"

Gillian felt an instant of real fear as the laird towered over her, glowering as though he had already decided she was fully responsible for his son's jeopardy.

"It was a mistake," she began.

"Damned right it was," Iain roared.

Alec's eyes grew wide. "Are you angry, Papa?"

His father took a deep breath. "Yes," he snapped.

"He isn't angry with you, Alec," Gillian whispered.

"He knows that."

"Don't snap at Gillian." Brodick, who had remained silent up until now, sounded as angry as Iain when he gave the command. "She is as innocent as your son in this. Sit down, and I'll tell you what I have learned. I know you're anxious to hear it all, but you cannot raise your voice to Gillian. I will not allow it."

Gillian could see that Iain was ready to explode and hurried to explain before the two lairds got into a real fight. "When I said it was a mistake..."

"Yes?" Iain asked.

"The men who took Alec thought they were stealing Ramsey's brother, Michael. They kidnapped the wrong boy."

"For the love of..." Iain was so enraged he couldn't go on.

"Sit down, husband," Judith suggested. "Listen to what Gillian has to say."

He nearly overturned the chair when he ripped it out from the table and sat down. Leaning back, he stared hard at Gillian for several seconds.

"Start talking."

"It's a very long story, Laird, and Ramsey should be here any minute now, shouldn't he? If you could please wait..."

Iain's jaw was clenched and he shook his head.

"Papa, you know what?" The little boy smiled up at his father when he spoke, and Iain reached over to pat him.

"No, what, Alec?" he asked gruffly.

"We sneaked away twice, but the first time we got dragged back, and it was all my fault 'cause I didn't wait like I was supposed to."

Iain blinked as he tried to sort out his son's confusing explanation. "What happened the first time you got away?"

"I climbed down into the gorge is what I did," he boasted. "But I didn't get a good rope."

"It was threadbare," Gillian interjected.

"My son climbed down into a gorge with a threadbare rope?" Iain lashed out. "And where were you while Alec was attempting this?"

"Papa, she told me to wait for her, but I didn't, and we weren't supposed to go into the canyon, but I thought it would be faster. Then I got good and stuck, didn't I, Gillian?"

"Yes, you did."

"I was supposed to wait in the stable."

"But you didn't," his mother said.

"No, and I thought Gillian was gonna puke 'cause her face turned green when she looked over the side and saw me. She told me she gets awful sick when she's got to look way down, and she sometimes gets dizzy too."

"You're afraid of—" Judith began.

Her husband interrupted with a question of his own. "But you climbed down to get Alec anyway?"

"I didn't have any other choice."

"She had to fetch me, Papa," Alec explained. "And she was just in time 'cause the rope broke right in half just after she grabbed me. She told me she was awful scared, but she didn't puke."

The child sounded a little disappointed over that fact. Neither one of his parents smiled, for they were both thinking about the near miss their son had had.

They were also realizing that Gillian had saved him.

"I will force myself to be patient a little longer and wait until Ramsey arrives to hear your accounting," Iain announced. "But at the very least, give me the names of the bastards who stole my child from me," he demanded. "By God, I want to know who they are and now, this minute."

"I've warned you not to take that tone with Gillian. Now I'm ordering you, Iain. I won't have her upset."

Judith Maitland couldn't make up her mind who was more surprised by Brodick's angry outburst. Iain looked flabbergasted, and Gillian appeared to be incredulous.

Iain quickly recovered. He leaned forward and in a furious hiss said, "You dare to order me?"

Brodick also leaned forward. "That's exactly what I—"

Gillian, hoping to avert the budding hostility, blurted out, "Shouting at me won't upset me."

"But it upsets me, Gillian."

Gillian wondered if Brodick realized he was nearly shouting at her now. She looked to Judith for help, but it was Alec who inadvertently turned his father's attention.

"Papa, don't yell at Gillian," Alec cried

out as he ran around the table to Gillian and climbed into her lap. "She never shouted at me, not even when the man beat her. She tricked him good, Papa."

"Someone beat her?" Iain asked.

Alec nodded. "She made him beat her so he wouldn't beat me."

The little boy suddenly remembered the ring Gillian had given him and pulled the ribbon over his head. "Gillian said she was gonna be my champion, just like Uncle Brodick, and she told me I could keep the ring until I got back home. She promised me she wasn't gonna let nobody hurt me and she didn't. I don't need the ring anymore to remind me I'm safe, but I still want to keep it."

"You can't, Alec," Gillian said softly.

He reluctantly handed the ring to her. "Uncle Brodick said I could keep his dagger forever."

She laughed. "I'm still not going to let you keep my grandmother's ring."

Judith placed her hand on top of her husband's. "You do realize that if it were not for this dear lady, our son would be dead."

"Of course, I realize—"

"Then I suggest, instead of shouting at her and treating her as though you hold her responsible for the actions of others, you thank her. I plan to get down on my knees and thank God for sending her to Alec. She was his guardian angel."

The emotional speech humbled Gillian, and she shook her head in protest. Judith

245

dabbed at her eyes with a linen cloth and then stood.

"Gillian," Iain began, his voice hesitant. "I do thank you for protecting my son, and I certainly didn't mean to imply that I in any way hold you responsible. If I gave you that impression, I apologize. As difficult as it will be, I'll wait for Ramsey to join us to find out what happened."

Judith beamed with satisfaction. "I do believe that is the very first time I've ever heard you apologize. It's a momentous occasion. And since you are now in such an accommodating mood, may I suggest that you and Ramsey wait until after the celebration to hear what Gillian has to say. Tonight is Alec's homecoming and our friends and relatives will be here soon." Judith didn't wait for her husband's agreement. "Gillian will want to freshen up now."

"Gillian likes to take baths, Mama," Alec said. "She made me wash too. I didn't want to, but she made me."

Judith laughed. "She took good care of you, Alec," she said as she clasped hold of Gillian's arm. "How would you like a hot bath now?"

"I would like that very much."

"I'll find clean clothes for you and have these washed right away," she promised. "The Maitland plaid will keep you nice and warm," she added. "Though the days are warm, it gets quite chilly at night."

Hearing that Gillian would wear the Maitland plaid didn't sit well with Brodick. Without thinking how his words would be interpreted, he said, "She'll wear the Buchanan plaid for this celebration."

Iain folded his arms and leaned back in his chair. "Why do you want her to wear your colors? Are you claiming—"

Brodick cut him off. "My soldiers would be... upset. They would surely rebel if they saw her in your plaid, Iain. They've taken a liking to the lass and have become very possessive and protective of her. While she's in the Highlands, she'll wear our colors. I won't have the Buchanan soldiers insulted."

Iain grinned. "You're worried that your men will be upset? Is that what I heard you say? For God's sake, they're warriors, not..."

He was going to say "women," but quickly changed his mind when his wife gave him a sharp look. With a smile he substituted "children."

Judith laughed, for she knew her husband was trying to be diplomatic for her sake. She started toward the stairs then, but Gillian paused to turn back to Brodick.

"Brodick, you did promise your brother, Winslow, you would see his wife and children."

"I remember what I promised."

"Then you'll be here when I return?"

Exasperated that she still couldn't get up the courage to ask him a direct question, he said, "Yes."

She nodded before hurrying after Judith. She tried to hide her relief that Brodick would stay a bit longer, and then she became angry with herself for feeling the way she did. She was acting like a fool because she was letting herself become dependent on him, and she had no right to lean on the man. No, she couldn't ask anything more of him.

She diligently tried to put him out of her thoughts for the next hour as she bathed and washed her hair. Judith brought her a pale yellow gown to wear. It was a little too snug across her chest and showed a bit too much of the swell of her breasts, but Judith thought it was still proper. Brodick had sent up one of the Buchanan plaids and Judith showed Gillian how to pleat it about her waist. Then she draped one end over her left shoulder and tucked it into the belt, explaining, "It took me a long time to figure out how to do this. For the longest while I could never get the pleats straight. The only way to get the hang of it is to practice," she added.

"The plaid is very important to the Highlanders, isn't it?"

"Oh, yes," Judith said. "They... I mean to say, we... are a very fanciful people. The plaid should always cover the heart," she added. "We wear our colors proudly." She stepped back and inspected Gillian. "You look lovely," she announced. "Now come and sit by the fire and let me brush your hair. It looks almost dry. Will you mind if I ask you a few questions?" She laughed then. "I'm terrible, I admit. I made my husband wait, and now I'm impatient."

"I don't mind answering your questions. What is it you want to know?"

"How did you end up with Alec? Were you also taken captive?"

"Yes, I was."

"But why? You're English and surely you could appeal to your king for help."

"My king is fast friends with the men responsible for the trouble Alec and I were in, and in a way John is fully responsible for it all."

While Judith brushed her hair, Gillian told her about Arianna's treasure. Judith was captivated by the story, and when Gillian told her about the death of her father, the dear lady looked genuinely saddened.

"Prince John fell in love with Arianna, and though it sounds quite romantic, 'tis the truth he was married at the time of his infatuation. It's tragic that Arianna was murdered, but I have no sympathy for my king. He betrayed his vows to his wife."

"He's been married twice now, hasn't he? And it's my understanding his first wife is still alive."

"Yes, she is," Gillian replied. "John was granted an annulment from Hadwisa after many years of marriage. They had no children," she added. "And they were second cousins. The Archbishop of Canterbury had forbidden the marriage, but John got a dispensation from Rome."

"If John's first marriage was recognized by the church, how, then, did he manage to marry a second time?"

"The Archbishop of Bordeaux and the

bishops of Poitiers and Saintes pronounced that the first marriage wasn't valid."

"On what grounds?"

"Consanguinity," she answered.

"Because they were too closely related as second cousins."

"Yes," Gillian said. "John immediately married Isabella and stirred up all sorts of trouble for himself because she was already betrothed to another. She was only twelve years old when they married."

"John takes what he wants," Judith remarked. "Doesn't he?"

"Yes, he does," she agreed.

Judith shook her head. "England has changed considerably since I lived there."

"John is the culprit for all the unpleasant changes. He's alienated many powerful barons and there are whispers of insurrection. Worse, he's alienated the church, and our pope has retaliated by placing all of England under interdict."

Judith gasped. "Has John been excommunicated?"

"Not yet, but I believe Pope Innocent will be forced to do just that if John doesn't bend, and soon, to the pope's decision. The issue centers around the position of Archbishop of Canterbury. John wanted the Bishop of Norwich, John de Grey, to be elected, and the younger monks of Canterbury had already selected Reginald and sent him off to Rome to be confirmed by the pope."

"And the pope settled on Reginald, then?"

Gillian shook her head. "No, he chose his own man, Stephen Langton. John was so furious he refused to let Langton enter England and took control of the monastery at Canterbury, and that is when our pope placed the entire country under interdict. No religious services can be performed. Churches are closed and locked, and priests must refuse to bless marriages. They can't administer any of the holy sacraments, except those that are of extreme necessity. It's a black time in England now, and I fear it will only get worse."

"I have heard that John acts out of anger."

"He's well-known for his ferocious temper."

"No wonder you didn't appeal to him for help."

"No, I couldn't," she said.

"Do you have family worrying about you?"

"My uncle Morgan is being held captive now," she whispered. "And I've been given a... task... to complete before the fall harvest. If I fail, my uncle will be killed."

"Oh, Gillian, you've had a time of it, haven't you?"

"I need your husband's help."

"He'll help any way that he can," Judith promised on Iain's behalf.

"The man who holds my uncle is a close adviser to the king, and John will listen to him, not me. I thought about asking one of the more powerful barons for help, but they are all fighting amongst themselves, and I didn't know who I could trust. England," she ended, "is in chaos, and I worry about the future."

"I'm not going to hound you to answer any more questions," Judith said. "You'll have to go through it all with my husband and Ramsey later."

"Thank you for your patience," she replied.

A knock sounded at the door, but before Judith could answer, Alec came running into the room. He stopped dead in his tracks when he spotted Gillian.

She stood up and smiled at him. "Is something wrong, Alec?"

"You look... pretty," he blurted out.

Judith agreed. Gillian's long hair had dried into a riot of curls that spilled across her slender shoulders and framed her delicate facial features. She was a striking woman who was going to cause quite a stir tonight, Judith predicted.

"Mama, Papa bids you come downstairs right this minute. He says, 'Can't you hear the music?' Everybody's here, and they're ready to eat the food. Gillian, you got to come downstairs too. Uncle Brodick said so."

"Judith, you go ahead," Gillian said. "I've gotten this bandage all wet, but I'm supposed to take it off, anyway."

Judith wanted to help, but Gillian insisted she join her husband. Once she was alone, she sat back down and slowly unwound the bandage, dreading what she was going to see. The wound was more appalling than she'd expected, but thankfully it wasn't seeping, and the swelling appeared to be gone. The skin was puckered, blistered in spots, raw, and horribly ugly. She reminded herself it was a sin to be vain and she shouldn't care about scars. Besides, the arm would always be covered by the sleeves of her gowns, and no one other than herself would ever see it. The injury was still extremely tender to the touch, though, and she grimaced while she cleaned the area with soap and cool water. By the time she was finished following Annie Drummond's instructions, her arm was throbbing.

She patted the skin dry, pulled the sleeve back down to her wrist, and put the matter of her paltry injury aside. There were so many more important matters to worry about. Her thoughts turned to her Uncle Morgan. Was he being treated well? If his own staff had been allowed to stay with him, Gillian knew he would do all right, but if Alford had moved him...

She buried her face in her hands. *Please God, take care of him. Don't let him catch cold or take ill. And please don't let him fret about me.*

The sound of laughter intruded on her prayers, and with a sigh, she stood up and reluctantly went to join the Maitlands.

CHAPTER THIRTEEN

Just as Judith had predicted, Gillian did indeed cause a commotion.

Quite a crowd had gathered to celebrate

Alec's return, and the mood was festive and loud. The hall was awash with candlelight. A young man was playing the lute in the corner as servants threaded their way through the throng balancing silver trays of drinks. A pig roasting on a spit was being watched over by an older woman with a poker in one hand and a wooden spoon in the other. She used the spoon as a weapon to discourage the soldiers from tearing off pieces of meat before it was ready to be served.

The lively music and joyful banter surrounded Gillian as she surveyed the great hall. She started down the stairs, and suddenly the music stopped. The lute player looked up, and then one by one the voices hushed as men and women turned their faces toward her.

Brodick was in the process of answering yet another question Iain had posed when he happened to glance up and see Gillian slowly descending the steps. He promptly lost his train of thought. He forgot his manners too, for he was in the middle of a sentence when he abruptly turned his back on his brother and his friend and walked to the stairs.

While Brodick had certainly noticed her shape before, the gentle curves of her body were more obvious to him now. He didn't much like the cut of her gown, thinking it flattered her figure a bit too much, and he seriously considered fetching another Buchanan plaid and draping it around her neck so that it would hang down and hide her feminine attributes from the spectators.

Damn, but she was lovely.

Gillian took one look at the scowl on Brodick's face and felt a sudden urge to turn around and go back upstairs. But she was already halfway down and wasn't about to look like a coward by retreating now. The attention was mortifying, the silence deafening. Several men, she noticed, appeared startled; others looked befuddled. Only Brodick's soldiers, loyal men, Robert, Stephen, Liam, Keith, and Aaron, smiled at her, and she decided to look at them and ignore the crowd, and Brodick, as she continued on.

Brodick wasn't about to be ignored, however. He waited at the bottom of the steps, and when she finally reached him, he put his hand out. Hesitantly, she placed her hand in his and looked up at him. Embarrassed to see that he was still glowering at her, she smiled sweetly and whispered, "If you do not stop glaring at me, I swear I will kick you soundly. Then you will have something to frown about."

He was so startled by her puny threat, he burst into laughter. "You think you could injure me?"

"Undoubtedly."

He laughed again, a wonderful booming sound, and, Lord, how his eyes sparkled with devilment. She suddenly felt much more in control and sure of herself. She barely minded her audience at all. Besides, they couldn't gawk at her now, because Brodick's men surrounded her on all sides as was their peculiar habit.

"Laird, you shouldn't allow the Maitlands

to stare at milady. It's unseemly," Robert muttered.

"And how would you have me stop them?" he asked.

"We'll be happy to see to that task," Liam offered, a glint of eagerness in his voice.

"Aye, we'll make them forget about their lustful thoughts," Stephen muttered.

Shoving an elbow into Liam's side, Aaron said, "Don't use the word 'lust' in front of milady."

Blessedly, the music started again, and the crowd resumed their celebration.

Brodick continued to hold her hand as he answered a question Liam had asked, and since he wasn't watching her, she pretended to be listening to what he was saying so she could stare at him. He was so ruggedly good-looking, she wondered if he had any idea how he surely affected women.

He also looked dangerous tonight, with his long golden hair about his shoulders and his day's growth of whiskers. He'd obviously washed, as his hair was only partially dry, and he was wearing a clean white shirt that either he had packed with him or Iain had loaned to him. His skin looked even more bronzed against the white fabric, and a strip of Buchanan plaid was draped over one of his broad shoulders.

He caught her watching him. The gleam in his eyes made her feel breathless, and she had a sudden urge to move into his arms and kiss that scowl right off his face. She sighed instead and thanked God the man couldn't read her unladylike thoughts.

"I say we take the Maitland soldiers outside and have a word with them, Laird," Robert suggested.

"A fist is more powerful than a word, Robert," Liam said. "What say we take them all on?"

Gillian hadn't been paying much attention to the Buchanan soldiers' grumblings until she heard the word "fist."

"You will not fight tonight," she ordered. "This is a celebration, not a brawl."

"But, milady, a good fight is always cause for celebration," Stephen explained.

"Are you telling me you enjoy fighting?"

The soldiers looked at one another, obviously perplexed by her question. The usually dour-faced Robert actually grinned.

"It's what we do," Liam told her.

Gillian kept waiting for Brodick to put a stop to the outrageous talk, but he didn't say a word. When she squeezed his hand, he merely retaliated by squeezing hers.

"I don't care if you enjoy fighting or not," she began. "Laird Maitland will be most displeased if you cause trouble tonight."

"But, milady, his soldiers continue to stare at you. We can't allow that."

"Yes, you can."

"It's insolent," Stephen explained.

"If anyone is staring, then it's my own fault."

"Aye, it is your fault." Brodick finally spoke. "You're too damned beautiful tonight."

She couldn't make up her mind if she was pleased or irritated. "Only you could make a compliment sound like a criticism."

"It was a criticism," he told her. "You simply cannot look the way you do and expect to be ignored. It's your own fault people are staring at you."

She jerked her hand away from his. "And just exactly what could I do to change the way I look?"

"It's your hair, milady," Aaron said. "Perhaps you could bind it up for tonight and cover it with a cloth."

"I'll do no such thing."

"It's also the gown she's wearing," Liam decided. "Milady, couldn't you find something less... fitted... for tonight?"

She glanced down at herself and then looked up. "Would a wheat sack do, Liam?" she asked.

The daft soldier looked as though he were actually considering the possibility. She rolled her eyes in vexation. "Those soldiers who might have glanced my way were probably just perplexed because they've noticed I'm wearing the Buchanan plaid. I shouldn't have put the thing on."

"Why not, milady?" Robert asked. "We like seeing you in our plaid."

"Only a Buchanan should wear your colors," she replied. "And I shouldn't proclaim to be something I'm not. If you'll excuse me, I'll just go back upstairs and put my old clothes on."

"No, you won't," Brodick said. He grabbed

her hand and pulled her along behind him. His goal was to get her to Iain and Judith so that they could introduce her to those they wanted her to meet, but the Maitland soldiers kept interfering with eager requests to meet Gillian. One upstart, built like a bull, was a little too enthusiastic and persistent for Brodick's liking, and he had to knock the man to his knees to get him out of their path as they made their way forward.

Gillian was appalled by his behavior. "You're the Buchanan laird," she reminded him in a whisper.

"I know who I am," he snapped.

If he wasn't going to worry about being overheard, then she wouldn't worry about it either. "Then act like it," she snapped back.

He laughed. "I am. In fact, I'm upholding our reputation and our traditions."

"You and your soldiers are acting like bullies."

"It's good of you to notice."

She gave up trying to reason with him. Elbow shove by elbow shove, they finally reached Iain and Judith. The Maitland laird bowed to her before turning his attention and his obvious displeasure on Brodick.

"Control your soldiers," he ordered. "Or I will."

Brodick grinned. Gillian turned around to find out what Brodick's men were up to and was further distressed to see that they were all doing their best to incite the Maitlands to fight.

She had no right to give orders to the Buchanan soldiers, but she still felt somehow responsible for their actions. She had become quite fond of all of them in a very short while, and she didn't want them to get on Iain's bad side even though the five rascals seemed to thrive on trouble. Fighting, it appeared, was as enjoyable to them as sweets to a child.

"Pray excuse me for one moment, Laird Maitland. I would like to have a word with Brodick's soldiers."

She made a curtsy to her host and hostess, ignoring Brodick altogether because she was having to do his duty for him, and then hurried over to his soldiers, who were in the midst of antagonizing a large group of Maitland warriors.

In a voice loud enough to be overheard by the Maitlands, she said, "It would please me if you act like gentlemen tonight."

They looked crestfallen, but quickly nodded their agreement. She smiled as she turned to the Maitlands.

"Your laird has decreed that none of his soldiers will fight tonight. I realize what a disappointment that must be for all of you good men, but as you know the Buchanans are honorable men, and they will not provoke you further."

"If they cannot fight us, why bother?" Liam said. "Your laird has taken the fun out of the game."

One of the Maitland soldiers slapped his shoulder. "Then what say we break open a keg of ale? We'll show you how Eric can down a full jug without once swallowing. I wager you can't top that feat."

Aaron disagreed, and after bowing to Lady Gillian, the Buchanans followed the Maitlands to the buttery to fetch the ale.

The competition, it seemed, was on.

"Children, every one of them," she muttered as she picked up her skirts and hurried back to the Maitlands.

Judith pulled her away from the men to introduce her to her dearest friend, a pretty, freckle-faced, redheaded lady with two full names, Frances Catherine.

"Her husband, Patrick, is Iain's brother," Judith explained. "And Frances Catherine and I have been friends for many years."

Frances Catherine's smile made Gillian feel at ease in a matter of seconds.

"Judith and I have been whispering about you," she admitted. "You have captured Brodick's attention, and that is no small accomplishment, Gillian. He doesn't like the English much," she added, softening the truth.

"Did he tell you he and Ramsey went to England a long time ago to find brides?" Judith asked.

Gillian's eyes widened and she glanced at Brodick. "No, he didn't tell me. When did he and his friend go to England?"

"It was at least six or seven years ago."

"More like eight," Frances Catherine told her friend.

"What happened?" Gillian asked.

"They were both in love with Judith," Frances Catherine said.

"They were not," Judith argued.

"Yes, they were," she insisted. "But of course Judith was already married to Iain, so they decided they would find brides in England just like her."

Gillian smiled. "They were very young then, weren't they?"

"With foolish expectations," Frances Catherine added. "None of the ladies they met measured up to their Judith—"

"Oh, for heaven's sake, Frances Catherine. You needn't make me sound like a saint. They weren't looking for ladies like me. They were just restless and hadn't found mates here. They soon came to their senses, however, and came back home. Both vowed to Iain that they would marry Highlanders."

"And that was that," Frances Catherine said.

"Until you came along," Judith remarked with a smile.

"Brodick has been very kind to me," Gillian said. "But that is all there is to it. He's a very kind man," she added in a stammer.

"No, he isn't," Frances Catherine bluntly replied.

Judith laughed. "Do you have feelings for this kind man?"

"You shouldn't ask her such a question," Frances Catherine said. "But do you, Gillian?"

"Of course I care for him. He came to my

aid and helped me get Alec home. I shall be forever indebted to him. However," she hastily added when both ladies looked as though they were going to interrupt, "I must return to England as soon as my duty here is finished. I cannot entertain foolish... dreams."

"There are complications you aren't aware of, Frances Catherine," Judith explained.

"Love is complicated," her friend replied. "Answer one last question for me, Gillian, and I promise I'll stop hounding you. Have you given your heart to Brodick?"

She was saved from having to answer the question when Frances Catherine's husband interrupted them. Patrick Maitland resembled his brother, Iain, in coloring, but he was sparsely built in comparison. He was just as protective of his wife, however, and Gillian noticed that both brothers didn't have any trouble letting others see how they felt about their wives. Their love was apparent, heartwarming, enviable.

Frances Catherine introduced her to Patrick and then proudly pointed out their children, six in all, twin girls who looked like their mother and four handsome sons. The baby couldn't have been more than a year old and was diligently trying to wiggle out of his father's arms. When the baby smiled, two shiny teeth were visible.

Alec tugged on Gillian's hand to get her attention then and presented his brother, Graham, to her. The firstborn Maitland was quite shy. He wouldn't look at Gillian, but he bowed formally all the way to his waist, then ran away to rejoin his friends.

"Our son Graham was named after a valiant soldier who trained my husband," Judith explained. "Graham's been gone almost eight years now, but we still mourn his passing. He was a wonderful man and like a grandfather to me. Ah, there's Helen waving to us. The food must be ready. Come, Gillian, you and Brodick must sit with Iain and me. Frances Catherine, fetch your husband and join us."

Darkness descended and additional candles were placed about the gigantic hall. All the women helped carry in platters of food. Though Gillian offered, she wasn't allowed to lift a finger. She was astonished that such a grand feast could be so quickly prepared. There were pigeon pies and pheasant, salmon and salted trout, thick crusty bread (black and brown), sugared cakes, and sweet apple tarts, and to wash it all down were glistening pitchers of wine and ale and icy cold water, fresh from a mountain stream. There was also goat's milk, and Gillian drank a full goblet of the creamy liquid.

During the meal, Alec was passed around from soldier to soldier. He was too excited to eat and was talking so fast, he stammered.

"My son has dark circles under his eyes," Iain said. "And so do you, Gillian. You will both have to catch up on your sleep."

"They both have nightmares." Brodick made the comment in a low voice so that only Iain would hear. "Where will Gillian sleep tonight?"

"In Graham's old room," Iain replied. "You needn't worry about her. Judith and I will make certain she isn't disturbed."

The music started again and Patrick immediately stood up. He put the baby in Judith's lap, then pulled his wife to her feet. Frances Catherine's face was flushed with excitement as she followed her husband to the center of the room. Other couples quickly joined them. They danced to the accompaniment of men stomping their feet and clapping their hands to the lively rhythm of the tune.

Several bold young soldiers came forward to ask Gillian to dance, but one dark look from Brodick sent them scurrying away.

He was getting angrier by the second. By all that was holy, couldn't they see she was wearing his plaid? And couldn't they leave her alone for one damned night? The lass was clearly all worn out. Why even Iain had remarked about the dark circles under her eyes. Brodick shook his head in disgust. What in thunder did he have to do to make certain that Gillian got a little peace and quiet?

And what right did he have to be so possessive? She didn't belong to him. They had simply been thrown together for Alec's sake.

"Hell," he muttered.

"Excuse me?" Gillian's arm rubbed against his when she leaned toward him. "Did you say something, Brodick?"

He didn't answer her. "He said, 'hell,'" Iain cheerfully informed her. "Didn't he, Judith?"

"Yes, he most certainly did," she replied,

her eyes sparkling with mischief as she patted her nephew. "He said, 'hell.'"

"But why?" Gillian asked. "What's wrong with him?"

Iain laughed. "You," he answered. "You're what's wrong with him."

Brodick scowled. "Iain, let it alone."

"Milady, could I have a dance with you?"

Alec stood right behind Gillian, poking her between her shoulders to get her attention. When she turned around and smiled at him, he bowed low. Lord, he was adorable, and she had to resist the urge to scoop him up in her arms and hug him tight.

While Brodick was patiently explaining to the child that Gillian was too tired to dance, she stood up, curtsied as though the King of Scotland himself had honored her, and then put her hand out for Alec to clasp.

Alec thought that dancing meant circling until he was dizzy. Brodick moved to the side of the hall and leaned against a pillar with his arms folded across his chest while he watched. He noticed how Gillian's dark curls shimmered red from the light of the fire blazing in the hearth behind her, and he noticed her smile too. It was filled with such sweet joy.

Then he noticed he wasn't the only man noticing. As soon as the dance ended, soldiers, like vultures, came swooping in. At least eight men surrounded her, begging for her attention.

All of them wanted to dance with her, but she politely declined their requests. She found

Brodick in the crowd, and without even thinking about what she was doing, she walked over to him and stood by his side. Neither looked at the other and neither spoke, yet when she moved closer to him, he moved toward her, until their bodies touched.

He stared straight ahead when he asked, "Do you miss England?"

"I miss my Uncle Morgan."

"But do you miss England?"

"It's home."

Several minutes passed in silence as they watched the dancers, and then she asked, "Tell me about your home."

"You wouldn't like it."

"Why not?"

He shrugged. "The Buchanans aren't like the Maitlands."

"And what does that mean?"

"We're... harder. They call us Spartans, and in some ways I think perhaps we are. You're too soft for our way of life."

"There are other women living on the Buchanan land, aren't there?"

"Yes, of course."

"I'm not certain what you meant when you said I was too soft, but I have a feeling it wasn't flattery. Still, I'm not going to take offense. Besides, I'd wager that the Buchanan women aren't any different than I am. If I'm soft, then so are they."

He smiled as he glanced down at her. "They'd have you for their supper."

"Meaning?"

"Your feelings would be destroyed in a matter of minutes."

She laughed, and heads turned in response to the joyful sound.

"Tell me about these women," she asked. "You've made me very curious."

"There isn't much to tell," he replied. "They're strong," he added. "And they can certainly take care of themselves. They can protect themselves against attack, and they can kill as easily and as quickly as any man." With another glance at her he added, "They're warriors, and they sure as certain aren't soft."

"Are you criticizing them or praising them?" she wanted to know.

"Praising them, of course."

She moved so that she stood directly in front of him. "What was your purpose in telling me about the women in your clan?"

"You asked."

She shook her head. "You started this conversation. Now finish it."

He sighed. "I just wanted you to know that it could never work."

"What couldn't work?"

"You and me."

She didn't try to pretend she was outraged by his impudence or insulted by his arrogance. "You're a very blunt man, aren't you?"

"I just don't want you to get your hopes up."

He knew he'd pricked her temper with his last comment—her eyes had turned the color of an angry sea—but he wasn't going to take the words back or soften the truth.

He dealt in reality, not fantasy, yet the thought of walking away from her was becoming more and more unacceptable to him. What the hell was the matter with him? And what was happening to his discipline? It fairly deserted him now, for though he tried, he found it impossible to make himself look away from her. He focused on her mouth, remembering all too well how wonderfully soft her lips had been pressed against his. Damn, but he wanted to kiss her again.

His eyes narrowed, and he looked as though he were about to start growling at her any moment.

"You probably feel you're being very noble by telling me you could never love me..."

Surprised by her interpretation, he replied gruffly, "I didn't say I couldn't love you."

"You most certainly did," she argued. "You just told me that a life together is out of the question."

"It *is* out of the question. You'd be miserable."

She closed her eyes and prayed for tolerance. She was riled and trying not to let it show. "Let me get this straight. You could love me, but you could never live with me. Have I got it right, now?"

"Just about," he drawled out.

"Since you've felt compelled to make your position clear, I believe I shall do the same. Even if I should suffer the misfortune of falling in love with an arrogant, opinionated, obstinate Spartan like you—which, I might add,

269

is about as likely as being able to fly like a bird—I couldn't possibly marry you. So you see it doesn't matter a twit that you believe a life together is out of the question."

"Why?"

"Why what?"

"Why can't you marry me?"

She blinked. The man was making her crazy.

"I must return to England..."

"So that the bastard who beat you near to death can have another opportunity to kill you?"

"I will protect my Uncle Morgan at all costs."

He didn't like hearing that. He clenched his jaw, causing the muscle to flex, his frustration more than apparent.

"And when you find your sister, will you ask her to give up her life as well?"

"No, I won't," she whispered. "If I can find Arianna's treasure... that will have to be enough to placate my uncle's captor."

"I find it curious that in all the time we've been together, you've never once said his name."

"We haven't been together all that long."

"Why haven't you spoken his name? You don't want me to know who he is, do you, Gillian?"

She refused to answer him. "I would like to sit down. Would you excuse me please?"

"In other words, you're through discussing the matter?"

She started to nod, then changed her mind.

"As a matter of fact, I do have one more thing to say to you."

"Then say it," he ordered when she hesitated.

"I could never love a man who finds me so lacking."

She tried to walk away, but he caught her by her shoulders and pulled her back.

"Ah, Gillian, you're not lacking." His head slowly bent toward her. "You're... just... so... damned... sweet."

His arms went around her and he roughly pulled her against him. His mouth brushed against hers. The mere touch of her sweet lips was so intoxicating that what happened next was surely inevitable and meant to be.

Brodick stopped running.

His mouth covered hers with absolute possession. Yet there was an urgency there as well to make her feel the way he was feeling. He knew she cared about him, but he wanted and needed much more. The music and the crowd and the noise were completely forgotten in that suspended moment of time as Brodick kissed her long and thoroughly. He felt her tremble when his tongue swept inside her sweet mouth with blatant ownership, and he tightened his hold around her waist, thinking that he never wanted to let go. Then he felt her twine her arms around his neck and lean into him until their thighs were pressed against each other. She met his kiss with an equal fervor that was so honest and giving he actually shuddered with raw desire.

He was thinking hard about throwing her

over his shoulder and finding the closest bed when someone shouted and he came to his senses in a flash. He ended the kiss so abruptly, her arms were still around his neck when he stepped back.

It took her several seconds to realize where she was and what had happened, and when her head finally cleared, she was promptly horrified by her own shameful behavior. Dear God, there were at least sixty strangers watching, and what would her Uncle Morgan say about her sinful exhibition of lust?

She was so confused she didn't know what to do. She wanted to tell Brodick never to kiss her like that again, yet at the same time she wanted to demand that he do exactly that, and right this minute. What was happening to her? She didn't know her own thoughts any-more. Angry and frustrated, she lashed out at him.

"You will not kiss me like that ever again." The command shook with emotion.

"Yes, I will."

He sounded gratingly cheerful, and she wasn't about to stand there arguing with him. She turned around and tried to walk away.

He grabbed her hand and jerked her back. "Gillian?"

"Yes?" she replied, rudely refusing to look at him.

"Ramsey's here."

Her head snapped up. "He is?"

Brodick nodded. "You will remember my kiss when you meet him. In fact, you're going to be thinking about it the rest of the night."

It wasn't a hope; it was a command, and she didn't know which offended her more, his arrogance or his bossy disposition.

"I will?" she challenged.

He smiled. "Yes."

Determined to have the last word, she took a step closer to him so she wouldn't be overheard and then said, "I will not love you."

He took a step toward her, no doubt trying to intimidate her, she supposed, and then he leaned down close to her ear and whispered, "You already do."

CHAPTER FOURTEEN

Every unattached female in the Maitland clan sprang to attention the second Laird Ramsey and the Sinclair entourage entered the hall. A collective sigh went up from the young girls, who acted very like a covey of quail following Ramsey as he crossed the long hall to get to Iain Maitland.

Brodick watched Gillian's reaction to the Adonis. Before Ramsey came inside, Brodick had suggested rather firmly that she sit in the corner and wait until the greetings were over to speak to him.

Her response to his friend pleased Brodick considerably. Unlike the other women, she didn't leap to her feet and go chasing after the laird. Instead, she appeared curious and somewhat relieved when she spotted Ramsey's little brother, Michael, trailing behind him. 'Twas a fact, she seemed far more interested in finding out who was with him. With a worried look on her face, she intently studied each man walking into the hall. When she suddenly relaxed in the chair, Brodick realized she had been waiting to see if the traitor was in the group.

Dylan was the last to enter. He immediately went to his laird to give his report, and when he was finished, he asked, "Where is Lady Gillian? I don't see her dancing with the others."

Brodick nodded toward the corner. Dylan turned, spotted her, and then smiled. "She wears our plaid," he remarked proudly. "Is she not the most beautiful lady here?"

"Aye, she is," Brodick agreed quietly.

"Laird, this is a celebration, yet I notice milady sits all alone. Why is that? Are the Maitlands ignoring her? Does the clan consider her an outsider? Hasn't Iain told his followers that she is the sole reason they have something to celebrate? By God, don't they realize Alec would be dead if it were not for her courage and strength?"

With each question he posed, Dylan became more outraged until his face was red with anger. The possibility that Lady Gillian was being slighted obviously infuriated him.

"Do you believe I would allow anyone to

ignore Gillian? Find your soldiers and you'll know the reason why she sits all alone. They won't let anyone near her."

Dylan glanced about the hall and relaxed. His anger quickly turned to satisfaction. Robert and Liam had stationed themselves near the hearth so that they could easily intercept any eager soldier foolish enough to attempt to get to Gillian. With the same determination, Stephen, Keith, and Aaron had taken up positions on the opposite side so that they could effectively block access to the lady from both the entrance and the south side of the hall.

Brodick changed the subject then. "How did Ramsey take the news that it was Michael they wanted?"

"I didn't tell him."

"Why not?"

"There were too many others there, including the bastard MacPhersons," he explained. "Not knowing who to trust—"

"You shouldn't trust any of them," Brodick interjected.

"That's true," Dylan agreed. "So I simply told him that Iain and you wanted a conference with him as soon as possible. I also insisted that Michael come with us. When I was finally able to get him alone, I told him that Alec had been found."

"I imagine Iain's telling Ramsey the full truth now," Brodick remarked when he saw the two lairds in deep discussion. Iain's anger darkened his expression and his gestures were animated as he related what had happened to his son, but Ramsey didn't show any reaction to the startling news. He stood with his hands at his sides, looking as though he were hearing complaints about the weather.

"Ramsey seems to be taking the news well," Dylan remarked.

Brodick disagreed. "No, he isn't. He's furious. Can't you see how his hands are clenched? Ramsey's better than Iain and me at masking his feelings," he added.

"Laird Maitland's beckoning you," Dylan said.

Brodick immediately went to join his friends. He showed his affection for Ramsey by slapping him on his shoulder and shoving him hard in his side with his elbow. Ramsey shoved back.

"It's good to see you again, old friend," Ramsey began.

"There's a foul rumor spreading through the Highlands about you, Ramsey, but I refuse to believe it. They say you've taken the MacPherson weaklings under your wing, but I know such odious gossip couldn't possibly be true."

"You know good and well the MacPhersons have joined my clan. They wanted to be Sinclairs," he added. "But they aren't weak, Brodick, only poorly trained. They didn't have the good fortune of a chieftain like Iain to train them properly the way you and I did."

"That's true," Brodick conceded. "Iain, what have you told him?"

"I told him Alec was taken by mistake and that Michael was the target."

"Where's the woman who brought Alec home?" Ramsey demanded. "I would have a word with her now."

"And so would I," Iain announced. "The party is over."

Iain signaled to the elders, and within minutes the crowd of well-wishers left. Ramsey said good night to his brother and asked him if he would like to stay with the Maitlands for a while.

Michael was thrilled. "Alec said his papa would take us fishing and he won't let us drown."

"I would hope not," Ramsey replied. "While you are here, you will remember your manners and you will obey Lady Maitland."

Michael went running up the stairs with Alec and his older brother, Graham, as Winslow came back inside. The Maitland commander went directly to Gillian, who had just said good night to Frances Catherine.

"My wife was upset with me because I didn't introduce her to you. If you could make time tomorrow..."

"I would love to meet your wife before I leave."

"Leave?" he repeated, sounding puzzled. "Where will you be going?"

"To the Sinclair holding with Ramsey."

"Brodick's allowing this?" he asked incredulously.

"I haven't asked his permission, Winslow."

"My brother would never let you go anywhere with Ramsey," he announced.

"Why wouldn't he?"

"My wife's name is Isabelle."

The abrupt change in topic was deliberate, of course. He wanted to end the discussion. His behavior reminded her of his brother's, for Brodick was just as abrupt.

And just as bossy, she decided when he told her she would like his wife. He hadn't made the statement as a hope. No, he'd ordered her to like Isabelle.

"I'm sure I will like your wife, and I look forward to meeting her."

Winslow nodded approval and then said, "The lairds are waiting for you."

With a deep breath, she straightened her shoulders and nodded.

The hall was still ablaze with light from the burning candles and the roaring fire in the hearth. The imposing assembly was gathered at the far end of the massive oak table, waiting for her to join them. Iain sat at the head with Ramsey to his left and Brodick to his right. As soon as the lairds saw Gillian coming, they rose to their feet. She pulled out a chair at the opposite end and sat down. Dylan and Winslow took their places behind their lairds.

"I would hear now exactly what happened to my son," Iain said.

Brodick dragged his chair to her end of the table, sat down next to her, folded his arms across his chest, and gave his friends a glare that suggested he'd bloody them if they said a word about his seating preference.

Ramsey kept his thoughts contained, but Iain

looked quite smug and satisfied. Dylan actually nodded, as though giving his approval, and then walked over to stand behind his laird.

Iain seemed amused as he watched Brodick, and it suddenly occurred to Gillian that the Maitland laird was actually a very kind man. When she had first met him, she'd found him intimidating and gruff, but she didn't any longer. Perhaps it was the affection she had seen him show his wife and children that had changed her opinion.

Ramsey, on the other hand, was more difficult to judge. He seemed far more relaxed than Brodick, which was amazing, given the fact that he had just learned that someone wanted to harm his brother. What would he do when he heard the rest of the story?

"I should have thought to have Dylan tell you to bring your commander," Brodick said to Ramsey.

"I'll tell Gideon what he needs to know when I return home," Ramsey said.

"My commander, Winslow, and Brodick's commander, Dylan, are here for a specific reason, Gillian," Iain explained.

She folded her hands on the tabletop. "For what specific reason, Laird?"

Brodick's arm rubbed hers when he leaned forward. "Retaliation." He said the word in a hard voice that sent chills down her spine. She waited for further explanation, her mind racing with questions, but Brodick didn't say another word.

"What kind of retaliation? Do you mean war?"

Instead of answering her, Brodick turned to Iain. "Let's get on with it. She's tired."

"Gillian, why don't you start at the beginning, and I promise not to interrupt," Iain said. "We'll get through this quickly and you can get some rest."

She had half expected Ramsey to rant and rave at her and blame her by association for the treachery of other Englishmen. Thankful she had been mistaken, she relaxed, leaning into Brodick's side.

"I'm not so overly tired tonight," she insisted. "But I appreciate your concern. I should start at the very beginning, the night my father awakened my sister and me and tried to get us to safety."

For the next hour Gillian took the men through her history. Her voice didn't falter and she never once hesitated in her recitation of the facts. She simply told them everything that had happened in concise, chronological order. She tried not to leave anything of importance out, and by the time she was finished, her throat was dry and scratchy.

The men never interrupted her, and only the burning logs crackling in the fire could be heard in the silence that followed. She must have sounded hoarse because Brodick poured a goblet of water for her. She drank it down and thanked him.

To their credit, Iain and Ramsey were amazingly calm, considering what they had just heard. They took turns questioning her, and for another hour she was subjected to an intense grilling.

"Your enemy thought to use your brother to draw you out, Ramsey, so he could kill you," Brodick said. "Who hates you so much that he would go to such extremes?"

"Hell if I know," Ramsey muttered.

"Ramsey, do you know Christen?" Gillian asked. "Have you heard of the family who might have taken her in and claimed her for their own?"

Ramsey shook his head. "I'm only just now getting to know all the members of my clan," he said. "I had been away from home for many years, Gillian, and when I returned to the Sinclairs and became laird, I only knew a handful of my father's followers."

"But Christen isn't a Sinclair," Gillian reminded him.

"Yes, you told me she's one of the MacPhersons, but unfortunately, I haven't had time to get to know many of them either," he admitted. "I honestly don't know how we'll find her."

"Then you'll help me?"

He seemed surprised by her question. "Of course I'll help."

"The old men will know about Christen." Brodick drew everyone's attention when he made the comment.

Iain agreed with a nod. "You're right. The old men will remember. They know all the families and all the gossip. How old was Christen when she came here?"

"Six or seven years old," Gillian answered.

281

"If a family suddenly claims a little girl as their daughter—" Ramsey began.

Iain interrupted him. "But Gillian just told us that the family lived near the border for several years before going north to join their relatives."

"Still, word would have gotten out if she wasn't their own child," Brodick insisted.

"I'll make inquiries," Ramsey promised.

"Finding her may not be as difficult as you're assuming," Iain said. "Brodick's right about the old men. When Graham and Gelfrid were alive, they knew everything that went on."

"Aye, they did," Ramsey agreed before turning to Gillian again. "Tell me, what will you do when you find her? Will you ask her to return to England with you?"

She bowed her head. "No, I won't," she said. "But it's my hope that she'll remember Arianna's treasure and that she might even know where it's hidden."

"She was very young when she was given the box," Iain said. "You're expecting her to have a strong memory. I doubt she'll remember anything."

"She may not even remember you," Brodick said.

Gillian refused to believe that possibility. "Christen is my sister. She'll know me," she insisted.

"You told us that Christen is a year older than you are," Ramsey said.

"Almost three years older," Gillian corrected.

"Then how is it you remember the details so vividly? My God, you were little more than a baby."

"Liese, my dearest friend, God rest her soul, helped me hold on to the memories. She constantly talked about that night and what she had learned from the others who survived. Liese didn't want me to forget because she knew that one day I would want…"

Brodick nudged her when she suddenly stopped. "She knew you'd want what?"

"Justice."

"And how do you plan to accomplish that?" Ramsey asked.

"I'm not sure yet, but one thing I do know. I won't have my father's name slandered. The man who holds my uncle Morgan captive thinks he can prove that my father killed Arianna and stole the treasure. I mean to prove he didn't. He will rest easy in his grave," she added, her voice shaking with emotion. "I do have a glimmer of a plan," she said then. "Greed motivates the monster," she added, referring to Baron Alford, though she deliberately withheld his name. "And he likes games. He thinks he's so clever, but perhaps I can find a way to turn that against him. That is my hope, anyway."

Weary from having to revisit the past, she took another drink of water and thought to end the discussion. "I don't think I've left anything out," she said. "I tried to tell you everything."

She was about to add her request that she

be excused for the evening, but Iain changed her mind with his comment.

"Not quite everything," he said softly.

She leaned back in her chair and put her hands in her lap. "What did I leave out?" she asked, feigning innocence.

Brodick put his hand on top of hers. "They know you saw the Highlander who made this pact with the English devil," he said.

"You told them?"

"Alec told his father, and he told Ramsey," he explained. "But just so you understand, Gillian. If the boy hadn't mentioned it, I sure as certain would have."

"Why did you ask Alec not to tell us about the traitor?" Ramsey asked.

She took a deep breath. "I worried that you might think to keep me here until I pointed out the man who betrayed you."

Iain and Ramsey exchanged a quick look, and she instinctively knew that was their exact plan. They were planning to keep her in the Highlands. She wanted them to admit it. "Is that what you're thinking to do?"

Both lairds ignored the question. "What did he look like?" Ramsey asked.

"He was a big man with long dark hair and a firm jaw. He wasn't unpleasant to look upon," she admitted.

"You've just described most of the men in the Highlands, Gillian. Were there no distinguishing marks that would help us find him?"

"Do you mean scars?"

"Anything that would help us recognize him."

"No, I'm sorry, there really wasn't anything unusual about him."

"I was just hoping... it would make it easier," Ramsey said, and then he leaned forward once again to ask her more questions. She was surprised by the Sinclair laird's restraint. He sounded so calm and in control, yet she knew he had to be sickened and furious by what he had heard thus far. He wasn't letting his emotions get the upper hand, though, and she thought his self-control was quite admirable.

Alec came running down the steps. "Papa, can I bother you?" he called out.

His father's smile was all the permission the child needed. Barefoot, he ran across the hall.

"Alec, why are you still awake?"

"I forgot to kiss you good night, Papa."

Iain hugged Alec, promised he'd look in on him before he went to bed, and sent him back upstairs.

Gillian watched Alec take his time crossing the room, obviously trying to delay going to bed. The young fought sleep, she thought, but the old relished it, and at the moment, she felt absolutely ancient.

"Are there any more questions?" she asked wearily.

"Just one," Ramsey said.

"Yes, just one," Iain agreed. "We want their names, Gillian, all three of them."

She looked from one laird to the other and

then said, "And when you know who they are? What do you plan to do?"

"Let us worry about that," Iain said. "You don't need to know."

She disagreed. "Oh, but I think I do need to know. Tell me," she insisted.

"What the hell do you think we're going to do?" Brodick asked in a low voice.

Jarred by his anger, she ordered, "Don't you dare take that tone with me, Brodick."

He was astounded by her outburst and wasn't quite sure how to respond. Had they been alone, he probably would have pulled her into his lap and kissed her, just for the hell of it, but they weren't alone, there was an audience watching and waiting, and he didn't want to embarrass her. He did want to kiss her, though, and that realization irritated him. Where had all his discipline gone? When he was close to her, he couldn't seem to control his own thoughts.

"Hell," he muttered.

"And don't curse in front of me either," she whispered.

He grabbed her arm, pulled her into his side, and bent down to whisper into her ear. "It pleases me to see you've got the courage to stand up to me."

Would she ever understand him, she wondered. "Then I'm about to make you delirious, Laird."

"No," he countered. "You're about to answer the question. We want the names of the Englishmen."

No one noticed that Alec was still lingering in the hall. When he had heard the briskness in his father's voice, he'd turned around to watch and listen, then slowly crept forward. He was worried his papa might be angry with Gillian, and if that turned out to be true, then the boy decided he would become her champion. If that didn't work, he would go and get his mama.

Brodick had leaned back in his chair and was now patiently waiting for her to do as she had been instructed by all three lairds.

"Yes," she suddenly said. "I will be happy to give you their names, just as soon as you promise me you will not do anything until after the fall festival."

"We need their names now, Gillian," Ramsey insisted, completely ignoring her demand.

"I need your promise first, Ramsey. I will not let you put my Uncle Morgan in danger."

"He's already in danger," Iain pointed out.

"Yes, but he's alive now, and I mean to keep him that way."

"How can you be certain he's still alive?" Ramsey asked.

"If he were killed, I would have no reason to return to England. The monster knows that. I won't give him anything until I see my uncle," she explained. "He won't harm him."

Iain sighed. "You're putting all of us in a difficult position," he began, trying to be diplomatic. "You've brought my son home to me and for that I will be eternally grateful. I know how much your uncle means to you, and

I promise that I will do everything within my power to free him, but Gillian, I want the name of the man who locked my son away like an animal, the man who beat you near to death—"

"Papa, don't be mad at Gillian." Alec shouted his plea as he ran to his father. Tears clouded the boy's eyes. "She didn't do anything wrong. I know the man's name."

Iain lifted Alec into his lap and tried to reassure him. "I'm not angry," he promised. "And I know Gillian didn't do anything wrong."

"Alec, did you hear all the names?" Brodick asked.

The little boy leaned against his father's chest and slowly nodded. "Yes," he said. "I heard all of the names, but I don't remember the other two... just the man who hurt Gillian."

"That's the name I most want," Brodick said softly. "Who is he, Alec?"

"Alec, please," Gillian began.

"Tell me, Alec. Who is he?"

"Baron," Alec whispered. "His name is Baron."

CHAPTER FIFTEEN

The screams began in the middle of the night. Judith Maitland awakened with a start, realized she was hearing Alec's bloodcurdling cries, and threw the covers off, but before she could get out of bed, Iain had already reached the children's chamber.

Graham and Michael were sitting up on their mats wide-eyed with fear. Alec fought his father, kicking and scratching. The boy was trapped in his nightmare, and no amount of soothing or shaking could bring him back. His son's tormented screams were unbearable, and Iain didn't know what to do to make him stop.

Judith sat down next to her son, took him into her arms, and rocked him. After several minutes, the child calmed down. His body relaxed against his mother, and he appeared to be sleeping peacefully again.

"Dear God, what hell did my son go through?" Iain whispered.

Tears streamed down Judith's face. She shook her head, her sorrow so overwhelming she couldn't speak. Iain lifted Alec from her lap, kissed the top of his head, and then put him back into bed. Judith covered him with his blanket.

Within the next hour they were awakened twice more by their son's screams, and both times they ran to his side. Judith wanted to bring Alec into their bed, and Iain promised her that if he screamed again, he would let Alec sleep with them.

It took a long time for Judith and Iain to get back to sleep, but when they finally did, they weren't disturbed again. They both slept late, past dawn, until their older son, Graham, came running into their chamber. He went to his father's side of the bed, touched his shoulder, and whispered, "Papa, Alec's gone."

Iain didn't panic. Assuming his son was already up and about, he motioned for Graham to be quiet so he wouldn't disturb his mother. Then he got out of bed, washed and dressed, and went out into the hallway, where Graham waited with Michael.

"He's probably downstairs," Iain whispered as he pulled the door closed behind him.

"He wouldn't go downstairs, Papa," Graham blurted.

"Stop worrying," he ordered. "Alec hasn't disappeared."

"But he did before, Papa," Graham whispered, growing more fretful by the second.

"Both of you, go downstairs and find Helen and have your breakfast. Let me worry about Alec."

Neither boy moved. Michael's head was bowed, but Graham looked his father right in the eyes when he said, "It's dark down there."

"And you don't like the dark." Iain tried his best not to sound perturbed.

"I don't like the dark neither," Michael admitted, his gaze still directed on the floor.

The main door opened, and Brodick and Ramsey came inside. As was their preference, they had both slept outside under the stars. They didn't like being cooped up with walls pressing in on them. They were used to being lulled to sleep with the scent of pine and the brisk wind surrounding them. 'Twas a fact, the only time they liked beds was when they had women with them, but they never slept the night through with any of their female companions.

Michael spotted his brother and went running down the stairs. "Ramsey, Alec's gone."

"What do you mean, he's gone?"

"He's not in his bed."

Iain came bounding down the stairs then. He went into the great hall and pulled the tapestries back from the two windows near the entrance. Light flooded the room.

"He's around here somewhere," Iain said, trying not to become alarmed.

"The guards would have seen him if he'd ventured outside," Ramsey said. "Where the hell is he?"

Ramsey was obviously concerned, but Brodick, on the other hand, wasn't the least fazed.

"He's with Gillian."

Both Ramsey and Iain looked at their friend. "Why would he be with Gillian?" Iain asked as he rushed back up the stairs.

"He feels safe with her."

Iain whirled around. "And he doesn't feel safe with his mother and his father?"

Brodick started up the stairs. "Of course he does, but he knows she'll let him in her bed. He's sleeping with her, and you aren't going in her room unless I'm with you."

"For the love of..." Iain didn't finish his thought. He strode down the hallway, and without bothering to knock, opened Gillian's door. The room was dark. Brodick brushed past him and went to the window. He lifted the tapestry, tied it with the cord hooked to the wall, and then turned around.

Alec was in her bed all right, just as Brodick had predicted. He was cuddled up against her, his head resting on her shoulder. Gillian was sleeping on her back with her right arm wrapped around the little boy as though she were trying to protect him, even in sleep. Her other arm was stretched across the bed, palm up, and in the light, the scars and raw abrasions were startling to see.

Ramsey stood in the doorway, and though usually diplomatic, he reverted to the days when Brodick's manners had rubbed off on him. "What the hell happened to her arm? It's a mess."

Fortunately, he'd whispered the comment and hadn't disturbed Gillian or Alec.

Brodick pulled the tapestry back in place so that the sun wouldn't bother them, and nudged Iain to leave.

Iain didn't budge. "One angel protects another," he whispered. He turned then and went into the hallway. "We will do what she asks," he told Ramsey.

"We wait to retaliate?" Ramsey asked, already frowning over that possibility.

"Yes, we wait."

Brodick was still in the bedchamber. He'd spotted his plaid on the chair, picked it up, and covered Gillian and Alec with the Buchanan colors. He looked at her once again as he was pulling the door closed and felt a strange contentment wash over him. It suddenly dawned on him that he was never going to let her go.

Like it or not, she was going to belong to him.

Gillian awakened an hour after dawn and felt thoroughly rested. She washed and dressed with care in her own clothes. The servants must have washed her gowns last night and then hung them in front of the fire, for they were dry and spotless.

The tunic she wore over her pale yellow gown was a deep, emerald green that her uncle had often told her enhanced the color of her eyes. After securing the braided cord around her waist so that it would droop just so on the tilt of her hips, she brushed her hair, pinched her cheeks for color, and went downstairs.

She ate breakfast with Judith and the boys. Graham begged his mother to let him take Michael and Alec to the field to watch the soldiers training, and after she gave her permission, they grabbed the wooden swords they would spar with and went running out the door.

"Now we can talk," Judith said. "Did you sleep well? You're up early. I was sure you'd stay in bed until noon at the very least. You have to be exhausted."

"I did sleep well," she replied. "And I wanted to get up early. I must leave today."

"Leave us so soon?"

"Yes," she replied.

"Where are you going?"

"Home with Ramsey."

Judith's eyes widened. "Does Brodick know?"

"Not yet. Do you know where he is?"

"He's down at the stables with Iain and Ramsey. Would you mind if I tagged along? I really would like to see Brodick's reaction to hearing you want to leave with Ramsey."

"Why would he object? He knows I have to search for my sister, and he also knows she's a MacPherson, so he surely understands I have to go to the Sinclair holding to look for her."

"With Ramsey."

"Why do you look so incredulous? Do you know Winslow acted the very same way last night when I mentioned I'd be going home with Ramsey today. He also asked me if Brodick knew about my plans. It was most peculiar."

"I can see I'm going to have to explain."

"Yes, please," Gillian said.

"Ramsey and Iain and Brodick are like brothers," she began. "And they are extremely loyal to one another. But surely you've noticed in the time you've been with Brodick that he's a very possessive man. All the Buchanans are," she added with a nod.

"What are you trying to tell me?"

Judith sighed. "When Iain and I were newly married, my husband didn't like it when Ramsey was near me."

"Why? Didn't he trust him?"

"Oh, yes, he trusted him all right, and so does

Brodick, but women, you see, tend to lose their heads over Ramsey. You've got to admit he's a handsome devil."

"Yes, but so are Iain and Brodick."

"Iain was a bit... insecure... but after a while, he calmed down because he knew my heart belonged to him. Brodick doesn't know, you see, and he's therefore going to be difficult about you leaving with Ramsey."

"He won't be difficult," Gillian assured her.

Judith laughed. "You think you know him so well, then?"

"Yes, I do," she said.

"There's also a little rivalry between Ramsey and Brodick. It should have caused a rift, but it didn't. As I told you last night, about eight years ago, the two of them went to England to find brides. What I didn't tell you is that Brodick found a woman he thought might do."

"What happened?" she asked when her friend hesitated and began to blush.

"This woman gave herself to Brodick."

"They were betrothed?"

Judith shook her head. "No, but she gave herself to him. Do you understand?"

"Do you mean she took him to her bed?"

Their voices had dropped to whispers and they were both blushing now.

"Knowing Brodick as I do, I'd say he took her to his bed, but she had to have agreed or he wouldn't have touched her."

"And he told you this?"

Gilllian looked flabbergasted. Judith laughed as she answered, "Good Lord, no, he didn't tell me. Iain did, but it took a good six months of nagging to get my husband to finally confide in me. You mustn't ever let the men know I've told you this story. Promise me."

"I promise," Gillian hastily agreed so she could hear the rest of the tale. "What happened to the woman? Brodick is a very honorable man and he wouldn't take an innocent—"

"But she wasn't innocent," Judith whispered. "She had been with other men."

"Oh, dear," Gillian whispered, thinking that it was a pity the woman was English.

"One of the men happened to be Ramsey."

"No."

"Hush," Judith whispered. "I don't want the servants to overhear."

"Both of them took her to their beds?"

"Yes, but neither knew for a time that she was playing one against the other."

Gillian's mouth dropped open. "No wonder Brodick dislikes the English so. What happened when they figured it all out?"

"Neither one of them wanted her, of course. They came home and vowed they would marry one of their own or not marry at all."

"Did Brodick love her?"

"I doubt that he did," she replied. "If he'd loved her, he would have been furious with Ramsey, but as it was, he was barely bothered."

"What about Ramsey?"

"He took it all in stride. Women throw

themselves at him," she added. "And that's why Brodick will be difficult about your leaving with him."

"You told me he trusts Ramsey."

"It's you he'll be concerned about," Judith told her bluntly. "As I said before, women tend to lose their heads over Ramsey."

"And he'll be concerned that I... oh, for heaven's sake," Gillian cried out, and then laughed. "You're wrong, Judith. Brodick won't care one way or another."

Judith stood up. "Shall we go find out?"

The two women walked side by side down the hill. The lairds were easy to spot, for they stood together beyond the stables, like towering trees in the center of a field, as they observed the soldiers sparring with their swords.

All three turned as the two ladies came toward them. Gillian noticed that Iain couldn't seem to take his eyes off his wife. Love obviously hadn't lessened in the years they had lived as man and wife.

"Gillian has something to tell you," Judith announced.

"Laird," she began.

"Iain," he corrected.

With a quick nod, she began again. "Iain, I would first thank you for your kindness and your hospitality."

"It is I who should be thanking you, Gillian, for bringing my son home to me."

"She wants to go home with Ramsey, and I think she should," Judith announced emphatically so that her husband would know she supported Gillian's plan. "She wants to leave today."

"Is that so?" Iain replied with a glance at Brodick.

"Ramsey, did you plan to go home today?"

"I did," he answered, and she noticed he, too, looked at Brodick.

"I know how important it is for you to find the man who betrayed Ramsey."

Iain interrupted. "He betrayed all of us, lass."

"Yes." She hurriedly agreed so she could explain her position before she lost her nerve. Telling the giants what they were going to do took courage, especially when she was standing so close to them. She wanted to get the speech she'd rehearsed with Judith on the way down the hill said as quickly as possible.

"I have until the fall festival to accomplish what I came here to do, which means I don't have much time. I'm going to find my sister, God willing, and since she's one of the MacPhersons and the MacPhersons are now part of Ramsey's clan, I'm going home with him today to start searching. I expect all of you to cooperate."

After giving her speech, she folded her arms across her waist and tried to look confident.

"I see your mind's set," Iain said dryly. "We expected you would want to go to Ramsey's holding."

"You had me worried for nothing," she whispered to Judith.

"We'll see," Judith whispered back.

"Ramsey, what say you? Will you take Gillian home with you today?" Iain asked.

"We can leave immediately if that is Lady Gillian's wish."

"What about you, Brodick?" Judith asked. "What do you think of Gillian's plan to go home with Ramsey?"

Gillian didn't give him time to answer. "Brodick's going to come with me," she blurted out.

"Is that right?" he asked quietly.

Her heart was suddenly pounding a furious beat and she could barely catch her breath. She realized then that she was in a panic, and it was all because she was terrified Brodick would leave her. Dear God, why and how had she allowed herself to become so attached to him in such a short time? She knew she shouldn't involve him in her problems, and yet the thought of watching him walk away from her knowing she would never see him again was simply unbearable.

"The Buchanans are feuding with the MacPhersons," Judith whispered softly. "I think perhaps you ask too much of Brodick."

"She has yet to ask me anything," Brodick said.

"Judith, the Buchanans aren't feuding with the MacPhersons." Iain corrected his wife's misconception. "They just don't like them. They don't like anyone they perceive as a weakling."

"Not everyone can be as strong as you are, Brodick. You should defend the weak, not trample on them," Gillian said.

All three lairds grinned as they glanced at one another, and it dawned on her then that they were actually amused by her attitude. They obviously thought she was naïve.

"Is this not so?" she challenged.

"No, it isn't so," Brodick answered. "The weak don't survive in the Highlands."

Both Ramsey and Iain nodded their agreement.

"The MacPhersons are leeches," Brodick said, addressing his remarks to Ramsey now. "They'll drain the strength out of all the Sinclairs, including you. They like being taken care of," he added. "And they sure as certain don't want to be strong. Once they've used up and destroyed you, they'll simply go to another compassionate laird and beg him to take them in."

"You make compassion sound like a sin," Gillian said.

"In this instance it is," he answered.

"Ramsey has only been laird for a short time, but he's already earned the reputation of a compassionate man," Iain remarked. "That's why the MacPhersons came to him."

"I, too, have little tolerance for a fit man who would deliberately embrace sloth and let others take care of him and his family. However, I think you're both mistaken about the MacPhersons. Their soldiers are poorly trained, and that is all there is to it. They aren't weak; they're inept."

The discussion continued, but a movement to the east caught Gillian's attention. There were four young ladies standing together near the tree line watching the lairds. All of them were busy primping. One redheaded woman kept pinching her cheeks, while the others groomed their hair and smoothed their skirts. All of them were giggling. Their carefree attitude made Gillian smile. She assumed the women wanted to look their best when they spoke to Laird Maitland, but were politely waiting until he was no longer engaged in conversation.

"That's exactly our concern, Ramsey," Iain said. "You'll train the MacPhersons, and then they'll turn on you."

"Fortunately, Iain and I won't let them destroy you," Brodick said. "If you won't watch your back, we will."

"I know what I'm doing," Ramsey announced authoritatively. "And you will both stay out of my affairs."

"Do you think it was a MacPherson that Gillian saw? Could one of them be your traitor?" Judith asked.

"The thought has crossed our minds," Iain replied.

Judith looked at Brodick. "If this man hears that Gillian has seen him... if he knows she can point him out, then won't he try to silence her? Alec told us there were three men who took him, so we know this traitor isn't acting alone."

"But he doesn't know I saw him," Gillian argued. "So I am quite safe."

"Who besides the three of you know that

301

Gillian saw the traitor?" Judith asked her husband.

"My brother, Patrick, was told, and while I'm away, he will watch over you, our sons, and Ramsey's brother. Dylan and Winslow were also told, and Ramsey plans to explain the situation to his commander, Gideon, as well."

Turning to Ramsey, he added, "Patrick won't let Michael out of his sight until this is over."

"My brother couldn't be in safer hands," Ramsey replied.

"Why was Winslow told?" Judith asked softly.

"Surely you trust Brodick's brother," Gillian stammered. "You cannot be concerned he would break his laird's confidence."

"I trust Winslow with my life," she said. "That isn't why I asked my husband the question, but as you know, Winslow is commander over our troops," she explained. "And I know Iain had a good reason for telling him. I want to know what it is."

Iain looked uncomfortable. He glanced at Gillian and then turned to his wife.

"Winslow needed to know so that he could prepare."

Judith wouldn't let it go. "Prepare what?"

"Our troops."

Gillian stiffened. "For battle?"

"Yes."

"You're going into England?"

"Yes."

"When?" Gillian demanded.

"When you give us the names of the Englishmen," Brodick answered.

She took a step toward him. "Us? Then
Dylan is also going to prepare your soldiers?"

He smiled. "My soldiers are always prepared. He will simply see to the details."

"But why?"

"How can you ask me such a question?
Iain's my ally and my friend, and Alec is my
godson. It's my duty to retaliate on the boy's
behalf."

"But there's another reason as well, isn't
there?" Ramsey asked.

Brodick, guarded now, slowly nodded.
"Yes, there is another reason."

"And what would that reason be?" Judith
asked.

Brodick shook his head to let her know he
wasn't going to explain. Gillian turned to
Ramsey. "What about your commander? Is he
going to prepare your troops?"

"Yes."

Incredulous, she addressed the one person
she believed was still sane. "Judith, they
cannot think to invade England."

"They think they can," Judith answered.

"We're only going after three men, not the
entire country," Iain said dryly.

"But they are three powerful barons," she
said. "If warriors ride into England armed for
battle, I assure you King John will hear of it.
You will risk war with England, whether you
intend to or not."

"Ah, lass, you don't understand," Brodick

told her. "Your king won't even know we're there. No one's going to see us."

"Do you think you're going to become invisible?"

"Now, Gillian, there's no need for sarcasm," Ramsey said, flashing a heart-stopping grin she would have found charming if the topic hadn't been so obscene.

"Of course King John will know you're there," she cried out in frustration. "Tell me, Brodick. When exactly are you planning this invasion no one's going to know about?"

"Iain already answered that question," he replied. "We'll leave as soon as you give us the names of the English pigs."

"I see," she said. "Now that I thoroughly understand your plans, I'm never going to give you their names. I'll find a way to deal with them. One way or another, justice will prevail."

Iain scowled. "Gillian, what do you think you could do? You're a woman—"

Brodick defended her. "She's strong, and she's determined, and very clever. I honestly think she would find a way to defeat the bastards."

"Thank you."

"It wasn't praise," he countered. "I'm simply stating what I know to be true. However, I cannot let you rob us of our rights, Gillian. We have just as much at stake in this as you do."

"Revenge isn't my primary motive," she argued. "But it's yours, isn't it?"

He shrugged. She turned to Ramsey in

hopes of ending the discussion. "I could be ready to leave in just a few minutes."

Ramsey nodded. "Are you coming with us, Brodick?"

"It's time for that direct question, lass."

"Brodick, I seem to remember that when Annie Drummond was about to pour that godawful mother's fire on my arm, you told her I wouldn't make a sound."

"And you didn't, did you?"

"No, I didn't," she answered. "But you didn't ask me. You told me. I'm just following your lead."

"For the love of God," he muttered, his patience at an end. "If you want me to come with you, then ask. Do it now, Gillian, or I'm leaving."

"You would leave me?" she whispered, appalled he would threaten such a thing.

He looked like he wanted to throttle her. "Ask me," he demanded again.

"I don't want you to think that I need you..."

"You do need me."

She took a step back. He followed. With a sigh, she tried again. "It's just that I've gotten to know you quite well and I trust you."

"I already knew you trusted me."

"Why are you making this so difficult?"

"I'm a difficult man."

"Aye, he is," Ramsey agreed.

The others had obviously heard every word she'd said. Feeling like a fool, she asked, "Will you come with me?"

"Yes."

"Thank you."

Brodick tilted her chin up with his thumb. "I'll stay with you until you get back home. I give you my word," he promised. "Now you can stop worrying."

Oblivious to their audience, he leaned down and kissed her. It was a gentle touch of his mouth against hers, and it was finished before she even had time to blink, yet it still made her heart race.

A burst of laughter startled her, and she turned to the sound. Her eyes widened then, for now there were at least twelve women waiting by the trees.

"Laird Maitland, there are quite a few young ladies waiting to speak to you," Gillian said.

Judith laughed. "They aren't waiting to speak to my husband. He's already taken."

"Taken?" Gillian asked.

"Married," Judith explained.

"For as long as Gillian is in the Highlands, she's my responsibility," Iain began. "She is the reason my son is alive," he added. "I will therefore act as her guardian."

"I also feel a tremendous responsibility for Gillian," Ramsey said. "Because of her, my brother will remain safe, and I now know I have an insurrection on my hands."

Iain stared at Brodick now and said, "I won't have her reputation blackened."

"Meaning?" Brodick demanded.

"People are going to talk," Judith said. "I don't want Gillian's feelings injured."

"And what will they say?" Gillian asked.

Judith deliberately avoided giving a direct answer so that she wouldn't embarrass her new friend. "Some will be cruel. Not the Maitlands, of course, but others will say terrible things."

"She's trying to tell you that there will be speculation you're Brodick's mistress."

"Iain, must you be so blunt?" Judith cried out.

"She needs to understand."

"Is there talk now?" Gillian asked.

Iain shrugged.

"That isn't a satisfactory answer," Brodick said. "Is her reputation being blackened now?"

He sounded outraged by the possibility. Gillian straightened her shoulders. "I don't care what the talk is," she said. "I will admit I hadn't thought about... that is to say, with everything else on my mind, I didn't stop to consider..." She suddenly stopped trembling, and though she could feel her face burning with mortification, her voice was firm when she said, "People who spend their time gossiping are petty and foolish. They may call me harlot for all I care. I know what's in my heart, and I only have to answer to God."

"I damn well do care," Brodick said angrily. "And I'm not going to let anyone slander you."

"How do you plan to stop them, Brodick?" Ramsey asked.

"Yes," Iain said, "tell us what you plan to do about it."

In Brodick's mind there was really only one possible solution. With a long drawn out sigh he said, "Marry her, I suppose."

Gillian's gasp nearly knocked her over. "You suppose wrong."

Everyone, including Judith, ignored her protest. "It makes sense to me," Iain said.

"Yes, it does," Ramsey agreed. "Brodick's been acting very possessive of her. Last night he wouldn't let me near her except when he was by her side."

"He's well aware of how women tend to forget themselves when they're around you," Iain remarked. "And there was that unfortunate incident in England when you and Brodick went to find brides. He's probably still chafed about that."

"I'm not chafed," Brodick snapped.

His friends ignored his protest. Ramsey shrugged. "It happened over eight years ago," he reminded Iain. "Besides, Brodick wouldn't have been happy with a woman who could so easily turn her attentions to other men."

"Which is why neither one of you brought her home."

"Neither one of us wanted her. She lacked morals."

"That's an understatement," Iain said with a chuckle.

Brodick looked as if he wanted to kill Iain and Ramsey, but his friends remained unconcerned.

"There's more to this story than you're telling, isn't there?" Judith asked.

No one answered the question. Iain winked at her, and she decided she would find a way to get the details later.

"She was wearing your plaid last night, Brodick," Ramsey said then.

"He insisted she wear his colors," Iain said. "It's little wonder people are speculating about her position."

"I heard that during the celebration you kissed her in front of the entire Maitland clan."

Brodick shrugged. "Not the entire clan, just some."

"You wanted everyone to know—" Iain began.

Brodick cut him off. "Damned right I did."

"He wanted everyone to know what?" Judith asked after giving Gillian a worried look.

"That Gillian belongs to him," Iain explained.

"That's why he kissed her in front of witnesses all right," Ramsey said.

Poor Gillian looked as though she'd just been struck hard on her head. Judith took mercy on her, for she knew she didn't understand the blunt ways of the Highlanders.

"I'm sure it was just a friendly little kiss, the kind one cousin would give another in greeting."

Gillian was frantically nodding when Brodick muttered, "The hell it was."

With a little sigh, Judith gave up. If she'd learned anything in her years living with Iain, it was that none of the Highlanders knew how to be subtle. If they wanted something done, they did it themselves, and if one of them wanted a woman, he took her. It was that simple. The men respected women, of course, and for that reason they usually married them before they took them to their bed, but once they made the commitment, they kept it until the day they died. In this instance, Brodick obviously wanted Gillian, and no amount of arguing would change his determination. He would take her, and his two loyal friends with their outrageous banter were simply letting him know they approved the match and would do anything they could to help.

None of them, however, were considering Gillian's feelings in the matter. Judith patted her friend's hand to let her know she sympathized. Gillian looked positively dazed.

"Brodick?"

"Yes, Judith."

"Do you love Gillian?"

Dead silence followed the question. If looks could kill, Iain would be without a wife by now, Judith thought. It was very apparent that Brodick didn't like being pinned down with such a personal question. Judith didn't back away, though; she had Gillian's best interests at heart after all. "Do you?"

"Sweetheart, that isn't a question you should be asking," Iain said.

"I think it is," she argued. "Someone has to look out for Gillian."

"We're looking out for her," Ramsey said.

"And Brodick obviously wants her," Iain interjected.

"Wanting isn't enough," Judith said. "Have you all forgotten she's English?"

"She used to be English," both Ramsey and Iain said at the same time.

Judith let them see how exasperated she was. "Didn't you and Brodick vow to marry Highlanders or not marry at all?" she asked Ramsey.

"Yes, they did," Iain answered. "After that unfortunate incident in England—"

"Will you quit calling it an 'unfortunate incident?'" Brodick demanded.

"We did make that promise," Ramsey admitted. "But Brodick has obviously changed his mind."

"I'm thinking of her reputation," Brodick muttered.

"Then simply stay away from her," Judith suggested.

"That is not an acceptable solution," Brodick said.

"Why isn't it?" Judith prodded.

"Because he doesn't want to stay away from her," Ramsey said. "That much should be obvious to you, Judith."

She decided to try another direction. "Brodick, have you told her what her life will be like living with the Buchanans?"

He shrugged. "I only just decided to marry her," he admitted.

"He told me I'd be miserable." Gillian's voice was but a hoarse whisper. She was still reeling from Brodick's outrageous impudence in dictating her future, but anger was quickly replacing disbelief, and within seconds she was trembling. She kept telling herself that any minute now they would have their laugh and tell her it was all just a game.

And when that happened, she knew she'd feel a glimmer of disappointment.

"Aye, she will be miserable," Brodick said.

Ramsey burst into laughter. "You told her the truth, then. I don't envy anyone, man or woman, who would try to fit in with those savages you call Buchanans."

"I won't be miserable," Gillian cried out. "And do you know why?"

The men acted as though they hadn't heard her question. Iain siezed on her first comment. "There, do you see? She already has an optimistic outlook. That's a fair start."

"Will you gentlemen stop jesting?" Gillian demanded. She had finally regained her senses and was determined to put an end to the discussion.

"I don't think they're jesting," Judith said. She moved closer to Gillian and whispered, "If you haven't already figured it out, I feel I should probably explain..."

Gillian threaded her fingers through her hair in agitation. "Explain what?" she asked frantically.

"They never jest. I do believe Brodick means to marry you."

CHAPTER SIXTEEN

"**B**rodick, I would like a word in private with you." Her clipped words didn't leave room for discussion, and she didn't even try to mask her anger. She wanted him to know she was furious.

"Not now, Gillian," he replied impatiently, seemingly unaffected by her show of temper. "Ramsey, we'll leave in ten minutes. Can you be ready by then?"

"Of course," Ramsey answered, and after bowing to Gillian and Judith, he started back up the hill.

Iain threw his arm around his wife's shoulders and turned to the west. "Before I go back to my duties, let's look in on the boys. They just went to Patrick and Frances Catherine's home."

Judith didn't have much choice, for her husband was pulling her along. "You promised to take them fishing," she reminded him.

"No, Alec promised on my behalf."

"But you will take them?"

"Of course I will." He laughed. "And I won't let them drown," he added, repeating Michael's promise to his brother.

Brodick continued to stand beside Gillian, but he wasn't paying any attention to her. He was fully occupied trying to locate Dylan in the field below, where over a hundred Maitland soldiers were training.

Gillian watched the group of women as they picked up their skirts and ran together up the hill. Most of them were giggling like little girls.

"What *are* they doing?"

Brodick glanced at the women. "Chasing Ramsey," he answered very matter-of-factly before returning to his task of scanning the field.

"Why?"

"Why what?" he asked as he continued to search.

She sighed. "Why are the ladies chasing him?"

The question startled him, for what should have been obvious to Gillian appeared not to be obvious at all. With a shrug, he said, "It's what they all do."

"All the ladies chase him?" she asked, still not understanding.

He finally gave her his full attention. "Yes, they do," he said quietly.

"But why?"

"You don't know?"

"I wouldn't ask if I knew, Brodick," she said, thoroughly perplexed.

"They find him... handsome," he finally said for lack of a better word. "That's what I've been told anyway."

"He's very nice and quite polite, but I can't imagine chasing after him just because he's attractive."

"The women don't care about his behavior or his character. They like looking at him."

She shook her head. "I know what you're trying to do. You're just trying to make me laugh so I'll forget about your arrogant claims in front of your friends."

"I swear to you, I'm telling the truth. Women like to look at Ramsey, and that's why they chase after him. You don't think him handsome?"

"I hadn't really thought about it until now, but I suppose he is," she said. "Yes, of course he is," she added with a bit more conviction so Brodick wouldn't think she was trying to find fault with his friend. "Iain's also very handsome. I'm surprised that the ladies don't chase after you. After all, you're much more..."

She stopped herself in time. Heaven help her, she was about to tell him how attractive he was. His earthy masculinity bordered on downright sinful. Just being near him made her want to think about things that were wanton and certainly unladylike, but strumpets had those kinds of thoughts. They were lustful; she wasn't. At least not until Brodick came into her life and turned it upside down.

Oh, she wasn't about to let him know how he affected her. The last thing she wanted to do was build his arrogance. Brodick already had enough to last a lifetime.

"I'm much more what?" he asked.

She shook her head and tried to ignore his penetrating gaze. "I know why ladies don't chase you," she said. "It's because you scare them."

He laughed. "That's good to know."

"And you frown all the time."

"Ah, there's Dylan."

Without so much as a fare-thee-well, Brodick strode away. She couldn't believe his lack of courtesy; he hadn't even bothered to glance her way first. He just took off.

"Oh, no you don't," she whispered. "You're not getting away from me." Muttering to herself, she picked up her skirts and hurried down the hill.

"Brodick, I insist on having a word with you, and I don't care if you want to listen or not," she called out, but since he was so far ahead of her, she doubted he heard a word she said.

She didn't mean to pick up the pace, but the hill was much steeper than she'd judged, and before she realized what was happening, she was running and couldn't seem to slow down.

She propelled herself right into the middle of a sword fight. "I beg your pardon," she stammered when she bumped into a soldier.

The man didn't hear her, but he obviously felt her ram into his back. Believing another soldier was trying to best him from behind, he whirled around, raised his sword, and was swinging it downward in a wide arc when he discovered whom he was about to strike.

His startled shout reached the treetops. Gillian jumped back and collided with another soldier. She quickly turned to him and said, "I'm so sorry."

Then *he* shouted. Mortified by the turmoil she was causing, and not knowing where to turn, she whirled in a circle and then stood in the thick of the mock battle, surrounded by large, panting soldiers who were fighting as though their lives depended on it. None of them seemed to realize they were merely training.

In the chaos, she lost sight of Brodick.

"Please excuse me for interrupting you," she apologized as she gently pushed her way through the crowd.

Brodick let out a roar that caused her heart to miss a beat. Then everyone began to shout. With a resigned sigh, she knew that she was the reason why.

The fighting had stopped, and she was circled by a ring of incredulous warriors staring down at her as though she had just dropped out of the sky.

"I'm so sorry, gentlemen. I didn't mean to interrupt your training. I really am... oh, there's Brodick. Please let me pass."

The men appeared too stupefied to move. Brodick's bellowed command got through to them, however, and within seconds a wide path was formed. Brodick stood at one end with his legs braced apart, his hands on his hips, and a scowl on his face.

She thought it would be a good idea to go the other way, but when she glanced over her shoulder, she saw that Dylan and Winslow were blocking that end. Winslow looked as though he wanted to kill her. Dylan just looked plain astonished.

Feeling trapped, she decided she was going to have to bluster her way through this embarrassment, and straightening her shoulders, she slowly walked to the man who she believed was solely responsible for turning her into a simpleton.

"For the love of God, Gillian, what were you thinking? You could have been killed."

A loud grumble of agreement washed over the crowd. Her face burning, she forced herself to turn to her disgruntled audience. She folded her hands together as though in prayer and repeated, "I am so sorry. I started down the hill, and before I knew what was happening, I was running. I apologize, gentlemen, for interrupting you and causing you concern."

The sincerity in her voice and her heartfelt apology both placated and pleased the soldiers. Several actually bowed to her, while others nodded to let her know they forgave her her transgression.

She was beginning to feel better, but then she turned back to Brodick, and that feeling immediately evaporated. His scowl was hot enough to make the sun break out in a sweat.

"I wanted to speak to you," she said.

His head down like a bull, he charged toward her. When he reached her, he didn't slow down. He simply clasped hold of her hand and kept right on going. She didn't have any choice. She could either walk with him—which meant run, because his stride was much longer and quicker than hers—or she could be dragged along behind him like a rag doll.

"Let go of me or slow down," she demanded as she tried to keep pace with him.

He slowed down. "I swear to God, you try the patience of a saint."

"You aren't a saint, Brodick, no matter what your mother might have told you."

The bull actually smiled. "Ah, but you do please me, Gillian. 'Tis the truth you do."

She wasn't in the mood for compliments, especially when given in such a bewildered tone.

"Then I'm about to make you—"

"Delirious?" he asked, remembering her comment from the night before.

"Yes, you will be delirious, and do you know why?"

"No," he replied dryly, "but you're going to tell me, aren't you?"

He sounded resigned. She refused to take insult. "I'm letting you off the hook."

"Meaning?"

"You don't have to worry about my reputation any longer. If I'm not going to be concerned about it, then why should you?"

"I see."

"You don't have to marry me."

"Is that right?"

He suddenly veered to the line of trees where Ramsey's admirers had gathered earlier.

"Where are you dragging me now?"

"We need some privacy."

She didn't argue or point out the fact that she had asked him for a moment of privacy just minutes before he went chasing after Dylan. The sooner she explained her position the better, she thought, before they were interrupted or he went running away again.

"I know why you offered."

"Offered what?" he asked with a glance at her.

"Will you please pay attention. You were just being gallant when you made the suggestion to marry me."

"Suggestion?" he scoffed. "Gillian, I don't make suggestions. I give orders. See the difference?"

She refused to waste time trying to appease him. "This isn't the time for diplomacy," she said. "I have to make you understand that you don't have to be noble. It's all my fault, really it is. I realize that now. I shouldn't have asked you to come with me to Ramsey's home. I backed you into a corner, and that was wrong of me."

"No one's ever backed me into a corner," he said, highly insulted by her remark. "I did what I wanted to do and what I felt was necessary."

"You aren't responsible for me."

He pulled her along to a secluded spot in the woods as she rambled on and on about his reasons for doing what he had done. She had obviously thought it over and worked it all out in her mind. She had it all wrong, of course, but he decided to wait until she was finished explaining his motives to him before he set her straight.

When they reached an open circle of trees, he let go of her hand, leaned back against a fat tree trunk, folded his arms across his chest, and waited for her to finish lecturing him.

He tried to concentrate on what she was saying, but he became distracted. She was such a sight with her cheeks flushed and her golden brown hair curling about her shoulders. He knew she didn't have any idea how beautiful she was. Appearances weren't important to her, and he thought that a refreshing difference between her and other women he'd known. Her eyes had turned a deep emerald color. There was definitely passion simmering below the surface, and he had a sudden, almost overwhelming need to take her into his arms and never let go.

"Now do you understand?"

What the hell was she talking about now? "Understand what?" he asked, realizing then he hadn't heard a word she'd said.

"Haven't you been listening?" she cried out in frustration.

"No."

Her shoulders slumped. "Brodick, I'm not going to marry you." She shook her head. "I won't let you be noble."

"Gillian?"

"Yes?"

"Do you like being with me?"

She pretended not to understand because it was safer than allowing him to push her into admitting all those feelings she was desperately trying to keep hidden.

"Do you mean... now?"

"You know exactly what I mean."

"Brodick—"

"Answer me."

She bowed her head. "Yes, I do like being with you... very much," she admitted. "But that doesn't matter," she added in a rush. "We've known each other a very short time, and you have to go home. I'm sure you have many pressing duties waiting for you. You are the Buchanan laird, after all."

"I know what the hell I am," he snapped.

She snapped back, giving him a dose of his own tactics. "Don't you dare take that tone with me. I won't put up with it."

When he suddenly broke into a grin, her temper flared. "Do you find my criticism amusing?"

"I find you utterly refreshing."

She had trouble catching her breath. "You do?"

"Yes, I do. Not many women would speak to me the way you do. 'Tis the truth you're the first," he added a bit sheepishly. "I shouldn't allow such insolence," he added.

"I don't believe I was being insolent, and I'm not usually critical of others, but you make me lose my senses."

"That's good to know."

Exasperated, she took a step toward him and shook her head. "I wish you would stop trying to confuse me by changing the subject. You're making this very difficult for me. I'm simply trying to—"

"Let me off the hook?"

She sighed. "Yes."

He reached for her, but she backed away and put her hand out as a command for him to stay where he was. "Don't."

"Don't what?"

"Kiss me. That's what you were going to do, isn't it?"

He leaned back against the tree again. "Do you want me to?"

She threaded her fingers through her hair in agitation. "Yes... I mean, no. Oh, stop asking me questions," she cried out. "You're making me daft. I can't marry you. I have to find my sister and that cursed box and go back to England. If I married you, you'd end up alone."

"Have you so little faith in me? Don't you think I can protect you?"

She didn't hesitate. "Of course I have faith in you. I know you can protect me, but this isn't your battle. It's mine, and I will not put you in the middle of it. If anything happened to you, I don't think I could bear it."

A sudden thought struck him and shook him to the core. "Is there a man in England waiting for you?"

For the first time since they had begun the heated discussion, he sounded unsure of himself. His vulnerability was endearing. Though she knew she could lie and end the discussion now and forever, she felt compelled and honor-bound to tell him the truth.

"No, there isn't any other man. I'm going home to my Uncle Morgan... but no other."

"Has your uncle chosen a husband for you?"

"No."

He tilted his head as he studied her, and then

quietly said, "He would find me acceptable."

She didn't argue with him. "Yes, he would."

"Would it please him to know you married a laird?"

Brodick's armor was fully back in place, and any uncertainty she had glimpsed in him had completely vanished. The arrogant warrior faced her now, cocky and full of himself.

"It would please my uncle to know you had attained such an important position in your clan, but that isn't why he would find you acceptable."

"Why then?" he asked curiously.

"Because he would easily see through your gruff exterior. You're hot-tempered and passionate in your beliefs, and you're extremely loyal to those you love. You're an honorable man, Brodick, and you couldn't fool my uncle. He would know what's in your heart."

"What about you, Gillian? Do you know what's in my heart?"

His voice was whisper soft, and a jolt of longing rushed all the way down to her toes. In the sunlight filtering through the branches of the trees surrounding them, Brodick's body had taken on an iridescent glow. His skin glistened and his long golden hair shimmered. Looking at such a fit man made her mouth dry and her stomach churn. Her fantasies heated her face, and when she realized she was staring at his mouth, she forced herself to look at the ground until she could get her errant thoughts under control. She had never thought much about mating with a man until she had met Brodick, and thanks to him, she knew she was going to have to spend a good deal of time in the confessional, telling a priest how depraved she had become.

"Have you been with many women?" She couldn't believe she had the nerve to ask him such an intimate question, and more than anything she wished she could take the words back. "Don't answer," she blurted out. "I shouldn't have asked."

"You can ask me anything," he said. "And yes, I've been with women," he answered very matter-of-factly. "Would you like me to speculate on the number?"

"No, I would not," she answered. She continued to stare at the ground when she asked, "Is there a woman waiting for you?"

"I imagine there are several waiting for me."

Her gaze flew to his. "You cannot marry several women, Brodick. Only one."

Her cheeks were flushed. It took all he had not to laugh. "There are always women waiting and willing to share my bed," he explained. "None of them have the expectation of marriage."

She decided she hated every single one of those women. The burst of jealousy she felt didn't make a lick of sense but made her feel miserable. She wasn't going to marry him, yet she detested the thought of Brodick sharing his bed with another woman.

Unable to hide it, the anger radiated in her

voice when she asked, "And will these women continue to share your bed after you are married?"

"I hadn't thought about it," he admitted.

"Then think about it now," she snapped.

She realized he knew exactly what was going on inside her head when he smiled at her. Oh, yes, he knew she didn't like hearing about his women, and he was thoroughly enjoying her reaction. She suddenly wanted to kick him and kiss him at the same time.

She chose to behave instead. "Your wife would not wish you to take other women to your bed."

"Gillian, when we marry, I will have only you and no other. We will both be faithful to each other, during the good and the bad times we share. You needn't worry about such inconsequential things. I want only you. Will your Uncle Morgan know I will take care of you?"

"He would know I could take care of myself. I'm not a weakling. My uncle taught me how to defend myself. Did you get the notion that I was weak because Alec told you I was beaten?"

"No," he answered. "You showed strength, not weakness. You protected the boy from harm by turning the bastard's rage on yourself. Besides," he added arrogantly, "I would never marry a weakling."

The warmth in his voice and his praise were almost her undoing. Oh, how she wanted to throw herself into his arms and hold him.

She didn't know how to protect herself from him, and she was already beginning to mourn her loss, for when she returned to England, she knew she would never be the same.

"Tell me you love me," he said.

"I do love you," she confessed. "But I'm not happy about it. I don't know how it happened... so fast... I didn't have time to protect myself from you, and I certainly didn't mean to fall in love." She shook her head as if to settle her thoughts. "It doesn't matter, though. I still can't marry you."

Brodick's entire body relaxed. Although he already believed she loved him, hearing her say the words reassured him. The tension eased out of him and he suddenly felt reborn. She made him feel clean and new and indestructible.

"I will have you, Gillian."

Taken aback by the vehemence in his voice, she shook her head. "No."

"Yes," he countered, his voice hard now, determined. "Know this. No other man will ever touch you. You belong to me."

"When did you make that decision?"

"When you told me you loved me. I already knew, but it seems I needed to hear you say the words."

She burst into tears. "Why won't you understand? I can't ever have Annie Drummond's house. Not now, not ever. You're trying to put foolish thoughts into my head, and I want you to stop. It's cruel to make me long for what I can never have. No," she added in a near shout, "I will not dream. It's dangerous."

"You want Annie Drummond's house?" he asked, thoroughly puzzled by the bizarre wish. "Why?"

"Oh, never mind. You wouldn't understand."

"Explain then so that I will understand."

"It's what Annie's cottage represents," she said, her voice hesitant. "She has a home and a husband who loves her, and her life is... idyllic."

"You cannot know what her life is like unless you walk in her shoes," he countered.

"Stop trying to be logical," she demanded. "I'm simply trying to make you understand that I can't ever have a life like Annie's. I have to go back to England."

Brodick suddenly stiffened. The truth struck him hard. He finally guessed her real reason for refusing to marry him, and he realized that even now she was trying to protect him.

"You believe you're going back to England to die, don't you, Gillian? That's what you're not telling me."

She looked away when she answered him. "There is that possibility." She burst into tears again.

"I don't like seeing you cry. You will stop it at once."

She blinked. Only Brodick could give such a ludicrous command. Did he think she was crying on purpose just to upset him?

"You are the most difficult man, and I will not marry you."

He moved so quickly she didn't have time to react. In two long strides he had her in his arms.

"You've already made your commitment to me when you admitted you loved me. Nothing else matters. I don't give a damn how complicated it all becomes. You're mine now. Do you honestly believe I'm ever going to let you go?"

Telling herself she had to remain strong and not give in to him, she shook her head and struggled to get free. She pushed against his chest with all her might, desperately trying to put some distance between them. When she was close to him, all she wanted to do was wrap herself in his warmth and let the world pass her by. She wanted time to stop... and that was impossible.

Her struggles proved useless. She couldn't get him to budge. His superior strength was at least ten times her own, and after a moment she ceased squirming and bowed her head.

"What are we going to do?" she whispered, once again on the brink of tears.

She had no idea how telling her question was. She hadn't asked what she was going to do, but what they would do. Content for the moment to simply hold her, he bent down, kissed the top of her head, and closed his eyes as he inhaled her light feminine scent. Her hair smelled of roses. She was unlike the Buchanan women, and he realized he was actually a little in awe of her. Her skin was as smooth and soft as he imagined a cloud would be, and her smile enchanted him. It was as beautiful as baby's first, and just as pure. There wasn't a hint of cunning in her. No, she wasn't like other women. He remembered that when he'd first met her, he'd judged her almost painfully prim and proper, and frail, too frail for his way of life. Yet almost immediately he had seen the steel strength inside of her. She was courageous and honorable, and those were but two of the hundred or so reasons he was never going to let her leave him.

"I'll give you a promise," he said gruffly. "And then you will cease your worrying."

"And what is this promise?"

"If you go back to England, I'll go with you."

"If I go back?"

"It hasn't been decided yet."

"What are you saying? I don't understand. The decision is mine to make."

He didn't argue, and his silence worried her. She once again tried to get him to explain his remark, but he stubbornly refused.

"When I go back, I'll go alone. You must stay here. I couldn't bear it if anything happened to you."

Her voice shivered with emotion, and the fear he heard surprised and pleased him. He'd never had anyone care about him the way she did. His only family was his brother, Winslow, but it was a distant, rigid relationship. They loved each other as brothers did, but never showed any outward affection.

"You will have confidence in my ability to protect you," he ordered.

"You don't know what you're up against. These aren't ordinary men. They have the king's support and friendship, and surely the Devil's on their side."

"None of them have Highland blood running through their veins, and that makes them vulnerable."

"Will you be serious?" she demanded. "A Highlander can bleed as easily as an Englishman."

"You will have faith in me. I command it."

She gave up arguing with him, feeling as though it would be easier to get a stone wall to understand.

"I do have faith in you, and I will try not to worry, but that's all I will promise. You can give me as many commands as you wish, and it won't change how I feel."

"Every man has a weakness," he patiently explained. "I'll find theirs, I promise you."

"Every man?"

"Yes," he answered emphatically.

His hand moved to the back of her neck. Twisting her curls around his fist, he jerked her head back. His face loomed over hers, his breath warm and sweet as he stared down into her eyes.

"What is your weakness, Brodick?" she asked.

"You."

CHAPTER SEVENTEEN

He lowered his head and kissed her, effectively sealing any protest she might have made. It wasn't a gentle caress of his lips against hers, but a hard, demanding kiss that let her know in no uncertain terms how much he wanted her. His tongue sank into her sweet warm mouth to stroke and caress, and within seconds she was kissing him just as thoroughly. Timid at first, the tip of her tongue touched his fleetingly, but when she felt him tighten his hold and heard him growl low in his throat, she grew bolder. His passion overwhelmed her, yet she wasn't frightened, trusting him to know when to stop. He didn't seem inclined to at the moment, though, and, Lord, his mouth was doing such magical things to her body. A yearning deep in the pit of her stomach burned for more, and as his mouth slanted over hers again and again, all she could think about was getting closer.

His hands stroked her back, then splayed wide as he lifted her up against the junction of his thighs so that they were pressed intimately against each other. Her breasts rubbed against his chest and his thighs felt like hot steel. He made her burn for more of him, and she couldn't seem to catch her breath as she frantically returned his kisses.

"Brodick, I want—"

He kissed her once again, almost savagely, and then he abruptly pulled back and let her slowly slip down to the ground. His face was buried in the crook of her neck, and he took several long deep, shuddering breaths as he tried to regain his discipline.

She didn't want to let go of him, and when he began to nibble on her earlobe with his teeth and his tongue stroked her sensitive skin, she felt a jolt of pleasure course through her.

"Don't..." Her voice cracked and she shivered in his arms.

He kissed his way down the side of her neck. "Don't what?" he asked.

She tilted her head to the side to give him better access and with a sigh said, "Don't stop."

He gently lifted her away from him and would have let go of her if she hadn't swayed. Displaying a wicked look of male satisfaction, he was arrogantly pleased he'd been able to arouse and confuse her in so little time. Her passion matched his own, and he knew that once he rid her of her shyness, she would be as uninhibited and wild as he planned to be on their wedding night. God help him, they'd better be wed soon because he didn't think he could wait much longer, and he certainly didn't want to disgrace her by taking her before their vows were spoken and blessed. But she was making it difficult. Just looking at her stirred a burning desire in him. Those incredible green eyes looked thoroughly ravaged now. Her hair was a riot of curls about her shoulders, and her mouth was rosy and swollen from his kisses.

Waiting for her to come to her senses and agree to marry him was out of the question. By the time she got around to making up her mind, they could have at least two children.

The world around them intruded, forcing both of them back to the present. Ramsey shouted Brodick's name, and with a long, regretful sigh, Brodick stepped back.

"Go and collect your things. It's time for us to leave." He turned and started back toward the fields.

She ran after him. "Thank you for understanding."

"Understanding what?"

"That I cannot marry you."

As he continued on his way, his hardy laugh echoed back to her.

By the time Gillian returned to the Maitland home, Helen, the housekeeper, had her things packed, and as Gillian was thanking her for her help, she remembered a promise she'd made. Fortunately, Helen was able to help and showed her a shortcut to her destination out the back door.

Ten minutes passed and then ten more, and Brodick, impatient by nature, was growing more irritated by the second as he waited for Gillian in the courtyard.

Ramsey and Winslow waited by his side, and every couple of seconds one or the other would glance toward the doors.

"What in thunder's keeping her?" Brodick muttered.

"Maybe she's waiting for Iain and Judith. Here they come now. Gillian surely wants to say good-bye to them."

Ramsey was the first to see Gillian walking toward the courtyard from the opposite side of the hill.

"Here she comes."

"She didn't forget," Winslow said, smiling.

His wife, Isabelle, was walking with Gillian, and Winslow's two boys trailed behind. His younger son, Andrew, soon to be five years old, ran forward and took hold of Gillian's hand. Winslow watched her as she smiled at his son and spoke to him. Whatever she said amused Andrew, for he burst into laughter. Isabelle was trying hard not to laugh.

"What didn't she forget?" Brodick asked his brother.

"I told her Isabelle was upset with me because I hadn't introduced her. She didn't forget."

Winslow suddenly figured out why his family was so amused with Gillian. "I don't think Isabelle understands a word she's saying. Your woman's Gaelic needs improvement."

Brodick nodded. "She has a quick mind. She'll learn."

"Are you going to keep her?"

"Yes."

"Does she know it?"

"Not yet."

Ramsey overheard the conversation and laughed heartily. "I assume you've considered all the problems, Brodick."

"I have."

"It won't be an easy life for her living with—" Ramsey began.

Brodick finished his sentence for him. "Living with the Buchanan clan. I know, and I worry about her adjustment."

Ramsey grinned. "That's not what I was going to say. It won't be easy for her living with you. Rumor has it, you're a difficult man to be around."

Brodick didn't take offense. "Gillian's aware of my flaws."

"And she'll still have you?" Winslow asked.

"As a matter of fact, she has refused to marry me."

Knowing Brodick as well as they did, both Ramsey and Winslow began to laugh again.

"So when's the wedding?" Ramsey asked.

CHAPTER EIGHTEEN

Love wasn't supposed to happen this suddenly.

Gillian spent most of the ride to Ramsey's holding thinking about Brodick and wondering how in heaven's name he had managed to capture her heart so completely in so little time. The man had all but robbed her of her senses. She was well aware of his flaws, most of them anyway, but she still loved him all the same, and how was such a thing possible? Love was supposed to be nourished. It was a slow realization that occurred after months and months of courting, and sometimes that awareness took years. Love certainly didn't strike like lightning.

Maybe it was lust, and if it was, then how was she ever going to be able to tell that atrocious sin in the confessional without dying of mortification? Was it lust? Brodick was a handsome devil, and she would have had to be dead not to notice. Yet Ramsey and Iain were also handsome, and her heart didn't race when either of them was near. Brodick had a mesmerizing effect on her, though. All he had to do was glance her way and she became quite breathless.

He wasn't paying her the slightest bit of attention now. He and Ramsey rode well ahead of their soldiers and Gillian, and Brodick never once looked back to see how she was doing. She spent a good deal of time staring at his broad shoulders while she tried to figure out how she could regain her senses.

She didn't want to think about her reason for going to Ramsey's home, yet reality kept intruding, no matter how she tried to block her worries. What if her sister wasn't there? What if she had married and moved away from the MacPhersons? Worse, what if Christen didn't remember her? Her sister hadn't had

Liese to help her keep the memories alive the way Gillian had, and what if Christen had forgotten everything that had happened?

So caught up in her thoughts, Gillian didn't notice that Brodick and Ramsey had stopped. Dylan reached over and grabbed Gillian's reins, forcing her mount to halt. She and the soldiers waited a good distance behind the lairds, and just as she was about to ask the commander why they weren't continuing on, she saw a horse and rider galloping up the hill from the west. Making a wide sweep around them, the stranger rode on ahead to join Brodick and Ramsey.

Gillian patiently waited to find out what was going on as she watched what appeared to be an argument between the stranger and Brodick. It couldn't have been much of a disagreement, though. Even though Brodick was scowling and the stranger was repeatedly shaking his head in obvious disapproval, Ramsey, Gillian noticed, was smiling.

"Dylan, who is that man shaking his head at your laird?" Gillian asked.

"Father Laggan. He serves the Sinclairs, the Maitlands, and many others."

"Does he serve the Buchanans as well?"

"When there's no getting out of it, he does."

"I don't understand. Doesn't he like the Buchanans?"

Dylan chuckled. "No one likes us, milady. We're proud of that fact. Most of the clans leave us alone, as do the clergy, including Father Laggan."

"Why don't they like you?"

"They fear us," the Buchanan commander explained cheerfully. "Father Laggan believes we're savages."

"Where would you get such an idea?"

"From Father Laggan. It's what he calls us."

"I'm certain he doesn't really believe any such thing. You aren't savages. You're just a bit... intense... that's all. The priest seems to be holding his own with Brodick now. Do you see how he's shaking his head?"

"Brodick will still win," Dylan predicted. "He always does."

As though he knew they were discussing him, Brodick suddenly turned in his saddle and looked at her while the priest continued to argue with him. Obviously upset, Laggan was now waving his hands in agitation.

Then Brodick winked at her. She didn't know what to make of his behavior. It wasn't like Brodick to be flirtatious in front of others, and the silly little gesture warmed her heart.

"Do you know what they're discussing?" she asked Dylan.

"I do," he answered.

Father Laggan then twisted in his saddle to look at her. He had shocking white hair and deeply tanned and leathered skin. His lips were pinched together, indicating his displeasure, and for that reason she neither smiled nor waved to him. She simply inclined her head in silent greeting.

As soon as the priest turned back to Brodick, Gillian demanded, "Tell me what they're arguing about."

"You."

"I beg your pardon?"

"I do believe you're the topic of their discussion, milady."

"Surely not," she said. "The priest doesn't even know me."

"Iain sent him to Brodick, and I do believe that now Laggan is acting as your guardian. He wants to make sure you aren't being forced to do anything you don't want to do."

"But I want to go to Ramsey's," she countered. "Iain must have explained my situation to Father."

Dylan sincerely hoped she wouldn't ask him to elaborate on the priest's motives. In his opinion, the less she knew, the better.

Brodick motioned for her to come forward as the priest, still frowning, nudged his horse to the side to give her room. Ramsey flanked Gillian on one side and Brodick on the other. Gillian smiled at the priest as Ramsey made the introductions, but that smile vanished in a heartbeat when she realized where she was. She had thought Brodick had stopped at the edge of a gentle slope, but now that she was only a few feet away from the edge, she could see the sheer drop below her. So forcefully did she pull on the reins, the horse reared, but Brodick's quick action saved her from being thrown.

He had to pry the reins away from her hands. "Gillian, what's come over you?"

She made herself look at him and only him. "I don't like looking down at such depths," she whispered. "It makes me lightheaded."

Seeing the panic in her eyes, Brodick quickly forced both mounts to back up several feet. Ramsey did the same.

"Better now?"

She exhaled as she relaxed. "Yes, much better, thank you," she whispered before turning to Father Laggan.

"Ramsey, I'll need your help with this," Brodick said quietly.

"I'll do what I can," his friend promised just as softly.

Curious, Gillian looked at Brodick. "Would you also like my help?"

He grinned. "Your help is a definite requirement."

"Then tell me, please, what it is you need assistance with, and I shall be happy to help in any way that I can."

He glanced at Ramsey, who quickly said, "The priest is waiting to speak to you. Do you want him to think you're ill-mannered?"

The possibility that she might have inadvertently insulted a man of God made her blush. "No, of course not," she said hastily. "Good day to you, Father. I'm happy to meet you."

"Good day," he replied with a hint of civility that was gone in the blink of an eye when he continued. "Now, I have a few important questions to ask you to satisfy the Church."

"You wish to satisfy the Church?" she asked, jarred by his sudden abrupt manner and his strange announcement. Surely she hadn't heard correctly.

"I do," he answered emphatically. After pausing to give Brodick what could only be interpreted as an extremely hostile glare, the priest added, "We will not move forward until I know for a certainty that you have not been coerced."

"Father, it's extremely important that I go to—"

Before she could finish her explanation, Ramsey forcefully interrupted. "Didn't Gillian have to climb into a gorge to get Alec Maitland? Iain told me his son was trapped on a ledge."

"She's right in front of you, Ramsey. Ask her," Brodick suggested.

She wasn't paying any attention to the two lairds now. "Father, why would you need to ask—"

"Did you, Gillian?"

Once again Ramsey had interrupted her, and had she not known better, she would have thought that he'd done it on purpose, but that was ridiculous, of course. Unlike Brodick, Ramsey wouldn't deliberately be impertinent. If anything, he was diplomatic to a fault.

"Did I what?" she asked somewhat absentmindedly as she continued to study the priest. Why in heaven's name did she have to satisfy the Church before she could continue on to Ramsey's holding?

Repeating his question, Ramsey demanded that she look at him when she answered. Because he was so insistent, she begged the priest's indulgence before turning her back on him.

"Yes, Ramsey, I did climb into the gorge to get Alec."

Before he could ask her another question, she gave the priest her undivided attention once again. "Father, are you telling me that I cannot go any further until I satisfy the Church? Did I hear you correctly?"

"Yes, milady, that's exactly what I said. No one's going to budge from this very spot until I'm completely satisfied. I mean what I say, Laird," he added with another piercing glare at Brodick.

"You will be satisfied," Brodick assured him.

"I don't understand..." she began.

"I will make certain you do understand," the priest said. "The Buchanans are experts in trickery and deception. They will do whatever it takes to get what they want, and since your parents and your confessor are not here to protect you, I feel it's my duty to speak as your guardian and your priest. Now do you understand?"

She didn't understand at all. She started to shake her head and thought to ask Father why he felt she needed someone to look out for her. Didn't he realize that Brodick was there to help?

"Father, I asked Brodick—"

The priest was so startled, he didn't let her finish. "*You* asked him? Then you weren't coerced?"

Gillian was beginning to think that Father Laggan might be a bit addled in the head. Once again she patiently tried to explain. "If anyone has done any coercing, it is I. Brodick would have gone back home if I hadn't asked him to—"

Brodick cut her off. "She has her own mind, Father. I have neither forced nor manipulated her. Isn't that so, Gillian?"

"Yes, it is so," she agreed. "But Father, I'm still not understanding why you feel it necessary to play my champion. Can you not see that I am in good hands?"

Father Laggan looked as though he wanted to weep for her. "Dear Lady, you cannot possibly know what you're getting into," he cried out, stunned by her calm acquiescence. "Answer me this," he demanded. "Have you ever been to the Buchanan holding?"

"No, I haven't..."

The priest threw up his hands in despair. "There you have it," he said triumphantly and in a near shout.

"What I have seen of the Highlands is very beautiful," she said. "And I imagine that Brodick's land is just as lovely."

"But you've never met any of the savages who call themselves Buchanans, now have you, lass?" the priest asked in a shrill voice.

It was more than apparent that Father Laggan was highly upset, and hoping to soothe him, she responded, "No, I haven't met many of his followers, but I'm sure they're very pleasant people and not savages."

"Dear God above, she thinks they're pleasant. Did you hear her, Ramsey? Did you?"

Ramsey struggled not to laugh when he answered. "I heard, Father, but I would remind you of what Brodick has said. Gillian has her own mind. 'Tis my belief she will find his followers very pleasant."

"How could she—" the priest began.

"She finds the Buchanan laird pleasant enough. He wouldn't be by her side if she did not. Brodick can be quite... charming... when he puts his mind to the task." Ramsey choked on the last of his words and then burst into laughter.

The priest returned to Brodick. "She can't possibly know what's in store for her."

"Are you suggesting that I will not look out for her or that any of my clan will mistreat her?"

Father Laggan realized he'd overstepped his bounds and hastily tried to repair the damage he had done. Raising his hands he said, "No, no, I was merely suggesting... the lass appears to be such a gentle lady... and I cannot imagine how she will survive such a harsh environment."

Gillian couldn't understand what had precipitated this peculiar conversation and why Father Laggan was so obviously distressed. She looked at Brodick, hoping he would explain what in heaven's name was going on, but he ignored her as he spoke to the priest in rapid Gaelic. His brogue was thick, his hostility apparent, and she was horrified that he would speak to a man of the cloth in anger.

He was telling the priest how much Gillian meant to him and that he would die before letting any harm come to her. He knew she didn't understand a word he was saying, but Father Laggan did, and at the moment that was all that mattered.

Brodick was vastly amused when Gillian blurted out, "You mustn't speak to a priest so harshly. God won't like it." Turning to Father, she said, "He doesn't mean to be insolent."

"You need not apologize for me," Brodick said.

"I'm guarding your soul," she snapped.

"You are mindful of his soul?" the priest asked.

"Someone has to be," she answered. "He isn't going to get to heaven without assistance. Surely you realize that, Father, for you have known him longer than I."

"Gillian, enough of this foolish talk," Brodick ordered.

She ignored him. "But he also has a good heart, Father. He just doesn't want anyone to know it."

The priest smiled. "You have seen this goodness within him?"

"Aye," she answered softly. "I have seen it."

The priest squinted as he studied her. "You were raised in a peaceful household?"

"Yes, I was. My uncle's home was very peaceful."

"Yet you're willing..." Father Laggan shook his head. "As I said before, I do not know how

346

you will ever survive in such a harsh environment."

"Father, Brodick and I are going to Ramsey's holding," she said, hoping to correct any misunderstanding.

"But you will not stay there forever," he shouted in frustration. "You will have to go home sometime."

"Yes, of course I will. I must go back to—"

"Gillian, how did you manage it?" Ramsey shouted.

Startled, she turned to him. "Manage what, Ramsey?"

"If you're afraid, how did you manage to climb into the gorge to get Alec?"

"You want to discuss this now?"

"I do."

"But I was just explaining to Father Laggan that I must—"

"Answer Ramsey's question, Gillian," Brodick ordered.

She gave up trying to control the conversation then and there. "How did I climb down to get Alec? It was simple. I closed my eyes."

"It must have been difficult for you. I saw how your face turned gray a few minutes ago when you were close to the ledge."

"I didn't have a choice, and I didn't have much time. Alec's rope was tearing."

"Now, lass, if I could gain your cooperation for a moment, I would like to ask a few pertinent questions," Father Laggan insisted.

At the very same time Ramsey said, "Of course you had a choice. To do something

347

you're so obviously afraid of required bravery."

"Gillian did what needed to be done. Of course she's brave," Brodick said.

She disagreed. "No, I wasn't brave at all. I was so scared I was shaking. And I cried," she thought to add.

"Gillian, you will not argue with me about this. I have said that you are brave, and you will accept that I know what I'm talking about."

She didn't like being contradicted. "Brodick, the pope is infallible. You are not. Therefore, you cannot possibly know—"

"I really would like to continue," the priest urged. "Now, lass, I need to know this. Are you in good standing with the Church?"

"I beg your pardon?"

"He wants to know if you're in good standing with the Church," Brodick repeated.

She looked from one to the other. "I believe I am."

"And when was your last confession?" Laggan asked.

She hesitated.

"Answer him," Brodick ordered.

Her temper flared. "I have asked you not to take that tone with me," she whispered. "I don't like it."

Father Laggan heard her. His mouth dropped open, his eyes bulged, and he stammered, "You dare to criticize Laird Buchanan?"

Embarrassed because he had heard her rebuke, she tried to justify her actions. "He dared to snap at me, Father. You heard him, didn't you? Shouldn't I stand up for myself?"

"Yes, of course you should, but, lass, most women wouldn't. They would fear his retaliation."

She scoffed at the notion. "Brodick would never harm a woman."

Father Laggan surprised her then by laughing. "I have heard it said that there is a special woman for every man, no matter how contrary and barbaric that man might be, and now I must admit that it is certainly so."

"Can we get on with this?" Brodick demanded.

"Yes, of course," Father agreed. "Lady Gillian, I ask you again. When was your last confession?"

She blushed. "It's been a long while."

Laggan didn't like hearing that. "And why haven't you partaken of this most holy sacrament?"

"I must answer these questions before I can continue to Ramsey's?" she asked.

"You must," Ramsey said.

"Father's waiting for your answer," Brodick reminded her.

Her head was beginning to ache. She seemed to be the only one who thought the priest's inquisition was strange, but when she got Brodick alone, she was going to demand that he explain. For the moment, she decided to placate all of them. "I haven't gone to confession because England has been placed under an interdict and priests are not allowed to administer the sacraments except in dire emergencies. Surely you've heard of our pope's...

349

unhappiness... with King John. The two are waging war over who will be the Archbishop of Canterbury."

Father Laggan nodded. "The interdict. Yes, of course. What was I thinking? I forgot you came to us from England. Now then, would you like me to hear your confession now?"

"Now?"

She hadn't meant to shout the question, but she was so appalled by the suggestion that she recount her sins in front of Brodick and Ramsey, and without a veil separating her from Father Laggan, she simply couldn't control her reaction.

"She hasn't done anything to warrant forgiveness," Brodick assured Laggan.

"How would you know?" she asked, clearly rattled.

Brodick laughed. "I know."

She glared at him. "I have sinned," she said, inwardly groaning because she sounded as though she were boasting.

"No, you haven't."

His contradiction was the last she was going to put up with. "I have too," she insisted. "Thanks to you, I've been plagued with impure thoughts, and they've all been about you, so you see? I have too sinned."

Only after the words were spoken did she realize what she had said. "My sins are all your fault, Brodick, and if I have to go to purgatory, then by God, you're going with me. Ramsey, if you do not stop laughing, I swear I shall toss you over this cliff."

"Do you love him, lass?" Father asked.

"I do not," she answered emphatically.

"It isn't a requirement," Laggan pointed out.

"I should hope not," she cried.

"But it would make your life easier," he countered.

"Gillian, you will tell the truth," Brodick demanded.

He grabbed hold of her hand. She tried to pull back, but he wouldn't let go.

"I have told the truth. I don't love Ramsey, and if he doesn't stop laughing at me, the Sinclairs will soon be looking for a new laird."

"Not Ramsey," Laggan shouted so he could be heard over Ramsey's laughter. "I'm asking you if you love Brodick."

"Did you tell Father I love you? Who else did you tell?"

In Brodick's opinion, the question didn't merit an answer. He quietly asked her to tell him again that she loved him.

"Brodick, now is not the time..."

"It's the perfect time."

She didn't agree. "What I said to you was private."

"Do you love me?"

Reluctant to admit the truth in front of an audience hanging on her every word, she bowed her head. "I do not wish to discuss matters of the heart now."

Brodick wouldn't be denied, and after nudging her chin up, he asked her again, "Do you love me?"

He squeezed her hand to get her to respond. "You know that I do," she whispered.

His expression solemn, he pulled the strip of plaid from behind his shoulder and draped the end over their joined hands.

Gillian understood what was happening then. In a panic, she tried to pull her hand free, but Brodick wouldn't let go of her, and after a few seconds of struggling, she stopped fighting.

Her heart belonged to him.

Staring into her eyes, he commanded, "You will give the words."

She stubbornly remained silent. He stubbornly persisted. "I want the words, Gillian. Don't deny me."

She could feel everyone watching her, and she knew how relentless Brodick could be. He would continue to prod her until he had what he wanted. Besides, it wasn't possible for her to deny him her love, and if he needed to hear the words again, then she would say them.

With a sigh she realized she had lost the battle, yet victory was hers. "I love you," she said in the barest of whispers.

"Now and forever?"

She paused for a moment and then put all her worries and fears aside, and made up her mind.

"Yes."

"And I will honor and protect you, Gillian," Brodick said. His hand moved to the back of her neck, and he roughly pulled her close. Out of the corner of her eye she saw Father Laggan raise his hand and make the sign of the cross.

She was powerless to resist when Brodick lowered his head to kiss her. There was such blatant possessiveness in his touch. Her hand stroked the side of his face, and for the moment she ignored her audience and the cheers echoing in her ears. When he finally let go of her, she had to grab hold of the pommel to keep from falling off her horse. She tried to repair her appearance while Brodick tossed the strip of plaid back over his shoulder and secured it in his belt.

She kept waiting for Brodick to say something to her, but he seemed content to remain silent, and so she turned to Father Laggan.

"God be with you," he said.

Ramsey, grinning like a culprit, slapped Brodick's shoulder. "We must celebrate tonight."

"Celebrate what, Ramsey?" she asked innocently.

"You have satisfied the Church."

"Then we may continue on?"

"Yes."

Before she could ask him any further questions, he hastily turned to the priest. "Father, will you be dining with us tonight?"

"I promised Laird MacHugh that I would stop by, but if darkness doesn't catch up with me on my way back, I'll gladly accept your hospitality. 'Tis the truth these old bones of mine have grown accustomed to a warm bed at night. An *empty* warm bed," he added with a glare in Brodick's direction.

"An empty bed will be waiting for you," Ramsey promised with a grin.

After giving Gillian a pitying look, Father Laggan blurted out, "There's still time... it isn't unheard of for a lass to change her mind before it's too late. Lady Gillian, if you should have second thoughts before tonight, or if you should come to your senses and realize the folly—"

"What's done is done, Father. Let it be," Ramsey said.

Laggan's shoulders sagged. "I warn you, Laird Buchanan. I'm going to continue to watch out for her."

Ramsey laughed. "Does that mean you'll break your own vow and return to the Buchanan holding? I seem to remember you telling Iain Maitland that the Buchanans were all heathens and that you would never step foot on their soil again."

"I remember what I said," the priest snapped. "And I certainly haven't forgotten the unfortunate incident. However, my duty's clear to me. I'm going to keep an eye on Lady Gillian, and if I see that she is unhappy or wasting away, then you'll be answering to me, Laird. You'd best take good care of her. You've got a treasure here, you realize."

After giving his passionate speech, Laggan took up his reins and guided his horse through the throng of soldiers. "God be with you," he called out.

Gillian watched the priest ride away, but Brodick tugged on her hair to get her attention. He brushed her curls over her shoulder. "I'll treat you well," he fervently promised.

"I shall make certain that you do," she responded. "Shall we go now?"

Brodick motioned to Dylan to take the lead, then turned to speak to Ramsey. Gillian saw the commander ride ahead to the cliffs. Instantly horrified, she goaded her mount in the opposite direction. One second she was beside Brodick and the next she was halfway down the southern slope.

"Where the hell is she going?" he asked Ramsey as he goaded his stallion into a gallop. He caught up with her, grabbed her reins, and tried to turn her around. She resisted by pushing his hand away and urging her horse forward again.

"You're going the wrong way."

"Is the right way over that cliff?" she asked, frantic.

"Now, Gillian, it isn't..."

"I won't do it."

"If you'll only let me explain..." he patiently began again.

He swore he had never seen anyone, man or woman, move as quickly as Gillian did then. Since she couldn't get him to let go of the reins, she slipped off her horse and was walking at a fast pace away from him before he could summon a good argument to persuade her to take the shortcut.

He caught up with her again. "What do you think you're doing?"

"What does it look like I'm doing? I'm

walking. I feel the need to stretch my legs."

"Give me your hand."

"No."

"It isn't a cliff," he began.

"I'm taking the long way around."

"All right," he agreed.

She came to a quick stop. "Do you mean it? You won't force me?"

"Of course I won't force you. We'll take the long way around."

He let out a shrill whistle and raised his hand. Dylan immediately turned back.

She knew she must be embarrassing Brodick because she couldn't go down a stupid hill. All of the soldiers were watching her, but fortunately they stayed where they were and therefore couldn't hear what she was saying.

"I don't wish to disgrace you in front of your good friend and your soldiers, but I swear that if you make me go down that cliff, I'll do just that."

"As terrified as you are, your concern is in the possibility of disgracing me? Ah, Gillian, you could never disgrace me. We'll take the long way around."

Anxiety blended with relief. "How much longer will it take us?"

"It depends on how fast we ride."

"How long?" she persisted.

"A full day," he admitted as he once again put his hand down to her.

"That long? Even if we hurry?"

"That long," he replied. "Give me your hand."

"I can ride my horse."

"I would rather you ride with me."

She backed away. "Brodick?"

"Yes, lass?"

"I have to go down that cliff, don't I?"

"You don't have to do anything you don't want to do."

She took a deep breath, squared her shoulders, and then clasped hold of his hand. Instead of swinging her up behind him, he changed his mind and lifted her onto his lap.

He could feel her shaking and sought only to comfort her. Wrapping his arms around her, he hugged her tight. "This worry of yours..."

"It's most unreasonable, isn't it?"

"Do you know what has caused this fear? Did something happen that has made you so cautious?"

"Don't you mean cowardly?"

Clasping her chin in his hand, he forced her to look up at him. "Don't ever let me hear you say that about yourself again. You are not a coward. Do you understand?"

"Yes," she agreed.

"Say it," he commanded.

"I'm not a coward. You can stop squeezing me now," she suggested.

She waited until he had relaxed his hold, then said, "I've made up my mind. We'll go down the cliff. We should go last, though," she hastened to add, hoping she'd find a little courage while they waited their turn.

"You're certain?"

"Yes," she insisted, though her voice was so

weak she wasn't sure he heard her. "And I'll ride my own horse," she added in a much stronger voice. "I'll not have your men think I'm a weakling."

"They could never think such a thing," he said as he prodded his horse back up the hill.

He didn't stop at the crest, nor did he slow his stallion's pace as he started down the narrow, winding path that led to Ramsey's holding. She buried her face in his plaid, wrapped her arms around his waist and demanded that he wait until everyone else had gone first.

He told her no.

There was still time to stop before they reached the steepest drop in the path, and she was going to make certain he did just that. She needed time to gather her courage. Why couldn't the mule-headed man understand that?

"I want to be last."

"I like to be first."

"We're going to wait," she demanded shrilly. Panic was making her throat close, and all she could think about was falling down into an endless dark hole and never, ever stopping. The need to scream was overtaking her control, and, God help her, she was either going to throw up or faint at any second.

"Brodick... I can't..."

"Tell me about all those impure thoughts you've been having about me."

"What?"

He patiently repeated the question. His stallion stumbled, rocks trickled down the sheer rock into the mouth of the ravine below, making quite a clatter, but Brodick merely shifted his position in the saddle to help the horse regain his footing, and continued on.

Gillian, hearing the noise, was turning to look down when Brodick asked, "In these impure thoughts, did we have our clothes on?"

Her blush warmed her face. "Our clothes?" she whispered.

"In your fantasies about me..."

"They weren't fantasies."

"Sure they were," he countered cheerfully. "You told Laggan you were having impure daydreams."

"Impure thoughts," she cried out.

"And you also said these... thoughts... were about me. Is that not so?"

"Oh, do be quiet."

He laughed. "So did we?" he asked again.

Her shoulders sagged. "Did we what?"

"Have our clothes on?"

Thoroughly rattled, she shouted, "Of course we had our clothes on."

"Then they couldn't have been very interesting impure thoughts."

"Will you stop talking about this?"

"Why?"

"It isn't proper, that's why."

"I think I have a right to know. You did say your impure thoughts were about me, didn't you?"

"Yes."

"Well then? I want to know what I was doing."

She closed her eyes. "You were kissing me."

"That's it? Nothing else?"

"What did you expect?"

"A whole lot more," he said. "Where was I kissing you?"

"On my lips," she answered. "Now will you stop this—"

"Nowhere else?" he asked, sounding disappointed again. "Shall I tell you about some of my fantasies about you?"

Her eyes widened. "You've had... thoughts... about me?"

"Of course I have, but my daydreams are far more interesting."

"Is that so?"

"Would you like me to tell you about them?"

"No."

He laughed and ignored her protest. "You weren't wearing anything in my fantasies. No, that's not exactly true. You were wearing something."

She knew she shouldn't ask, but she couldn't stop herself. "What was I wearing?"

He bent down and whispered into her ear, "Me."

She jerked back and pushed against his chest with both hands. "Oh, Good Lord," she cried out. "We're both going to land in purgatory if we continue this sinful conversation. How could you know what I look like without my clothes on?"

"A calculated guess," he answered. "You're perfect, by the way."

"No, I'm not."

"Your skin's silky and smooth, and in my fantasies, when I lie between your soft—"

She clasped her hand over his mouth to get him to stop. His eyes sparkled with pure devilment. He was outrageous, and perhaps it was that very trait that drew her to him. Brodick had somehow managed to free himself of all restrictions. He didn't seem to care what anyone else thought about him, and he didn't particularly want to impress anyone.

She wished she could be that free. "Being with you is a... liberating... experience," she whispered.

"That wasn't so bad, was it, milady?"

Gillian jumped at the sound of Dylan's voice. "I beg your pardon?" she asked as she slowly removed her hand from Brodick's mouth. He grabbed it and kissed the palm. Shy all of a sudden, she pulled her hand back before Dylan caught up with them.

"The ride down wasn't so bad, was it?" Dylan repeated.

She glanced up at the rocks, shook her head, and burst into laughter. "No, it wasn't bad at all."

A few minutes later, she was once again riding her own horse. Deciding to take the lead, she nudged the mare into a trot, and as she passed Brodick and Ramsey, she called out, "You used trickery."

"Yes, I did," he admitted. "Are you angry with me?"

She laughed again. "I don't get angry. I get even."

Unbeknownst to her, she had just recited the Buchanan creed.

CHAPTER NINETEEN

Ramsey Sinclair's home was majestic. It sat atop a plateau rising up in the middle of a magnificent valley that was bordered by steep cliffs on one side and lofty, rolling hills on the other. A glistening carpet of grass, sprinkled with the new sprigs of heather the wind had planted, covered the land for as far as the eye could see, and the scent of heather and pine drifted on the afternoon breeze and blended with the pungent aroma of smoke pouring from the thatched cottages. The laird's massive stone castle towered protectively over the houses that dotted the landscape beneath it, and a wall of timber and stone circled the perimeter of the entire community, offering safety to the clan within.

The heavy, iron-hinged gates opened, and Ramsey and his guests entered his estate. A resounding cheer echoed around them as soldiers came running to greet their laird. A fair number of young ladies also came running.

Immediately Gillian was surrounded by Brodick's overly protective guard. Aaron moved in front of her, Dylan and Robert positioned themselves beside her, and Liam rode behind.

As impossible as it was for her to see much of anything with the guards' wide shoulders blocking her view, she still tried to look at every face in the crowd. Though it would be wonderful, as well as miraculous, if she could find Christen immediately, Gillian knew it wasn't going to be that easy. Yet each time she spotted a yellow-haired woman, her heart leapt with that impossible hope.

Brodick and Ramsey had dismounted and were now surrounded by soldiers. Gillian patiently waited for Brodick to remember her.

"Do you see him, milady?" Dylan asked in a low voice.

"Him?"

"The traitor," he whispered.

"No, I'm sorry. I wasn't looking for..." she said as she once again tried to search through the crowd. "Not yet," she whispered back. "There are so many here..."

"Most of Ramsey's men aren't here," Dylan explained. "They are most likely still training in the field behind the castle. Aye, I'm certain they are, or Gideon would be here to greet his laird."

While Gillian continued to look over the crowd, a few curious and bold MacPherson soldiers, wearing their clan's plaid, moved closer to get a better look at her. One young, foolish man dared to step a little too close.

Black Robert nudged his mount forward,

forcing the man to step to the side or be run over. In a voice dripping with venom, he ordered, "You will stop staring at the lady."

The burly soldier glanced at his friends, then turned back to Robert with an insolent sneer on his face. "Or what?" he challenged.

Robert wasn't impressed with the man's bluster. Before the soldier realized his intent, Robert leaned down, grabbed him by the throat and lifted him up to eye level.

"Or I'll break every bone in your body."

The MacPherson soldier was a big man, but Robert had lifted him as though he weighed no more than a twig. The remarkable feat of strength astounded her. And so did his poor manners.

"Robert, please put that boy down."

"As you wish, milady," Robert grumbled.

Brodick happened to turn just as Robert sent the soldier flying. The man landed in the center of his friends. Shaking his head, Brodick threaded his way through the crowd, but stopped in front of the prone and dazed MacPherson.

"Robert?"

"I didn't like the way he was staring at milady, Laird."

The soldier tried to get up, but Brodick put his booted foot on his chest to hold him down. "How was he staring at her?"

"With insolence," Robert answered.

"She's very beautiful," the soldier said somewhat defiantly. "If I want to look upon her, I will."

Brodick glanced down at the man and began to apply pressure on his chest with his foot. "Yes, she is very beautiful," he agreed pleasantly. "But I don't like it when any other man stares at her." Increasing the pressure until the soldier's face was bright red and he was gasping for breath, Brodick added, in a decidedly menacing voice, "I don't like it at all."

Ramsey appeared at his side. "Let him up," he ordered.

Brodick stepped back and watched as the soldier regained his feet. Then Ramsey stepped forward and shoved the man so forcefully he landed on his backside again.

"You will apologize to Laird Buchanan now," he roared.

"Buchanan?" he gasped. "He's Laird Buchanan? I didn't know..."

Ramsey took another threatening step toward him. The soldier scrambled to his feet and blurted, "I apologize, Laird Buchanan. I will not ever look upon your woman again. I swear it on my father's head."

Ramsey wasn't satisfied. He'd noticed that the soldier and his friends were still wearing the MacPherson plaid. "You will wear my colors or you will get the hell off my land."

Gillian watched Ramsey in amazement. Until that moment she had thought he was a mild-mannered gentleman. Judith Maitland had told her that whenever Iain wanted an alliance, he always sent Ramsey as his spokesman to work out the details because he was so diplomatic. He certainly wasn't being diplomatic now. In fact his temper rivaled Brodick's. Knowing that she was the cause of his anger embarrassed her, and she glared at Robert to let him know what she thought about his behavior in inciting the incident, but the soldier defended his actions by whispering, "He was being insolent, milady."

"I did not think he was," she whispered.

"But I did, milady."

The set of his jaw indicated he thought he was right, and Gillian decided not to argue further with him.

"There's Gideon," Aaron said. "You should speak to him, Dylan. Word has it he believes he's your equal."

A large group of soldiers came swarming over the hills on both sides of the castle, and Gillian, squinting against the sunlight, couldn't see their faces.

Robert drew her attention when he remarked, "Gideon is Ramsey's commander. Is he not then Dylan's equal?"

"No one is my equal," Dylan answered as he swung down from his mount. "But I will placate Gideon by lowering myself to speak to him. If you'll excuse me, milady?" Dylan asked as he took the reins in preparation to lead the horse away.

"Of course," she answered. "I, too, would like to dismount, Robert. Would you please move your horse so that I may have room?"

"You must wait for your laird," he answered.

"Aye, you must," Liam agreed as he reined his horse forward to take Dylan's place.

"Milady, you could make it easier for us if you would wear our plaid."

"Make what easier?" she asked.

"Letting them know that you are..."

He suddenly stopped. She prodded, "That I am what?" she asked.

"With us," Robert said.

He was saved from having to give further explanation when Ramsey motioned for him to move his horse so that he could get to Gillian's side.

He lifted her to the ground. "Do not judge my clan by a handful of boys," he cautioned.

"Her feet are on the ground now," Brodick said from behind his friend. "You can let go."

Ramsey ignored him and continued to hold Gillian. "Come inside. It's nearly noon, and you must surely be hungry."

Brodick shoved Ramsey's hand away from Gillian and gestured for her to come to him. Annoyed with his behavior, she stood her ground and made him come to her.

"I'm not hungry," she told Ramsey.

"Then tonight we will have a fine feast," he promised. "But before then, you'll have met every one of my soldiers in the holding. If the man you saw isn't among them, then tomorrow we'll head out to look over the others. It will take time, Gillian," he warned. "Now that the Sinclairs and the MacPhersons have joined, there's a vast amount of land to cover."

"What about her sister?" Brodick asked.

"I would like to meet all the women as

well," she said, slipping her hand into Brodick's. "I know the importance of pointing out the man who betrayed you, and I will do all that I can to help you find him, but I implore you to do the same for me. I must find Christen."

Ramsey nodded. "You have told us that she was taken in by the MacPhersons, and as Iain suggested, the elders will have surely heard about her."

"Then why were the requests for information ignored? King John sent emissaries to all the clans, and no one responded."

Ramsey smiled. "Why would they?"

"I don't understand."

"We don't like King John," Brodick bluntly explained.

"No, we don't," Ramsey agreed.

They continued to walk toward the chiseled stone steps that led up to the broad timbered doors of the castle, the crowd giving them a wide path. Gillian noticed two elderly men hovering near the steps. One was tall and as thin as a walking stick, and the other was but half his size and as round as a full moon. Both men bowed to Ramsey as he strode forward.

After presenting them to her, Ramsey turned to Gillian, "It's my hope that Brisbane and Otis will be able to help you find Christen. Both are MacPhersons."

Ramsey filled the men in on the necessary details about Gillian's sister. "With your memories, I'm sure you'll be able to recall a family taking in a young girl. She would have been around six years old."

"But if the family came to us from the Low-lands with the child, how would we know the lass wasn't actually theirs?" Brisbane said.

"You'd know. You know everything that goes on here. You both would have heard the gossip."

"Perhaps we can be of service to the lady," Otis said. "But I'm wondering why you're helping her, Laird. Has the lady come to mean more to you than she should?"

"She has come to mean a great deal to me," Ramsey said, his voice curt now.

"But she's English." Brisbane pointed out the obvious. "And that is why Otis is concerned, Laird."

"I know what she is," Ramsey said. "Lady Gillian is Brodick's woman, and Brodick is my friend."

The announcement cheered both men. Otis looked vastly relieved. "Then you are not—"

"No," Ramsey interrupted. "Her heart belongs to Brodick."

Brisbane turned to Brodick. "Even though she's English... you still claim her?"

"I do."

Annoyed by the turn in the conversation, Gillian said, "I'm happy to be English."

Otis gave her a sympathetic look. "Ah, lass, you cannot possibly be happy being English, but it's courageous of you to pretend. Come along with me," he added as he motioned Ramsey out of his way so that he could latch onto her arm, "and we will talk about your sister."

Brisbane wasn't about to be left out. "My

369

memory's much stronger than yours, Otis," he said as he took hold of Gillian's other arm, rudely nudging Brodick out of his way. "Why don't we take a stroll around the lake and put our heads together. I do recall one family in particular. They have a lass about your age, and they did come to us from the Lowlands."

Because both men were holding on to her, she couldn't curtsy and beg permission to be excused from her host. She glanced back at Brodick, caught his nod of approval, and then gave her full attention to her escorts as they led her away.

Ramsey and Brodick watched her leave. "She'll be all right?" Brodick asked, though he was already motioning to Robert and Liam to follow.

"Of course she'll be all right," Ramsey replied. "Let your men relax their guard."

"Very well," Brodick agreed, and quickly rescinded his command to his men. He followed Ramsey inside, where a crowd had gathered to speak to their laird.

"Do you think Otis and Brisbane will be able to help Gillian?" he asked.

"The question isn't *if* they can help, but rather, *will* they help." Ramsey poured a cup of wine and handed it to his friend and then poured one for himself. "They probably have a good idea where Christen is," he explained. "But they'll talk to her family before telling Gillian anything. If Christen wants to meet her sister, then they'll arrange it. If not..."

"You'll command it."

"Yes," he agreed. "But it will be difficult. The old men will be stubborn."

"They would seek to protect her because she's a MacPherson?"

"Yes."

"Why would they think they have to protect her from her own sister?"

"Her English sister," Ramsey said. "Stop worrying, Brodick. If Christen is here, we'll find her. Ah, there's Gideon with Dylan. Let me take care of any pressing business, and then we, too, will put our heads together and decide our plans."

An hour passed quickly as Ramsey first listened to the concerns of his clan, then heard Gideon's report on the problems that had arisen while he was away from the holding. He wasn't surprised to hear that the majority of those problems involved the MacPherson soldiers. Ramsey held his patience while Gideon recounted incident after incident on the training fields.

By the time the Sinclair commander was finished listing the grievances, his face was bright red. "You've ordered me to be tolerant," Gideon reminded his laird. "But I tell you this: It's dangerous to allow such insubordination. The leader of this group of misfits grows more powerful with each passing day. When I give an order, the majority of MacPhersons look to him first, and if he gives his nod of approval, then they follow my command. It's unacceptable," he added in a voice shaking with anger.

Ramsey stood calmly in front of the hearth and watched his commander pace about the hall. Brodick leaned against the table as he, too, listened to the tirade against the MacPhersons. Dylan stood beside him.

When Ramsey had heard enough, he raised his hand for silence. "And what would you have me do, Gideon?" he asked softly.

The commander whirled to face his laird. "Throw the bastard out."

"Does the bastard have a name?" Dylan asked.

"Proster," Gideon replied.

"And you want me to banish him?" Ramsey demanded.

"I would rather you let me kill him, Laird, but I would be content if he were cast out."

"What about his followers? What would you have me do to them?"

"The truth?"

"Of course."

Gideon sighed. "I would have you throw them all out. You know I was against this union of clans, Laird, and I do recall telling you that it wouldn't work."

"And you believe your prophecy has been fulfilled?"

"I do."

"You knew there were going to be problems, Gideon. It is your duty to find a way to solve them, but not by casting the misfits out," he added curtly. "Find Proster and send him to me," he commanded then. "I'll deal with him and his cohorts."

Gideon seemed relieved to be rid of the problem and eagerly nodded. "I welcome your interference, Laird, for I swear the troublemakers have pushed me to the wall. I do not have your patience."

No one had Ramsey's patience, Brodick thought to himself. Gideon obviously didn't know his laird well, for if he did, he would have known that under that thin layer of civility and diplomacy beat the heart of a savage warrior whose temper put Brodick's to shame. Unlike Brodick, Ramsey was slow to ignite, but once he had reached his limit or had been prodded too far, his reaction was explosive and most impressive. He could be far more brutal than Brodick, and perhaps that was one of the reasons they had become such good friends. They trusted each other. Aye, Brodick trusted and admired Ramsey as much as he trusted and admired the man who had trained them to be leaders, Iain Maitland.

Now *there* was a ruthless leader, Brodick thought. Iain rarely showed mercy, and was known for his impatience, which was why in the past he had relied on Ramsey to speak on his behalf at council meetings. Whereas Iain would have killed anyone who disagreed with him, Ramsey used persuasion to get what he wanted, and only if and when that didn't work, did he, like Iain and Brodick, resort to brute force.

Once Gideon had aired his complaints, his disposition improved dramatically. "There's one more matter to attend to before you rest," he announced with a grin.

Ramsey raised an eyebrow. "The matter amuses you?"

"Aye, it does," Gideon replied.

Ramsey sighed. "Let me guess," he said. "Does the matter involve our Bridgid Kirk-Connell?"

Gideon laughed. "You're most perceptive, Laird, for it does indeed involve our Bridgid. There has been yet another request for her hand in marriage."

A resigned look on his face, Ramsey asked, "Who is it this time?"

"The soldier's name is Matthias," Gideon said. "He's a MacPherson and I would warn you that if Bridgid agrees to marry him after turning down so many of our worthy and proud Sinclair soldiers, there will be hell to pay."

Now Ramsey laughed. "If Bridgid is anything, she's predictable. We both know she isn't going to agree to have this Matthias, so you needn't worry about the repercussions. Send her in, and I'll put the question to her. I'd like Brodick to meet her."

"Why?" Brodick asked.

"She's... intriguing," Ramsey explained.

"Begging your indulgence, but her mother requests an audience first, Laird. She wishes to speak to you before Bridgid is summoned."

"Is she waiting now?"

"No," Gideon answered. "I'll send someone to fetch her."

"When we're finished," Ramsey said. "I want you to give the order for all the men to gather in the courtyard at sunset. Every single man must attend," he added.

"Accept no excuses," Brodick interjected.

Gideon immediately nodded. "As you wish," he said. He studied Ramsey for several seconds and then asked, "Are you planning to make an announcement then? Do I congratulate you?"

"No," Ramsey replied.

Curious about Gideon's remark, Brodick asked, "Congratulate you on what?"

"I've been asked by the elders to consider marriage to Meggan MacPherson. I still haven't decided what I'm going to do. 'Tis the truth I haven't had time to think about it. I'll admit it would make my life easier if the two clans were joined by marriage."

"You'll break a lot of hearts," Dylan couldn't help remarking. "There were quite a few pretty young ladies following after you, but I noticed none had the courage to come forward and speak to you."

"They usually hound him," Gideon said. "Today, however, they were most timid. I believe I know the reason why they stayed away."

"And what would that reason be?" Brodick asked.

Gideon decided to be blunt. "You, Laird. You were standing with Ramsey, and that's why the women didn't come forward. Though they're clearly besotted with their laird, they're more frightened by you."

Dylan grinned. "'Tis good to know that

you can still make the ladies fainthearted, Brodick."

"We don't have time for foolish banter," Ramsey muttered, clearly uncomfortable with the talk about the young ladies' behavior. Brodick knew it embarrassed Ramsey to be chased after because of the way he looked, and as his friend, Brodick used that knowledge to his advantage. Whenever he could increase Ramsey's discomfort, he did exactly that.

"It must be sheer hell for you to be cursed with such a pretty boy's face," he drawled. "The agony of finding a different woman in your bed every night must wear you thin. I don't know where you get your stamina with this terrible burden you bear."

The muscle in Ramsey's jaw flexed, which pleased Brodick considerably.

"We know you've had as many women in your bed as I have," Ramsey snapped. "But I meant what I said. There are more important matters to discuss."

Weary now, he walked to the table, deliberately shoving Brodick out of his way when he tried to block him and gaining a good laugh from his friend. Motioning to Dylan and Gideon to take their seats, Ramsey sat down at the head of the table, grabbed a pitcher of cold water, poured another drink, and asked the young squire waiting by the doorway to fetch them some warm bread and cheese to ease their hunger until supper was ready.

As soon as the boy left the hall, Ramsey suggested that Brodick fill Gideon in on all that had transpired. "Our commanders are going to have to coordinate their efforts for the attack," he said. "Iain wants Winslow and Dylan and you to handpick the soldiers who'll ride with us into England."

"We're attacking England?" Gideon asked, astonished.

"No," Brodick answered. "Though the thought of it warms my heart."

He leaned back and then told Gideon what had happened and how Gillian had saved Alec Maitland. Gideon had trouble taking it all in. When Brodick finished, the soldier, shaking his head, whispered, "Dear God, it's a miracle Alec survived."

"His miracle was Gillian," Brodick said. "If it were not for her, Alec would be dead."

"And no one would have known there was a traitor in our midst," Ramsey pointed out.

"Who would do such a thing?" Gideon asked the question, then pounded his fist on the tabletop as he offered an answer. "It must be a MacPherson because they are the only ones who would gain in this. There are many who would cheer your death, Laird, and all of them are under Proster's thumb. Though he's little more than a boy, he has gained their loyalty. They are rebels, pure and simple."

"My mind is not so set as yours, and I will be certain before I act," Ramsey said.

He raised his hand for silence as the squire came hurrying into the hall with a platter of bread and cheese. After the boy placed the food on the table, Ramsey ordered him to wait in the kitchens and then resumed the discussion. "We must help Gillian find her sister. I have given her my word."

"It's a certainty that the woman is a MacPherson?" Gideon asked, rubbing his jaw as he considered the matter.

"Yes," Ramsey answered. "Her name's Christen, and she's a few years older than Gillian."

"The family surely changed her name in order to protect her," Brodick interjected.

"Still, I'm hopeful that Brisbane and Otis will know who she is. Nothing escapes their notice."

"I might be able to help," Gideon said. "My father also has a strong memory and knows most of the MacPhersons. He hates them, but he's civil to them," he added. "His sister married a MacPherson. She's dead now, but she was ill-treated by her husband, and my father will never forget that. Still, he would help you, Laird, if he can. If a family took a child in, then my father would most likely know about it. Now that he's feeling better, he detests being confined and this puzzle will help distract him. With your permission, Laird, I'll go to him as soon as possible."

"Gideon's father broke his leg in a bad fall," Ramsey explained to Brodick and Dylan. "It's good news to hear that he's going to mend. For a time, we thought he wasn't going to make it, and Gideon rushed home to be by his side."

"If he cannot walk again, he would rather

die," Gideon commented. "But now there is a glimmer of hope. If you don't need me for a couple of days, I could leave now. I could be halfway there before darkness falls."

"Yes," Ramsey agreed. "The sooner you speak to your father, the better. Brisbane and Otis will take days worrying about their duty to the MacPhersons, and you could be back with the information we need before those old men make up their minds to tell us the truth."

"Christen might come forward on her own," Dylan suggested.

Gideon started to stand up, then changed his mind. "Laird, you said that we'll be riding into England, but where exactly will we be going?"

"We don't know... yet," Ramsey admitted. "Gillian hasn't given us the names of the Englishmen who held Alec captive and made the bargain with the traitor."

Perplexed, Gideon asked, "Why hasn't she told you, Laird?"

Brodick answered. "She has it in her mind that if she tells us who the men are, then we'll attack, leaving her uncle vulnerable. She also worries that I'll force her to stay here."

"But that is what you're going to do, isn't it?" Ramsey asked. "You surely won't allow her to return to England."

"It's complicated," Brodick said. "Gillian's headstrong."

"Which is why you were drawn to her," Ramsey pointed out.

Brodick shook his head. "How can I demand her trust knowing all the while in my heart that I'm going to betray that trust? Hell, I don't know what to do. I don't like the idea of breaking my word to her, but the thought of her in such danger is unacceptable."

"You're going to have to work this out with her and quickly. We need the names," Ramsey said.

Gideon stood and bowed to his laird. "With your permission, I'll take my leave now."

"Give your father my good wishes for a full recovery."

"I will," he promised. He started toward the entrance, then turned. "Laird, with all this news I forgot to ask..."

"Yes?"

"Do you still want the men to gather in the courtyard tonight? I'll have Anthony give the order," he hastily added. "But if you aren't going to announce your decision to marry Meggan, then may I ask why you wish to address your men? Perhaps I should stay."

Ramsey realized then that an important detail had been left out of the telling. "We have an advantage in finding the traitor," he said. "Gillian saw the man as he was riding toward her estates."

"She saw him?" Gideon asked, astonished.

"Aye, she saw the bastard," Dylan confirmed. "From the description of where she was hiding, I'd say she was close enough to spit in his face, but the fool never knew she was there."

"And that's why I want every man to come

to the courtyard. Gillian will look at each one of them, and if the man is there, she'll spot him," Ramsey said.

Gideon shook his head. "And she'll recognize the traitor for a certainty?"

"Yes," Ramsey said.

"Then she must be protected at all costs. If this man knows she can point him out, he'll surely try to silence her before—"

"She's well protected," Dylan announced. "We Buchanans aren't going to let anything happen to her. She belongs to us now."

Gideon blinked. "Lady Gillian belongs to the Buchanans?" he asked Ramsey, confused by Dylan's boast.

His laird nodded. "Aye, she does. She just doesn't know it yet."

CHAPTER TWENTY

Ramsey's audience with Bridgid KirkConnell's mother, Leah, left a bitter taste in his mouth. When the woman had walked into the great hall, Ramsey's first impression of her was positive. Though in her middle years, Leah was still a striking woman. Aye, time had been kind to her. After listening to what she had to say, Ramsey's opinion of her radically changed, and by the time she left the hall, the sight of her sickened him.

He and Brodick had gone to the lake to wash and change into clean clothes, but as soon as he'd heard Leah's petition regarding her daughter, Ramsey felt the sudden need to wash again. Leah's perfidy blasphemed motherhood.

Brodick returned to the hall a few minutes after the encounter frowning, as was his usual inclination, because Gillian was still talking to Brisbane and Otis. He was anxious to hear what news they'd given her. There was also the fact that he wanted her by his side, an admission that made his frown intensify, for even he realized he was acting like an infatuated boy.

He found Ramsey slumped in a chair, his head bowed as though in prayer.

When his friend looked up and Brodick saw his sour expression, he asked, "What ails you? You look like you've swallowed lye."

"I feel as though I have," Ramsey admitted. "I just finished an audience with Bridgid KirkConnell's mother, Leah."

"I take it the meeting didn't go well."

"The woman is foul," Ramsey muttered. "How in God's name am I going to tell Bridgid that her own mother..."

"What?"

He sighed. "Leah's jealous of her daughter," he explained, shaking his head over such a sin.

"Did she say as much?"

"No, but it was very apparent that's the root of her trouble. Leah is newly married, and she doesn't like the way her husband looks at Bridgid. She thinks he lusts after her daughter, and she wants Bridgid out of her house."

"Maybe she's thinking to protect Bridgid," Brodick suggested.

Ramsey shook his head again. "No, her daughter's welfare is the last of her concerns. She went on and on about how old she looks when she's standing near Bridgid."

"For God's sake," Brodick muttered. "Why must you deal with such petty matters?"

"Like you, I, too, must look out for all my clan, and Bridgid is part of my family. Stay and meet her," he urged. "Then you'll understand why I'm so sickened by her mother's behavior."

"Does Bridgid know her mother wants her to leave her home?"

"I don't know," he answered. "Leah sent her to her sister to stay for a spell, using the excuse that Bridgid's aunt needed help with the new baby."

"Then maybe she can return to the aunt's house."

"It was only a temporary solution," Ramsey explained. "The aunt has five children and lives in a small cottage. There simply isn't room for Bridgid."

"Then marriage is the only answer."

"That's the problem," Ramsey said, and then quickly explained about the promise given to Bridgid's father.

"Do you mean to tell me that Bridgid decides who she marries?"

"Unless I break that promise."

"I know you well," Brodick said. "You won't do any such thing."

"So what's the answer to this problem?" he asked. "Got any ideas?"

Brodick thought about it for a moment, then said, "Iain could find a place for her."

"She belongs here. This is her home," he argued. "She would think she was being banished."

"She would adjust."

"I will not hurt her tender feelings. She's done nothing wrong."

Brodick studied Ramsey for several seconds and then said, "You care for this woman, don't you?"

"Of course I care. She's part of my clan."

Brodick smiled. "Then why don't you marry her?"

Ramsey stood up and began to pace in front of the hearth. "Because she's in the Sinclair clan," he explained. "I know my duty. If I am to make this union work between the MacPhersons and the Sinclairs, then I should marry Meggan MacPherson. It makes perfect sense, doesn't it? I get what I want out of the bargain. The MacPherson land is a dowry I cannot turn down."

"You've always been a practical man," Brodick remarked.

"And so were you," he countered, "until Gillian entered your life."

Brodick agreed with a nod. "I never saw it coming."

Because Brodick sounded disgusted with himself, Ramsey laughed. "When exactly did you know..."

Brodick shrugged to cover his discomfort. "When Annie Drummond poured liquid fire on Gillian's open cuts. I held her hand down so that she couldn't move during the atrocious treatment. She never made a sound."

"Ah, so it was her bravery that captivated you."

"No, it was the way she glared at me," he admitted with a laugh. "Honest to God, she looked like she wanted to kill me for making her suffer such an indignity. How could I not become infatuated with such a strong, stubborn woman?"

Anthony put an end to the discussion when he announced that Bridgid KirkConnell was waiting to speak to her laird.

A moment later, Bridgid came inside. The sight of her smile lifted Ramsey's spirits, though he was amazed that she would have anything to smile about.

"Good day, Laird," she called out as she walked forward and curtsied. "And good day to you, Laird Buchanan."

She couldn't quite look Brodick in the eye when she greeted him, as she, too, had heard all the rumors about him and was therefore wary.

Brodick could see that he scared her, but he was impressed that, even so, she moved close to him and curtsied once again.

"Isn't it a fine day?" she asked in an effort to ward off the topic she knew Ramsey wanted to discuss.

"And what's so fine about it?" Ramsey asked.

"Oh, everything, Laird. The sun is bright and the breeze is warm. It's a very fine day."

"Bridgid, I just spoke to your mother..."

She lowered her eyes and clasped her hands behind her back. "Is that so?"

"Yes," he agreed.

"And has she convinced you to break the sacred promise made to my father?"

She deliberately used the word "sacred," Ramsey knew, to make him feel guilty if he had indeed done such a thing.

"No, she has not convinced me to break the promise given to your father."

Bridgid was once again smiling. "Thank you, Laird, but I have taken up too much of your time. With your permission, I'll leave you now," she added.

She was halfway out of the hall before Ramsey stopped her. "You don't have my permission, Bridgid. Come back here. There is an important matter to talk about."

Brodick heard her sigh before she turned around. She obviously knew what the topic was and had hoped to avoid it.

She took her time returning to her laird. And then she simply stood in front of him, looked him in the eye, and waited for him to speak.

"There has been a request for your hand in marriage."

"I graciously decline."

"You don't even know the name of the man who wants to marry you. You cannot decline yet."

"I'm sorry," she said, though she didn't

386

sound the least contrite. "Who is this man?"

"His name is Matthias," Ramsey said. "He's a MacPherson, and I'll admit I don't know much about him. However, I'm certain that if you agree, he will treat you kindly."

He waited a full minute for her to respond, but Bridgid remained stubbornly silent.

"Well?" he demanded. "What say you?"

"May I decline now?"

"For the love of... Do you know this man?"

"Yes, I've met him, Laird."

"Can you not find anything acceptable about him?"

"Oh, I'm sure he has many wonderful qualities."

"Well then?"

"I won't have him."

"Why not?"

"Laird, are you aware you're shouting at me?"

Brodick coughed to cover his laughter. Ramsey shot him a dark look before turning to Bridgid again. He watched her brush an errant lock of hair over her shoulder in a dainty feminine gesture, and for a second he lost his train of thought.

"You try my patience."

"I apologize, Laird. I don't mean to try your patience. May I be excused now? I've just heard that there is a lady here from England, and I must make her acquaintance."

"Why must you?" Brodick asked.

She jumped at the bark in his voice but quickly recovered. "Because I've never been to England," she explained. "And I have a thou-

387

sand questions to ask her. I'm curious to know what life is like in England, and she is the only one who can tell me. I cannot imagine living anywhere but here, and I find myself wondering if she feels the same way about her home in England. I have already decided that I will like her," she added.

"Yes, you will," he predicted.

"You have much in common with Lady Gillian," Ramsey remarked. "You're both stubborn women."

"Is she being forced to marry, then?" Bridgid asked, unable to mask her irritation.

Ramsey took a step toward her. "No one is forcing you to marry, Bridgid."

"Then may I please be excused?"

"No, you may not," Ramsey snapped. "About this Matthias..."

Impatiently settling her hands on her hips, she asked, "Are we back to that?"

"Bridgid, I warn you, I will not tolerate insolence."

She was immediately contrite. "I'm sorry. I know I spoke out of turn, but I have already declined the offer."

Ramsey didn't want to give up. "Do you realize how many requests you've turned down?"

"Yes, I do."

"You've broken many hearts."

"I doubt that, Laird. None of those men know me well enough to have their hearts broken. If I could get them to stop asking, I assure you I would. It's very upsetting for me to have to go through this audience again and again. 'Tis the truth I'm beginning to dread..."

"Dread what?" he asked when she abruptly stopped.

Her face turned pink with embarrassment. "Never mind," she said.

"You may speak freely. Now tell me, what is it you dread?"

"The sight of you," she blurted. "The only time you speak to me is when you want me to hear a proposal. I know how distressing this is for you. You don't wish to waste your valuable time on such inconsequential matters."

"You are not inconsequential."

"But I am difficult, aren't I?"

"Yes, you are."

"Are we finished now?"

"No, we are not. Bridgid, don't you want to get married?"

"Of course I do. I want children," she said, her voice fervent now. "Lots of children, and I'm going to love them the way a mother should."

"Then why have you declined so many requests? If you want to have children—"

She wouldn't let him finish. "I love another."

The announcement took Ramsey by surprise. "You do?"

"Yes, I do."

"Who is this man?"

She shook her head. "I cannot say his name."

"Then marry him," he suggested impatiently.

She sighed. "He hasn't asked me."

"Does he know how you feel?"

"No, he doesn't. He's a very stupid man."

Brodick did laugh then, he couldn't help it. "Yet you love him?" he asked.

She smiled as she answered. "I do. I don't want to love him, but I do, with all my heart. I must be as stupid as he is. That is the only excuse I can give. Matters of the heart are most perplexing, and I'm not smart enough to sort them all out." Turning to Ramsey again, she said, "I will not have Matthias. I won't settle for any man I don't love."

Ramsey's reaction to her announcement puzzled him. When she had admitted she loved another man and therefore wouldn't accept Matthias, he was at first surprised, but that feeling was quickly replaced by what he could only describe as irritation. Though he couldn't figure out why, the thought of her loving someone didn't sit well with him. His reaction didn't make any sense. Here he was trying to persuade her to marry Matthias, and if she had agreed, would he have had the same disappointment? No, he thought, and all because he knew she would never agree.

Shaking himself out of his confusing thoughts, he said, "Tell me who the man is and I will speak to him on your behalf."

"I thank you for your suggestion to help, but the man I love must decide without interference."

"I wasn't making a suggestion. I was giving an order. Tell me his name."

He took another step forward, but Bridgid stood her ground. It wasn't easy. Ramsey was such a big man his nearness was overwhelming, and she had to remind herself that as her laird, it was his duty to protect her, not harm her. She was a loyal member of his family, and like it or not, he had to look out for her best interests. Besides, she knew him to be a kind, generous man. He might scare the breath out of her, but he would never raise a hand against her.

She decided to try to turn his attention in hopes he wouldn't notice she hadn't answered his demand. "Laird, where's Michael? I haven't seen him today, and I had promised him some time ago that I would take him tree climbing."

"Tree climbing?"

"All boys should know how to climb a tree."

"And you think you could show him how it's done?"

She slowly nodded.

"He's staying with the Maitlands," he said. "He and Alec have become good friends, but when Michael returns home, you won't be showing him how to climb a tree. It's unladylike, Bridgid."

"I suppose it is," she agreed reluctantly.

Ramsey once again demanded the name of the man she had declared she loved.

Disgruntled because her ploy to make him forget the question hadn't worked, she said, "I don't wish to tell you his name, Laird."

"That much is obvious," he replied. "But you're still going to tell me."

"No, I'm not."

He couldn't believe she had the audacity to defy him. "I'm not going to give up," he warned. "Tell me his name."

The man was as relentless as a dog chasing after a cat, and she had no one to blame but herself because she had foolishly told him what was in her heart.

"You have an unfair advantage," she said.

"How's that?"

"You're Laird," she said. "You can speak freely, while I—"

He wouldn't let her finish. "You've been speaking freely since the moment you came inside. Now answer my question."

His voice had a definite bite to it, and she flinched. She didn't know how she was going to get out of the corner he had backed her into.

"Unless you order me to..."

"I've already ordered you to give me his name," he reminded her.

His curtness embarrassed her. She lowered her head so he wouldn't see her face and said, "I'm sorry, but I cannot tell you his name."

Ramsey gave up and decided to let the matter go for now. He was disgusted with himself. It wasn't like him to let his temper flare with a woman. Yet, this particular woman did try his patience.

"Is it a sin to defy you, Laird?" she asked.

The question gave him pause. "No, of course not."

She smiled again. "That's good."

He let her see his irritation. "You know damn good and well it isn't."

Ignoring his comment, she said, "I've taken up too much of your valuable time. With your permission, I shall take my leave now."

She curtsied and tried to leave but he stopped her with his next remark. "If you're not going to marry Matthias, then there is another matter I wish to speak to you about."

"There is?"

"Yes."

She waited, but Ramsey couldn't seem to get the words out. How could he crush her by telling her that her mother didn't want her? He couldn't do it.

"I seem to have forgotten..."

Brodick came to his aid. "Michael."

Ramsey glanced at his friend. "Michael?"

Brodick nodded. "You were telling me you were going to ask Bridgid to help you with your brother because of his tender years, remember?"

Ramsey leapt at the idea. "Yes, that was it. Now I remember. Michael's with the Maitlands now."

"Yes, Laird, you already told me he was visiting with his friend."

"Yes, I did," he said, feeling like an idiot. "But when he comes home..."

"Yes?"

Ramsey looked to Brodick for help.

"Ramsey doesn't have time to devote to his brother, and he also feels that Michael needs a woman's influence."

"Yes, that's right," Ramsey agreed. They were

both making up the story as they went along, but Bridgid didn't seem to notice.

"I would be happy to help with Michael."

"Then it's settled."

"What's settled? What exactly do you want me to do?"

"Move in here," he explained. "There are three empty chambers upstairs. Choose one and move your things in as soon as possible. You're going to have to leave your home, of course, and I know that it will be difficult for your mother and you," he added, proud of the fact that he hadn't choked on the lie.

"You want me to live here? Laird, it wouldn't be proper. People would talk."

"Then sleep with the servants in the quarters behind the castle."

She contemplated him for several seconds without saying a word, then slowly nodded. The sadness he saw in her eyes was heartbreaking, and it was then that he realized she understood everything.

Straightening her shoulders, she took a deep breath and said, "I'll be happy to help with Michael, but shouldn't I wait until he returns home before I move my clothes?"

"No, I want you to get settled as soon as possible."

"Then if you'll excuse me, I'll get my things now."

Ramsey granted her permission and watched her walk away. Her proud bearing impressed him, more so because he had seen the tears

394

brimming in her eyes before she turned her back to him.

She paused at the entrance and called out, "Laird?"

"Yes?"

"Don't judge my mother too harshly. She cannot help the way she feels. She's newly married and wishes privacy with her husband. I'm in the way. Besides, it's time that I left home."

"Do you think that's the reason I asked you to move in here? Because your mother wants privacy?"

"Isn't it?" she asked. "What other reason could there be?"

Lust and jealousy, Ramsey thought, but he wasn't about to tell her the shameful truth, that her stepfather lusted after her and her own mother was jealous of her daughter's beauty.

"I've explained my reason. You will help with Michael, and that's all there is to it."

"You're a kind man, Laird," she said. "But..."

"But what?"

Her smile was fleeting. "You really don't lie all that well."

CHAPTER TWENTY-ONE

Nothing was ever easy. After a long and tedious conversation with Brisbane and Otis, Gillian's head was pounding from all of their evasive answers. They were sweet, gentle men, but terribly stubborn. Though neither one of them would admit it to her, it soon became apparent that, while they knew where Christen was, they weren't going to tell until they had spoken to her and gained her permission. Gillian tried to be patient and was finally rewarded when Otis accidentally let it slip that Christen did live on MacPherson land. Gillian's heart leapt with joy, and she began to prod them relentlessly, but to no avail.

So certain was Gillian that Christen would come running as soon as she heard her sister was there, she agreed to wait until the men had talked to her. She begged them to speak to Christen as soon as possible, explaining that time was running out and that she must return to England soon. She didn't tell them why.

Feeling edgy and frustrated after the elders took their leave, Gillian wanted to be alone for a few minutes, and so she took a walk along the stone path that meandered among the buildings of Ramsey's holding. Reaching the top of a hill, she found a shady spot under a tree and sat down. She spread her skirts over the soft tufts of grass and then closed her eyes and cleared her mind, letting the mild, sweet breeze brush against her face. When she opened her eyes again, she took a long look around her. Ramsey's estate was beautiful... and peaceful. Beneath her, the people of his clan carried on the daily routine of their lives. Soldiers sharpened their weapons, while other men bent over their tools, tilling the land for their next crop. Women sat in doorways visiting as they ground the grain for their next loaves of bread, and their children skipped nearby, playing a rambunctious game with a large smooth stone and a stick.

For a brief moment, she was at peace too, taking in the tranquillity of the scene. But then her mind wouldn't let her rest. It raced with all the questions she wanted to ask Christen when she saw her again. She prayed that her sister would remember her, and that her memories would be fond ones. Liese had kept Christen's memory alive with amusing stories about the two of them. She told them over and over again so that Gillian wouldn't forget her sister. Christen didn't have anyone to help her remember, but Gillian hoped that, because she was older, she wouldn't have forgotten.

A woman's shout pulled her from her thoughts, and Gillian turned around just as a young, fair-haired lady came running up the path. Her brow was wrinkled by distress, and Gillian soon understood the reason why, for hot on her trail was a big brute of a man with a look of determination gleaming in his eyes.

On closer inspection, she realized the brute was more boy than man.

"I've told you to leave me alone, Stewart, and I mean what I say. If you don't stop pestering me, I'll..."

She stopped suddenly when she spotted Gillian. Almost immediately, she smiled and hurried forward, oblivious now to her unwanted suitor. Stewart stopped and backed away to listen.

"Good day, milady."

"Good day to you," Gillian replied.

"My name's Bridgid," she said as she curtsied haphazardly. "Don't get up," she added. "You're the lady from England, aren't you?"

"Yes," she answered. "My name's Gillian."

"I've been searching everywhere for you," she said. "I was hoping that if you weren't too busy, you would take a few minutes to answer my questions about England. I'm very curious about the people who live there."

Gillian was surprised and pleased. "I'd be happy to answer your questions, though I must confess you are the very first person I've met who has shown any interest at all in my country. Do you like England then?"

"I don't know if I do or not," she answered with a laugh. "I've heard terrible stories about the English, but I'm determined to find out if they're true or not. The men here tend to exaggerate."

"I can assure you without even hearing those stories that they are false. The people of England are good men and women, and I'm proud to be one of them."

"It's noble of you to defend your countrymen."

"I'm only being honest, not noble. Tell me some of these stories and I will convince you they're false."

"If the stories are exaggerations, then I'll probably change my mind and want to see England one day, though I cannot imagine my laird would allow it. Is your country as beautiful as mine?"

"Oh, yes," Gillian replied. "It's... different, but just as beautiful."

Another soldier had joined Stewart and stood beside him gawking at Bridgid and Gillian. He, too, was little more than a boy. He was tall and gangly with splotches on his face. She thought they were being terribly rude to listen in on their conversation, and she would have shooed them away but Bridgid was ignoring them, and so she decided to do the same.

"My mother told me that husbands living in England must beat their wives every Saturday night so that their women will have done their penance before Sunday mass," Bridgid said.

The lie so amused Gillian she burst into laughter. "That isn't true. Husbands in England are kind and thoughtful and wouldn't ever harm their wives. At least most wouldn't," she qualified. "They're no different than the men who live here. They hold the same values and want the same things for their families."

"I suspected that story was made up," Bridgid admitted. "And now I'll wager the story I was told about the pope was also false."

"What were you told?"

"That our holy father placed an interdict on England."

Gillian's shoulders slumped. "Actually, that's true. The pope is having a disagreement with King John. It will be resolved soon."

"That's not what I heard," Bridgid replied.

"What have you heard?"

"That John will be excommunicated first."

Gillian made the sign of the cross, so atrocious was Bridgid's prediction. "I sincerely hope not," she whispered. "My king has enough troubles on his hands now, what with the barons rebelling."

"Your king makes his own troubles."

"But he is my king," she gently reminded Bridgid. "And it's my duty to be loyal to him."

Bridgid thought about that for a moment and then nodded. "Yes, I, too, would be loyal to my leader unless or until he did something to betray that loyalty. May I sit with you? I've just finished dragging my things to the castle, and I'm exhausted. Besides, I have a hundred more questions to ask you, and I promise none of them concerns your king, for I can see that topic makes you uncomfortable."

"Yes, please do sit with me," Gillian said. Then she spotted Stewart running toward Bridgid. The other young man followed in his wake. "Oh, dear, the scoundrels are coming."

As Gillian stood up, Stewart lunged and grabbed Bridgid around her waist. She let out a yelp and tried to pry his arm away. "Let go of me, Stewart."

"You heard her," Gillian ordered, determined to help. "Get away from her."

Stewart grinned at Gillian. "This here is between Bridgid and me. I'm wanting a kiss, that's all, and then I'll let her go. Maybe I'll steal a kiss from you too. You're as pretty on my eyes as Bridgid is."

"Will you get away from me? You smell like a wet dog," Bridgid muttered.

The young man who had joined Stewart now raced forward. "You already caught a woman. I'll catch the other," he boasted. "And I'll steal a kiss from her."

Stewart howled in pain as he let go of Bridgid and jumped back. Staring down at his arm, he shouted, "You bit me. You little..."

Her hands on her hips, Bridgid whirled around to confront her offender. "You little what?"

"Bitch," he mumbled.

Shocked by the insult, Gillian's hand flew to her throat and she gasped, but Bridgid didn't seem to be the least bit offended. Shaking her head, she said, "If you were not such a stupid little boy, I would immediately report you to our laird, Stewart. Now go away and leave me alone. You're a nuisance."

"You're fair game," he told her.

"I'm no such thing," she scoffed.

"Yes, you are. I saw you carrying your clothes up the hill. Your mother tossed you out on your ear, didn't she? And you ain't married, so that makes you fair game. I'm not a boy," he added, scowling now. "And I mean

401

to prove it to you. I'm getting my kiss, with or without your permission."

"Then I'm getting my kiss too," the other soldier boasted, though Gillian noticed he kept swallowing loudly and glancing over his shoulder, obviously to make sure he wasn't being overheard.

"That boy's name is Donal," Bridgid said. "He's as young and ignorant as Stewart." She leaned into Gillian's side and whispered, "Are you afraid? If you are, I'll call for help."

"I'm not afraid. I am vexed, though. These boys need to learn some manners."

Bridgid grinned. "What say you we toss them down the hill?"

The plan sounded outrageous and fun, and Gillian was sport enough to give it a try. She followed Bridgid's lead and slowly backed up until the two of them were close to the slope.

Donal and Stewart, grinning like lunatics, moved forward. With the crook of her finger, Bridgid bid them to keep coming.

"Do what I do," she whispered to Gillian, and then she ordered Stewart to turn around and close his eyes, promising him that she would give him a reward.

As eager as puppies waiting for a meaty bone, the two boys turned.

"Quit peeking," she ordered. "Close your eyes tight."

"Are you ready?" Gillian asked Donal.

He was vigorously nodding when she gave him a hard shove backward. Bridgid pushed Stewart at the same time. Donal went flying, but Stewart proved to be far more agile. With a shout of victory, he put his foot back to keep from falling, then whirled around to watch his friend rolling down the hill. Bridgid and Gillian seized on his inattention. Lifting their skirts, they kicked him soundly in his backside and sent him on his way.

Unfortunately, Bridgid lost her balance in the process. She'd rolled halfway down the hill before she could stop. Her shrieks of laughter echoed through the treetops. Gillian, thinking to help, chased her, tripped on her own skirt, and ended up crashing into Bridgid.

They were both covered in grass, dirt and leaves, but neither one of them cared. They were so overcome with laughter and making such a racket the soldiers in the fields below paused in their training exercises to look up at them. The women tried to gain control, but when they sat up and spotted Donal and Stewart running away, the sight so amused them, they became hysterical again.

Bridgid wiped the tears away from her face. "I told you they were stupid."

"Yes, you did," Gillian agreed as she staggered to her feet. She heard her blouse rip, looked down, watched her left sleeve fall to her waist, and began to laugh again.

"Do I look as horrible as you do?" Bridgid asked.

"You've got more leaves than hair on your head."

"Stop," Bridgid pleaded. "I cannot laugh anymore. I've got a stitch in my side."

Gillian put her hand down for Bridgid to clasp and pulled her to her feet. Her friend was several inches taller than she was, and she had to look up at her as they walked side by side up the hill.

"You're limping," Bridgid noted. "Did you hurt yourself?"

Gillian began to laugh again. "I've lost my shoe."

Bridgid found it and handed it to her. Just as Gillian was bending down to put the slipper on, Bridgid grabbed her arm and whispered, "Dear Lord, don't look."

"Don't look where?" she asked, squinting against the sunlight at the soldiers below.

"One of the Buchanan soldiers is watching us. Oh, heavens, I think it's their commander. He's standing at the top of the hill. Don't look," she whispered when Gillian tried to turn around. "Do you think he saw what we did?"

Gillian pulled away from Bridgid and turned around to look. "It's Dylan," she said. "Come, I'll introduce you. He's really quite nice."

Bridgid took a step back. "I don't want to meet him. He's a Buchanan."

"Yes, he is."

"Well then, he can't possibly be nice. None of them are," she added with a nod. "But you're from England, and so you wouldn't know..."

"Know what?"

"That they're... ruthless."

Gillian smiled. "Is that so?"

"I'm telling you the truth," Bridgid insisted. "Everyone knows they're all brutal. How could they not be? They follow their leader's example, and Laird Brodick Buchanan is the most frightening man alive. I know what I'm talking about," she insisted. "I could tell you stories that would turn your hair gray. Why, I've known women who have burst into tears just because Laird Buchanan glanced in their direction."

Gillian laughed. "That's absurd."

"It's true," Bridgid continued. "I was in the hall speaking to my laird, and he was there."

"And did he make you cry?"

"No, of course not. I'm not a weakling like some of the women here. But I'll tell you this. I couldn't look him in the eye."

"I promise you, he isn't so fierce."

Bridgid patted Gillian's arm and gave her a look that suggested she thought she was terribly naïve. Then she glanced at the top of the hill again. "Oh, dear, he isn't leaving. I think he's waiting for us."

Gillian latched onto Bridgid's arm and pulled her along, forgetting for the moment that she still held her shoe in her other hand. "I promise you that you'll like Dylan."

Bridgid snorted. "I doubt that. Gillian, do listen to me. Since you're going to be my friend, I must advise you to stay clear of all the Buchanans, especially their laird. He won't hurt you, but he'll scare you half to death."

"I don't scare easily."

"I don't either," she said. "You just don't understand. Take my advice and stay away from him."

"That's going to be difficult."

"Why?"

"I'm betrothed to the man."

Bridgid stumbled and would have fallen down if Gillian hadn't held tight to her arm. Bridgid gasped, then burst into laughter. "For a minute there, I thought you were serious. Do all the people in England have your wicked sense of humor?"

"It's the truth," Gillian insisted. "And I'll prove it to you."

"How?"

"I'll put the question to Dylan, Brodick's commander. He'll tell you."

"You're daft."

"You want to know something else positively shocking?"

"Of course I do."

"I love Brodick."

Bridgid's eyes widened. "You love Laird Buchanan. Are you sure you don't have him mixed up with someone else? All the women love Ramsey. They don't love Brodick," she explained authoritatively.

"I don't love Ramsey. I like him," she replied. "But Brodick—"

Bridgid interrupted her. "You cannot possibly know what you're—"

"Getting into?" Gillian supplied when Bridgid didn't finish her thought. "Odd, but those were Father Laggan's very words to me. I do know what I'm doing, though. If I'm able to accomplish a... task... in England and come back here, I will marry Brodick."

Bridgid kept laughing. She absolutely refused to believe Gillian was serious, so outrageous was the notion that any sane woman would willingly pledge herself to such a man.

They argued all the way up the hill. Bridgid wanted to take a wide path around Dylan, but Gillian wouldn't let her. She made her face the commander.

Dylan did look a little fearsome, she supposed, with his legs braced apart and his arms folded across his chest. He towered over the two of them and appeared to be angry, but Gillian knew it was all bluster.

"Good day, Dylan," she said. "I'd like you to meet my friend, Bridgid. Bridgid, this impressive soldier is Dylan, and he's commander over all the Buchanan soldiers."

Bridgid paled. Bowing her head, she said, "It's a pleasure to meet you, sir."

Dylan didn't say a word, but he did incline his head ever so slightly. Gillian found his arrogance delightful.

"Lady Gillian, what happened to you?"

"You didn't see the men—"

Bridgid shoved an elbow into her side. Dylan's frown intensified. "What men?" he demanded.

She turned to Bridgid. Her friend promptly stepped forward to answer. "The men in the fields. We saw them."

"Didn't you?" Gillian asked.

"Didn't I what, milady?"

"See the men... the men in the fields," she stammered, trying desperately to maintain a straight face.

"Of course I saw them," he replied, clearly exasperated. "I see them now. I'm asking you—"

"But that's what we were doing," Bridgid volunteered.

"Yes," Gillian agreed, nodding vigorously. A dried leaf floated down from her hair in front of her face, and she giggled. "We were watching the soldiers."

"You aren't going to tell me what happened, are you?" he asked.

A dimple appeared in her cheek, and Dylan tried not to notice how attractive it was. She was his laird's woman, and he shouldn't be thinking about anything but protecting her. Still, it was a point of pride that Brodick had managed to capture such a beautiful woman.

"No, I'm not going to tell you."

"But you will tell Brodick, won't you?"

"No, I don't believe I will."

"I'll wager you will."

"Ladies don't make wagers," she replied before turning the subject. "Dylan, I have a request to make."

"I'll do whatever you ask of me," he replied, his tone once again formal.

"I told Bridgid that I was betrothed to Brodick, but she doesn't believe me. Would you please confirm it for her? Why are you looking so surprised?"

"You think you're betrothed to..."

"Brodick," she supplied, worried now because of his poor attempt to cover his amusement.

"I knew you made it up," Bridgid said, nudging Gillian again. "She has a wicked sense of humor," she told Dylan.

"I didn't make it up. Dylan, tell her."

"To my knowledge, milady, you are not betrothed to Laird Buchanan."

"I'm not?" she whispered.

"No, you're not," he confirmed.

Her face turned scarlet. "But I thought... the priest was there... I saw him bless..."

Realizing she had just made a complete fool of herself, she stammered, "Then I was wrong. I would appreciate it if you didn't mention this to Brodick," she hastily added. "I don't want him to think I'm an... idiot. It was just all a misunderstanding, and I thank you for clearing the matter up."

"But, milady—"

She put her hand up. "I really don't want to talk about this any longer."

"As you wish."

Gillian had trouble getting past her embarrassment but tried to pretend that she hadn't thoroughly humiliated herself in front of the commander. Noticing her sleeve was back down at her elbow, she tugged it up to her shoulder and let out a sigh.

"Brodick would like to speak to you," Dylan said, finally remembering why he'd come after Gillian.

Realizing she still held her shoe in her hand, she took hold of Dylan's arm to balance herself as she bent down to put her slipper back on.

"Where is he?"

"In the courtyard with Ramsey."

"Bridgid and I are going to the lake. I really would like to change into clean clothes before I see him."

"Brodick doesn't like to wait, and I'd like for him to see you in your present condition," he admitted with a grin.

"Very well," she agreed.

Bridgid kept silent until Dylan had bowed and taken his leave. "Count yourself blessed," she said.

"I feel like such a fool. I really thought Brodick and I were betrothed. He did ask me to marry him. Honestly. No, that isn't quite true. He told me he was going to marry me."

"You cannot be upset about this."

Gillian shrugged. "I don't know what to think or feel," she said. "Come. We mustn't keep Brodick waiting. He lacks patience."

Bridgid walked by her side along the curving path. "I don't know if I should admire you or feel sorry for you."

"Why?"

"Because you looked disappointed."

"I was embarrassed."

"Oh, I know all about that. Today I was thoroughly humiliated. Did you hear what Stewart said? My mother tossed me out of her home... I thought it was my home too, but she corrected that misconception. If Stewart knows, then everyone else does too. And do you know what's worse?"

"What?"

"My laird knows. He had me move my things to the castle, using the excuse that he needed someone to help with his brother, Michael, but that isn't the reason. It was my mother. She asked him to do something about me."

"Do something?"

"Those were the words she shouted at me while I was packing. She's disgusted with me because I've refused to marry."

Bridgid explained the details, and by the time she was finished, Gillian forgot all about her own embarrassment. "Your mother was wrong to make you leave your home."

"She wants me to be Ramsey's problem," she said. "My mother's newly married, and I'm a difficult daughter."

They strolled along the path, stirring the scent of the bordering flowers with the rustle of their skirts and sharing confidences in whispered voices, as comfortable with one another as if they were already old friends. Neither Bridgid nor Gillian wished to hurry. Bridgid wanted to pour her heart out to someone who wouldn't judge her, and Gillian wanted to forget her own problems for a while.

"So you see, I can't blame my mother. She cannot help the way she feels. I'm weary of talking about my problems. I want to hear more about you. Do you really love Brodick?"

"Yes, I do."

"Have you known him long?"

"Actually, no, I haven't known him long at all."

"There you have it," Bridgid exclaimed.

"When you get to know him, you'll come to realize it was just an infatuation."

Gillian shook her head. "I didn't choose to fall in love with him. It just happened, but I do love him with all my heart."

Bridgid sighed. "I, too, am in love," she admitted.

Gillian glanced at her. "You don't sound very happy about it."

"I'm not. I'm plain miserable, as a matter of fact. I don't want to love him."

"Why not?"

"Because he doesn't love me."

"Are you sure?"

"He's a very stupid man."

Gillian laughed. "Yet you love him."

"I do."

"Who is he?"

"A Sinclair."

"Does he know how you feel about him?"

"No."

"Are you going to tell him you love him?"

"I've given the matter a great deal of thought, and I've tried to get him to... notice me. I've been hoping that he would be perceptive, you see, but thus far he hasn't figured it out."

"I think you should tell him. What have you got to lose?"

"My self-respect, my dignity, my pride, my—"

"Never mind, then."

"I know you're right. I should tell him. If I continue to wait, I'll be an old woman before he gets around to realizing I'm the best thing that ever happened to him. No one will ever love him the way I do. I know all of his faults, and there are many, I assure you, but still I love him."

"When?"

"When what?"

"When will you tell him?"

"Oh, I won't."

"But you just said—"

"That I should tell him. I won't do it, though. What if he doesn't want me to love him? He may not even like me. Come to think of it, I don't believe he does. He's always telling me how difficult and stubborn I am."

"Then he is noticing you, isn't he?"

"Yes, but only as a nuisance. The men here court the ladies. Is it the other way around in England?"

"No, it's the same."

"Then he should chase me, shouldn't he? No, I won't tell him how I feel. When did Brodick tell you he loved you?"

Three soldiers came striding up the path, and Gillian waited until she wouldn't be overheard before she answered, "He hasn't told me he loves me, and to be completely honest, I'm not sure that he does. I know he's fond of me, though."

"Yet you told him you loved him?"

"Yes, I did."

Bridgid was clearly impressed. "You're more courageous than I am. The fear of being rejected pains me to even think about, yet you boldly told Brodick how you felt, even though he hadn't spoken his feelings."

"Actually, he told me I loved him."

Bridgid laughed. "How like a man. They're all arrogant, you know."

"Most are, anyway," Gillian agreed. "But Brodick also happened to be right, and when he pressed me to admit I loved him, I did. I couldn't lie to him."

"And he told you he was going to marry you. It's terribly romantic, but it's also a little... shocking."

"Why?"

"Because he's a Buchanan. May I ask you a personal question... really personal? You don't have to answer it if you don't want to," she hastened to add.

Gillian could hear the hesitation in Bridgid's voice. "What is it you wish to know?"

"Has Brodick ever kissed you?"

"Yes, he has."

"What was it like?"

Now Gillian's face felt warm. "It was very nice," she whispered. She glanced at Bridgid and grinned. "The man can make me shiver just by looking at me."

Bridgid sighed with longing. "I've only been kissed once, and he didn't make me shiver. I wonder what it would feel like if the man I love kissed me."

"Your knees will go weak, your heart will race, and you won't be able to catch your breath. And do you know what else?"

"What?"

"You'll never want the kiss to end."

They sighed in unison, then laughed over

414

their own behavior. Bridgid turned the topic then when she commented, "I have never understood how Ramsey and Brodick could be such close friends. They're nothing alike."

"Oh, I think they have a lot in common."

"No, they don't. Ramsey's generous to a fault, and kind, and thoughtful—"

"So is Brodick," Gillian insisted. "He just growls while he's being generous to a fault and kind and thoughtful. Ah, there's the man of my dreams now," she added with a laugh.

Brodick and Ramsey were crossing the courtyard when they spotted Gillian and Bridgid strolling toward them. The warriors came to an abrupt stop.

"We can't possibly look that bad," Gillian remarked as she brushed her hair over her shoulder.

"Oh, yes, we do," Bridgid replied. She turned to Gillian and tried to help her pull her sleeve up to her shoulder, but the material immediately drooped back down to her elbow.

"What the hell happened to you?" Brodick demanded in a lion's roar.

Bridgid grimaced at the sound of his voice.

"Bridgid, explain yourself," Ramsey demanded.

Gillian leaned into her side and whispered, "What say we toss them down the hill?"

Bridgid bit her lower lip to keep herself from laughing as she followed Gillian across the yard.

"I asked you a question. What happened to you, Gillian?" Brodick repeated.

She stopped several feet away from the men, gave up trying to repair herself and folded her hands together. Bridgid moved to stand by her side.

"What makes you think something happened?" she asked innocently.

Given their appearance, Ramsey thought the question ludicrous.

Brodick wasn't amused, however. He took a step toward Gillian. "Your gown's torn; your face is covered with dirt, and your hair is full of grass and leaves." The smudge on the side of her nose was driving him to distraction. He reached for her chin and used his thumb to wipe the dirt away. The sparkle in her eyes sidetracked him, and he couldn't make himself let go of her. In a much softer voice he asked her yet again to tell him what had happened. "Dylan said that you mentioned something about men on the hill with you. Who were they and what did they do?"

"There weren't any men with Bridgid and me."

"Gillian..."

"There weren't any men with us."

Before he could press her further, she placed her hand on his chest, leaned up on tiptoes, and whispered into his ear. "I was having a lovely time, and that's all there is to it. I missed you, though. Did you miss me?"

"I'm a busy man," he replied gruffly, trying to ignore her wonderful scent. Her hand was warm against his skin, and it occurred to him then how he liked her casual and open show of affection. He'd learned early on to shield his feelings, and it had become second nature for him to back away. She was the complete opposite. All he had to do was look at her face to know exactly what she was thinking and feeling. There was no speciousness or guile in her. She was refreshingly honest, headstrong, and apparently unafraid. She was also irresistible. He hadn't even had time to guard himself; she'd gotten to his heart that quickly.

She tried to step back, but his hand covered hers against his chest.

"Do you think you could spare me a moment of privacy?" she asked.

"For what purpose?"

Her voice dropped to a whisper again, her sweet breath tickling his ear. "I wish to shamelessly throw myself into your arms and kiss you passionately until your head begins to spin."

She kissed him on his cheek and stepped back, looking quite pleased with herself.

"And you believe you can accomplish all of what you have just proclaimed in one minute?"

"I do."

"Accomplish what?" Ramsey asked.

Brodick grinned. "She thinks she can—"

"Brodick!" She cried out his name with a gasp.

"Yes?"

"What I said was private."

Ramsey let the matter go. "Gillian, all of the Sinclairs will gather here at sunset."

She had trouble concentrating. The way Brodick was looking at her made her stomach flutter. It was sinful, really, the effect he had on her.

"I'm sorry. What were you saying?"

"Everyone will be here at sunset," he patiently repeated.

"Men and women?"

"Yes."

"Good."

"Perhaps you'll see your sister then," Bridgid exclaimed.

"Yes," Ramsey replied, smiling over her enthusiasm. Directing his question to Gillian he asked, "Did Brisbane and Otis tell you she was here?"

"Not exactly," she replied. "One of them let it slip that he knew who she was, though, and when I pressed, he said that if the woman was indeed Christen, then she lives on MacPherson land. I don't know how far away that is."

"Not far," Ramsey said.

"If you'll excuse me, I'd like to go to the lake with Bridgid and wash. I must do something about my appearance before sunset."

"Not yet," Brodick said as he grabbed Gillian's hand, practically swept her off her feet, and headed toward the castle. She had to run to keep up.

"What are you doing?" she whispered.

He didn't answer her. Throwing open the door, he gave her a decisive jerk. The entrance was dark and musty when the door slammed shut behind them. She could barely see him as he backed her against the door, braced his hands over her head, and leaned into her. She could feel the heat and strength in him, yet he was so incredibly gentle when he touched her.

"It's your minute, Gillian. Are you going to waste it or are you going to make good your boast."

Suddenly feeling a bit uncertain, she battled her shyness and then slowly reached around his neck and buried her fingers in his hair drawing him closer. Her mouth touched his. Her teeth caught his lower lip and gently tugged on it. She heard his sharp intake of breath and knew her boldness had pleased him. Tightening her grip, she tilted her head back, opened her mouth, and kissed him with uninhibited enthusiasm.

His knees buckled.

Trained to be the aggressor, he couldn't let her have the upper hand. Growling low in his throat, his strong arms lifted her up as his mouth slanted over hers again and again, his tongue sweeping inside to duel with hers, his control damn near shattered when she made that seductive sound of pleasure. He couldn't get enough of her. His hands stroked her back, then moved lower to lift her up against his groin.

They were both panting for breath when she ended the kiss. She clung to him, her faced pressed into his neck as she placed fervent kisses along the column of his throat.

"Don't let go of me," she whispered, knowing that if he did, she'd collapse. The kiss had temporarily robbed her of her strength, and yet all she could think about was kissing him again. She was thoroughly wanton and didn't care a twit.

"Never," he answered. "I'll never let go of you."

He slowly eased her down until her feet were touching the floor again, but he continued to hold her in his arms as he nuzzled the side of her neck. Her sigh was filled with longing.

Reluctant to let go of him, she lay her head down on his shoulder and closed her eyes. Her hand rested over his heart, and she could feel the rapid beat.

"I did make your heart race, didn't I?"

"Yes," he admitted. "You're a temptress, Gillian. You cannot kiss me like that and expect to go on your merry way."

"What would you have me do?"

God, she was innocent. "I'll explain tonight," he promised.

He slowly pulled her arms away from him and reminded her that she was going to the lake with Bridgid.

She had turned toward the doors when he stopped her. "Dylan told me he thought some of the Sinclair soldiers were bothering you."

"There weren't any men with Bridgid and me," she told him once again. "But if there had been and they had been bothering me, I would have handled them."

"No, you would not," he insisted. "You would tell me who they were and I would handle them."

"And what would you do?"

He didn't have to think about his answer long at all. "If any man ever touched you, I would kill him."

The glint in his eyes and the set of his jaw told her he was serious. He suddenly looked quite dangerous. She wasn't the least afraid and she wasn't about to back down.

"You cannot kill—"

He wouldn't let her finish. "It's the Buchanan way," he said emphatically. "You belong to me, and I would not allow any other man to touch you. Now enough of this. There's something I've been meaning to tell you, and now is just as good a time as any."

She waited a long minute for him to continue before she prodded him. "Yes?"

"We do things different here."

"We?"

"The Buchanans," he qualified. "When we want something, we take it."

"That doesn't seem right."

"It doesn't matter if it seems right or not. It's what we do."

"But it does matter. You could get into trouble with the Church if you take something that doesn't belong to you."

"I'm not worried about the Church."

"You should be," she countered.

Gritting his teeth, he said, "Don't argue with me."

"I'm not arguing. I'm simply stating fact. You needn't get surly."

He gripped her shoulders and hauled her

close. "I'm starting over. I'm going to explain, and I want you to follow along."

"Are you insulting me?"

"No, sweetheart. Just listen."

She was so surprised by the endearment, her eyes got misty. "All right," she whispered, "I'll listen. What is it you want to explain?"

"You told me you loved me. You did admit it, didn't you? You can't take the words back."

His vulnerability was showing, and she immediately sought to assure him. "I don't want to take the words back. I do love you."

He relaxed his grip on her arms. "Tonight..."

"Yes?"

"I... that is, we... ah, hell."

"Brodick, what in heaven's name is wrong with you?"

"You," he muttered. "You're what's wrong with me."

She pushed his hands away. "Your moods change with the wind. Now, if you'll excuse me, I have more important things to do than to stand here and listen to you grumble at me." She swung around, pulled the door open with both hands, and marched outside.

He gave up. He knew he'd made a muck of things, but he figured everything would work tonight. Gillian was an astute woman. Surely by the time he'd taken her clothes off her and carried her to bed, she'd have worked it all out in her mind. If not, then he'd tell her.

Ramsey walked inside, saw Brodick, and immediately guessed what had happened. "You still didn't tell her, did you?"

"No, but God knows I tried."

"It's simple enough, Brodick."

"No, it isn't."

"How about, 'Gillian, you're married'? How complicated is that?"

"I'm telling you, I tried, damn it. If you think it's so easy, you tell her."

Ramsey laughed. "By God, you're afraid to tell her, aren't you?"

"Of course not."

"Yes, you are. What do you think she'll do?"

Brodick quit trying to bluster his way through the conversation. "Yes, I am afraid. She'll run. She'll panic, and then she'll try to run. Damn it, I tricked her, and I shouldn't have done that."

"You also deceived a priest."

"Yes, well... I'm more worried about Gillian. I'm telling you, I shouldn't have tricked her. It was wrong."

"But you'd do it again, wouldn't you?"

With a shrug he admitted he would. "Yes. I can't imagine living without her, and if you laugh at me for admitting such a weakness, I swear I'll put my fist through your face."

Ramsey slapped Brodick's shoulder. "Take heart," he suggested.

"What the hell does that mean?"

"Gillian might panic when she first hears she's married to you. Hell, any woman would."

"Ramsey, you're not helping."

"But she won't run, Brodick."

"I'll tell her at supper. Yes," he added with a firm nod, "I'll tell her then."

Brodick all but ripped the door off its hinges as he pulled it open to leave.

CHAPTER TWENTY-TWO

The anticipation of finally being reunited with her older sister was almost more than Gillian could handle. As she dressed to meet Ramsey's followers, her hands actually shook and her stomach felt as though it were filled with butterflies.

She wore a golden colored gown with embroidered threads along the hem of the skirt and the wristband of the fitted sleeves. A servant helped her pleat the Buchanan plaid around her waist and drape one end over her shoulder. The fabric was secured with a braided leather belt.

Gillian still wasn't ready to go downstairs just yet, and so she stayed in the chamber Ramsey had assigned to her at the end of the hallway, pacing back and forth in front of the hearth and rehearsing what she would say when she greeted Christen.

Bridgid was sent up to get her. She opened the door, took a step inside, spotted Gillian in the firelight of the hearth, and came to a sudden stop. "Oh, Gillian, you look beautiful. The color suits you."

"Thank you, but I'm pale in comparison to you."

Bridgid laughed. "Aren't we a pair? Praising one another like silly girls."

"I'm sincere. You look radiant, and the man you love will surely notice you tonight."

Bridgid snorted. "I predict he will continue to look right through me. He always does. I'm getting used to it," she added with a nod. "Are you ready to go downstairs?"

"Yes," she answered as she turned to put her brush back on the chest. She steadied her hands and forced herself to take a deep breath. "I'm so excited about seeing my sister again I'm actually trembling."

"Do you think you'll meet her tonight?"

"I do," she answered. "And I've been practicing what I will say to her. I want our reunion to be perfect, and I want her to like me. Isn't that a foolish worry? Of course she'll like me. I'm her sister, for heaven's sake."

"Come along," Bridgid said then. "We mustn't keep Laird Ramsey waiting. Brodick's with him, by the way, and so are Brisbane and Otis. I'll warn you none of them look very happy. Something's wrong, but no one will tell me what it is. I'll wager it has to do with the MacPhersons, though. That man Proster is always making trouble. Anthony and Faudron are constantly complaining about him and his cohorts."

"Who are Anthony and Faudron?" Gillian asked as she pinched her cheeks for color and followed Bridgid out the doorway.

"They're Gideon's close friends, and Gideon is—"

"Ramsey's commander."

"Yes," Bridgid said. "You rarely see one without the other two, and whenever Gideon is away from the holding, then Anthony takes over his position."

When they reached the bottom step, the door opened and a soldier came hurrying inside. He was tall, thin, and had deep creases in his brow.

"That's Anthony," Bridgid whispered. "I'll introduce you after you've spoken to Ramsey. You shouldn't keep him waiting."

The men were at the far end of the hall. Ramsey and Brodick stood together talking in low whispers while Brisbane and Otis sat at the table watching the lairds. The old men looked as though they'd just lost their best friend. Otis noticed her coming toward them, nudged his friend, and then stood up.

Gillian's smile of greeting faltered when she saw Brodick's expression. He looked furious, and after she had bowed to Ramsey, she folded her hands together and waited to find out what was wrong.

The duty of breaking her heart fell on Brodick's shoulders, and he decided to get it over and done with as quickly as possible. "Your sister has refused to meet with you."

She wouldn't believe what she had just heard. She made him repeat the news.

"Why would she refuse to see me?"

Brodick looked to Brisbane for an answer. The old man scraped his chair on the floor as he pushed it aside and rounded the table.

With a long face, he explained, "She's been a MacPherson for almost as long as she can remember, and she feels no loyalty to England."

"What about her family?" Gillian cried out. "Does she feel no loyalty to me and our Uncle Morgan?"

"Her family is here," Brisbane said. "She has a mother and father and—"

She cut him off. "Her mother and father are buried in England."

Brisbane's shoulders sagged even more than was their usual inclination. "And she has a husband," he hurriedly added. "She is... content."

"Content? She's content?" she repeated in a near shout. The picture of her Uncle Morgan came into her mind and she began to shake with fury. A kind, gentle man's life was at stake, and Gillian didn't care how content Christen was.

She took a step toward Brisbane, but Brodick stopped her by putting his arm around her waist and pulling her into his side.

"Try to understand, Lady Gillian," Brisbane pleaded.

"I don't have time to understand," she countered. "I must speak to my sister as soon as possible."

"Did she tell you she wouldn't see Gillian or did her husband speak for her?" Brodick asked.

The question surprised Brisbane, and he mulled it over for several seconds before admitting, "Her husband explained. She didn't speak at all, but she was there, and she

427

heard every word he said. If she didn't agree, she could have protested."

"Does she know that I only want to talk to her? That I won't make any demands?"

"Yes, I told her that you only wanted to see her again, but I don't think she or her husband believed me. Remember, lass, in the past there have been inquiries about her whereabouts. She fears you'll force her to return to England or tell others where she is."

Gillian put her hand to her forehead. "I would do no such thing."

She leaned into Brodick and tried to think. How could she rid her sister of her fears? And how could Christen believe that her own sister would betray her?

"Ramsey?" Brodick called out. "What the hell are you going to do about this?"

"I'll give her one day to change her mind."

"And if she doesn't?" Brisbane asked.

"Then I'll speak to her on Gillian's behalf. If she still refuses, I'll order her to come forward. If I have to drag her here, I will. I would prefer, however, that she come to this decision on her own."

"Her husband won't like it," Brisbane blurted.

"I don't give a damn if he likes it or not," Ramsey said.

"He's a proud MacPherson." Otis stepped forward to join in the heated discussion.

"He's a Sinclair now," Ramsey snapped. "He pledged his loyalty to me, did he not?"

"All the MacPhersons did," Brisbane said.

428

"The MacPherson soldiers are all loyal to you, Laird," Otis said. "But since you have brought up this issue, I will tell you that every one of them has been made to feel as though they are outcasts, especially the soldiers. Your commander, Gideon, and his soldiers, Anthony and Faudron, constantly ridicule and mock their efforts. The MacPhersons have still not been trained properly, and I tell you this, there will be an insurrection if something isn't done and soon."

Ramsey didn't immediately respond to the fervent speech, but Brodick knew he was furious.

"Are you suggesting that Ramsey pamper or give special consideration to the MacPherson soldiers?" Brodick asked.

Otis shook his head. "I'm suggesting they only be given a fair chance to show their strength."

"Tomorrow I will take charge of the training, and when Gideon returns, I'll discuss the problem with him," Ramsey stated. "Does that satisfy you?"

Otis appeared vastly relieved. "Yes, thank you."

Brisbane sought to be as accommodating as Ramsey. "With your permission, Laird, I would like to return to Lady Gillian's sister first thing in the morning. I'll stress the fact that Lady Gillian has promised me she only wants to talk to her sister." He looked pointedly at Gillian when he made the last remark.

"Yes, that is all I want," she assured him.

After Ramsey agreed, Brodick said, "Brisbane, when you speak to her, make certain her husband isn't in the room. He could be making the decisions for her."

"Why do you think that?" she asked.

"It's what I'd do."

"But why?" she pressed.

"Your sister's husband would certainly try to protect her."

Brisbane rubbed his jaw. "Now that I reflect upon the meeting, I'll tell you I believe that's exactly what happened. I don't believe she had a say in the matter."

What they said made sense, and Gillian began to relax. She grabbed hold of the idea that it was Christen's husband who was denying her and not her sister. She didn't fault the man, for as Brodick had suggested, he was only trying to protect his wife. But she believed with all her heart that if she could just spend a few minutes with Christen, she would be able to put her fears to rest.

"You're going to have to be patient a little longer," Brodick said.

"I don't have time to be patient."

He kissed her forehead and whispered, "I don't want you to worry about this tonight. Put it aside for now. Tonight should be a joyous occasion."

"Why? What happens tonight?"

Her face was turned up toward his, and he simply couldn't resist the temptation. He kissed her sweet, soft lips. Because they weren't alone, he didn't deepen the kiss, but it damn near killed him, and when he pulled back, his frustration was palpable. He wasn't used to denying himself, and even though he only had to wait a few more hours to make her completely his, he was tense in anticipation.

And worried. In truth, he wasn't sure how she was going to react to finding out she was married, and the not knowing was making him as edgy as a caged animal.

He swallowed, took a deep breath, and then said, "Gillian, I have something to tell you." He cleared his throat again and said, "I want you to know that..."

"Yes?"

"You see... damn, your eyes are pretty."

What in heaven's name was the matter with him? If she didn't know better she would have thought he was actually nervous. That was ridiculous of course, because Brodick was one of the most self-assured men she'd ever known. She waited another couple of seconds for him to tell her what was on his mind, then tried to help him. "Did you want to tell me something about tonight?"

Sweat broke out on his brow. "Yes," he said. "It's about tonight." He gripped her arms as he added, "I don't want you to be upset. What's done is done, and you're just going to have to come to terms with it."

Thoroughly confused, she asked, "Come to terms with what?"

He let out a loud sigh. "Hell," he muttered. "I cannot believe I'm having so much trouble getting the words out."

"Brodick, what's going to happen tonight?"

Brisbane and Otis were hanging on their every word, but Ramsey diverted their attention by escorting them outdoors. Having privacy didn't make Brodick's task any easier, and he decided to wait a little longer. He'd do it during supper, he decided. Yes, he'd take her aside and tell her then.

"I asked you a question," she reminded him. "What happens tonight?"

"You're going to make me very happy."

It wasn't what he said but how he said it, in such a sensual gruff whisper, that sent tremors racing through her middle. All he had to do was look at her with those beautiful eyes of his and she melted. His smoldering gaze robbed her of the ability to think. She couldn't even remember what he had just said to her, and since he seemed to need a response, she said on a sigh, "That's nice."

CHAPTER TWENTY-THREE

For the next two hours Gillian stood on the steps with Ramsey at her side as each man came forward to meet her. Brodick stood behind her, and when weariness set in and she began to shift her weight from foot to foot, he coaxed her to lean back against him.

A good number of the followers brought their wives with them, and Gillian noticed that all the females stared starry-eyed at Ramsey and warily at Brodick.

How in heaven's name was she going to find the traitor among so many? Impossible, she thought, as impossible as finding a Highlander who was fond of King John.

It seemed to her that she looked at a thousand faces by the time sunset colored the sky. The light was rapidly fading, and with Ramsey's command, soldiers lit fiery torches around the perimeter of the courtyard and the edge of the path beyond.

"What reason did you give your followers for assembling?" she asked Ramsey in a whisper.

"I didn't give them a reason," he replied. "They're here because I have requested their presence."

His arrogance made her smile. Then Brodick, gruff as usual, suggested she pay attention to the task at hand.

Yet another hour passed as she greeted each man and woman who came forward. Her stomach began to rumble, and she was shivering from the cold breeze, so she pressed her back against Brodick to gain more of his heat.

There was one moment of levity. The two boys who had tried to steal kisses from her and Bridgid came forward together. They looked as though the blood had drained from their faces as both, with eyes bulging, stared at Brodick.

"Good evening, Donal," she said.

The soldier's knees buckled and he went down hard. His friend grabbed him by the arm and hauled him upright, but he never once looked at him. No, his gaze was glued to Brodick.

"Do you know this man?" Ramsey asked.

Donal held his breath while he waited for her to answer. She heard Bridgid laugh.

"Yes, I do know him. I was introduced to him earlier today."

"And the other one?" Brodick asked.

Stewart looked as if he were going to cry. "I met him as well," she said.

"Where did you meet them?" Brodick asked, a decided chill in his voice now. "Were you on the hill by chance?"

She gave him an indirect answer. "Donal and Stewart are friends of Bridgid's. She introduced me to them."

"Gillian..."

She put her hand on top of Brodick's. "Let it go," she whispered.

He decided to let her have her way. The last group to come forward was led by an angry looking young man with an arrogant swagger much like Brodick's. His brown hair hung down in his face as he strutted forward, gave a curt nod to his laird in lieu of a formal bow, and then turned to leave.

Ramsey stopped him. "Proster, come back here."

The soldier stiffened, then did as he was ordered. The young men who had come forward with him quickly moved back to give him room.

"Yes, Laird?"

"You and your friends will train with me tomorrow."

Proster's demeanor changed in a flash. He acted as though he'd just received manna from heaven.

"All of my friends with me now? There are eight of us."

"All of you," Ramsey said.

"And will I have an opportunity to fight you, Laird?"

"You will."

"But eight men against one. It hardly seems fair."

"To you or to me?"

"The numbers are in our favor, not yours," the soldier pointed out.

Ramsey glanced at Brodick. "Are you interested?"

"Definitely," Brodick answered.

Ramsey turned back to the soldier. "Laird Buchanan will join me. Don't worry, Proster. I won't let him kill you or your friends."

The young soldier openly scoffed at the notion. "I look forward to sparring with both of you on the battlefield. Do you wish to fight with weapons or without?"

"You may use your weapons if that is your inclination. Laird Buchanan and I will use our bare hands."

"But, Laird, when I... I mean to say, if I beat you, I want it to be fair."

Ramsey smiled. "I assure you it will be fair," he said. "Be on the field at dawn."

Proster bowed and then went hurrying away with his comrades, no doubt to plan their strategy for tomorrow's games.

Bridgid had watched and listened to the exchange from the side of the steps. She couldn't stop herself from interfering. "Laird?"

"Yes, Bridgid?"

"Proster and his friends will use their swords. How can you defend yourself against them?"

Gillian responded as well. Whirling around to confront Brodick, she said, "Don't you dare hurt those boys."

"You aren't concerned that they will have weapons?"

"We both know that you and Ramsey will rid them of their swords before they've even gotten them out of their scabbards. I mean what I say, Brodick. I don't want you to hurt them. Promise me," she insisted.

He rolled his eyes. "When Ramsey and I are finished with them, their arrogance and insolence will be gone. That I promise you."

Ramsey was in full agreement. "They'll have humility when they leave my battlefield."

The discussion ended when another group of latecomers hurried forward to bow to their laird. Ramsey watched Gillian for some sign of recognition, but she shook her head.

Feeling as though she had somehow failed, she whispered, "I'm sorry. I don't see him."

"I thought for certain you'd recognize one of Proster's friends," Ramsey admitted.

"You don't believe they're loyal to you?"

"They have resisted the union of the clans," he explained. "Still, I find I'm glad it wasn't one of them. They're very young, and I would hate..."

He didn't give her any further explanation, and she didn't press him.

Brodick said what she was thinking. "You're so certain it's a MacPherson?"

"I was," he admitted. "I'm not any longer. Hell, the Hamiltons or the Boswells could be hiding the bastard. Both clans have good reason to want to see the union with the MacPhersons fail."

The men continued to discuss the matter as they went in for the banquet the servants had prepared. Gillian wanted Bridgid to join them at the supper table, but she had disappeared. Gillian didn't see her again until the meal was over.

Her friend motioned to her from the back hallway.

"Gillian, may I have a word in private with you?" Bridgid asked. "I was listening when Brisbane told you that your sister refuses to see you, and I wanted you to know how sorry I am. I know you must be terribly disappointed."

"I was disappointed," she replied. "But I'm still hopeful that she'll change her mind."

"Ramsey will order her to come forward. I heard him say so."

"Yes, but not until the day after tomorrow at the earliest. He wants to give her a chance to do the right thing, I suppose. Still, I hate having to wait."

"If you knew where she lived, what would you do?"

Gillian didn't have to think about her answer. "I would immediately go to her. I don't have unlimited time to wait for her to change her mind."

"I might be able to help you," Bridgid whispered. "Anthony also heard what Brisbane said, and he's offered to follow him tomorrow morning when he goes to plead with your sister again."

"Will he get into trouble for doing me this favor?"

"He thinks he's doing me the favor," Bridgid explained. "Besides, Anthony's second-in-command under Gideon, and he can pretty much do whatever he wants. If anyone gets into trouble, it's going to be me, but I'm not worried because no one's going to find out. Anthony will tell me where she lives, and then I'll tell you. If my laird bows to pressure from Brisbane and decides to delay your meeting with Christen, then you can take matters into your own hands."

"Why would he bow to pressure?"

"Brisbane is an elder in the MacPherson clan, and my laird respects him. He also doesn't want to order Christen if he doesn't have to. Her family has gone to great lengths to make sure her identity has remained secret."

"I'm her family."

"I know," Bridgid whispered. She patted Gillian's hand. "Brisbane could come back with Christen tomorrow."

"But you don't think he will, do you?"

"She's remained hidden for years. No, I don't think she'll willingly come."

"Will you take me to her?"

"Yes."

"I want to go tomorrow afternoon."

"You've been ordered to wait."

"Not ordered," Gillian argued. "Brodick suggested I be patient."

"All right, then. We'll go tomorrow afternoon."

Gillian glanced at Brodick, then whispered, "I'm going to have to figure out a way to get rid of Brodick's men. They follow me like shadows."

"They didn't follow you to the lake."

"No, of course not. They knew I was going to bathe."

Bridgid grinned. "Well then? Simply tell them you're going to the lake."

"I hate having to lie to them. I've become quite fond of Brodick's guard."

"But if we do go to the lake first, then you wouldn't have to lie, would you?"

Gillian burst into laughter. "You have the mind of a criminal."

"What are you two whispering about?" Ramsey called from the table.

"Foolish matters," Bridgid replied. "Laird, Fiona has graciously offered to sew some new gowns for Gillian so that she won't have to borrow from others, but she needs to measure her. Could we see to this chore now? It shouldn't take long."

As soon as they were out of earshot, Ramsey

asked Brodick, "When are you going to get the names of the Englishmen from Gillian? Iain grows impatient. He wants to move, and so do I."

"Tonight," Brodick promised.

"The women have prepared one of the new cottages for you and Gillian, unless you'd rather use one of the chambers upstairs."

"The cottage will afford more privacy," Brodick said. "But I'd rather we stayed outside."

"Your bride deserves a bed on her wedding night," Ramsey said, and Brodick nodded in agreement.

The revelry began with Father Laggan's arrival. Calling out his congratulations, he demanded supper, and while the servants saw to the priest's needs, Brodick paced and waited for Gillian.

In a very short while, the hall was filled with Sinclairs. Brodick's soldiers didn't mingle with the others until kegs of ale were carried in and a rowdy Sinclair boasted that he could arm wrestle any Buchanan to the floor without breaking a sweat. Black Robert meant to prove him wrong, and the game was on.

When Gillian came downstairs, for a second she thought she was back at the Maitlands'. The noise was certainly just as deafening. She stared into a sea of faces and spotted Father Laggan in a corner eating and drinking. He pushed the bench back as he stood to wave and beckon her forward. Gillian grabbed Bridgid's hand and threaded her way toward him.

Ramsey watched Gillian bow to the priest, then nudged Brodick so he'd turn around. "Laggan's with Gillian."

"Ah, hell."

"You really ought to tell her before the priest lets it slip. He's bound to say something."

Brodick pushed through the crowd to get to Gillian. One of the MacPherson soldiers was having a heated argument with a Sinclair, and just as Brodick reached them, the two men lunged with fists at one another.

Ramsey moved forward with lightning speed. "This is a celebration, not a brawl," he muttered in disgust as he grabbed the Sinclair by the back of his neck with one hand and took hold of the MacPherson's neck with his other. With the flick of his wrists he slammed their heads together, then shoved them apart and watched them crash to the floor. The blow rendered both men unconscious.

With a grunt of approval, Brodick continued on. Ramsey ordered the fallen men removed from the hall and then hurried after his friend. Nothing was going to prevent him from seeing Gillian's reaction when Brodick finally found the gumption to tell her the truth.

The priest was busy chiding Bridgid because she was still unmarried. "It's your duty to wed and have children," he said. "It's what God intended."

"I do plan to marry, Father," she countered, a faint blush tingeing her cheeks. "As soon as I am asked by the right man."

"She's in love, Father," Gillian interjected. "And she's hopeful that the man she's given her heart to will marry her."

"Does this man know you would marry him?" the priest asked. He took a long swallow of his drink while he waited for her to answer.

"No, Father, he doesn't know."

It was apparent from the way Bridgid was squirming that she didn't want to talk about marriage any longer, and so Gillian stepped forward.

"Father, I made a foolish mistake today."

The priest scowled. "It's a little late for second thoughts, lass."

"Excuse me?"

"You heard what I said. I asked you if you knew what you were getting into and you said... No, I believe it was Brodick who said that you did. You told me in your own words that you loved him."

He was becoming highly agitated. "It was just a misunderstanding," she said. "But when I asked Dylan, he cleared it up for me."

The priest cocked his head to the side. "What misunderstanding are you talking about?"

"It's silly, really, and embarrassing. You see, when you blessed Brodick and me, I jumped to the conclusion that we were betrothed. I told Bridgid that we were, but she didn't believe me, and so I asked Dylan to confirm it for her. That was the misunderstanding," she added, her voice trailing off, for she had just noticed how dumbfounded Father Laggan looked.

442

The poor man was choking on his wine. He'd taken another drink just as she'd said the word "betrothed."

His eyes bulging, his face bright red, he stammered, "You're telling me... you're saying you thought you were betrothed to the Buchanan?"

Gillian wished he hadn't shouted the question because he'd drawn attention to them. Brodick's guard was already moving toward her. She hastily smiled at Dylan to let him know everything was all right, then turned back to the priest. In a low whisper, she said, "I did think that, but Dylan cleared the matter up for me."

Father Laggan shoved his goblet at Bridgid and then folded his hands together as though in prayer. His gaze piercing now, he demanded, "And how did the commander clear up the matter for you?"

Gillian was thoroughly confused by the priest's behavior. He was acting as though she had just confessed an obscene sin. "He told me I wasn't betrothed."

"She isn't, is she?" Bridgid asked.

"No, she isn't," he snapped. Then in a whisper, he said, "Good Lord Almighty."

"Excuse me?"

"You aren't betrothed, lass..." The priest clasped one of Gillian's hands in both of his and gave her a sympathetic look. "You're married."

"I'm sorry, what did you say?"

"I said you're married," he repeated in a

shout. He was so rattled he could barely control his temper. "That's why I blessed you. You said your vows."

"I did?"

"Yes, you did, lass. I asked you if you had been coerced, and you assured me you hadn't... and there were witnesses."

"Witnesses?" she stupidly repeated.

"Aye," he agreed. "Don't you remember? You and the others had just ridden to the rise above the holding... that's when I joined you, and the Buchanan took hold of your hand..."

"No," she whispered.

"It was proper and binding."

She frantically shook her head. "I cannot be married. I would know if I was... wouldn't I?"

"It was sheer trickery," the priest cried out. "Good Lord Almighty, the Buchanan tricked me, a man of the cloth."

The priest's explanation was finally settling in her mind, and with the realization came a blinding burst of fury that almost knocked her over.

"No!" she shouted.

A servant happened by with a tray full of goblets brimming with wine. Bridgid grabbed one and thrust it into Gillian's hand.

Before she could drink it, the priest snatched it out of her hand and gulped it down. She reached for another. And it was at that precise second that Brodick, with Ramsey hot on his heels, reached her side.

"Gillian—"

She whirled around to face him. "We were married today?"

"Yes," he answered calmly as he took the goblet away from her and handed it to Ramsey.

"On a horse? I was married on a horse?"

Ramsey passed the goblet to Bridgid before turning to Gillian. "We should celebrate this joyous occasion," he suggested with a straight face. Gillian looked as if she wanted to kill the groom; Brodick looked stoic, and the priest appeared to be on the verge of hysteria.

"This can be undone," Father Laggan threatened.

"The hell it can," Brodick snapped.

"What's done is done," Ramsey interjected.

The priest glowered at him. "Has this marriage been consummated?"

Ramsey raised an eyebrow. "You're asking me?"

Gillian's face turned scarlet. Bridgid, taking mercy on her, handed her another full goblet of wine.

Brodick stopped her hand as she raised it to her lips. He grabbed the goblet, thrust it toward Ramsey, and then said, "You will not get drunk. I want you clearheaded tonight."

She was so angry, tears blurred her vision. "How could you?" she whispered. "How could you?" she repeated in a shout.

"You're upset..." Brodick stopped to give Ramsey a hard shove. "This isn't funny, damn it," he muttered.

"You're upset? That's the best you can

come up with to calm your bride?" Ramsey asked.

"I'm not his bride," Gillian cried out.

"Now, sweetheart," Brodick began again without having the faintest idea what he could say that would calm her. "You're going to have to come to terms with this."

"No, I'm not," she declared emphatically.

It was apparent she wasn't in the mood to listen to anything he had to say. When he tried to take her into his arms, she backed away, stepping on Father Laggan's foot in the process.

"I asked a question, and I demand an answer," the priest snapped. "Has this marriage been consummated?"

Since he was staring at Bridgid, she thought he expected her to answer. "I honestly don't know, Father. I don't believe I should know... should I?"

Father Laggan grabbed the goblet out of Ramsey's hand and emptied it in one huge swallow. Ramsey quickly snatched another full goblet from the tray and gave it to the priest.

Laggan, beside himself with the ramifications of the Buchanan's deceit, wasn't paying any attention to what they were doing. "In all my days, I've never... It's the Buchanan who's responsible..." He quit rambling as he reached for the sleeve of his robe and began to vigorously mop his brow. "Good Lord Almighty. What's to be done?"

"On a horse, Brodick?"

"She's having a bit of trouble getting past that fact," Ramsey remarked dryly.

"You could have gotten off the mare," Brodick told her, trying to be reasonable. "If you'd wanted to get married with your feet on the ground, then you should have said something."

She really wanted to throttle him. "But I didn't know I was getting married, did I?"

"Gillian, there isn't any need to shout. I'm standing right in front of you."

She threaded her fingers through her hair in frustration and tried to gain control of herself.

"We knew," Ramsey volunteered.

It suddenly dawned on her that there was an audience watching and listening to every word. She was surrounded by Brodick's guard, and as she glanced from face to face, she vowed that if one man dared to smile, she would start screaming.

"Did all of you know?" she demanded.

Every last one of them nodded. Then Brodick commanded that she look at him. Her eyes blazed with anger when she complied. "I didn't know," she cried out. "You tricked me."

"No, I didn't," he countered. "I told you I was going to marry you, didn't I?"

"Yes, but I—"

He wouldn't let her finish. "And you told me you loved me. Isn't that also true?"

"I've changed my mind."

He took a step toward her and gave her a hard look to show he wasn't happy with her answer. Under his penetrating stare she couldn't continue to lie. "Oh, all right," she relented. "I do love you. There, are you happy now? I love you, but only God knows why because *I* certainly don't. You're the most difficult, stubborn, arrogant, mule-headed man I've ever known."

He seemed unimpressed with her tirade. "We're married now, Gillian," he said in a calm voice that made her want to tear her hair out.

"Not for long," she threatened.

He didn't like hearing that. He looked as if he was going to grab her, so she quickly backed away and put her hand out in a puny attempt to ward him off. "You stay where you are," she demanded. "When you touch me, you know I can't think, and I need to think clearly now so I can figure out what to do."

Ramsey handed the priest yet another drink.

Father Laggan's head was reeling from the Buchanan's trickery and the heavy wine. Believing it was his duty to look out for the poor lass, he mopped the sweat from his forehead with the cowl of his robe and stepped forward to take charge.

"*Has* this marriage been consummated?" he demanded, unaware he'd shouted the question.

Gillian was mortified. "Should you be asking me such a personal question in front of a crowd?"

"I've got to know," the priest whispered loudly. "Lord, it's hot in here," he added, his voice slurred. He then wiped the back of his neck with his hood as he repeated his question. "Was it consummated?"

Gillian answered in a bare whisper. "No."

"Then it's possible that I can undo this tangled mess."

"You'll do no such thing," Brodick commanded.

The priest squinted up at the Buchanan laird and tried to bring the giant into focus. "Good God Almighty, there's two of them." Shaking his head in an effort to clear it, he said, "You used deception to catch this sweet lass."

Brodick didn't deny the allegation but merely shrugged. Father Laggan turned to Gillian to console her in her darkest hour. "You've got to stay away from him, lass, until I can figure out how to straighten this out. Do you understand what I'm telling you? You can't let him touch you if you're truly wanting out of this union. You've just got to stay away from him, lass. I can't stress that enough," he added as he patted her hand. "Once he's... and you've been... well, you see, don't you, I can't have it undone. Do you understand what I'm telling you?"

"Yes, Father, I understand."

"All right, then. Now you sleep on the problem, and tomorrow we'll put our heads together and decide what's to be done. I've never encountered a situation like this before, and it shocks me, yes it does, but I shouldn't be shocked at all because it's the Buchanans you see, and their laird's the worst of the lot. They're all heathens," he added with a nod. "Tricking a man of the cloth. Wait until my superiors hear about this. Why, I'm certain

449

they'll figure out a way to remove the blessing from this union. I just may petition the pope to excommunicate every last one of them."

"Oh, Father, please don't do that. I don't want the Buchanans to get into trouble with the Church."

Brodick heard every word of the exchange and was highly amused by the priest's fervent speech. Leaning toward Ramsey, he asked, "Where is it?"

His friend understood what he wanted to know and in a low whisper answered him.

Gillian's wrath was now directed at Dylan. Poking him in the chest, she demanded, "Why didn't you tell me?"

"You didn't ask me, Lady Buchanan."

"I'm not your Lady Buchanan," she cried out, so rattled her words tripped over each other.

"Don't you want to belong to us, milady?" Robert asked.

"I don't want to belong to anyone."

"Then why did you marry our laird?" Liam asked.

"I didn't know I was marrying him."

"We knew," Aaron cheerfully announced.

"We want to keep you, milady," Stephen interjected. "You love our laird. We all heard you say so."

"Aye, we heard you," Robert agreed. "And you belong to us, milady."

Perhaps it was because they were all pressing in on her looking so earnest and worried that she couldn't hold on to her anger any longer.

She did love Brodick, and she did want to be married to him. Now and forever. Dear God, they'd all made her daft.

Father Laggan sagged onto the bench and braced one hand on his knee. "You'd best bolt your door tonight," he suggested. "Do you understand what I'm telling you? You've got to stay away from him."

"Gillian?"

"Yes, Brodick?"

"I want a word in private with you. Now."

She wasn't given time to think about it. Clasping her hand, he marched out of the hall dragging her along with him.

As soon as the doors closed behind them, a resounding cheer went up. Bridgid was thoroughly perplexed. What in heaven's name was there to cheer about?

Father Laggan had also watched the couple leave. Shaking his head he cried out, "Didn't the lass hear a word I said? Good Lord Almighty."

Ramsey suggested a toast then. Bridgid thought he was crazy. Hadn't he been listening to the conversation? "Laird, I believe you should wait until Laird Brodick and Gillian come back before you give a toast. As to that, why would you toast them? Didn't you hear what Father Laggan said? Tomorrow he's going to... Why are you smiling?"

"Ah, Bridgid, I forgot how innocent and naïve you are," Ramsey said.

"I'm not so naïve."

"Are you waiting for Gillian to come back?"

When she nodded, he laughed. "But you're not naïve?"

"No, I'm not," she insisted.

"Then you understand."

"Understand what?"

He laughed again. "They aren't coming back."

The priest continued to shake his head. "Good Lord Almighty. He's got her now."

CHAPTER TWENTY-FOUR

He swept her off her feet and carried her into the night. She put her arms around his neck and patiently waited for him to tell her where he was taking her. In truth, she had already come to terms with the inevitable. She loved this man with all her heart, and at the moment that was all that mattered.

She traced a line down the side of his face with her fingertip to get his attention. "Brodick?"

"You will not argue with me," he commanded. "You're sleeping with me tonight and every night for the rest of our lives. Understand me?"

She didn't protest or scream, which surprised him.

A moment passed in silence and then she said, "I have just one question for you."

He warily glanced down at her. "What is it?"

"What am I going to tell our children?"

He came to an abrupt stop. "What?"

"You heard me. What am I going to tell our children? I refuse to tell them I married their father while I was riding a horse, but then you'll probably expect me to give birth on a horse too, won't you?"

His eyes were filled with tenderness when he replied to her outrageous question. "I think we should concentrate on making my son before we worry about what we're going to tell him."

She kissed the side of his neck. "Then I'm in trouble."

"Why?" he asked.

"I can't concentrate when I'm around you, but I'll do my best."

He laughed. "That's all a man could want."

"You aren't always going to get your way."

"Sure I am."

"Marriage is about compromise."

"No, it isn't."

She bit his earlobe. "Nothing's changed, you know. I'm still going back to England to finish what I've started."

"Everything's changed, sweetheart..."

Following Ramsey's directions, Brodick veered off the main path and continued down the hill. A gray stone cottage sat at the bottom isolated from the other homes and surrounded by thick, towering pines. He flung the door open and carried his bride inside. Then he kicked the door shut, leaned back against it, and let out a sigh of male satisfaction.

453

The cottage was warm and cozy and smelled faintly of freshly cut wood. A fire crackled in the hearth and gave an amber glow to the room. The mantel was covered with candles, and after putting Gillian down, Brodick went to light them. She stood by the door and watched, suddenly feeling shy and nervous, her attention fully centered on the plaid-covered bed adjacent to the hearth. The cottage had seemed quite roomy until Brodick began to move around. He took up a good deal of the space, and the bed seemed to take up the rest.

Gillian saw her satchel on the floor next to the little table in the corner of the room. She thought she should probably get her sleeping gown out, but then how could she possibly change her clothes with Brodick just a few feet away and no privacy screen to separate them?

She couldn't do it. The walls seemed to be closing in on her. She backed up until she was pressed against the door. Then she reached behind her for the door latch. *Calm down,* she told herself, as she began to take rapid breaths. She was suddenly having difficulty drawing in enough air, and she couldn't understand why. The faster she inhaled, the less air she got.

Brodick took one look at her and knew she was in a panic. He blamed himself, for he had allowed her time to think, and that was his mistake. He went to her, tilted her head up so she could look at him, and then gently pried her hand away from the door. Her

454

panting escalated until she sounded like a trumpeter.

"Having a little trouble, are you, sweetheart?"

The amusement in his tone irritated her. "I cannot breathe," she gasped. "You could show a little sympathy."

He laughed right in her face. Astounded by his callous attitude, she stopped panicking. "Does my fear amuse you, Brodick?"

"Yes, but you love me anyway, don't you?"

His hands moved to her waist, and he pulled her forward as his mouth settled possessively on top of hers. She was tense against him, almost rigid, but he wasn't in any hurry, and after lazily exploring her mouth for long minutes without rushing or making any other demands, he felt her relax in his arms.

He wanted to woo her with sweet, loving words so that she would know how much she meant to him, but he didn't know what to say because he was unschooled in the gentle ways of seduction. He was a warrior, a savage and a heathen, just as Father Laggan had said, and for the first time in his life, he wished that he knew the poetic jargon that came so easily to Ramsey.

He was making a sacrifice for her. Going slowly was a first for him, but important and necessary because she was a virgin and he knew she had to be scared of the unknown.

He was driving her crazy with his gentle caresses and his sweet kisses. Tearing her mouth away from his, she demanded that he

455

stop teasing her. She pulled on his hair and sought his mouth again and was richly rewarded for her impatience. With a low growl mingled with laughter, he gave her what she wanted. He kissed her hungrily and deeply, his tongue stroking and coaxing, and she began to tingle everywhere. Her heart pounded, her stomach fluttered, and she was suddenly gripping his shoulders so that she wouldn't fall down.

Lord, did he know how to kiss. She moved restlessly against him, giving him all the encouragement he needed, and he continued to devour her as he quickly undressed her. So consumed was she by the passion he elicited, she didn't realize what he was doing until he was pulling her undergarment down over her arms.

She tried to push his hands away and tell him to wait until she was under the covers, but he kept kissing her and tugging on her clothes, and before she could draw a breath and demand that he wait, it was too late and she was stripped bare. How he had managed to get her shoes and stockings off without her knowing was beyond her.

He'd removed his own clothes too. She realized that when he roughly wrapped his arms around her and pulled her against his chest. He groaned from the touch of her soft breasts against him; she sighed from the heat of his body against hers.

His hands were suddenly all over her. He stroked her shoulders, the curve of her spine, her silky thighs.

Their kisses became wild, ravenous, and when they drew apart, they were both panting for more. Gripping her shoulders, he whispered, "You set me on fire."

She didn't know if that was good or bad, and she didn't care. She wrapped her arms around his middle and kissed him with all the longing and passion he had ignited inside her.

Brodick was shaken to the core, for he had never had a woman react the way his sweet bride did. He buried his face in her neck, inhaled her womanly scent, and believed that this was as close to heaven as he was ever going to get.

"Damn," he whispered again. "We've got to slow down."

"Why?" she demanded.

It took all he had to concentrate enough to answer her. "Because I want this to be perfect for you."

She stroked his back, nearly overwhelmed by the strength in him. She could feel his muscles rippling under his skin, and, Lord, the heat of his body pressed intimately against hers was making her so incredibly hot she wanted to close her eyes and let the feelings rioting through her body take control.

"It already is perfect," she whispered. "Take me to bed now."

Her beautiful green eyes were misted with passion. Arrogantly pleased that he could rattle her as much as she rattled him, he lifted her into his arms and carried her to bed.

Her hands shook when she cupped his face

and sought his mouth again for another deep kiss. He didn't stop kissing her as he tore the covers back and fell into bed with her cushioned in his arms, then gently rolled her onto her back and covered her with his body. The feel of her soft skin was almost more than he could bear, and he actually shook with his desire. She was pinned beneath him, but he braced his arms on either side of her so that his weight wouldn't crush her. Her glorious hair spilled across the plaid, and when he lifted his head and looked at her, he saw that she was smiling.

"I've got you right where I want you, Brodick," she whispered.

"Nay, my sweet, I've got you where I want you." And then he began to nuzzle the side of her neck, as he once again tried to think of the poetic words she deserved to hear. "You please me, Gillian."

She tilted her head to give him better access to her neck, shivering when he kissed the sensitive spot just below her ear.

"Tell me what you like," he ordered gruffly.

With a sigh of longing, she answered, "You. I like you."

He continued his tender assault on her senses, stroking and kissing her until she nearly was consumed. Her toes rubbed against his legs restlessly, and she began to caress his back, loving the feel of his hard body under her fingertips. How could anyone this strong be so amazingly gentle?

His touch became more demanding and far more intimate, jarring her out of her sweet lassitude. His hands stroked her thighs, then moved between to caress the heat of her. She nearly came off the bed. She tried to move his hand away, but he silenced her protest with another deep kiss. And still he continued his erotic love play until she was shaking with her need.

She gripped his shoulders, kissing him almost frantically now, desperately wanting to please him as much as he was pleasing her, but she didn't know what she was supposed to do, and she couldn't seem to think long enough to ask.

He was driving her out of her mind, and she could feel her control slowly slipping away. Frightened by the intensity of the raw emotions erupting inside her, she cried out, "Brodick, are we supposed to be doing this?"

He slowly moved down her body, his mouth hot against her skin as he placed wet kisses along her collarbone.

"Hush, love, it's all right. We can do whatever we want to do," he said in a ragged voice. He tried to control his pace, but it was the most difficult thing he'd ever had to do. His heart was pounding furiously, and he was hard and hot. He was throbbing with his need to be inside her.

Loving her was going to be the death of him, but damn, he'd die happy.

"I want to please you," he whispered. "Tell

me," he demanded as one hand slid down between the fragrant valley of her breasts. "Does this make you happy?"

A scant second after asking the question, his mouth covered her breast. She reacted as though she'd just been struck by hot, white lightning. She sucked in her breath, groaned low in her throat, and dug her fingernails into his shoulders.

She squeezed her eyes shut and breathlessly answered him. "Oh, yes, that makes me happy."

He nipped the skin above her navel, causing the muscles to flex. Her indrawn breath told him she liked that too, and so he did it again.

"Then this is going to make you delirious," he said, using the promise she had often used on him. He slowly moved lower, caressing and kissing her intimately until she was writhing in his arms.

Never in her wildest fantasies had she ever imagined making love to be like this. She never could have believed she'd completely lose her control either, but she did just that. He wouldn't let her hold back, and as he made love to her with his mouth, she arched up against him, screamed his name, and scored his shoulders with her nails.

Her response fueled his own. He couldn't wait any longer to make her his. His hands shook, and he wasn't at all gentle as he pushed her legs apart and positioned himself between her thighs. Covering her mouth with his, his hands gripping her hips, he tried to enter her slowly, thinking that it would be less painful for her, but then she moved ever so slightly, and that was all it took. He was lost. Thrusting deep, he penetrated her completely and captured her soft cry with another hungry kiss. His tongue delved into her sweet mouth to coax a response and make her forget the pain he had caused.

He stayed completely still, his discipline in threads now, and burying his face in the crook of her neck, he took deep, ragged breaths to try to make himself slow down. She needed time to adjust to his invasion, but damn, it was killing him not to move. She was so hot and wet and tight and perfect. He knew he'd hurt her, and he hoped to God that the pain would soon be forgotten. Damn, she felt good.

The pain had taken her breath away, but it receded almost immediately. The feel of him inside of her thrilled and frightened her. He made her throb with desire for more, but Brodick wasn't moving, and he seemed to be having trouble breathing. She began to worry that she hadn't pleased him at all.

"Brodick?" she whispered his name, letting him hear the fear in her voice.

"It's all right, love. Just don't move... just let me... ah, hell, you moved..."

She had shifted slightly, then gasped, shocked by the incredible sensation the movement caused. A burst of raw pleasure coursed through her body so intensely she cried out. She tried to lie perfectly still, but she couldn't control the fire burning inside her now. She moved again and the pleasure intensified.

He groaned in reaction. He was planted solidly inside her, yet still he tried to temper the ravenous demands of his body. Then she moved again, and the battle to take it slow and easy was lost. His discipline vanished. He slowly withdrew, then sank deep inside her again.

She thought that was the most amazingly wonderful thing he had ever done. She became wild, for the erotic feelings controlled her movements now. Instinctively she drew her legs up to take him deeper inside. The more aggressive he became, the more uninhibited she became until she was mindless to anything but finding a release to the burning sensations. Sobbing his name over and over again, she clung to him when the first tremors ignited, squeezing him tightly inside her.

Terrified by the magnitude of her climax, she tried to stop it, but he wouldn't let her retreat. He stoked the fires of passion with each hard thrust. She screamed his name as wave after wave of ecstasy poured over her, and only then when he knew she had found her fulfillment did he give in to his own. With an almost violent shudder, he thrust deep and poured his seed into her.

He didn't move for long minutes. The only sound was harsh panting as each tried to recover. Gillian was overcome by what had just happened. She continued to hold on to him as she tried to calm her racing heart.

Brodick wanted to kiss her and tell her how much she had pleased him, but he couldn't find the strength to move. He heard her whisper, "Good Lord Almighty," and he laughed, but he still couldn't make himself move, and so he kissed her earlobe and stayed where he was.

"I knew you'd be good, but damn, Gillian, I didn't know you'd kill me."

"Then I made you happy?"

He laughed again and finally lifted his head and looked at her. Her eyes were still misty with passion, she looked thoroughly ravaged, and he suddenly thought it might be a good idea to make love to her again.

"Yes, you made me very happy."

"I didn't know... when you... and then I... I didn't know we could do... what we did... I didn't know."

His hands cupped the sides of her face, and he kissed her lazily and thoroughly. When he shifted his position ever so slightly, his chest hairs tickled her breasts, and she sighed in reaction. He kissed her again then rolled to his side and pulled her into his arms.

He felt an overpowering possessiveness. He didn't know how he had managed to capture her or why she loved him, but she belonged to him now. She was his wife and for the rest of his life he would protect and cherish her.

She stroked his chest as she snuggled closer to him and closed her eyes. She was just drifting off to sleep when a sudden thought jarred her wide awake. "Brodick, what am I going to tell Father Laggan tomorrow?"

In graphic detail, using every lusty word he

could think of, he described what they had just done and then suggested she simply repeat those words to the priest.

She told him she'd do no such thing, and after mulling the matter over in her mind for several minutes, she decided she wasn't going to tell him anything at all.

"I don't want Father to remove the blessing," she worried out loud.

With a yawn, he answered, "He won't."

"You tell him."

"All right," he agreed. "Now you tell me."

"Tell you what?" she whispered.

"That you love me. I want to hear the words again."

"I love you."

She fell asleep waiting for him to tell her that he loved her.

CHAPTER TWENTY-FIVE

Loving Brodick was exhausting. She didn't get much sleep that night, unaccustomed as she was to having a man in her bed, a big man at that, who took up most of the space. Every time she tried to move, she bumped into him. She finally slept pinned under one of his hard thighs.

Brodick wasn't used to sleeping in a bed, and so he had just as much trouble. It was too soft, and he much preferred the ground out-doors with the brisk wind cooling his body and the stars to gaze at until he drifted off, but he wasn't about to leave his bride on their wedding night, and so he stayed where he was and dozed off and on. In between he made love to her. He tried to be gentle because he knew he'd hurt her the first time he'd mated with her, and Gillian was too sleepy at first to resist him; then she was too caught up in the magic of his touch to care if he hurt her or not.

She was dead to the world when he finally got out of bed. He was late meeting Ramsey on the field—dawn had already come and gone—and after kissing Gillian on her fore-head, he covered her with the plaid blanket and then quietly left the cottage.

The training session went well in spite of the fact that he was in such a good mood. He really didn't want to hurt anyone. Ramsey did most of the damage and impressed the MacPherson boys in no time at all. Brodick did accidentally break the nose of one of the MacPherson soldiers with his elbow, but he snapped it back in place with his hand before the soldier could regain his feet and told him he'd be as good as new once the bleeding stopped. It wasn't an apology, but it was damned close, and Brodick began to worry that marriage had already turned him into milk toast.

Ramsey of course noticed his cheerful dis-position. He took great delight in ribbing him about showing up late and yawning every other minute until Brodick seriously considered breaking one of Ramsey's bones.

When the training session had begun, Proster, the leader of the faction, refused to use a weapon against the laird. He was being honorable, and foolish, for though he was vastly superior to the other MacPherson soldiers in skill and technique, he wasn't by any means Ramsey's equal. After his laird had knocked him to his knees a couple of times, Proster's cloak of arrogance began to shred. All of the other soldiers reached for their swords, thinking that would give them the advantage, but Proster still stubbornly refused.

It didn't really matter, though. Brodick and Ramsey quickly disarmed all of the soldiers, and then got down to the business of teaching them how to stay alive on the battlefield. It was a lesson in humility, and by the time the two lairds strolled off the field, the ground behind them was littered with groaning bodies.

The two friends went to the lake to wash the blood off them. They passed Bridgid on their way back. She greeted Ramsey with a curt nod, smiled at Brodick and wished him a good day, and then continued on with her head held high.

"What was that all about?" Brodick asked. "She seems irritated with you."

Ramsey laughed. "That's an understatement. She's furious with me, but because I'm her laird, she has to be civil. I think it must

466

be killing her. Did you see the fire in her eyes? She's something else, isn't she? That smile of hers could make a man..."

"What?" Brodick prodded.

"Never mind."

"You want her, don't you?"

Ramsey didn't have to guard his words with his friend, and so he was bluntly honest. "Sure I want her. Hell, she's a beautiful woman, and most of the men here want to bed her. God help the man she ends up with, though, for I swear she'll lead him a merry chase."

"Are you going to tell me what happened?"

Sighing, Ramsey admitted, "I embarrassed Bridgid. The widow Marion wanted to warm my bed," he explained. "Bridgid must have seen her going into my chamber and she went in after her. Honest to God, Brodick, I've never seen such a temper in a woman before. Bridgid rivals you," he added. "Poor Marion wanted to be discreet and had gone to considerable trouble making certain no one knew she was going to share my bed, and then Bridgid marched in there and made such a ruckus, all hell broke loose. Marion had already gotten undressed and was waiting in bed for me, and that shocked the hell out of Bridgid, and it also infuriated her. She thought I was being... duped. Will you stop laughing so I can finish this?"

"Sorry," Brodick said, though he didn't sound the least contrite. "What happened then?"

"Bridgid dragged Marion out of bed, that's

467

what happened. By the time I got upstairs, Marion was running down the back steps, screaming at the top of her lungs and only barely clothed. Fortunately the hall was almost empty and Father Laggan had already passed out."

"And?"

"I slept alone."

Brodick laughed again. "No wonder you're in such a foul mood today."

"That I am," he agreed. "Bridgid seemed to think that I should have thanked her for saving me from Marion."

"But you didn't."

"Hell, no, I didn't."

"Did you explain that you had invited Marion to share your bed?"

"Yes, I did, but that was a mistake. I'm never going to understand women," he said, his voice bleak now. "I swear Bridgid looked... wounded. I hurt her and I..."

"What?"

Ramsey shook his head. "Bridgid is innocent and naïve."

"But you still want her in your bed, don't you?"

"I don't take virgins to my bed. I would never dishonor Bridgid in such a way."

"Then marry her."

"It's not that simple, Brodick."

"You still getting pressured to marry one of the MacPhersons?"

"Meggan MacPherson," he countered. "And I am still considering it. It would solve a lot of problems, and I have to do my duty as laird. I want their land and resources, and I also want peace. It seems the only way to get that is to join the clans by marriage."

"What's this woman like?"

"Admirable," he replied. "She wants the best for her clan. She's strong and stubborn," he added. "But she doesn't have Bridgid's..."

"What?"

"Fire."

"When will you decide?"

"Soon," he replied. "Enough talk about me," he added as he turned the conversation to what he considered a much more serious matter. "Did Gillian give you the names of the Englishmen?"

"No."

"Why the hell not?"

"I forgot to ask," he admitted sheepishly.

Incredulous, Ramsey stared at him for several seconds and then snapped, "How could you forget?"

"I was busy."

"Doing what?" Ramsey asked before he realized how foolish the question was. Now he sounded as naïve as Bridgid.

Brodick glanced at him. "What the hell do you think I was doing?"

"What I wasn't," Ramsey replied drolly.

They walked along in silence, each lost in his own thoughts. Brodick had always been able to tell his friend whatever was on his mind, but he was hesitant now as he asked his advice.

"Marriage changes a man, doesn't it?"

"You should ask Iain that question, not me. I've never been married."

"But you're more astute about these matters than I am, and Iain's not here."

"Matters of the heart?"

"Yes."

"You've only been married one day," Ramsey pointed out. "What is it you're worried about?"

"I'm not worried."

"Yes, you are. Tell me."

"I've just noticed..."

"What?" Ramsey asked in exasperation.

"I'm... cheerful, damn it."

Ramsey laughed. Brodick didn't appreciate his friend's reaction. "Look, forget I said anything. I'm not used to talking about such..."

"You never talk about what you're thinking or feeling. I shouldn't have laughed. Now tell me."

"I just did," he growled. "I mean it, I'm cheerful, God help me."

"That is unusual," he admitted.

"That's what I mean. I've been married one day and marriage is already changing me. Gillian confuses me. I knew I wanted her, but I didn't know I'd become so possessive."

"You were possessive of her before you married her."

"Yes, well, it's worse now."

"She's your wife. It's probably just a natural inclination."

"No, it's more than that. I want to take her home and—"

Ramsey cut him off. "You can't, not yet. She's got to help me find the bastard who tried to kill my brother."

"I know she needs to stay here, but I still want to take her home, and if I could, I swear I'd keep her under lock and key," he admitted, shaking his head over his own foolish thoughts.

"So she'd be safe."

"Yes, and also because I don't like other men..."

"Staring at her? She's a beautiful woman."

"I'm not the jealous sort."

"Sure you are."

"She's turned my mind upside down."

"You sound like a man in love with his wife."

"Lovesick men are weak men."

"Only if they were weak before they fell in love," Ramsey said. "Iain loves his wife. Would you consider him weak?"

"No, of course not."

"Then it stands to reason that love doesn't make a man less than what he already is."

"It makes him vulnerable."

"Perhaps it does," Ramsey agreed.

"And if his mind is constantly consumed with thoughts of her, then he becomes weak. Is that not so?"

Ramsey smiled. "I'll tell you what is so. You love her, Brodick, and that scares the hell out of you."

"I should have broken your nose."

"Get the names first; then you can try. Are you certain that she'll tell you who they are?"

"Of course she will. She's my wife, and she'll do whatever I tell her to do."

"I wouldn't use those exact words when you talk to her. Wives don't like being told what to do by their husbands."

"I know Gillian," he said. "She won't refuse me. I'll have the names of all the Englishmen by sundown."

CHAPTER TWENTY-SIX

No one was more surprised than Brodick when his sweet, she'll-do-whatever-I-tell-her-to-do wife refused to give him the names of the Englishmen.

Astounded that she would deny him, he was at a loss as to what to do next. Gillian sat at the table with her hands folded in her lap, as calm as could be in the eye of his storm.

"What do you mean, no?" he demanded.

"You forgot to kiss me when you came inside. I think you should."

"What?"

"You forgot to kiss me."

"For the love of..."

He hauled her to her feet, planted a hard kiss on her mouth, and then sat her back down again. "You're going to tell me who those bastards in England are."

"Yes," she agreed, and then qualified her answer. "Eventually."

"What does that mean?"

She refused to answer. She picked up her brush and ran it through her hair. Damn, she looked pretty tonight, he thought. She wore a flowing blue sleeping gown that delicately clung to her soft curves. Her cheeks were pink, her eyes were bright, and she smelled like roses. The woman was nearly irresistible. He glanced at the bed, then back at her before he realized where his thoughts were leading.

It was already way past sunset, and he still hadn't gotten the names from her, though in truth, he hadn't seen her since he'd left at dawn, and he'd been too busy until this minute to think about it. Now, however, he was determined to get what he wanted before they went to bed, and with that thought in mind, he said, "A wife must do whatever her husband orders her to do."

The command didn't sit well with her. "This wife doesn't."

"Damn it, Gillian, don't turn stubborn on me."

"A husband doesn't curse in his wife's presence."

"This husband does," he snapped.

She didn't like hearing that either. Tossing her brush on the table, she got up and took the long way around him to get to the bed. Then she kicked her slippers off and sat down.

Ramsey had been right after all. Some wives

473

really didn't like taking orders from their husbands, and Gillian obviously fit into that category. He noticed the tears brimming in her eyes and knew he'd injured her feelings. Marriage was far more difficult than he'd anticipated.

"Don't do that."

"Do what?"

"Cry."

"I wouldn't think of it," she haughtily replied. She stood up, pulled the covers back, and got into bed.

He blew out the candles and was going to bank the fire in the hearth when she asked him to please add another log. "It's hot in here."

"I'm cold."

"I'll keep you warm."

When he sat on the bed to take his boots off, she rolled to her side to face the wall. In a whisper, she asked, "Are you sorry you married me?"

The question caught him off guard. Gillian was obviously feeling a bit insecure, and he knew he was responsible because he'd been acting like a bear from the moment he'd joined her.

"It's too soon to tell," he told her with a straight face.

She didn't appreciate the humor. "Are you sorry?"

He put his hand on her hip and forced her to turn toward him. "I'm sorry you're so stubborn, but I'm happy I married you."

"You aren't acting happy."

"You defied me."

"And you aren't accustomed to anyone refusing you, are you?"

He shrugged. "'Tis the truth I'm not."

"Brodick, when we are with others, I will never argue with you, but when we are alone, I will tell you exactly what's on my mind."

He thought about that for a moment and then nodded. "Did something happen tonight that's upset you? When I left you this morning, you were happy."

"When you left, I was sleeping."

"Aye, but you had a smile on your face," he teased. "You were no doubt dreaming about me."

"As a matter of fact, I've had an aggravating day."

"Tell me about it," he suggested.

"You really want to hear my complaints?" she asked, amazed.

His nod was all the encouragement she needed, and she sat up and proceeded to tell him everything. "First, Ramsey made me sit in the hall all morning long and look at face after face as more of his followers came inside. Then when I still hadn't found the man who betrayed him, he dragged me all over kingdom come to look at more faces. He was too busy to speak to Christen on my behalf," she added. "And Brisbane had already come back to report that my sister still hasn't changed her mind. I'm not going to continue to be patient, Brodick. I'm giving Ramsey until noon tomorrow to order Christen to come forward, and if he doesn't, then I'm going to take matters into my own hands."

She took a deep breath and then continued. "I finally met Bridgid at the lake, but it was already close to suppertime by then, and when she joined me, she had disappointing news."

"What was her news?" he asked.

"She asked a friend to follow Brisbane to find out where Christen lives, but the friend didn't return to the holding. Bridgid thinks he forgot."

Brodick stood up and stretched. Gillian watched the muscles across his shoulders flex and was taken aback by the sheer might of his body. Then he removed his belt and stripped out of his clothes, and she promptly lost her train of thought altogether. Her husband was so incredibly beautiful.

"So you thought that if you knew where Christen lived, you would simply go to her?"

He waited a long minute for her to answer, then repeated the question.

"Yes," she stammered, flustered. "That's what I thought."

"Christen's a MacPherson and now part of the Sinclair clan."

"I realize that."

"Ramsey's her laird and you shouldn't interfere. Let him handle this. He promised you he'd force her to see you."

He dropped to the bed on his stomach, his weight all but knocking her to the floor.

Though he was loath to admit it, he was exhausted.

"Ramsey promised me he'd talk to her today, but he didn't."

With a loud yawn, he said, "He's a busy man, Gillian."

"I know he is. People are constantly hounding him with problems, and the women here won't leave him alone. They make up all sorts of petty worries just so they can talk to him. It must drive him to distraction. Still, he promised me, Brodick, and he has until noon tomorrow to speak to Christen."

He didn't want her to stop talking because he loved the husky sound of her voice.

"What else happened today?"

"I hid from Father Laggan," she confessed. Brodick laughed, and she had to wait until he'd stopped to ask, "Did you perchance have an opportunity to speak to him?"

"Yes," he replied. "He had a hell of a hang-over."

"Ramsey got him drunk on purpose, didn't he?"

"Laggan was already well on his way, but Ramsey helped."

"That's a sin," she decided. "Why did he do it?"

"Because he's my good friend and he knew that one way or another, I was going to take you to my bed."

She put her hand on his shoulder, noticed how tense he was, and began to rub his muscles. He groaned with pleasure, and so she pulled her gown up, straddled his hips, and used both hands to work the tension out of him.

"Damn, that feels good."

She was also feeling relaxed, and she realized it was because she had shared her day with Brodick. "What did you do today?"

"I went home."

"But you told me your holding is a long way from here."

"I rode hard," he said. "But it was past sunset by the time I got back."

"What did you do at home?"

"Settled a few problems," he said.

She remembered another bit of news to share with him then. "Do you know what Bridgid told me today?"

"What's that?"

"A woman tried to sneak into Ramsey's room... at least that's what Bridgid thought. So she went in after her, and the sinful woman had taken her clothes off and was going to... you know."

Grinning, he said, "No, tell me."

"Seduce Ramsey, of course. Bridgid threw her out and made quite a scene. Now she's furious with her laird because he bluntly told her he had invited the woman to share his bed. If he's going to have women parading into his bedroom every night, Bridgid's made up her mind to leave."

"And where will she go?"

"We discussed that very problem on the way to chapel. We wanted to light a candle for Gideon's father and another one for Ramsey's soul. Bridgid is convinced he's on his way to purgatory."

The heat of her thighs pressed against his was starting to interfere with his ability to concentrate. "Why would you light a candle for Gideon's father? You don't know the man."

"Because the poor man took a turn for the worse. Bridgid heard Faudron tell Ramsey so when he was explaining why Gideon has been delayed. Faudron and Anthony will share the commander's duties until he returns."

"You've got a good heart, lass."

"Wouldn't you light a candle for me if I were dying?"

"Do not talk about such things. I would not let you die," he said vehemently.

She leaned down and kissed his shoulder. "I told Bridgid she could come and live with the Buchanans. She tried to hide her reaction to my suggestion, but it was obvious she was horrified by the idea. Isn't that peculiar?"

"It would be a difficult adjustment for her. Ramsey treats his followers like children. I don't."

"I won't have a difficult adjustment."

"Yes, you will."

"No, I won't, because you'll be there. I don't care where I live or how I live as long as you are by my side."

He was humbled by her faith and love. "Now that I'm married, I'll have to make some changes," he remarked.

"Such as?"

"You'll probably want a home."

"You don't have a home now?"

"No."

"Where do you sleep?" she asked, trying not to sound appalled.

"On the ground. I much prefer it to a soft bed."

"But what do you do when it rains?"

Her voice sounded strained, and he knew she was having difficulty staying calm. Her hands weren't rubbing his shoulders now; they were pounding them.

"I get wet."

She began to pray he wasn't serious. "What about your followers? Do they also sleep outside?"

"Some do, but the married men live in cottages like this one with their women."

"Why doesn't their laird?"

"I've had no need for one."

"You do now. I don't want to sleep outside."

"You will sleep with me."

"Yes, but I want a home."

"Like Ramsey's?" he asked.

"No," she answered. "It doesn't have to be grand. One just like this cottage would be nice."

She stopped rubbing his shoulders and traced a crescent-shaped scar below his right shoulder. "How did you get this?"

"I don't remember. It happened a long time ago."

"It must have hurt," she said. She kissed the jagged gray line, noticed his muscles tightened, and kissed him again. Then she stretched out on top of him and put her head down on his shoulder.

He groaned. "You're killing me, Gillian."

"Am I too heavy for you?"

"That isn't what I mean. If you don't stop wiggling, I'm going to make love to you, and I know you're tender."

The heat radiating from his body warmed her. "Not so very tender," she whispered. "And you weren't worried about that during the night."

"Then you remember? I thought you slept through it."

She knew he was teasing her. "Yes, I did sleep through it. It must have been a dream that made me scream."

"Aye, you were screaming," he agreed, smiling over the memory. "I made you burn, didn't I?"

"How would I know? I was asleep."

She began to stroke his arms, loving the feel of him. "You're so hard," she whispered.

She was far more accurate than she realized. He was hard from wanting her, but he was pleased by her boldness and curiosity.

"Brodick?"

"Yes?"

"Could we... if you're not too tired and you didn't have to move... could I..."

"Could you what?" he asked.

She finally got up the courage to get the words out. "Could I make love to you?"

"But I won't have to move?"

"No," she insisted.

He laughed. "Sweetheart, moving is a definite requirement."

Her hands caressed the sinewy ripples of his back as she slowly moved down his body. She wanted to kiss him everywhere.

"Gillian," he began gruffly.

"Hush," she whispered. "I'm making love to you this time. You said I could."

"May I offer a suggestion?"

"What is it?"

"It'll work better if you let me turn over."

He rolled onto his back, grabbed her, and kissed her hungrily as he helped her untie the ribbon of her gown and watched her blush as she pulled the gown over her head and tossed it aside.

"You are so beautiful," he whispered. He kissed her again.

The teasing ended then as passion flared. Trembling in his arms, she became more demanding. He entered her swiftly, completely, and the pleasure was so intense, so blissful, he closed his eyes and groaned loudly, "Lord, you feel good."

And then he began to move within her, slowly, deliberately until she was writhing out of control. The thrilling sensations drove him on, and when he felt her tighten around him and heard her cry his name, he climaxed deep inside her.

Spent, he collapsed on top of her and stayed there long minutes until his heart stopped slamming inside his chest and he could draw a decent breath.

"You've exhausted me," he whispered gruffly as he rolled to his side and pulled her up against him. Her back was against his chest and her sweet derriere was pressed against his groin. The scent of their love-making clung to their bodies; the only sound was that of the logs crackling in the hearth and Gillian's occasional sigh.

"I had no idea I was going to like this so much."

"I did," he told her. "I knew the first time I kissed you. I could feel the passion in you. I knew you were going to be wild, and I was right."

"Because I love you," she said. "I don't think I'd be so... free... with any other man."

"You aren't ever going to find out," he said. "No other man will ever touch you."

Before he could get riled up, she soothed him. "I don't want any other man. I want only you. I love you, now and forever."

Her fervent words pleased him. Lifting her hand, he kissed her wrist. "Does this still bother you?" he asked as he looked at the scars puckering her skin.

"No," she answered. She tried to pull her hand away then. "But it's unsightly."

He kissed her ear. "Nothing about you is unsightly."

And then he proceeded to kiss every mark on her arm, and by the time he reached her elbow, she was shivering.

Just as Gillian was contentedly drifting off to sleep, he nudged her. "Do you trust me?"

"You know that I do."

"Then give me the names of the Englishmen."

She was suddenly wide awake. Turning in his arms, she looked into his eyes. "I want you to promise me something first."

"What is it?"

She sat up, pulled the covers around her, and leaned against the wall. "You know that I have to return to England. You understood that before you married me, didn't you?"

He knew where this was leading and frowned. "Yes," he agreed. "I knew you wanted to return to England."

"I'll give you their names after you promise me you and Iain and Ramsey won't retaliate until I've accomplished my goal and my Uncle Morgan is safe. You're a man of your word, Brodick. Promise me."

"Gillian, I cannot let you go back. You'd be walking into a death trap, and I can't—"

"You cannot stop me."

"Yes, I can." His voice was forceful now, angry. He sat up and roughly pulled her into his arms.

"I have to go."

"No."

"Brodick, Morgan is now your uncle too, and it's your duty to look out for him, isn't it?"

"I'll find him for you, Gillian, and see that no harm comes to him."

She shook her head. "You wouldn't know where to look. I have to go back and finish this."

He tried to reason with her. "You told me that the bastard demanded you return with the king's box and your sister. You will be going back empty-handed. How then can you expect to save your uncle?"

"The baron's far more interested in getting the jeweled box back than anything else. I'm going to try to convince him that my sister's dead."

"But you don't have the box, do you? And you don't know where the hell it is, remember?"

"I'm praying that my sister remembers," she said quietly.

"And if she doesn't?"

"I don't know," she cried out. "I have to go back. My uncle's life is at stake. Why won't you understand?"

"I can't let you put yourself in such jeopardy. If anything happened to you..." His voice shook, and he couldn't go on, couldn't even think about Gillian being hurt without shuddering. "I wouldn't like it," he muttered.

"Promise me, Brodick."

"No."

"Be reasonable," she demanded.

"I am being reasonable. You aren't."

"You knew... before you married me... you knew what I had to do."

"Gillian, things have changed."

She tried another strategy. "You could protect me. You could make certain I was safe, couldn't you?" He didn't answer her. "If you and Ramsey and Iain came with me, I would be very safe. After I've found out where my uncle is, then you could retaliate... but not before."

"So it's your plan to walk into the demon's den alone? You're out of your mind if you think..."

"You could make it safe for me."

She wasn't going to bend, and he had to have the names.

"All right," he finally agreed, but before she could get excited over his promise, he qualified it.

"If your sister has the box or knows where it is and you then have something to bargain with, and if you do exactly what I tell you to do when we get there, then I'll let you go with us."

"And you will wait until my uncle is safe to retaliate?"

"Yes. I give you my word."

She was so pleased she kissed him. "Thank you."

"I swear to God, Gillian, if anything happens to you, I could not live with it."

"You'll protect me."

Heaven help him, he was already regretting his promise. How in God's name could he let her near the bastards?

She put her head down on his shoulder. "There are three of them," she whispered, and felt him tense in reaction. "All of them are barons and close friends of King John. When they were boys, their antics amused him. Baron Alford of Lockmiere is the most powerful. He's the adviser to the king. My Uncle Morgan told me that he was the one who introduced Arianna to John, and for that reason alone, John will always protect him. You're going to have to be very cunning and careful, Brodick. The king will not care what your reasons are if you harm Alford."

"Is Alford the one who killed your father and laid claim to your estates?"

"Yes," she answered. "He's called Alford the Red because of the color of his hair and his temperament. He's the one who struck the bargain with the Highlander, but he had help from the other two. Hugh of Barlowe and Edwin the Bald are always at Alford's beck and call. Both have estates adjacent to Alford's."

"Where is Alford now?"

"Waiting for me in Dunhanshire," she answered.

"Do you think your uncle is there as well?"

"I don't know."

"You're going to have to accept the possibility that Alford has already killed your uncle."

"No," she replied. "Oh, I know Alford would if he could and not suffer a minute of remorse, and I've heard him proudly declare that he has never kept his word, but he needs to keep my uncle alive in order to gain my cooperation. Alford knows he won't get the box unless he can produce my uncle... and in good health... first."

"And then he's going to try to kill both of you."

"You won't let that happen."

"No, I won't," he agreed. "This is a dangerous game you're playing, Gillian, and I promised to let you go with us if you had something to bargain with."

"You'll take me with you," she said. "With or without the box."

Brodick didn't agree or disagree. For the next hour he made her describe in minute detail both her Uncle Morgan's estate and Dunhanshire, and once he was satisfied, he questioned her about the number of soldiers under Alford's command.

It was past midnight when he finally let her rest. She fell asleep sprawled on top of him, safe and protected in his arms.

He stayed awake another hour while he formulated his plans, and when he finally fell asleep, he dreamed of killing the man who had dared to touch her.

Aye, he dreamed of revenge.

CHAPTER TWENTY-SEVEN

Gillian was sick and tired of waiting for her sister to come to her senses. She was also angry with Ramsey because he still hadn't kept his promise to speak to Christen on her behalf, and though she had threatened that she would give him until noon today before she would take matters into her own hands, noon had come and gone, and so had Ramsey. One of the servants told her that he had left the holding early that morning with Brodick and a small band of soldiers. The servant didn't know where they had gone or when they were coming back.

She finally decided to find Brisbane and demand his help. With that intent she got up from the table just as Bridgid came running into the hall, carrying two sets of bows and arrows. She paused to smile at one of Ramsey's soldiers standing guard near the entrance, then continued on until she reached Gillian.

"Shall we go to the lake and swim?" she suggested in a loud voice.

"I don't want—"

"Yes, you do," she whispered. "Play along," she added with a barely perceptible nod at the guard.

"I'd love to go swimming," Gillian replied in a near shout.

Bridgid's eyes sparkled with merriment. "I've brought bows and arrows for both of us," she said. "If we're clever and quick, we will have rabbit stew for supper."

Gillian slipped the pack of arrows over her shoulder and carried the bow as she followed Bridgid through the buttery to the back door. They were outside and across the clearing in a matter of minutes.

Once they reached the cover of the trees, Bridgid, in her excitement, clasped Gillian's hand. "I know where Christen lives. Anthony didn't forget after all. He followed Brisbane yesterday morning just like he promised he would, but then he was ordered to relieve one of the border guards and didn't get back to the holding until dark. It was too late by then, of course. He even apologized," she added. "He's such a dear man."

"Yes, he is," she agreed. "Will you take me to Christen now?"

"Of course I will, but slow down, Gillian. People will notice if you run. Anthony's hidden two horses near the lake, and if luck stays on our side, we'll be on our way soon. You can't tell anyone where we're going. Anthony made me promise, and we can't let anyone know he helped us."

"I won't tell," she assured her friend. "I wouldn't like to see him get into trouble for doing a good deed."

"I doubt anyone will give us a second notice. It's the perfect opportunity. Brodick and Ramsey have gone to settle some trouble on the western border."

"Do you think Ramsey will be angry because I didn't wait for him to speak to Christen?"

"Probably," she replied. "But if he is, he'll talk to Brodick about it, not you. He would never let you see his anger."

"I'm worried about you," she countered. "I don't want you to get into trouble."

"Then we'll hurry and get back before anyone knows we've left," she said. "Besides, I'd be more concerned about your husband's anger if I were you. Brodick's known to have a fierce temper."

"He won't be angry with me. I told him I was

going to take matters into my own hands if Ramsey didn't keep his promise to me. And he didn't," she insisted vehemently.

"He would have," Bridgid said in defense of her laird. "Ramsey's a man of his word."

"I don't know what I would do without your help. I even thought about pounding on every door until someone told me where Christen was."

Bridgid lifted a tree branch for Gillian to duck under as she said, "You never would have found her. It's peculiar really. Your sister lives in a very remote area. I've never been that far north, but Anthony assured me it's part of the MacPherson territory."

"Did he tell you how long it will take us to get there?"

"Yes," she answered. "We should be there by midafternoon."

They finally found the horses Anthony had hidden for them. "The gray's yours," Bridgid decided as she ran to the chestnut mare and climbed into the saddle.

Gillian took one look at the beautiful horses and the ornate saddles and shook her head in disbelief. "He borrowed Ramsey's horses?"

"Ramsey won't miss them."

"But they're such grand horses, and if any-thing—"

"Will you stop worrying?"

Gillian was too close to finally finding her sister to change her mind now.

"Just think. In a very little while you'll be reunited with your dear sister."

Gillian was suddenly brimming with excitement. Slipping the bow over her shoulder, she swung up into the saddle and tried to get comfortable. It was no easy feat. Made of a thin layer of wood, then covered with wide, thick strips of leather, the saddle was stiff, unyielding, but smooth against her skin. Because it was constructed to accommodate a man, she, like Bridgid, rode astride, and after tugging her skirts down over her knees, she picked up the reins and followed her friend down the gentle slope into the valley.

They both spotted Proster on the rise when they crossed the meadow, and Gillian thought he was watching them leave, but Bridgid was just as certain he hadn't noticed them at all.

It was a beautiful day for a ride. The sky was clear, the sun was bright and warm, and the scent of summer was everywhere. They crossed a clearing golden with buttercups, and a few minutes later they climbed a hill. At the summit, Gillian turned to look back. The vista was so incredibly beautiful she imagined that this land surely resembled heaven.

They continued along at a quick pace and descended into a narrow glen, following its long winding corridor until they reached a dense forest. The farther they rode into the wilderness, the more nervous Bridgid became. She kept looking behind her to make certain they weren't being followed.

Gillian also began to worry. She wondered why Christen and her husband would deliberately isolate themselves from all the other

MacPhersons. It didn't make any sense to her, for everyone knew there was safety in numbers against hostile clans and marauders. No, it didn't make any sense.

Bridgid was having the same thoughts. "I don't like this," she whispered, as though she were concerned she would be overheard. Pulling on her reins she stopped her horse and waited for Gillian to catch up with her. "I don't like this at all," she repeated.

"We must have taken a wrong turn," Gillian suggested.

"I don't think so," her friend said. "I memorized Anthony's instructions, and I'm sure this is the way he said we should go. He was very specific, but I must not have—"

"Something's wrong," Gillian argued. "This cannot be the right way. Bridgid, do you notice how quiet it is? It's as though the birds have all left the forest."

"It's too quiet. I don't have a good feeling about this. I think we'd best turn around and go back."

"I think we should too," Gillian quickly agreed. "We've been riding most of the afternoon, and we should have found Christen's cottage by now."

"If we hurry, we can be home by sunset. Are you very disappointed? I know how much you want to see your sister again."

"It's all right. I just want to get out of here. I feel like the forest is closing in on us."

Their instincts were telling them to hurry, and both of them admitted that they had

493

acted rashly by going into the wilderness barely armed and without an escort.

Because the path was so narrow and broken, they had to back their horses to a wider area so they could turn around. Then Gillian took the lead. She had just broken through the thicket and was crossing a stream when she heard a shout. Turning toward the sound, she saw a soldier riding hard down the slope toward them. Squinting against the sun, she recognized the MacPherson plaid, but she couldn't see the man's face.

Bridgid rode forward to flank her side. She put her hand above her eyes to block the sunlight, then cried out, "It's Proster. He must have followed us."

"What in heaven's name is he doing?" Gillian asked, as she watched the MacPherson soldier swing his bow up and reach for an arrow, his gaze intently locked on the trees behind them.

The ambush took them by complete surprise. Gillian heard a whistling noise behind her and turned just as an arrow sliced through the air in front of her face.

And then more arrows whizzed past. Gillian's horse bolted into a gallop, keeping pace with Bridgid's strong mare as they raced up the bank of the stream. Thinking they were easy targets together, Gillian veered her horse away from her friend, screaming to Bridgid to get to Proster.

There was a fleeting moment when she thought she was going to make it to the cover of the trees. She flattened herself against the gray, lifted her knees, and tucked her head low beside his mane to make herself less of a target. And that was when the arrow caught her.

The force and speed of the weapon were so great, the tip went through skin and muscle and into the saddle. The pain was instant. She cried out softly, and instinctively tried to push the white hot agony away, but when she touched the arrow, a pang shot down her leg, and it was only then that she realized she was skewered to the saddle.

She suddenly became enraged and was turning to get a look at her attackers just as Bridgid's scream pierced the air. Gillian spun around and saw Bridgid's horse stumble and fall, throwing her to the ground. And then suddenly the screaming stopped and Bridgid lay completely still.

"No," Gillian shouted as she kicked her horse to get back to her friend.

Bridgid's arrows were strewn about the ground, and only then did Gillian remember she wasn't defenseless after all. She grabbed one of her arrows and swung her bow up. A man on horseback broke through the trees, racing to intercept her, but Proster rode toward her from the other direction, shouting at her to get away as he notched an arrow to his bow and took aim. A second later there was a bloodcurdling scream, and the man slumped to the ground, an arrow imbedded in his belly. He continued to howl, squirming like a snake in the dirt. And then the squirming stopped and the scream became a death rattle.

The other attacker rushed Gillian then. Proster notched another arrow. For the barest of seconds he hesitated as he recognized the man, but then he let the arrow go. His enemy threw himself flat against his horse, and Proster's arrow narrowly missed. Frantic, Proster searched for another arrow as the horse's thundering hooves galloped toward him. He flung the bow down and struggled to get his sword out of its sheath.

As the attacker closed the distance, his attention was on Proster, and Gillian seized the opportunity. She raised her bow, prayed for accuracy, and dispatched her arrow. Her aim was true. The arrow struck the man in the center of his forehead and flung him backward over his horse. He died instantly.

Gillian was panting with fear and then began to gag. She threw her bow to the ground and broke into sobs. God forgive her, she had just killed a man and had even begged for His help. She knew she had no choice. It was their lives or his, but the truth didn't ease her torment.

She took a deep breath and steadied herself. Now wasn't the time to fall apart, she told herself as she wiped the tears from her face. Bridgid was hurt and needed her.

Proster reached her friend first. He held Bridgid in his arms, but her head was slumped down and she wasn't moving. There was blood trickling from her forehead.

Even as she heard Bridgid groan, she cried out, "Is she breathing?"

"Yes," Proster answered. "She struck her head on a stone, and it knocked the wind out of her."

Bridgid groaned again and slowly opened her eyes. Gillian was so relieved, she began to cry. "Thank God," she whispered. "You're all right, Bridgid? You didn't break anything?"

Dazed, it took her a moment to figure out what Gillian was asking, and then she answered. "I think I'm all right," she said as she put her hand to her forehead. Grimacing from the pain her touch triggered, she let her hand drop back to her lap and noticed then that it was covered with blood. Turning in his arms, she looked up at the soldier. "Proster, did you save us, then?"

He smiled. "It seems so."

"You followed us."

"Yes," he admitted. "I saw you crossing the meadow and I wondered where you were going. Then you turned to the north and I became more puzzled. I kept expecting you to come back, and when you didn't, I decided to go after you."

"Thank God you did," Gillian said.

"Who were they?" Gillian demanded. "Did you recognize the men who attacked us?"

"Yes," he answered, his voice grim now. "Durston was one and Faudron was the other. They're both Sinclairs."

"Faudron?" Bridgid cried out. "But he's one of our laird's commanders."

"He isn't any longer," he said bluntly. "Lady Gillian killed him."

497

"Were there more than two?" Bridgid asked, and before he could answer her, she said, "They could come back—"

"There were only two."

"You're certain?" Bridgid asked. "If there were more—"

"There weren't," he insisted. He looked at Gillian when he added, "It was an ambush, and you were their target, Lady Buchanan."

"How could you know that?" Bridgid asked.

"The arrows were all aimed at her," he answered patiently. "Their goal was to kill you, milady," he added. "And if Bridgid had seen their faces, they would have killed her too. I'm sure they didn't think they would need more than two men to kill one woman. The element of surprise was on their side as well."

"But why would they want to kill her?" Bridgid asked.

"Do you know why, milady?" Proster asked.

She didn't hesitate in answering. "Yes, but I cannot speak of it without permission from Ramsey and Brodick."

"This is my fault," Bridgid said then. "And I will tell my laird so. I shouldn't have—"

Gillian cut her off. "No, it's my fault for taking matters into my own hands. Bridgid, you and Proster both could have been killed." Her voice shook, and she took a deep breath to calm herself. She wanted to weep, for the pain in her thigh was burning intensely and she was becoming sick to her stomach.

Proster helped Bridgid stand, then swung up onto his horse's back. He was going to get

Bridgid's mare, but Gillian whispered, "I need help."

"The danger's over now," Bridgid said. "Don't be afraid."

Gillian shook her head. Proster noticed the arrow protruding from her saddle when he rode forward and, without thinking, reached over to pull the arrow out.

Gillian screamed. "Don't touch it."

And that was when he and Bridgid both noticed the blood dripping down her leg.

Bridgid was horrified. "My God, you must be in terrible pain."

"It's not so bad if I don't move, but I need help getting it out."

Proster leapt from his horse and rushed to her side. Gently lifting her skirt away, he said, "I can't see the tip. It's in deep. It went clear through the leather into the wood. Milady, this is going to hurt," he added as he tried to get a grip on the arrow by sliding his fingers between the saddle and her thigh.

The blood made his hands slick and twice he lost his grip. The third time he tried, she cried out and he let go of her. He couldn't put her through the torture any longer.

"I can't get it out without assistance."

"I could help," Bridgid offered. She reached up and took hold of Gillian's hand to offer her friend comfort.

Proster shook his head. "It will require more strength than you have. I'm not sure what to do."

"It isn't as bad as it could be," Bridgid

announced in hope of cheering Gillian. "The arrow didn't go through bone. It looks like it just caught the edge of your skin."

"But it's firmly lodged," Proster pointed out.

"Maybe if we removed the saddle—" Bridgid suggested.

"Dear God, no," Gillian shouted.

"Removing the saddle will only pull the arrow further through," Proster said.

"I'll stay here," Gillian said. "You and Bridgid go and get help. Find Brodick. He'll know what to do."

"I won't leave you."

"Please, Proster."

"I'm not leaving you either," Bridgid insisted.

"Then you stay with me and Proster can go."

"I will not leave you." Proster's voice was firm, and she knew it was pointless to continue to argue with him. He obviously felt honor-bound to stay with her.

"Then what are we going to do?" Bridgid asked.

"If we take it slow and easy, and if I hold my leg down, we could try to go back."

"We'll see how you do," Proster decided. "I'll go get your mare, Bridgid. Do you think you can ride? You took quite a spill."

"I'm fine," she replied.

The two of them watched Proster ride down the hill and when he was out of earshot, Bridgid whispered, "I lied. My head's pounding. It's going to get worse too when my laird finds out what I've done."

"You haven't done anything wrong," Gillian

insisted. "Anthony sent us this way. If anyone's to blame, he is."

"You cannot think that Anthony had anything to do with this. He's one of Ramsey's most trusted... he's second only to Gideon..."

"And Faudron was third under Gideon, wasn't he?"

"Yes, but—"

"He betrayed Ramsey," she argued. "And now he's dead."

"Yes, but Anthony—"

"How can you not think he's responsible? Bridgid, it was an ambush. They were waiting for us and Anthony set the trap."

"But why?" Bridgid cried out. Stunned, her mind rebelled against the truth. "My God, it's too much to take in. My head is spinning."

Gillian was immediately contrite for losing her temper. "Why don't you go to the creek and put some cold water on your cut. You'll feel better."

Bridgid nodded and then started down the hill. She stopped suddenly, turned around, and asked, "You do trust Proster, don't you?"

"Yes, I do, but I think you should tell Ramsey what happened and no one else."

"I've never killed anyone before, but I swear to you, when I see Anthony again, I'm going to kill him."

While her friend continued on to the creek, Gillian held her leg steady against the saddle and slowly maneuvered her horse back down the hill so that she could get a closer look at the fallen men. She'd seen Faudron before, but she didn't remember meeting anyone named Durston. She shuddered at the bloody sight, and after one quick, necessary glance, she knew that Durston wasn't the man she had seen riding into Dunhanshire.

When Bridgid called to her, she turned around and went back to the top of the hill. She found that if she gripped her thigh tight and pushed down hard, the wound wasn't jarred by the movement of the horse's gait and the pain was bearable.

Proster had collected Bridgid's bow and arrows and was now helping her onto her mare.

"You're certain you can ride, Bridgid?" he asked.

"Yes."

Proster swung up onto his mount, glanced up at the sun to judge the angle of descent, and then said, "Hopefully we won't have to go far before they find us."

"Do you think they're looking now?" Bridgid asked.

"I hope they are," he answered.

The three of them set out at a snail's pace. Gillian had to keep stopping because of the discomfort. She finally got up the nerve to look closely at the laceration and was relieved when she saw it wasn't as horrible as she thought. The arrow had caught the outside of her thigh and had gone through flesh, just as Bridgid said. Now that she knew the injury wasn't severe, the discomfort didn't seem so bad. Until she tried to pull the arrow out. She nearly passed out from the bolt of pain that shot through her.

"Do you think they're looking for us?" Bridgid asked.

"We've been gone a long time," Gillian said. "Surely someone's searching for us by now."

"Ker and Alan both saw me leave," Proster said. "I told them I was going to follow you."

Bridgid jerked on her reins and turned to Gillian. "They'll tell their commander," she whispered. "They'll tell Anthony, and he'll send more men..."

Gillian tried not to panic. "No," she said. "He doesn't know his men failed."

Proster turned back when Bridgid and Gillian didn't follow. He assumed Gillian needed to rest for a few minutes.

A mist was rolling into the forest. The thick swirling fog may have been harmless to touch but it was deadly to ride in, for like a thief, it would rob them of their sight.

"We've got to get to high ground before dark," Proster said.

"No one will find us in this mist," Gillian said, feeling miserable now and disheartened.

"Anthony won't find us either," Bridgid pointed out.

Unaware that Anthony had sent them into an ambush, Proster misunderstood Bridgid's comment. "Ker and Alan should tell Anthony that I followed you, but I don't think they will."

"Why not?" Bridgid asked. "In Gideon's absence, he's their commander."

"It won't matter," Proster said. "They don't respect or trust him. He's made it clear he has no use for any of the MacPherson soldiers, and he's humiliated Ker and Alan and all the rest of us countless times. No, they won't tell him."

"But when it's noticed that we're gone, Anthony will have to send out search parties, won't he?"

"Yes, but I doubt he'll send any soldiers this far north. He'd send soldiers to search the more populated areas. Why did you take this route? Did you get lost?"

"No," Gillian answered.

"Yes," Bridgid said at the same time.

"We went riding and lost track of the time," Gillian lied. "And we... no, that isn't true, Proster. We thought that my sister lived in this area, but we were mistaken."

Proster saw the tears in Gillian's eyes and rushed out, "It isn't hopeless. Ker and Alan will tell Ramsey, and I'm sure that Brodick is already looking for you, Lady Buchanan."

"But if he—"

Proster smiled. "Milady, you are the Buchanan's wife. I imagine that Brodick and his guard are tearing the hills apart now looking for you. Don't despair. Your husband will come for you."

CHAPTER TWENTY-EIGHT

Gideon gave them the bad news. Ramsey and Brodick had only just returned to the holding when the Sinclair commander came running across the courtyard to intercept them.

One look at his grim expression told both lairds there was serious trouble.

"What is it?" Ramsey demanded.

Gideon panted as he explained. "Lady Buchanan and Bridgid KirkConnell have disappeared. We've searched everywhere and cannot find them."

"What the hell do you mean, they've disappeared?" Brodick roared.

"How long have they been missing?" Ramsey demanded.

Gideon shook his head. "I'm not certain. When I got back from my father's, Anthony had already left the holding with soldiers to search for them. I was just about to join them."

"They can't have gone far," Ramsey told Brodick. "It's nearly sunset now. We'll have to hurry if we're going to find them before dark. Which way did Anthony go?"

"South," he answered. "Laird, I take full responsibility for this. If I had been here instead—"

Ramsey cut him off. "You were needed at home," he snapped. "No one saw them leave?"

he asked then. Incredulous, he shook his head. "How was it possible for them to get away without anyone seeing them?"

Gideon didn't have any answers. Brodick swung onto his stallion's back. "We're wasting time," he muttered. "I'll search the west. Gideon, take soldiers and search the east, and Ramsey, you go north."

"There's no reason to go north," Ramsey argued. "If they went out alone, they wouldn't have gone into the wilderness. Bridgid knows better."

Two scared young MacPherson soldiers waited on their horses near the base of the valley. They watched Gideon lead a band of soldiers down the hill and then head east.

"You tell Laird Buchanan," Alan whispered.

Ker shook his head. "You tell him. I don't want him to break my nose again. I'll tell Ramsey."

Brodick and Black Robert took the lead, followed by Dylan, Liam, and Aaron. They had just crossed the grassy plain when they heard a shout. Dylan turned back when he saw the MacPherson soldier chasing them, but the others continued on.

Alan's freckled face was bloodred, more from fear than exertion as he blurted out his important news. "Proster... he followed the ladies, and they went north."

Dylan whistled and within seconds Brodick and the others surrounded the boy.

"Proster followed my wife?"

The steely gaze of the laird so unnerved the soldier, he could barely get the words out. "He saw your wife and Bridgid KirkConnell riding north."

"Were there soldiers with them?" Aaron demanded.

"No, they went out alone, and that's why Proster followed them. He said he was going to bring them back... that it wasn't safe..."

"Then why the hell didn't he bring them back?" Liam demanded.

"I don't know," Alan stammered. "Something must have happened to delay them. Ker and I were going to look for them, but then Gideon arrived, and on his heels, you and Ramsey returned."

"If you aren't telling us the truth, I swear I'll flay you alive," Black Robert threatened.

"As God is my witness, I'm telling you the truth. I swear it on my mother's grave. My friend... Ker... he went to tell Ramsey to go north."

"Bring him with us," Brodick ordered. Goading his stallion into a gallop, he raced toward the forest. He kept telling himself not to panic, but it didn't do any good. My God, what was she thinking to ride out into the wilderness without protection? One boy protecting two women? Something had happened all right, or Proster would have brought them back by now.

For the first time in his life, Brodick prayed. *Dear God, let her be all right. I need her.*

CHAPTER TWENTY-NINE

Gillian had had enough. She simply couldn't go on, and it was too dangerous anyway, as darkness was fast approaching and the gray mist was getting thicker. They had stopped beside a creek, and she was about to tell Proster that with or without his help she was going to get rid of the arrow, but then she heard a rumbling in the distance. Within seconds the ground beneath her began to tremble.

Proster grabbed his sword as Bridgid frantically reached for her bow and arrows. Gillian pulled her dagger from her belt and moved closer to Bridgid.

"Get ready," Proster called, grimacing over the tremor he heard in his voice.

"Maybe it's Ker and Alan." Bridgid whispered the hope out loud.

"Too many horses," Proster said as he nudged his horse forward to put himself in front of the women.

Seconds later, Brodick emerged from the mist. He saw the three of them and pulled hard on the reins. The sight of his wife, apparently safe and sound, filled him with such relief, his knees almost buckled when he leapt to the ground.

His soldiers followed. They, too, dismounted and headed straight for Proster. The boy was shaking so violently it looked as though he was waving at them with his sword. But he didn't back down or run. As terrified as he was, he held his ground, willing to risk his life for the women.

"Put your sword away, boy," Dylan commanded.

Brodick rushed to his wife. "Gillian, you are all right?"

He expected a quick yes, and then he was going to give her hell. Didn't the woman understand how much she meant to him? How dare she take such a risk? By God, he would demand that she beg his forgiveness for putting him through such torture. And it would be a month of Sundays before he forgave her.

She was so overwhelmed with relief and joy that Brodick had found her, she didn't care that he was furious. "No, I'm not all right, but Brodick, I'm so happy to see you."

Proster, his hands still trembling, after three attempts had finally gotten his sword back into its sheath. He had just swung one leg over and was jumping off his horse when Brodick reached for his wife. The soldier lunged at the laird and shouted, "Don't touch her."

Brodick reacted with amazing speed. Proster's feet hadn't even touched the ground before he was thrown backward with such force he landed on his backside in the grass.

"What the hell's the matter with him?" Brodick demanded as he turned back to his wife.

Dylan grabbed the crazed soldier by the scruff of his neck and hauled him to his feet. Then he began to shake him. "You dare to give my laird orders?" he roared.

"She's pinned to the saddle," Proster shouted. "An arrow—"

As soon as the words registered, Dylan let go of the soldier. Brodick had already noticed the arrow and had moved to the right side of the horses to get a closer look.

Gillian put her hand against Brodick's cheek. "I'm so happy to see you," she whispered.

"And I'm happy to see you," he whispered back. "Now let me see what you've done to yourself," he ordered gruffly.

Her spine stiffened. "I didn't do anything," she cried out. "Except try to get away. If it weren't for Proster, Bridgid and I would have been killed."

Suddenly the three of them were talking at the same time as each tried to explain what had happened.

"They were Sinclairs," Proster announced.

"They weren't trying to kill me," Bridgid said. "They were after Gillian."

"They would have killed you too," Gillian countered.

"Proster killed one of them," Bridgid told Brodick then.

"Their names were Durston and Faudron," Proster said.

Brodick was taken aback when he heard the name of one of Ramsey's most valued commanders. "Faudron tried to kill you?"

"Yes," Bridgid answered for Gillian. "He and Durston were waiting for us."

"It was an ambush," Gillian said.

"I killed Durston," Proster boasted.

"What about Faudron? Did he get away?" Brodick asked.

"Nay," Proster answered. "Your wife killed him."

Brodick's gaze flew to Gillian.

"I had to," she whispered.

"One arrow, Laird, that went through his forehead. Her aim was true."

Brodick was trying to wedge his hand beneath Gillian's thigh so that he could get a proper grip on the arrow, but when he saw her flinch, he pulled his hand back.

"Proster tried to get the arrow out, but he couldn't," she told him.

The soldier began to move away from the commander, but Dylan grabbed him by the neck again.

Exasperated, Gillian called out, "Dylan, please let go of him."

Brodick took Gillian's dagger, lifted her plaid, and then slit her underskirts all the way up to the top of her thigh. The soldiers crowded around their laird to watch what he was doing and Gillian, trying to maintain some semblance of modesty and decorum, hastily tugged the plaid down over her leg.

"This isn't the time for shyness," Brodick told her.

She knew he was upset. "It isn't as bad as it looks."

"Could have fooled me," he countered.

"She might wish to sleep through this, Laird," Robert suggested.

"You're going to wait until she falls asleep?" Bridgid asked. She'd pushed her way through the men so that she could take hold of Gillian's hand.

Gillian was more astute than her friend. She was also outraged by Robert's suggestion. "No one's going to knock me out. Have I made myself clear?"

"But milady," Robert began.

She stopped him cold. "I cannot believe you would suggest such a thing."

"A light tap is all it would take," Aaron argued. "You wouldn't feel a thing."

"We don't like seeing you in pain, milady," Liam rasped.

"Then close your eyes," she snapped.

Brodick finally noticed Bridgid squeezed up against him. She had tears in her eyes as she stared at Gillian. He told her to move back so that he could do what was needed, but Bridgid didn't budge, and Aaron had to lift her out of the way.

"What are you going to do?" Robert asked from behind.

In answer, Brodick pulled his sword free. "Dylan, hold the arrow steady. Liam, grab the reins."

Dylan moved forward, grabbed the arrow with both hands and pressed down against Gillian's thigh to keep it from moving.

Aaron pulled Bridgid out of the way, while

Robert hurried to the other side of the horse and told Gillian to lean toward him.

"Are you still thinking about punching me, Robert?" she asked suspiciously.

"Nay, milady, I would never strike you without gaining permission."

She decided to trust him and put her hands on his shoulders as she slowly leaned down toward him.

"Brodick?"

"Yes?"

"Don't miss."

And then she closed her eyes and waited. She heard the whistle of the sword as it sliced through the air, felt only a slight jarring as the blade cut the arrow, and then it was over. When she opened her eyes again she saw that the arrow had been cleanly cut in half just a thumb's width above Dylan's hands.

She knew what was going to happen next, and, Lord, how she dreaded it. Brodick was slipping his arms under her knees. "Put your hands on my shoulders," he ordered.

"Wait."

"What is it?"

"I don't want to go back to Annie Drummond's cottage. Do you hear me? I don't want to go back there ever again."

He tightened his grip. "I thought you liked Annie's house."

Bridgid was wringing her hands in agitation. She could barely stand to watch her friend in such pain. "You'll feel better if you scream," she blurted. "I would."

Brodick looked into his wife's eyes, saw the tears, and said, "She will not make a sound."

He got just the reaction he wanted. Instantly furious, she shouted, "I'm supposed to say that, not you. If you tell me to be brave, then when I am, it doesn't count. I..."

She didn't make a sound, except her deep indrawn breath when Brodick lifted her and the arrow slid through her leg. She threw her arms around him and held tight, and when the tears fell, she buried her face in the crook of his neck.

He wasn't sure which one of them was shaking more. Without a word, he turned and carried her to the creek. Bridgid tried to follow them, thinking she could help bind the injury, but Dylan grabbed her and told her to wait until they returned.

"It's over with," Brodick whispered, and his voice was hoarse with relief. He held her tight against him and couldn't seem to make himself let go. It was going to take some time for him to get over the scare of losing her. He kissed her forehead and then begged her to stop crying.

She wiped her face with his plaid. "You're dying to yell at me, aren't you?"

"Damn right I am," he admitted. "But I'm a thoughtful man, and so I'll wait until you have recovered."

She didn't believe a word of it. "That is thoughtful of you," she agreed.

"What in God's name were you thinking, to

leave without... my God, Gillian, you could have been killed."

He had only just gotten warmed up, and he continued to rant at her all the while he splashed cold water over her leg to wash off any dirt or dried blood. He stopped long enough to grudgingly admit the wound wasn't nearly as awful as he'd first thought, but he went right back to shouting at her while he tore strips from her skirt and wrapped them around her thigh to stop the bleeding. By the time he was finished, her thigh didn't hurt much at all, but her pride had taken quite a blistering.

He wouldn't let her walk, and she wouldn't let him carry her anywhere until he had finished giving her a piece of his mind. She wasn't about to let him scold her in front of the men.

Scooping her up into his arms, his tirade continued. "When we get home, I swear I'm putting two guards in front of you and two behind you. You're never going to get another chance to scare me like this again."

She put her hand against his cheek, a simple caress that magically calmed him. Then she ruined it by trying to explain her actions, inadvertently getting him riled up again.

"I didn't deliberately leave the holding in hopes of getting attacked."

"But you did leave the holding, didn't you? And without a proper guard to protect you. How could you leave Sinclair land without—"

"I didn't know I was leaving Ramsey's territory."

He closed his eyes and told himself for the hundredth time that she was all right. The thought of losing her scared the hell out of him and infuriated him at the same time. How had he allowed himself to become so vulnerable?

"Shouting at me isn't going to accomplish anything."

"Sure it is," he snapped. "It's making me feel a hell of a lot better."

She didn't dare smile, guessing he would take grave offense if she did. She wanted to soothe him now, not incite his wrath further.

"Will you please be reasonable?"

"I am being reasonable. Haven't you figured it out yet? It took me a while, but by God, I finally have."

"Figured out what?"

"Trouble follows you like a shadow, Gillian. You're prone to injuries. I swear to God, if a tree decided to fall right now, it would find your head to land on."

"Oh, for heaven's sake," she muttered. "I'll admit that I have had a run of bad fortune, but—"

He wouldn't let her continue. "A run of bad fortune? Since I've known you, you've been beaten, stabbed, and now shot with an arrow. If this keeps up, you'll be dead in another month, and if that happens, I'm going to be damned angry."

"I was beaten, yes, but that was before I met you," she said, believing she was being quite logical. "And Alec didn't stab me. He cut my arm, but only because he was so frightened.

516

It was just bad luck that it didn't heal. As for the arrow," she continued. "it only pinched my skin. You saw the cut; it wasn't bad."

"It could have pierced your heart."

"But it didn't."

She demanded that he put her down, and when he did, she walked to a tree so that he could see she was as fit as ever. Then she leaned against it to take the weight off the throbbing leg. Forcing a smile, she said, "Do you see? I'm quite all right."

Brodick turned away from her and stared out into the night, brooding. He didn't say a word for several minutes.

"I made up my mind a long time ago that no woman would ever unsettle me again. I will not let it happen."

"What are you telling me?"

His temper exploded. "You and I struck a bargain when we married, and you're going to live up to your end of it."

"What bargain?" she asked quietly.

"You married me for my protection."

"I married you because I love you. Now, tell me, Brodick. Why did you marry me? What did you get out of this bargain?"

He wouldn't answer, but she wasn't about to give up. Prodding him, she asked, "Did you marry me because you loved me?" She held her breath until he answered.

"Love weakens a man, and I'm not weak."

His hard words shattered her heart. She bowed her head so he wouldn't see how he had hurt her. "You told me you wanted to protect my reputation. I remember that conversation, but even then I knew that wasn't the real reason you married me. I thought... I hoped, anyway... that you cared for me. I knew you were grateful because I helped Alec and you're his guardian, but surely you didn't marry me out of gratitude. A simple thank you would have been enough."

"I had a responsibility to you, Gillian, and that is all that need be said about my reasons."

"You care for me, Brodick. I know you do."

He turned away from her. He was acting like a cornered animal. He had never hedged or skirted an issue before. No, he'd been honest and blunt, but now he was deliberately being evasive. It made her worry all the more. What he wasn't telling her frightened her.

Why was it so difficult for him to admit what was in his heart. "I ask you again. Why did you marry me?"

He refused to answer. "Ramsey's here," he said then. "I'll carry you back, and then you're going to start at the beginning and tell both of us what happened today."

"I can walk," she assured him. "You go ahead. I'll be there in a few minutes."

"You're coming with me now," he told her, and before she could argue, he picked her up and carried her back to the clearing.

One of the soldiers had started a campfire in the center of the grassy flat, and all the Buchanans sat in a circle around the flames. Proster, Ker, and Alan stood together near

Ramsey and his men while Proster waited to give his laird their accounting. Bridgid faced her laird, and after one quick glance, Gillian knew her friend was hearing Ramsey's displeasure.

Brodick settled Gillian on the plaid Dylan had spread out for her, but she didn't stay there. As soon as he turned his back and walked away, she got to her feet and went to Bridgid.

"Ramsey, don't blame Bridgid for what happened. She isn't responsible."

"Then Bridgid was forced to leave the holding?"

His voice was deceptively mild, but Gillian knew he was seething with anger. "No, of course she wasn't forced."

"I take full responsibility for my actions," Bridgid said.

"If anyone is responsible for what happened today, you are, Ramsey. Yes, you are," Gillian added when he looked so incredulous. "If you had kept your promise to me, this incident could have been avoided."

"What promise?" he demanded.

"It meant so little to you that you have already forgotten?"

Ramsey glared at Brodick, obviously seeking his assistance. "Your wife believes I'm responsible."

"She's wrong."

Folding her arms defiantly, she boldly turned to Brodick. "I warned you that I would give Ramsey until noon today to do as he promised and order my sister to see me, but he didn't,

519

and so I took matters into my own hands. Bridgid was kind enough to help me."

Ramsey was seething now. "I haven't had time to speak to your sister, and your impatience nearly got you killed."

Bridgid tried to deflect some of her laird's anger. "It was all for the good," she blurted out, and when Ramsey and Brodick looked at her as though she'd lost her senses, she hastened to explain. "You never would have known that Faudron and Durston wanted to hurt Gillian, and now perhaps you can figure out why."

"I'm sorry you're angry with us," Gillian said then. "And I'll admit we did take a needless risk, but in our defense, I would point out that neither one of us knew we were leaving your territory."

"Laird, may I speak freely?" Bridgid asked.

"What the hell have you been doing?" he countered.

She shook her head. "You're my laird and I respect you, and for that reason I will not lose my temper. I would appreciate it if you would treat me with the same consideration, for I am one of your most loyal followers."

"Bridgid, I'm going to assume that the bump on your head has addled you and that's why you dare to speak to me this way."

"Please don't be angry with her," Gillian pleaded on her friend's behalf. "This is all my fault. It's just as you have said, Ramsey. I was impatient."

"I'm the one who came up with the idea to follow Brisbane," Bridgid insisted.

"No, you didn't," Gillian countered. "You told me that Anthony came up with the idea."

Ramsey's roar stopped the discussion. "What does Anthony have to do with this?"

Gillian realized then that Bridgid hadn't told her laird everything. "Anthony told Bridgid that he would follow Brisbane."

"And?" he demanded when she hesitated.

"He told me he did follow him," Bridgid said. "He gave me specific directions, and I memorized them so we wouldn't get lost."

"He sent us into a trap."

Ramsey was shaking with rage. "I'm going to kill the son of a bitch with my bare hands."

"No, you're not," Brodick countered. "He tried to kill my wife. I'm going to kill him. It's my right."

"The hell it is," Ramsey muttered. "By God, he's going to suffer before he takes his last breath."

CHAPTER THIRTY

It was late, well past midnight, and Bridgid and Gillian were so exhausted from their long day and their ordeal, they could barely keep their eyes open. They sat shoulder to shoulder with their backs resting against a tree trunk, their legs stretched out in front of them, trying to hear what their lairds were discussing.

Everyone else had gone to sleep, and the ground was covered in a maze of plaids. Ramsey and Brodick sat in front of the fire with their heads bent, their whispered conversation grave. Ramsey continuously stirred the embers with a long, crooked stick as though looking for a forgotten object, while Brodick gazed at some distant point in the darkness, nodding every now and again at what Ramsey was saying.

Gillian moved her head slightly and stared at Brodick's chiseled profile. She could see the tenseness in his shoulders, and though he sat motionless now, she felt as though he was about to spring.

Bridgid nudged her and whispered, "Ramsey thinks he's done a terrible injustice to the MacPhersons because he thought one of them was responsible for taking Alec Maitland. Does that make sense?"

"Yes," Gillian answered. "I'll explain later. Keep listening."

"I am," she whispered back, and a minute later she turned to Gillian again. "He said that when he came home and challenged for the position of laird, he made an error in judgment by allowing the old guard to stay in place. He acted out of kindness, and that was a mistake."

Bridgid continued to listen and after a while, Gillian nudged her again.

"Ramsey says he's going to stop procrastinating. He's... Oh, God."

"What?"

The look on Bridgid's face showed how

devastated she was. "He's going to marry Meggan MacPherson." Her voice trembled.

"Oh, Bridgid, he's the one, isn't he? He's the man you love."

A tear slipped down her cheek. "'Tis true. I do love him, and I have for the longest time."

Gillian took hold of her hand. "I'm so sorry."

Bridgid wiped a tear from her eye. "Men are stupid."

"Yes, they are," Gillian agreed. "What's Brodick saying?"

"He's trying to talk Ramsey out of it. He just advised him to think long and hard before he makes such a commitment."

"He didn't practice what he's now preaching," she whispered. "And he's very upset with me."

"He must be," she replied. "He just told Ramsey that marriage is a sacrifice." A minute later she whispered, "Now that doesn't make sense."

"What?"

"Ramsey said that in Brodick's case the sacrifice was worth it because he got the Englishmen's names. Do you know what he's talking about?"

Gillian was suddenly furious. "Yes, I do. Is Ramsey saying he believes Brodick married me just to get the names of the Englishmen?"

"What Englishmen?"

"I'll explain later," she promised. "Tell me. Is that what he says?"

Realizing how agitated her friend was, she hastened to answer. "Yes, Ramsey did say that, and your husband just agreed."

Gillian closed her eyes. "I don't want to hear any more."

"What's wrong?" Bridgid whispered. "You can tell me. I'm your dearest friend, aren't I?"

"You're my only friend," she answered. "I'm not going to believe it."

"Believe what?"

"That Brodick married me to get the names of the Englishmen. No, I won't believe it. No one would get married for such a reason. It's sinful."

Bridgid thought about what Gillian had just said, and then whispered, "Did these Englishmen insult one of the lairds?"

"Insult? Oh, Bridgid, they did something much worse."

"Then I'll tell you this. You don't poke a bear in the eye and expect to walk away unscratched. They will get even. The men here never forget a wrong done to them, and they will go to great lengths to get what they want."

"I still refuse to believe that Brodick only married me to get the names. No, I won't believe it. Marriage is a holy sacrament, and he wouldn't... no, he wouldn't do that. He's speaking out of anger now. That's all there is to it."

"Did he ask you for the names of these Englishmen before you were married?"

"Yes."

"But you didn't tell him?"

"No, I didn't." In frustration she added, "And even after we were married, I made him promise he wouldn't retaliate until I had accomplished my task. Then I gave him the names. He gave me his word, and I trust him to keep it. I know he cares for me. He's just too stubborn to admit it. He told me he felt a responsibility for me."

"Of course he cares for you."

"Maybe Brodick will talk Ramsey out of marrying Meggan MacPherson."

"No, I don't think so. Ramsey sounded as though he'd already made up his mind. He's putting the interests of the clan above his own, and that's as it should be because he's laird. He'll do what he thinks is right. I don't think I can stand watching him with her, though. I had already made up my mind to leave, and now I realize I must leave soon."

"Where will you go?"

Bridgid closed her eyes. "I don't know. I cannot stay in the servants' quarters. The new mistress won't like it."

"Maybe your mother will let you come back home."

"No. She's made it clear she doesn't want me around. No one does," she added, knowing she sounded pitiful but too miserable to care. Dabbing a tear away from her eye, she whispered, "The fall I took has made me weepy."

Gillian pretended to believe that nonsense. Ramsey was the reason Bridgid was brokenhearted. She shifted her weight to ease the throbbing in her thigh and closed her eyes. She fell asleep accepting that Bridgid was right. Men were stupid.

CHAPTER THIRTY-ONE

T he first golden streaks of dawn were bursting onto the horizon when Brodick nudged Gillian awake. She had slept in his arms, though she had no memory of being moved during the night, and she was so sleepy she didn't want to cooperate. Snuggling under the blanket, she groaned, "Not yet," and went back to sleep.

Bridgid had also been moved to a plaid blanket closer to the fire. Another plaid covered her, and when Ramsey squatted down next to her and saw how peaceful she was, he regretted having to wake her. She really was lovely, he thought, noticing for the first time how long her eyelashes were and how pure her complexion was. Her lips were full, rosy, and without a thought as to what he was doing, he brushed his thumb across her lower lip.

She batted his hand away as though he were a pest and grumbled something in her sleep he couldn't quite make out, but he was sure he heard the word "stupid."

"Open your eyes, Bridgid. It's time to get going."

She didn't wake up happy. "Do leave me alone," she mumbled.

Brodick stood over Gillian, wondering why the hell she wouldn't obey him, and once again ordered her to get up.

"Maybe we ought to throw them in the creek," Ramsey suggested. "That will wake them up."

Bridgid took the threat to heart and sat up. Shocked to find Ramsey so close to her, she leaned back on her elbows to put some distance between them. She knew she looked a sight. Her hair hung down over her eyes, and she squinted up at him, wondering how he could look so incredibly... perfect... at this ungodly hour of the morning.

Brodick pulled Gillian to her feet but didn't let go of her until he was certain she could walk. Her leg stung with each movement, but she suffered in silence, knowing that if she gave a single complaint, she'd hear another blistering lecture about her reckless behavior.

"Are you still angry with me, Brodick?"

"Yes."

"Good," she whispered, "because I'm furious with you."

Head held high, her attitude haughty, she took a step toward the creek, but her leg wouldn't support her. She would have fallen on her face if Brodick hadn't grabbed her.

"You can't walk, can you?"

"Of course I can," she replied, her voice as surly as his had been when he'd posed the question. "Now, if you'll excuse me, I'll go wash."

Brodick watched her limp away to make certain he wasn't going to have to catch her again. Ramsey had given Bridgid a gentle shove to get her moving in the direction of the creek, and Brodick relaxed his guard when she assisted Gillian.

The women took their time. Gillian redressed her bandage, grimacing when she saw how bruised her thigh was. The wound wasn't bad at all, though, and was already closing. Walking got rid of the stiffness, and by the time she and Bridgid returned to camp, they were both in much better spirits. Gillian wasn't limping much.

They set out for Ramsey's home right away. Gillian insisted she ride her own horse, and Brodick reluctantly agreed. Before long they reached the meadow and rode down the northern slope. To the west a fair distance away were the cliffs she and Brodick had ridden down the day they were married, and she remembered the foolish, carefree banter and the joy she had felt. Lord, it seemed an eternity had passed since then.

Her mind continued to wander as they crossed the meadow and neared the gate to Ramsey's holding. They were riding next to the wall when Gillian glanced up. A soldier suddenly appeared on the catwalk above. Her breath caught in her throat and her heart began to pound. Pulling on the reins, she forced the horse to stop and shouted, "Brodick."

The man saw her and stepped back out of sight.

Brodick and Ramsey immediately turned back. "What's wrong?" Brodick demanded.

"Why did you stop?" Ramsey asked.

"Did you see the man up there on the catwalk? Did you see him, Ramsey?"

Brodick answered. "I saw him. It was Gideon. He's probably on his way to the gates now to meet Ramsey. You met him on the day we arrived. Don't you remember?"

She was frantically shaking her head. "No, Brodick, I didn't meet him."

"Yes, you did," Ramsey insisted.

"No, I didn't," she cried out. "But I've seen him before. He's the man who betrayed you."

CHAPTER THIRTY-TWO

Ramsey's battle cry rent the air, alerting the gatekeepers to call the men to arms. Within bare minutes every possible exit was sealed as tight as a tomb. Soldiers raced to the catwalks, their arrows already notched to their bows in preparation, as more of Ramsey's followers leapt upon their horses and galloped out into the valley to surround the perimeter of the holding. No one would get into the estate, and no one was going to get out.

Every able-bodied man came running to support their laird, and for the first time since the MacPhersons had joined the Sinclairs, there was no prejudice or rivalry. United, they stood together, five deep, in a wide circle around the courtyard, waiting and watching, with but one single intent—to protect Ramsey.

Gideon waited in the center of the courtyard with eleven other traitorous men, all Sinclairs, and all loyal to the man they believed should have been laird. Gideon was eager and confident. His moment had finally arrived, and soon now he would become laird of the Sinclairs, and he was anxiously looking forward to killing Ramsey. He believed that once Ramsey was dead, the clan would give him their loyalty.

Brodick ordered Liam and Aaron to take the women to the cottage, but Gillian countered his command with one of her own.

"You will stay and protect your laird."

Brodick heard her and nodded his agreement. Gillian motioned to Bridgid then and took the lead to the cottage. She wanted to call out to Brodick, to tell him to be careful and not take any foolish chances, but his thoughts were on the battle ahead of him, and she didn't want to distract him. She prayed to God instead and asked Him to keep Brodick and Ramsey safe. When she turned to Bridgid, she saw her make the sign of the cross and knew she was doing the same thing.

Ramsey and Brodick leapt to the ground before their horses had stopped, and drawing their swords, they closed the distance.

Proster tried to follow his laird, but Dylan shoved him aside. "You haven't earned the right to protect your laird's back."

"Then who will?" the soldier demanded.

"The Buchanans, of course. Watch and learn, boy."

Liam put his hand on Proster's shoulder. "You did well protecting our mistress," he said. "And we are thankful, but until you are properly trained, you are a hindrance to your laird, forcing him to protect you. Patience, boy. Do as my commander orders. Watch and learn."

Gideon boldly stepped forward to confront Ramsey. "I challenge you now, Ramsey, for the right to rule the Sinclairs," he shouted.

Ramsey laughed, the sound harsh in the sudden stillness. "You challenged me once before, you son of a bitch. I should have killed you then."

"You dared to come back here and steal what belonged to me. Me!" Gideon shrieked. "I should have been laird, not you. I am worthy."

"Worthy?" Ramsey roared. "You think you're worthy? You prey on children and women to get what you want, and you believe that makes you worthy? Only a coward would strike a bargain with the English devils to steal my brother and kill him. When Alec Maitland was taken by mistake, you thought you could rectify that blunder by going back to England and ordering the death of a five-year-old boy. No, you aren't worthy. You're a coward and a traitor, you bastard."

"I did what needed to be done to gain the loyalty of all the Sinclairs. You and Michael will both die. I'm strong, Ramsey, not weak like you. You allowed Bridgid KirkConnell to deny me," he shouted. "And you listened to the whining of old men and let them foul our land with the MacPherson scum. How dare you believe they are equal to us. When I'm laird, I'm going to rid my land of their plague."

With the crook of his finger, Ramsey motioned for Gideon to attack. "Come and kill me," he taunted. "Show me your strength."

Screaming, Gideon raised his sword and charged. His friends advanced at the same time, their plan to overwhelm the laird with their sheer number, but Brodick and Dylan moved forward, their swords swift as they cut down two of the enemy before they could swing their weapons. A weathered Sinclair soldier, flanked by two MacPhersons, joined the fight then, thinking to even the odds.

Brodick never took his gaze off Anthony and moved with deadly intent toward his prey. Seeing the look in his eyes, Anthony tried to run, but Dylan blocked his retreat. Brodick wasted little time fencing with the soldier and killed him with one quick thrust across his throat. He died standing, then crashed to the ground. Brodick spit on him as a final insult before turning to watch Ramsey.

A loud piercing squeal issued from Gideon's

throat as Ramsey's sword sliced down through his shoulder to his waist, nearly cutting him in half. The commander fell to his knees, a look of stunned disbelief on his face. As he was drawing his last breath, Ramsey kicked him onto his back and lifted his sword with both hands as he muttered, "You lose." And with all his might he thrust his sword into Gideon's black heart.

Ramsey stood over his enemy while he sought to control his anger. The silence was heavy; the only sound, that of his heavy breathing. The scent of blood hung in the air and filled his nostrils. He shuddered once, like a dog shaking his coat to rid it of water, then straightened and jerked his sword from Gideon's body.

"Does anyone else want to challenge me?" he roared.

"Nay," a man shouted from deep within the crowd. "Our loyalty is to you, Laird."

A resounding cheer went up then, but Ramsey paid it little attention. The ground around him was littered with the dead, the dirt and grass blackened with their spilled blood. Turning to the three soldiers who had stepped forward to fight the battle with him, he said, "Drag their bodies outside my walls and leave them to rot."

He noticed then that he, like Brodick, had splatters of blood on his arms and legs, "I want to wash their stench from my body."

Without a backward glance, Brodick followed his friend to the lake.

When they were well away from the others, Ramsey turned to him, "We leave for England tomorrow."

Brodick nodded. "At first light."

CHAPTER THIRTY-THREE

Proster told Gillian and Bridgid what had happened. In his enthusiasm, he went into excruciating and sickening detail as he described the fight, blow by bloody blow, and told them far more than either one of them wanted or needed to hear. By the time he was finished, Bridgid's face was gray and Gillian was sick to her stomach.

"You're certain Brodick and Ramsey were unharmed?" Gillian asked.

"Neither suffered so much as a nick," Proster replied. "They were both covered with blood, but it wasn't theirs, and they went to the lake to wash it off. Ramsey's going to let the bodies of the dead rot."

"I don't wish to hear another word," Bridgid said. She dismissed the soldier then and opened the door for him. "Gillian, I'll fetch some salve to put on your leg to help with the healing."

"You might want to wait," Proster advised. "Or take the back way. The grass in the court-yard is black from blood spilled, and I'm not certain all the dead have been dragged away yet."

"I'll go to my mother's, then, and get some salve from her. Proster, men died today and you should not be smiling."

"But they weren't good men," he countered. "They deserved to die."

They continued their argument as Proster closed the door.

Gillian sat down to wait for Brodick. She expected him to walk through the door at any moment. An hour later she was still waiting. By midafternoon she went searching for him and was told by one of the MacPhersons that her husband had left with Ramsey. It was speculated that the two lairds had gone to Iain Maitland to tell him the news.

She tried to wait up for her husband, but because she'd had so little rest the night before, she couldn't keep her eyes open. She finally fell into a fitful sleep.

Brodick woke her up in the middle of the night when he pulled her into his arms and made love to her. His hands were rough and demanding, and she felt a desperation in him, a violence barely controlled, but she didn't fight or reject him. Nay, she stroked and caressed him and tried to soothe the beast within. Their lovemaking was wild and frantic, and when he climaxed deep inside her, she came apart in his arms.

She told him she loved him, and he cherished her words because he knew that her love was going to be sorely tested in the days ahead. By tomorrow night, she could very well hate him.

Brisbane and Otis knocked on her door early the following morning. Gillian was dressed for the day and had just finished her morning meal.

"We have been instructed to take you to your sister," Brisbane announced.

"Did she finally agree to see me, then?" she asked as she stepped outside.

Otis shook his head. "She has been ordered to see you."

Gillian tried not to let them see how disappointed she was that her sister had once again refused her. They walked together to the stables, where their horses were saddled and waiting. Brisbane took the lead, and neither he nor Otis said another word until they reached a cluster of cottages near the border that once separated the MacPhersons from the Sinclairs.

Gillian was suddenly nervous and scared. Christen had already rejected her, and as painful and humiliating as that was, she had accepted it, but if her sister didn't know where the king's treasure was or had forgotten all that had happened, then everything was lost and Uncle Morgan was doomed.

"Please, God, let her remember," she whispered as she dismounted and walked toward the cottage Brisbane had pointed out.

"We'll wait here for you," Brisbane said.

"You needn't wait. I know the way back."

The door opened then, and a woman Gillian never would have recognized as her sister stepped into the sunlight. Her husband, tall and gaunt, followed her. His hostility was evident as he hovered protectively over his wife.

Christen was a good head taller than Gillian. Her hair was much darker too, and Liese had told Gillian that Christen had golden curls, but she didn't remember them. There wasn't a glimmer of recognition, and though Gillian knew this woman was her sister, she was a stranger to her.

She was heavy with child. No one had bothered to mention that fact to Gillian.

Had Christen not looked so sullen, Gillian would have embraced her and told her how happy she was to see her again. They stared at one another for a long minute before Gillian finally broke the uncomfortable silence.

"Are you Christen?"

"I am," she answered. "I used to be anyway. My parents changed my name. I'm called Kate now."

A burst of anger took Gillian by surprise, and she spoke before she could stop herself. "Your parents are dead and buried in England."

"I don't remember them."

Gillian cocked her head to the side and stared at her sister. "I think you do remember our father."

"What is it you want from me?" she asked, a note of defiance creeping into her voice.

Gillian suddenly felt like weeping. "You're my sister. I wanted to see you again."

"But you want more than that, don't you?"

Her husband asked the question. Christen remembered her manners and quickly introduced him. His name was Manus.

Gillian lied when she told him she was pleased to meet him. Then she answered his question. "Yes, I do want something more."

Christen stiffened. "I cannot and will not go back to England. My life is here, Gillian."

"Is that what you're so afraid of? That I'll force you to go home with me? Oh, Christen, I would never ask that of you."

The sincerity in her voice must have gotten through to Christen. She nodded to her husband and whispered something in his ear. Manus reluctantly agreed, and after bowing, he went inside and then carried out two chairs. Christen sat down and motioned for Gillian to do the same. Manus went back inside, and they were suddenly alone, two sisters who were strangers.

"Are you happy?" she asked, hoping to put Christen at ease by urging her to talk about her life with the MacPhersons.

"Yes, I'm very happy," she answered. "Manus and I have been married five years now, and soon we will welcome our first child."

Gillian decided to get to the heart of the matter before her sister decided to end the reunion. Twice she'd glanced at the door.

"I only want to talk to you," Gillian said.

"How did you find me?"

"One of the Sinclairs found out who you were

and told Baron Alford. Do you remember him?"

She nodded. "He's sent others in the past to try to find me and drag me back to England. So did the king. How did this soldier find out?"

"I don't know," she replied.

"It seems strange to talk of this. My parents urged me to forget."

"I need you to remember."

"Why?"

"Our Uncle Morgan's life is at stake. Do you remember him?"

"No."

"Christen, I swear to you that when I return to England, I will convince the baron and the king that you are dead. I give you my word. They won't hound you any longer."

Christen's eyes widened. "How will you make them believe you?"

"I'll find a way," she assured her. "But now I need you to try to remember that night our father died."

"What makes you think I would remember what happened? I was very young."

"You're three years older than I am," Gillian pointed out. "Even I remember being terrified."

"I don't want to talk about that night. I've spent years trying to forget."

Gillian tried everything she could think of to convince her sister to help her. She pleaded and begged, but it didn't matter, for Christen continued to refuse. When Manus came outside and announced that his wife needed to rest and that it was time for Gillian to leave, Christen looked relieved, as though she'd just been given a stay of execution, and that broke Gillian's heart.

Overwhelmed with disappointment, she stood up and slowly walked down the path. Tears streamed down her face as she thought about her uncle. What a fool she had been to believe that she could save him.

Suddenly enraged by her sister's attitude, she whirled around and shouted, "Christen, when did you become such a coward? You shame our father, and I thank God he's not alive to see what you've become."

Gillian's disdain slashed through Christen like a knife. Bursting into tears, she called out, "Wait. Don't leave." Pulling away from her husband, she hurried toward Gillian. "Please forgive me," she sobbed.

And suddenly her sister was there and not a stranger, and they embraced and wept for what they had lost. "I never forgot you," Christen whispered. "I never forgot my baby sister. Do you forgive me?" Christen asked as she mopped at her eyes with the backs of her hands. "For so many years I've lived with the guilt, and I knew it wasn't my fault, but I couldn't—"

"You have nothing to feel guilty about," Gillian said. "None of it was your doing."

"But I got away and you were trapped."

"Oh, Christen, you cannot blame yourself. You were just a little girl. You couldn't have changed what happened."

"I remember that night as though it happened yesterday. God knows I tried to forget. I remember father kissing us good-bye. He smelled of leather and soap. His hands were rough with calluses, but I remember liking it when he would stroke my face."

"I don't have many memories of our father."

"It's funny. I don't remember the color of his eyes or hair, but I remember his scent and his touch."

"You remember Liese, don't you?"

"Yes, I do," she replied, smiling.

"She kept my memory of you alive. She told me the soldiers called you Golden Girl."

Christen laughed. "They did, and my hair was golden then. It's turned dark over the years."

"Christen, tell me what happened that night."

"The soldiers were going to take us away because it wasn't safe. One of our father's enemies had attacked."

"Baron Alford and his troops," Gillian supplied.

"I don't remember being afraid. Father gave me a present, and you were upset because he didn't have one for you."

"The jeweled box," Gillian whispered. "He gave you the king's treasure. The soldiers told Liese that your guards were supposed to help you keep it safe until the battle was over and Father could come for you. Do you have it hidden away, Christen?"

"No," her sister answered. "And I don't know what happened to it."

Gillian's disappointment was wrenching. "I... had... hoped..."

A sudden burst of wind stirred the leaves at their feet. It was warm and sunny, but Christen began to rub her arms as though she could ward off the chill that came with the memories.

"I'm sorry," she whispered. "I don't know where the treasure is."

Gillian didn't say a word for a long time, for she was battling her despair and panic. How could she save her uncle now? Without the box or her sister, he was doomed.

"Father died that night, didn't he?"

"Yes," Gillian whispered.

"Were you there?"

She had to force herself to concentrate on what her sister was asking. "Yes, I was there, but my memories from that night are so hazy."

"Father wrapped the box in a cloth."

"Who was there in the chamber with us?"

"There were four soldiers and father," Christen answered. "Tom and Lawrence were to go with me, but I don't remember the names of the men assigned to take you to safety."

"Liese told me their names. They were William and Spencer, and they died trying to protect me. I pray for their souls every night."

"I don't know what happened to Lawrence and Tom. I was given to one of Tom's relatives and told that Father would come for me. Both he and Lawrence left me, and I can only guess that they returned to our father. I never saw them again."

"Did you have the box with you then?"

"No, I didn't."

"Then what happened to it?" Gillian asked, gripping her hands in frustration. Taking a deep breath, she forced herself to calm down, and then said, "Tell me exactly what happened after Father gave you the treasure."

"I dropped it," she said. "I was so afraid I'd broken it and I'd be scolded, but Liese's husband picked it up. Father wrapped it and gave it to me. Then he left."

"Ector was there?"

"Yes, that was his name. He was there, but only for a minute or two. He must have died that night too in the battle."

Gillian shook her head. "No, he didn't die, but he lost his mind. He frightened me," she added. "I heard stories about him over the years. He lived like an animal in the corner of the old stables, and he carried an old knapsack filled with dirt. Liese told me it was cowardice that broke his mind, and she didn't cry at all when she heard he died."

"And Liese? What happened to her?"

"She lived with me and Uncle Morgan, and I think she was very happy. She died in her sleep," she added, "and she hadn't been ill long at all. She didn't suffer. She knew about the passage door between our chambers, but she never let on that she did."

"But we didn't go through that doorway the night of the attack. We were in father's room, weren't we?"

"Yes, and the soldiers lit torches to take us out."

"We fell down the steps," Gillian said then. "It was very steep. I had nightmares for years, and I cannot stand to look down from a great height even now."

"But we didn't fall down the steps. We were pushed. I remember it clearly," Christen said, her voice shaking with emotion. "You were behind me, and you were trying to get the box away from me. I turned around to tell you to stop, and I saw him then. He jumped out of the shadows and threw himself at us. I think he must have taken the box then too. The soldiers lost their footing and we went flying down the steps. There was terrible screaming and then I struck my head on the stones, and when I awoke, I was in Lawrence's arms on his horse and we were well away from the holding."

Gillian's nightmares came back to her with a new clarity and understanding. "In my dreams there were monsters who leapt from the wall and chased us. I must have seen him too."

"I never saw his face," Christen said. "But whoever it was got away with the treasure."

"Then it must still be there... somewhere... unless whoever took it got away before the baron sealed off the holding. Oh, God, I don't know what to do."

"Stay here," Christen urged. "Don't go back to England. You're married to a laird and your life is here."

"Christen, could you turn your back on the family you've come to love?"

"No, of course not."

"Uncle Morgan is depending on me."

"He would want you to be happy."

"He raised me," Gillian cried out. "And he was loving and kind and generous. I would die for him. I must go back."

"I wish I could help you, but I don't know how. Perhaps if I put my mind to it, I can think of something I've forgotten about that night. I'll try," Christen promised.

They continued to sit together and talk about the past until Gillian noticed how weary her sister was. She kissed her on the cheek and promised to come and see her again.

"If I'm able to return from England, I would like to get to know you better. I won't ask anything more of you, Christen. I promise, but now that I've found you again, I don't want to lose you."

Christen slowly stood up. She couldn't quite look Gillian in the eye when she told her how she felt about their reunion. "I remember you as a little girl, but now I feel that we are strangers with little in common. I don't want to hurt your feelings, but I must be completely honest with you. Dredging up the past only brings painful memories back, and when I look at you, I'm reminded of a time I desperately want to forget. Perhaps I'll change my mind one day. Now, however, I believe it's best if we go our separate ways. I promise you, though, that if I remember anything that can be of help to you in your search, I'll send word to you."

Gillian was devastated and quickly bowed her head so that Christen wouldn't see how hurt she was.

"As you wish," she whispered.

Without another word, she turned and slowly walked down the path. She didn't look back.

CHAPTER THIRTY-FOUR

Gillian desperately needed Brodick to put his arms around her and hold her. Marriage had already changed her, she decided, because before she had met Brodick and fallen in love with him, she had always felt that she had to face her problems alone. Now she had a husband she wanted to share her worries with, and her heartaches. At the moment she didn't care why he couldn't tell her he loved her. In her heart she believed that he did, and she certainly didn't believe that he had made a lifelong commitment to her for any ulterior reason. No man would go to such lengths just to get revenge on his enemy, and Brodick would not have married her just to get the names of the Englishmen. Ramsey had simply jumped to the wrong conclusion, and Brodick, unwilling to give voice to his true feelings, didn't bother to correct him.

Brodick was stubborn to the core and so riddled with other flaws it would take her an hour to list them all. She still loved him, though, and she desperately needed his comfort now and his broad shoulder to cry on while she poured her heart out to him. How could her sister be so cold and unfeeling? She had made it abundantly clear that she didn't want Gillian in her life. For so many years she had dreamed of their reunion, and never once had she considered that Christen would reject her.

Gillian felt ashamed and inferior, and couldn't understand why. She knew she hadn't done anything wrong, yet she couldn't help feeling as though she had.

Shaken from their meeting, her only thought to get to her husband and tell him what had happened, she returned the horse to the stable and, despite the soreness in her leg, ran all the way to Ramsey's castle, hoping she would find Brodick there.

Proster met her and gave her the news. "Your husband's gone, milady," he explained. "They've all gone."

"They? Who?" she asked.

"The lairds," he answered. "Iain Maitland and my laird, Ramsey, and Laird Buchanan."

"Iain was here?"

"Aye, he was here just a bit after dawn this morning."

"Where did my husband go?"

"With Ramsey and Iain."

"Yes," she said, trying to control her frustration. "But exactly where did they go?"

547

He seemed surprised she hadn't been informed. "To the crest to join their soldiers. Surely you knew the call to arms went out days ago," he added.

"No, I didn't know," she admitted.

"The lairds have gathered their fighting men and by now they should have all assembled."

"At the crest."

"Yes," he said with a nod.

"And where is this crest?"

"A good ride to the south," he told her.

"Then they won't be back until late, will they?"

"Late? Milady, they won't be back for a long while."

She still didn't understand. Proster, seeing her confusion, hastened to explain. "They're going to England, and surely you know their purpose."

"I know they plan to go to England eventually, but you're mistaken in your belief that they're leaving now. If you'll excuse me, I'll go back to the cottage and await my husband's return."

"You'll have a long wait, then," Proster said. "He isn't coming back, and tomorrow you'll be leaving."

"Where will I be going?"

"Home," he answered. "I heard your husband give orders. There will be Buchanan soldiers coming for you tomorrow to escort you to your new home. Graeme and Lochlan are in charge of seeing to your safety until then."

Gillian's head was spinning, and her stomach felt as though it had been tied in knots. "And who are Graeme and Lochlan?"

"Graeme's a MacPherson," the young soldier told her proudly. "And Lochlan is a Sinclair. They're equal in their duties and their standing. We're all equal now, our laird has declared it so, and he says that we may keep our clan's name and still live in harmony as one."

"I see," she whispered.

"Are you feeling unwell, milady? You've gone pale."

Ignoring his question, she cried out, "Proster, you couldn't have heard correctly. When they go to England, they're taking me with them. I was promised... he wouldn't break his word to me. He knows... They all know that if the English see them, my uncle will die. No, you have to be mistaken. Brodick's going to come back for me."

Her distress alarmed the soldier, and he didn't know what to do. He wanted to lie to her, to tell her, yes, he must have been wrong, but he knew that eventually she'd have to accept the truth, and so he braced himself for her reaction, prayed she wouldn't faint on him, and then blurted out, "As God is my witness, I heard them correctly. Everyone knows... but you," he stammered. "They are going to England, and you are being taken to the Buchanan holding. Your husband was concerned about your injury, and he wanted you to have one day's rest before riding such a distance. It was very thoughtful of him, wasn't it, milady?"

She didn't answer him. She turned and started to walk away, then stopped. "Thank you, Proster, for explaining."

"Milady, if you still don't believe me, talk to Graeme and Lochlan. They'll confirm what I've just told you."

"I don't need to talk to them. I believe you. Now, if you'll excuse me, I'd like to go back to the cottage."

"With your permission, I'll walk with you," he offered. "You don't look well," he added. "Is your leg paining you?"

"No, it isn't," she answered. Her voice was flat.

She didn't say another word until they'd returned to the cottage. Proster had just bowed to her and turned to leave when she called him back. "Do you know where Kevin and Annie Drummond live?"

"All the soldiers know the Drummonds. When someone gets hurt, he goes to her for help. If he doesn't die on the way, she heals him. Most times, anyway," he added. "Why do you ask?"

"I was just curious," she lied. "In a little while, I would like to return to my sister's home. Would you please accompany me?"

Honored that the Buchanan's woman would choose him to escort her, he squared his shoulders. "I would be happy to ride with you, but didn't you just come from your sister's?"

"Yes, but I forgot to give her the presents I brought from England, and she's most anxious to have them. When I'm ready to leave, I'll send for you."

"As you wish," he said.

She closed the door softly, walked to the bed, and sat down, and then buried her face in her hands and wept.

CHAPTER THIRTY-FIVE

She moved with an urgency born out of desperation. Tearing the Buchanan plaid from her body, she threw it on the bed and reached for her English gown. She had already packed a small bag, filled it with the necessities she would need on her journey.

Bridgid interrupted her. Gillian heard her call out, opened the door a crack, and told her friend she wasn't feeling well. She tried to shut the door then, but Bridgid wouldn't let her. She pushed it open and rushed inside.

"If you're ill, I'll help you. Why are you dressed in those clothes? Your husband won't like it. You should be wearing the Buchanan colors."

With her back to her friend Gillian tossed her brush into the bag and then tied it closed. When she turned around, Bridgid saw her face and knew something was terribly wrong.

"What is it?" she demanded. "Tell me and I'll help you any way that I can."

"I'm leaving."

"Yes, I just heard, but not until tomorrow. Your husband's soldiers won't be here until then. Is that what's upsetting you? Don't you want to go to your new home?" she asked, trying desperately to understand.

"I'm going home to England."

"What? You cannot be serious..."

"And I'm never wearing the Buchanan plaid again. Never," she cried out. "Brodick betrayed me, and I will never, ever forgive him." The truth of it overwhelmed her, and she sat down on the bed before her legs gave out. "He gave me his word that he and Iain and Ramsey would wait..."

Bridgid sat beside her. "They've all gone to England."

"Yes," she answered. "Proster told me this morning that they had left. Brodick promised me that he would take me with him. I made him give me his word before I would tell him the names of the barons who helped Gideon take Alec Maitland."

"What was their reason for taking the laird's son?"

"They didn't mean to take him. They thought they'd kidnapped Ramsey's brother."

Bridgid's mind was racing with questions. "Start at the beginning and tell me what happened. Then maybe I can figure out a way to help you."

"You can't help me," she whispered. "Oh,

God, I don't know how I'll be able to protect my uncle now. I'm so scared and I..." Her voice broke on a sob.

Bridgid patted her arm and pleaded with her to explain.

And so Gillian told her everything, beginning with the night her father was murdered. By the time she was finished, she realized how hopeless her situation was.

"If you don't return to England with the box or your sister, how will you save your uncle?" Bridgid asked.

"It doesn't matter now. As soon as the lairds attack, Alford will order Morgan's death."

"What makes you think your uncle is still alive? You told me that Baron Alford has never kept his word."

"Alford knows I won't give him the treasure until I see my uncle is safe."

Bridgid in her agitation began to pace about the cottage. "But you don't have the box."

"I know I don't have it," she lamented. "I had hoped that my sister would know where it was..."

"But she didn't know," Bridgid said. "Tell me again who was in the chamber with your father the night he gave Christen the treasure."

"I already told you that there were four soldiers with my father," she explained once again. "And the reeve, Ector, but he was only in the chamber for a moment. Christen told me he gave Father a message and then left."

Bridgid mulled the puzzle over in her mind,

shook her head, and then asked, "The soldiers assigned to protect you were both killed?"

"Yes, they were."

"You're absolutely certain? Did you see them die?"

"If I did, I don't remember. I was very young," she reminded her friend. "But Liese told me they died protecting me. She was certain."

"But your sister isn't certain what happened to the soldiers who took her north. She's only guessing that they returned to your father's estate. Isn't that true?"

"Yes, but—"

Bridgid interrupted her before she could finish. "Then couldn't one of them have taken the treasure?"

"No," she said. "They were loyal and honorable men, and my father trusted them implicitly."

"Perhaps his trust was misplaced," she offered. "It has to be one of them, or the reeve, but you just said that Ector was only in the chamber for a very short while."

"Oh, it couldn't have been Ector. He was daft."

"He was crazed?"

"Yes," she answered impatiently. She stood up then and went to the door.

"Where are you going?"

"I asked Proster to accompany me to my sister's home, and I'm going to go get him."

"But you told me that Christen doesn't wish to see you again."

"Yes, that's true, but—"

"Then why are you going back?"

With a sigh she said, "I'm not really going to my sister's. Proster knows where the Drummonds live, and once we're on our way to Christen's, I'm going to insist that he take me on to Annie's instead."

"But why?" she persisted.

"Because Kevin and Annie know the way to the Len holding, and I know the way home from there."

Bridgid was stunned. "My God, you really are going back to England. You told me you were, but I didn't believe you."

"Yes, I am." When Bridgid ran to her, she hugged her farewell. "I want you to know how much your friendship has meant to me. I'm going to miss you."

"But I'll see you again, won't I?"

"No. I'm not coming back."

"What about Brodick? You love him."

"He doesn't love me. He used me, Bridgid, to get what he wanted. I meant so little to him that he couldn't..."

It was too painful to talk about. Straightening away from her friend, she said, "I must get going."

"Wait," Bridgid demanded when Gillian reached for the latch. "I'll go hunt Proster down while you change your clothes."

"I'm never wearing the Buchanan colors again."

"Be reasonable. Everyone will know you're up to something if you go outside wearing those clothes. You've got to change."

Gillian realized her friend was right, they would notice. "I wasn't thinking... I was so angry, and I... Yes, I'll change my clothes while you go get Proster."

"It may take me a while to find him, but you stay here. Promise me you'll wait inside."

"I'll wait. Remember," she warned, "Proster thinks I'm going to see Christen."

"I know," Bridgid said as she opened the door. She stepped out onto the stoop, then turned to pull the door closed. Still puzzling over the disappearance of the treasure, her mind raced with possibilities. "Could I ask you one more question?"

"What is it?"

"You said that Ector was crazed. Were you exaggerating because he was a little peculiar, or did you really mean it? Was he truly crazed?"

"Oh, yes, he was," she answered in a rush. "Now, please hurry, Bridgid. I must get going as soon as possible."

"But I was just wondering..."

"Now what?" she asked.

"Why would your father put a crazed man in charge of collecting the rents? That doesn't make any sense at all."

"Ector wasn't crazy then. Liese told me it was cowardice that broke his mind. After the siege he was never the same. I know Ector was mean-tempered, cruel, and terribly greedy. Now, please go and get Proster."

Bridgid finally closed the door. Gillian removed her gown and was reaching for the plaid when she suddenly froze and let out a loud gasp.

"My God, of course."

Bridgid was gone a long time, and when she returned to the cottage, Gillian was frantic with worry.

"What took you so long?" she demanded as soon as her friend came inside.

"I had to do a few things first," she said. "Proster's here, and he isn't alone. He's letting Ker and Alan ride along. They're acting like they're escorting a princess. You should have heard them carrying on. They're honored that you asked a MacPherson."

"They're young is what they are," she countered.

"I've been thinking about your plans," she said then. "I don't think you should ride to the Drummonds because their home could be out of your way. Take a direct route to the Len holding. I'm sure Proster knows the way."

"How can you be sure?"

"All the soldiers know the territory boundaries and where they can ride and where they can't. Their lives depend upon such knowledge."

"But I don't know how I can convince the soldier to take me there. I was going to tell him I needed Annie's treatment for my leg."

"Then do that," she advised. "But when we're on our way, then we'll tell Proster we must go to the Len holding."

"We? Bridgid, you cannot mean—"

"I'm going to England with you. I've already packed my things and rolled them in a plaid so the soldiers won't be suspicious. It's tied behind the saddle of my mare. That's what took me so long."

Bridgid's voice was calm, but her hands were fisted at her sides and she had a determined glint in her eyes. When Gillian began to shake her head, Bridgid hurried to convince her that her mind was made up and that nothing her friend would say could change her decision.

"There isn't anything for me here, and I won't stay and watch Ramsey marry Meggan. It would hurt too much. No, I can't stay. I won't. For God's sake, my own mother doesn't even want me around, and that's the truth of it. I don't know where else I could go. Please, Gillian. Let me come with you. I've always been curious about England, and you told me that your Uncle Morgan had Highland blood. I'm sure he'll let me stay with him for a little while... until I decide what to do."

"I can't take you with me. You could get hurt and I wouldn't be able to protect you from him."

"The baron?"

"Yes," she answered. "You don't understand what he's like. He's a monster."

"How do you plan to protect yourself? You were ordered to return with your sister and the treasure, but you're going back without either. If anyone should be afraid, it's you."

"I don't have a choice," she argued. "I have to go back home, and you have to stay here."

"I'm begging you, Gillian. I accept the danger, and I take full responsibility for anything that might happen to me. Please reconsider. I have a plan in mind."

"I couldn't live with myself if you were hurt."

"Then let me ride with you as far as the Len holding. I can help you persuade Proster. I know I can."

"And you'll come back here with them?"

"Yes," Bridgid promised and immediately felt a wave of guilt for lying to her dear friend. She did have a sound plan and her mind was made up, and with or without Gillian's permission or approval, she was going to help her.

"We... that is, you... could run into Brodick and the others."

"No, I don't think I will. They'll surely go to my Uncle Morgan's home first, and it's in the northwest of England, a remote area to be sure, and I'm heading east to Dunhanshire."

"Where is this Baron Alford's estate?"

"Due south from my uncle's home. God willing, by the time they reach Dunhanshire, the ransom will be paid and it will be over."

"What will be over?"

Gillian shook her head. She wasn't going to explain. Bridgid suddenly felt chilled to the bone. "Shall we go then?"

Straightening her shoulders, Gillian nodded. As she walked through the doorway, she whispered, "God be with us."

CHAPTER THIRTY-SIX

It was a desperate race against time. She knew she would reach Dunhanshire well before the fall festival, but her fear was that Brodick and Iain and Ramsey would get there before her. And God help them then. As angry as she was at her husband for deceiving her and as determined as she was never to return to the Highlands, she was still terrified for his safety. He had broken her heart, but she couldn't stop loving him. If he and the others tried to breach Alford's fortress, there would be a war and they would all die.

She was certain Alford had split his ranks and sequestered soldiers at his estate and at her Uncle Morgan's holding. He had boasted he had more than eight hundred fighting men at his beck and call, and though Gillian doubted any of them were actually loyal or beholden to the baron, she knew they feared him. Alford controlled his troops with tyranny, using torture as his method to make examples of the men who dared to deny him.

Her blood ran cold thinking about Alford's sadistic lessons, and all she could concentrate on was finding a way to protect the man she loved.

She was a full day's ride away from Dunhanshire when she was forced to stop. Exhaustion had taken its toll, and she was actually light-headed from lack of food and sleep.

Proster, Ker, Alan, and Bridgid were still at her side. She'd tried several times to get them to go home, but none of them would listen to her. Bridgid kept insisting that she had a plan, but she refused to tell Gillian what it was, and no matter how much Gillian argued and begged her to go back, she stubbornly resisted. The young soldiers were almost as maddening. Proster explained over and over again that, since she wouldn't return to the Sinclair holding with him, he and his friends were determined to stay by her and do their best to protect her.

It was getting dark when Bridgid suggested that they stop for the night. Gillian spotted a thatched roof in the distance and insisted on gaining permission to cross the farmland before they rested. Ignoring Proster's vehement protest, she dismounted at the door.

A family of five resided in the tiny house. The father, an older man with skin so weathered his face looked like a dried riverbed, was at first suspicious of their motives, for he had seen the Highlanders put their hands to their swords, but as soon as Gillian introduced herself and formally requested to spend the night on their land, his demeanor softened.

He bowed to his waist. "My name's Randall and the woman hiding behind me is Sarah. The land ain't mine, but you know that already, don't you? And yet you still ask my permission. I till the land for me liege lord, Baron Hardington, and I know he ain't gonna mind if you rest on his grass. I knew your father, milady. He was a grand man, and I'm honored to be of assistance to you. You and your friends are welcome to share our supper with us. Come inside and warm yourself by the fire while my boys see to your horses."

Although they had little to share, they insisted that Gillian and Bridgid and the soldiers join them. Bridgid was unusually quiet during the meal. She sat beside Gillian, the two of them squeezed in between two of Randall's strapping boys.

When they were leaving, Sarah gave them blankets from her bed. "It chills at night," she explained. "Just leave them be in the field when you leave tomorrow and Randall will fetch them."

"Is there anything more we can do for you?" Randall asked.

Gillian took the man aside and spoke to him in a low whisper. "There is something I need that would help immensely, but I must be certain that if you give me your word, you'll see it through, no matter what. Lives are at stake, Randall, so if you cannot do this errand, you be honest and tell me so now. I don't mean to insult you, but the importance—"

"If I can do it, I will," he promised. "Tell me what you need, and then I'll decide."

"You must take a message for me," she whispered. "Say these words exactly. 'Lady Gillian has found Arianna's treasure.'"

Randall repeated the words twice, then nodded. "Now tell me who I am to give this message to, milady."

Leaning close, she whispered the name in his ear. Randall's knees weakened.

"You're... certain of this?"

"Yes, I'm certain."

The old man made the sign of the cross. "But they're heathens, milady... all of them."

"What I ask of you will require courage. Will you take my message?"

Randall slowly nodded. "I'll leave at dawn."

CHAPTER THIRTY-SEVEN

Dunhanshire was swarming with soldiers. It was a black, moonless night, but the holding was as bright as the king's palace, for torches blazed orange red along the top of the parapets and the walkways, and from the distance the fires looked like the eyes of demons staring out at them.

The five stood clustered together, well hidden in the dense forest beyond the meadow, all silent as they listened to the clanking sound of the drawbridge being lowered and then watched yet another troop of soldiers riding into the holding.

"They go into the bowels of hell," Ker whispered. "I can feel the evil here."

"Why are there so many soldiers?" Proster asked. "The baron must be preparing for battle. I swear I've counted over a hundred men since we've been watching."

"He must have heard that our soldiers are coming," Alan speculated.

Gillian shook her head. "Alford always surrounds himself with a league of soldiers to protect him. He wants to make certain no one can sneak up on him and take him by surprise."

"He fears death, doesn't he?" Bridgid said. "He knows he'll burn in hell for his sins. Is he an old man?"

"No," Gillian answered. "When I was a child, I thought he was, but he was a very young man then. Because of his friendship with John, Alford was given power, and it has been his lifelong quest to gain more. Dunhanshire used to be a joyful place," she added. "But Alford and his greed changed all of that. He killed my father and destroyed my family."

"God willing, our soldiers will come thundering down the hills tomorrow and attack," Proster said.

"I pray to God they stay away until this is finished," Gillian countered.

"Do you think your uncle is inside Dunhanshire?" Bridgid asked.

"I don't know," she answered. "But I'll find out tomorrow. We'll rest here tonight." She untied the strap holding her blanket to the horse's back and then spread the woolen square under one of the large oak trees. Bridgid followed her and sat down beside her.

"This is as far as we go together," Gillian said. "I have to do the rest alone."

"You know that Proster isn't going to let you go into Dunhanshire alone."

"You've got to help me make him understand," she whispered. "I'll be safe as long as Alford thinks I have what he wants, but if Proster goes with me, I promise you he'll use him against me. He must stay here with you and Ker and Alan."

Proster dropped down on one knee beside Gillian. "We've been talking," he said with a nod toward his friends. "And we've decided that you should wait here until your husband arrives. Then you can go inside."

"Our minds are made up, milady," Ker interjected.

"I'll wait until the middle of the day," she said. "The baron doesn't awaken until then, but I won't wait any longer."

"Either you wait for your husband or I go with you," Proster argued.

"We will put off this discussion until tomorrow. Now we should rest." She closed her eyes to discourage the soldier from continuing to argue with her.

Bridgid fell asleep almost immediately, but Gillian dozed off and on through the night. The soldiers slept at her feet with their swords clasped in their hands.

None of them heard her leave.

565

By the time she crossed the meadow she was surrounded by Alford's soldiers and escorted inside the holding. She was then taken to the great hall and told to wait until Alford's senior officer arrived.

A young servant girl who obviously didn't know that the baron wouldn't have wanted her to see to Gillian's comfort carried in a tray of food and set it on the table. Two soldiers stood guard at the entrance watching Gillian's every move. For a long while she paced in front of the hearth, and when she grew weary, she sat at the table and forced herself to swallow bites of the cold meat and bread on the trencher. Gillian had little appetite, but she knew she'd need nourishment to strengthen her for the confrontation with Alford.

The soldier in charge finally came inside. He was a brute of a man with a broad, bulging forehead and small dark eyes as flat and lifeless as marbles.

"Baron Alford doesn't like to be disturbed while he's sleeping. He and his companions, Baron Edwin and Baron Hugh, were up quite late last night."

"I have nothing to say to Alford until I see my Uncle Morgan. Is he here?"

"No," he answered sourly. "But you are in luck. Last week the baron ordered soldiers to bring him here from his estate."

"Then my uncle was allowed to stay in his own home?" she asked.

"Since you've been gone, your uncle has been moved twice," he replied.

"Why is it taking the soldiers so long to bring him here? If they left last week..."

"The soldiers were also sent to Baron Alford's home to fetch his favorite cloak. They should be here any time now."

Gillian was taken upstairs and locked in the same chamber she and Alec had escaped from weeks before. Snickering, the soldier told her the passage had been sealed.

The wait continued until late afternoon. She spent a good deal of time praying and worrying about Brodick and the others. Please God, keep them safe and keep them away from this place until it's finished and Alford can't hurt them.

The brute unlatched the door and told her the baron was waiting to see her. "The rest of your family has arrived," he announced.

She wanted to ask him if her uncle was well, but she knew he wouldn't tell her anything more, and so she hurried downstairs to see for herself.

Edwin was waiting. She didn't give him a second glance as she hurried past him into the hall. Alford and Hugh were seated at the table side by side. They had obviously had too much to drink the night before, for Hugh's complexion was gray and his hands shook when he reached for his goblet. Red liquid sloshed over the rim onto the table as he greedily drank the wine like a man dying of thirst.

Alford rubbed his forehead to rid himself of the pounding headache.

"Where is my uncle?" she demanded.

"He'll be here soon," he answered. "Tell me, Gillian. Did you fail or succeed in your quest?"

"I won't tell you anything until I see my Uncle Morgan."

"Then perhaps your sister will. Bring her in, Edwin," he called out, then grimaced in pain and put his hand to his forehead again.

Because Alford was watching her closely, Gillian tried to hide her surprise and confusion. Bring her sister in? What in God's name was he talking about?

"Ah, there she is now," Alford crooned.

Gillian whirled around and nearly fell over as Bridgid sauntered into the hall. Dear God, what was she doing? The soldiers must have found their hiding place, Gillian decided then, and if that were true, what had happened to Proster and Ker and Alan?

She took a panicky breath. Bridgid smiled at her and then asked loud enough to be overheard, "Which one of the pigs is Alford?"

Alford lunged forward, bracing his hands on the table to support himself. "You will guard your tongue," he shouted, "or I'll have it cut out."

Bridgid didn't seem the least impressed by the threat. "You'll die trying," she shouted back.

Gillian grabbed her hand to get her to be silent. Inciting the beast in his cave was dangerous and foolish.

"Where is my uncle, Alford?"

He waved away her question. Then Hugh drew his attention with his comment. "I'm not disappointed in the way Christen turned out. She still has her yellow hair."

Edwin joined his friends at the table and snapped his fingers to alert the servants to bring food and more wine. "They don't look like sisters."

Alford studied the two women. "They didn't look like sisters when they were young. Christen was always the pretty one, and Gillian was the mouse."

"She isn't a mouse now," Hugh chortled. Reaching under the table he began to rub himself. "I want her, Alford."

Alford ignored the demand. "What clan did you live with?" he asked.

"The MacPhersons," Bridgid answered.

"And what name did those heathens give you, or have you always been called Christen?"

Gillian's heart started pounding, because she couldn't remember if she had told Bridgid the name Christen was given by the Highlanders.

"I'm called Kate," Bridgid answered. "I much prefer it to Christen."

"She has the same sour disposition as Gillian," Hugh remarked. "They're sisters, all right."

"Yes," Alford drawled, but the furtive look in his eyes said he still wasn't completely convinced. Impatient, he stood up and came around the table. "Do you have my treasure with you, Christen?" His beady eyes darted back and forth between the women as he waited for her answer.

He was so vile he made her skin crawl. She boldly faced him and summoned forth her most defiant look. "I thought the treasure belonged to your king."

"*My* king?"

Bridgid quickly recovered from her blunder. Forcing a shrug of indifference, she said, "I'm a MacPherson now, and I have lived in the Highlands for many years and have become loyal to the king of Scotland. I don't consider England my home."

"What about your Uncle Morgan? Do you consider yourself loyal to him?"

"I don't remember him," she said. "I'm merely helping my sister."

His eyes were piercing as he studied her. "I plan to see that the king gets the box back," Alford snapped. "Do you have it with you?"

Edwin came rushing forward to join his friend. Scratching his triple chins, he remarked, "Surely she was searched before she was brought in."

"Search her again," Hugh called out, snickering. "Take her to one of the chambers and give her a thorough examination, Edwin. Start with the neck and work your way down."

Gillian intruded before the situation got completely out of hand. "My sister doesn't have the box, and she doesn't know where it is."

Alford slapped Edwin's hand as he was reaching for Bridgid. "You can have her later," he promised. Sidling close to Gillian, he asked, "Do you have the treasure?"

"No."

"You may take Christen upstairs now, Edwin. Do what you want with her. Hugh, would you like to join them?"

With a hoot of laughter, Hugh drained his goblet and shoved his stool back as he stood. "I believe I will join them," he called out.

Alford was watching Gillian closely as he made his suggestion. She didn't show any reaction, but when Edwin lunged for Bridgid, she moved with amazing speed and shoved him back.

Incensed by her interference, Edwin lashed out and slapped her across her face. The force was enough to knock her into Bridgid, who grabbed her to keep her from falling.

"If you touch her again, I'll kill you," Bridgid shouted.

Alford raised his hand to let Edwin know he was to wait.

"Please, go and sit down," Gillian ordered Bridgid.

She wanted her out of harm's way, and Bridgid didn't have to be told twice. She backed away from Edwin and then hurried to a chair against the far wall. Her heart was pounding from fear and shame because she realized now that she was far more of a deterrent than a help to Gillian. Too late she understood what her friend had meant when she'd told Proster that if he went with her, the baron would use him to get what he wanted.

"This is between you and me, Alford," Gillian said. "It began in this hall, and it will end here. I know where the treasure is hidden, and I'll show you where it is as soon as Uncle Morgan and my sister are given safe passage out of here. I suggest you bring my uncle to me as quickly as possible, for I will not tell you anything more until I see for myself that he is well. Do we understand each other?"

"Did you notice, Edwin, that she doesn't ask safe passage for herself?"

His friend nodded, and realizing he wasn't going to get Bridgid upstairs now, he rejoined Hugh at the table. Reaching for the jug of wine, he called out, "Why didn't she include herself?"

"Because she knows I will never let her go." He stepped closer to Gillian and said, "You and I have been playing our game for years now, and one of us must lose. I swear to you the day will come when I will break that spirit inside you and you will learn to cower in my presence."

A shout disrupted his train of thought, and the brute came running into the hall pulling another soldier along in his wake.

"You know better than to interrupt, Horace," the baron snarled at the brute.

"We have good cause," he called out. "You'll want to hear this, milord." Turning to the soldier, he commanded, "Tell him, Arthur."

The pock-faced soldier nodded, swallowed loudly, and then blurted, "We have just returned... We went to Baron Morgan Chapman's holding to fetch him here for you, milord, just as you ordered, but when we—"

Alford cut him off. "You were told to go to my home first."

"Yes, milord, but it seemed quicker to us if we—"

"Did you bring me my favorite cloak?"

The question seemed too difficult for the soldier to understand. Horace shoved him. "Answer your baron," he commanded.

Arthur frantically shook his head. "No... no, we didn't think to look for your cloak."

"Where's Morgan?" Alford demanded then. "Bring him inside."

"I can't, milord. I can't. You don't understand what's happened. We went to his estate, and it was... empty. They're gone. All of them gone."

"What are you stammering about? Who's gone?"

"The soldiers," Arthur wailed, terrified because he knew that when the baron was given bad news, he often lashed out at the messenger. Stepping back to put some distance between them, he continued, "Morgan's home was empty and your soldiers have vanished."

"What do you mean, they've 'vanished'?" he roared.

Arthur cringed when he saw the murderous rage in the baron's eyes. "I'm telling you the truth. The men have vanished. The holding was completely empty, milord, and there was no sign of attack or struggle. Not a chair or a stool was overturned, and we couldn't find any arrows or blood anywhere. It's as though they all just got up and walked away."

"Where is my Uncle Morgan?" Gillian demanded.

"Silence," Alford shouted. "What did the servants tell you happened?" he asked Arthur.

"There were no servants there, milord. The place was deserted I tell you. We decided then that the soldiers must have gone to your home and taken the servants with them and that you had ordered them to do so."

"I gave no such order," Alford muttered, his anger barely controlled. "And they will pay with their lives for leaving their posts, every last one of them."

Horace cleared his throat and said, "There is more for you to hear, Baron."

Alford squinted at Arthur. "Well?" he snapped when the soldier stood there quivering in his boots.

"We rode like lightning to your holding, milord, but when we got there, the draw-bridge was down... and it was the same. Not a soldier was there."

"What say you?" Alford screeched.

"Your home was deserted."

"And the servants?"

"They, too, had vanished."

Alford became rigid. "My own men dare to desert me? Where could they have gone? Where?" he bellowed. "I will know who is responsible for this..." He suddenly stopped ranting. His head snapped up and he whirled to confront Gillian. "What do you know about this?"

"I know only what I have just heard."

He didn't believe her. He reached for his dagger at his waist, realized it was on the table, and went to get it. Then he slowly, deliberately walked back to her and held the blade in front of her face.

"I'll slice your throat, you bitch, if you don't tell me the truth. Where are my soldiers?"

"I don't know," she answered. "Would you like me to guess?"

He pressed the point of the blade against the side of her neck, a look of perverted pleasure in his eyes as he deliberately pricked her skin. He took yet another step closer to her and then froze, slowly looking down at the knife Gillian had pressed against his belly.

"Shall we find out whose blade is quicker?" she whispered.

He jumped back. "Seize her," he shouted to Horace.

Bridgid jumped up and ran to Gillian, but Horace saw her coming and shoved her aside. He grabbed Gillian's arm and tried to snatch the weapon away from her. She cut him twice in the palm of his hand before he was able to get the knife.

"I know what happened to your soldiers," Bridgid shouted.

"Move back, Horace," Alford ordered.

Shaken, Alford poured himself a drink, then turned and leaned against the table's edge. "Tell me what happened to them."

"They're dead," Bridgid answered. "All of them. Did you think you could take a child from a powerful laird and not suffer the consequences?" Gripping her hands together, she laughed. "You're next. You and your friends."

Edwin scoffed. "They won't come to the heart of England. They wouldn't dare."

"Yes," Hugh agreed. "If it was the Highlanders, they've gone back home by now. They've certainly finished—"

"Oh, they've only just begun," Gillian called out. "They don't care about gold or treasures. They want the three of you, and they won't stop until you're dead."

"She speaks lies," Horace shouted. "The Highlanders are savages, and our soldiers are vastly superior."

Gillian laughed. "Then pray tell, where are they?"

"How many soldiers do you have posted along the perimeter?" Hugh asked.

"Whatever the number, perhaps you should double the guards. One cannot be too cautious," Edwin interjected.

Alford shrugged at their worries. "If it will please you, I will double the guard. See to it, Horace," he commanded. "No one can get into this holding. I've made it impenetrable. Why, I've over two hundred men here, all hand-picked and all loyal to me. Add their number to the soldiers who escorted the two of you, and we are an invincible force."

"There were forty men who rode with me," Hugh said.

"Twenty-two came with me," Edwin said.

"So you see? We have nothing to fear."

The commander had only just left the hall when he came racing back. "Milord ... you have company coming."

"Who is it?"

"My God, it's the heathens?" Edwin shouted.

"Nay, Baron, it's not the heathens. It's the king himself and a full contingent of soldiers. The watch spotted their banner, milord, and the drawbridge has been lowered."

Alford was astounded. "John is here? The king of England is at my door?"

"Aye, Baron."

"How many soldiers do you suppose ride with him?" Alford asked.

"The watch reported near to sixty or seventy men."

Alford snorted. "So my troops outnumber his," he remarked.

Hugh laughed. "You always try to outdo him, don't you?"

"Whenever I can," he admitted. "He is king, however, and that puts me at a distinct disadvantage. Still, I do what I can."

"We can certainly relax our guard now," Edwin said.

Alford clapped his hands and ordered the servants to prepare a feast for their honored guest. Hugh and Edwin hurried upstairs to change their tunics, and Alford waited until they had left the hall before grabbing Gillian.

In a low hiss he whispered, "You listen to me. You will keep silent about the treasure. Do you hear me? You will not tell the king you know where Arianna's box is hidden. I swear I'll kill your uncle and your sister if you defy me on this."

"I understand."

He shoved her away from him. "Go and sit in the corner. Hopefully the king will pay you little attention."

Bridgid followed Gillian and sat next to her. "I've made a mess of things, haven't I?" she whispered.

"No," she answered. "Don't worry. It's going to be over soon."

"Are you afraid?"

"Yes."

The women fell silent when Hugh and Edwin came running back into the hall. Hugh was pulling his tunic down over his stomach as he joined Alford, and Edwin was trying to rub off the stain he'd just noticed on his sleeve.

Servants frantically rushed about preparing the great hall for their noble guest. Additional logs were added to the fire in the hearth, the table was cleared, and after a fine linen cloth was spread upon it, tapered candles in silver holders were placed in the center.

Hugh and Edwin stood with Alford off to the side and discussed the king's reasons for coming to Dunhanshire.

"Perhaps he's heard your soldiers have left their posts at your estate and Baron Morgan's," Edwin speculated.

"They didn't leave their posts," Hugh argued. "They fled in the face of battle, and they should all die for their cowardice."

"The king couldn't have heard that news yet," Alford pointed out.

"If he hasn't heard the news, then why is he here?" Edwin asked.

"I think I know what he wants," Alford said. "There's talk of another journey to France, and he's probably going to press me to go with him."

Bridgid nudged Gillian. "Did you see Alford's reaction when he heard that his soldiers had vanished? I thought the vein in his forehead was going to explode."

"Bridgid, when the king comes inside, don't lie to him. If he asks your name, tell him the truth."

"But then Alford will know I'm not your sister."

"You cannot lie to the king of England."

Bridgid stopped arguing and agreed to do as Gillian asked. "It's bad timing that John decided to visit his friend now. Why do you suppose your king is here?"

"I know why," Gillian answered. "I sent for him."

CHAPTER THIRTY-EIGHT

The day of reckoning had finally arrived. John, king of the realm, didn't walk into the hall; he strutted. At least twenty soldiers, all in shiny new garb, marched in behind him in pairs, then fanned out, forming a circular cocoon from one side of the entrance to the other. The walls were quickly lined with heavily armed soldiers who had but one intent—to make certain their king remained safe.

Gillian and Bridgid made a formal curtsy to one knee, bowed their heads, and waited for the king to grant them permission to stand.

Bridgid peeked. Curious to get a good look at the man she had been taught was the devil incarnate, she was a little surprised he didn't have horns growing out of his head. John was quite ordinary looking, actually, with dark, wavy hair in need of a trim and a thick, wiry, brown beard speckled with gray. His size was ordinary too, and she guessed that the top of his head wouldn't even reach the shoulders of Ramsey or Brodick or Iain.

The three barons genuflected to their king, and after John had granted them permission to rise, Alford crooned, "What a wonderful surprise, my lord."

"Yes, indeed," John replied. "What mischief have you gotten yourself into now, Alford," he drawled, a hint of amusement in his voice.

"No mischief," Alford assured him. "To what do I owe the pleasure of your company, my lord?"

"I haven't come to see you," John said, impatient as he turned his back on Alford and strode purposefully across the hall.

Gillian and Bridgid were suddenly staring at a pair of shiny boots.

"Stand," John commanded.

The ladies did as he ordered. Bridgid looked

the king right in his eyes, but then she noticed that Gillian's head was bowed and so she hastened to imitate her.

"Which one of you fair ladies is Gillian?"

"I am Lady Gillian, my lord," she answered.

Alford came running. "May I ask, my lord. What business do you have with my ward?"

"Your ward, Alford? Did I give her to you then?"

Gillian slowly raised her gaze, and the king was so startled by the intensity of her green eyes and her exquisite features he drew a sharp breath. He spoke his thought aloud. "She is magnificent. Why hasn't she been brought to my court?"

"I didn't think you would want the daughter of a murderer in your court," Alford said. "As you know, I firmly believe that Gillian's father was involved in the plot to kill Arianna and steal the treasure, and I felt that you would have been constantly reminded of the tragedy every time you saw Gillian. That is why I didn't bring her to court, my lord. I didn't think you should have to bear such pain."

John's eyes narrowed. "Yes, of course. You have been a very thoughtful friend, Alford."

The baron inclined his head and then remarked, "Gillian has been living in the north of England with her Uncle Morgan... Baron Chapman. And she has only just returned to Dunhanshire. I'll send her upstairs so you won't have to look upon her any longer."

"You'll do no such thing. Go and sit with Hugh and Edwin while I have a word in private with these two ladies."

Alford didn't dare argue. He gave Gillian a threatening glance before hurrying to join his friends. Too agitated to sit, he stood with Hugh and Edwin and strained to overhear the king's conversation.

John ignored the barons as he once again addressed Gillian. "Where is it?" he demanded urgently, and before she could respond, he asked, "Do you have Arianna's treasure with you?"

"No, my lord, but I think I know where it's hidden."

"You think?" he repeated in a near shout. "You aren't certain? If I have made this journey on a whim, I assure you I will be displeased."

His face was turning red, and she hurried to explain before he completely lost his temper and went into one of his famous rages.

"I didn't have time to look for myself, but I'm certain it's here... at Dunhanshire. Just a short walk away," she assured him.

Her explanation calmed him. "If the treasure is recovered, you do realize that it will prove without a doubt that your father was involved in the murder of Arianna?"

She knew she shouldn't argue with the king, but she couldn't stop herself from defending her father. "I was told... and I believe... that my father was an honorable man, and honorable men do not kill innocent women."

"I, too, believed your father was a loyal subject and a good man," John said, "... until he betrayed me."

"I cannot believe that he did betray you," she whispered. "My mother had only just passed away, and my father was mourning her at home... here, my lord, at Dunhanshire."

"I know he wasn't in court when Arianna died, but Alford is convinced that he was in league with another. Aye, the man who killed Arianna passed the treasure to your father. If the treasure is here, it proves Alford's theory is correct."

"I don't know what to say to convince you that my father was innocent," she said.

"Soon we may have proof that he was a blackheart. If you had kept silent about the treasure's whereabouts, I never would have known for certain that your father betrayed me. Why, then, did you send for me?"

"Alford imprisoned my Uncle Morgan and told me that he would kill him if I didn't go to the Highlands and find my sister. Alford believed she had the box, and I was ordered to bring her and the treasure back to him."

John glanced at Bridgid but otherwise continued to ignore her as he defended his baron's actions. "Alford's zeal in helping me with my search for Arianna's treasure has not dimmed over the years, and I cannot fault him for going to such extremes. Besides, it appears the end might justify the means." Smiling as though he were a father explaining his precocious son's behavior, he added, "But he has his faults, and one is greed. I'm sure he wanted you to bring the treasure to him so that he could give it to me and collect the reward. I would do the same thing, and so, apparently, would you."

"My lord, I don't want a reward. Truly I don't."

"Then what do you want?"

"My Uncle Morgan is one of your faithful barons, and I ask that you protect him."

"That is all you want?"

"Yes, my lord."

The king's disposition shifted as quick as a bolt of lightning, and he was suddenly charming and solicitous. Though she had heard about his radical changes of mood, she was still caught off guard.

"I have just spoken at length with Morgan," he announced.

Gillian's voice shook when she asked, "He is well, my lord?"

"He's old and tired and making outrageous accusations, but he is well. You'll see him soon."

Tears clouded her vision. "Thank you, my lord," she whispered. "I know you are anxious to see if the treasure is here, but if I may, I would ask..."

"Yes, my dear?"

"If I'm wrong and the box isn't here, please don't take your displeasure out on my Uncle Morgan. He had nothing to do with this. I alone am responsible."

"And I should therefore turn my wrath on you?"

"Yes, my lord."

John sighed. "I have waited over fifteen years for the return of the treasure, and I find that anticipation increases my joy and my sadness. I don't want to hurry," he explained. "For the possible disappointment will be very painful for me. As for Morgan," he continued. "I assure you that even if the treasure isn't here, your uncle will still have my protection, and so shall you. Do you think me an ogre? I will not hold you responsible for your father's crimes."

Though she knew that at this moment he was sincere, she also knew how swiftly he could change his mind. She didn't dare put her faith in his promise.

"You are very kind, my lord," she whispered.

"I can upon occasion be kind," he arrogantly agreed. "Now answer a question for me."

"Yes, my lord?"

"Are you married to the giant barbarian with the long golden hair named Laird Buchanan?"

Gillian swayed. "I am his wife, my lord," she stammered. "He is here... you have seen him?"

"Aye, I've seen him," he drawled. "And he is indeed here, with two other lairds and an army at their side. The Highlanders surround Dunhanshire."

Bridgid's deep indrawn breath drew the king's attention. "I've been ignoring you far

585

too long, my dear. Forgive me my poor manners and tell me, who are you?"

"She is my dearest friend," Gillian said. "Her name is Bridgid KirkConnell."

Bridgid smiled at the king, and within a heartbeat he was smiling back. "Ah, you are the lady the Laird Sinclair has come for."

"I do belong to his clan, my lord," she whispered, nervous to have the king's undivided attention. "And I am one of his many loyal followers, but he wouldn't come all this way just for me."

The king laughed. "From the way he was ranting at me, I believe you're mistaken. I must admit the Highlanders are an impressive and intimidating lot, to be sure. When I saw them, I considered returning to London to get additional troops, and I was certainly urged to do just that by my guard," he added. "But then the three lairds separated from their men and rode hard to intercept me. It seems they had only just found out that the two of you were inside, and they were... highly agitated. I commanded them to stay outside the walls, and I will tell you that I was most unhappy when Laird Maitland dared to argue with me. When I told him that you had sent for me, and that I would not allow any harm to come to you, they grudgingly agreed to wait. Why did you come all this way, Bridgid?"

She looked at Gillian, hoping she would explain.

"Baron Alford believes Bridgid is my sister."

"But she isn't," the king said.

"No, my lord, she isn't."

"We lied to Baron Alford," Bridgid blurted. "But Gillian told me I mustn't lie to you, my lord."

The king seemed amused by Bridgid's honesty. "And she was right," he said before turning to Gillian again. "And what of your sister?"

Gillian bowed her head. "She is forever lost to us, my lord."

John nodded, accepting what she said as fact. Alford interrupted the conversation then by offering the king refreshments.

"I'll dine with you when I return."

"Return, my lord?" Alford asked.

"Yes," John answered. "Lady Gillian is going to show me where she believes Arianna's treasure is hidden. We will not know for certain that it's here until we look for ourselves."

Alford took a step toward his commander and motioned for him to come to him.

John smiled at Gillian. "Shall we go then?" he asked as he stepped back and graciously offered his arm to her.

Her hand trembled when she placed it on the king's arm. Noticing her distress, John put his hand on top of hers, gave it an affectionate pat, and commanded that she cease being afraid of him.

"You are a loyal subject, are you not?"

"Yes, my lord, I am."

"Then, as I said before, you have nothing to fear from me. Do you know, Gillian, that you remind me of her?"

587

"Your Arianna, my lord?"

His face dropped, and he became melancholy. "Aye, she was my Arianna, and though your eyes are not the same color as hers, they are as beautiful. I loved her, you know, as I have never loved any other woman. She was... perfection. I often wonder what course my life would have taken had she lived. She brought out the good in me, and when I was with her, I wanted to be... different." He sounded like a very young boy now in the throes of his first love.

The king suddenly pulled away from her and turned to Alford, for he'd only just noticed his friend was in deep discussion with one of his soldiers. John lashed out, berating the baron for his rudeness, reminding him that when he was in the room, it was the law of England that he, and only he, be the center of attention.

Having just been duly chastised, Alford bowed his head while he gave John his apology.

"What were you discussing with your soldier?" John demanded. "It must have been important for you to be so impertinent."

"Horace is one of your most loyal soldiers, and I was telling him that I would ask you if you would allow him and three other worthy men the honor of escorting you and Gillian."

With a negligible shrug, John granted permission. "We won't be gone long," he said, and then he commanded his soldiers, "All of you stay here. No one leaves this hall until I return. Bridgid, my dear, will you please wait here?"

"Yes, my lord," she replied.

Alford drew the king's attention yet again. "May I accompany you and Gillian?"

"Sit down," John commanded.

Alford didn't heed the warning in the king's voice and dared to ask a second time.

Irritated with his baron, John decided to make him suffer. "No, you may not come along," he said once again. "And while Gillian and I are taking our stroll, I suggest that you and Hugh and Edwin stay away from the open windows."

Alford looked confused by the suggestion. John chuckled as he explained. "Did I forget to mention that Dunhanshire is completely surrounded by Highlanders? Ah, I can see from your expression I did forget. How remiss of me."

"The heathens are here?" Alford's eyes bulged, and he swallowed loudly as he tried to get past his surprise.

"I just said that they were," John replied. "You do know why they've come, don't you?"

Alford feigned ignorance. "No, my lord, I don't know why. How could I?"

John grinned, enjoying his friend's discomfort. He was annoyed with Alford for being so impudent in his presence and also because of the mischief he'd caused with Baron Morgan. The king had few loyal lords now, and even though Morgan wasn't a favored baron, he was well thought of by the others, and his voice in support of John's policies could well make a difference in the future.

Alford's zeal in trying to locate Arianna's treasure had put his king in the middle of a squabble, and he planned to make his friend suffer a bit longer before he forgave him.

In truth, he would always forgive him for the simple reason that Alford had brought Arianna to him. No matter how severe his transgressions were, John would never forget that most wondrous gift.

Thinking to make him squirm now, he explained the Highlanders' mission. "Would you like me to tell you why they've come all this way?"

"If you are so inclined," Alford replied smoothly.

"They want to kill you. Let me try to remember their exact words. Ah, yes, I recall now. The tallest one... his name is Maitland. He told me he's going to tear your heart out with his bare hands and shove it down your throat. Isn't that amusing? He's big enough to do it," he added with a chuckle.

The king didn't expect an answer and continued on. "All three of the lairds were arguing—and in front of me, mind you—as to which one has the right to kill you."

Alford forced a smile. "Yes, that is amusing."

"They've also made threats against you, Edwin, and you as well, Hugh. The Buchanan laird has gotten it into his head that one of you struck Lady Gillian. He believes he now has the right to cut off the culprit's hands. Oh, he also mentioned cutting your feet off, Alford, or did I already mention that threat?"

Alford shook his head. "You should kill them for threatening your friends," Alford cried. "Aren't we loyal to each other? You and I have been through many trying times, and I have always stood by your side against your enemies, including the pope. Kill them," he demanded with a shout.

"No," Gillian cried out.

John patted her arm. "See how you have upset this dear lady? Come along, Gillian. This discussion can wait until we return, but I assure you, I have no plans to kill the lairds. Even I know that I would have every man in the Highlands at my doorstep, and I have enough disruption in my kingdom at the moment. I don't need more."

The doors were thrown open and they stepped outside. Gillian was looking down at the steps as she lifted her skirts, and when she looked up again, she came to a dead stop and gasped.

There, standing in the center of the court-yard, were Iain and Ramsey and Brodick. They were all armed, with their swords in their scabbards.

Brodick's eyes seemed to blaze with anger, and he was staring at her. She couldn't take her gaze off him, and he looked as if he couldn't wait to get his hands on her.

John had given orders that they were to remain outside the walls, and he therefore didn't know what to make of the lairds' appearance. How, then, had they gotten inside? More curious than angry, he glanced at Gillian and asked, "You willingly pledged yourself to that laird?"

"I did willingly marry him, my lord," she answered. "And I love him very much."

"Then what they say is true. Love is surely blind."

Not knowing if he was jesting and expected her to laugh, or serious and expected her agreement, she remained silent.

As she moved closer to Brodick, he shifted his position until his legs were braced apart and he took up twice the space. Iain and Ramsey immediately did the same.

Their message was clear. They weren't going to let Gillian get past them, and she knew that if she and the king tried to walk around them, they'd block them.

The rest of the king's soldiers stood in the background with their hands on the hilt of their swords, watching and waiting for John's command.

The lairds seemed impervious to the soldiers, and Gillian was frantic with worry for their safety.

"Stand down," John ordered.

"My lord, may my husband accompany us on our walk?" Gillian asked softly. "I have not seen him in a long while, and I would be happy for his company."

"You would?" John asked, grinning once again. "He doesn't look too happy to see you, Gillian. None of them do," he added. "In fact your laird wears the expression of a husband who would like to beat his wife."

"Oh, no, he would never do such a thing," she assured him. "No matter how angry he becomes, he would not even think about hurting me. They are honorable men, all of them."

John stopped directly in front of Brodick, tilted his head back so he could look into the giant's eyes, and said, "Your wife wishes you to accompany us on our stroll."

Brodick didn't say a word, but he moved back so that John and Gillian could walk past. Her hand brushed his, a deliberate touch she couldn't resist.

She knew he was right behind her now, and she was tormented with conflicting emotions. She wanted to throw herself into his arms and tell him how sorry she was because she had put him in such danger, yet at the same time she wanted to shout at him because he had lied to her and placed revenge above his own safety.

Desperate to protect him, she prayed for God's help. The king let go of her arm, and they walked side by side across the barren courtyard. She saw Horace select three men, and her uneasiness intensified. She wished that John hadn't granted Alford's request.

Alford's soldiers fell into stride behind the king. Brodick stayed behind her, his back vulnerable to attack, and her panic became nearly uncontrollable.

Out of the corner of her eye she saw another group of Alford's men rushing up the steps into the castle. John drew her attention then when he asked, "Where are you leading me?"

"We're going to the old stable, my lord. It's

593

directly behind the new building Alford built after he seized control of Dunhanshire."

"Why didn't his men simply tear down the old when they put up the new?"

"Superstition," she answered.

"Explain what you mean, and while you're at it, tell me how you determined where the treasure was hidden."

Gillian began with the night her father was killed and finished her story just as they reached the dilapidated barn.

At the king's command, one of the soldiers ran to fetch a torch. John questioned Gillian while they waited. "You still haven't explained what you meant about superstition," he reminded her.

"After Ector became crazed, the soldiers feared him, and my lady's maid told me that every time he would walk past, the soldiers would drop to their knees and make the sign of the cross to ward off his evil. She saw them do it countless times," she added. "The soldiers feared that Ector had the power to snatch their minds and make them as crazed as he was. Liese also told me the men believed that Ector was possessed by the Devil, himself, and for that reason they didn't dare touch him or touch anything that belonged to him. Ector roamed the land during the day and slept in the corner of the stable at night."

"You paint my soldiers as superstitious fools, but if you're correct in your guess, their fear kept my Arianna's treasure safe for me all these many years."

The soldier returned with the burning torch, and John motioned for him to go inside first. Gillian was suddenly so filled with trepidation she couldn't get her legs to move. *Dear God, please, please let the box be there.*

She felt Brodick's hand on her shoulder, and she swayed back against him. She stayed there for no more than a second or two, but that was all the comfort she needed, and then she straightened and followed the king inside.

She could see specks of dust spinning in the bolts of fading gray sunlight filtering in through the holes in the rafters. The light wouldn't have been sufficient without the aid of the torch. The air was as stale as death and smelled of mold and mildew, which grew stronger with each step she took.

The king stopped when he reached the center of the corridor and motioned for her to take the lead.

"It's in the corner," she said as she hurried past him. She kept her attention on the floor now. It was cluttered with decaying flats of wood and nails.

When she passed the last stall, she slowly turned to look in the corner, and then she cried out. There it was, Ector's knapsack, still hanging from the hook on the wall.

"Shall we see if the treasure is inside?" John whispered.

He moved forward with Gillian at his side and lifted the filthy knapsack from the hook, and shoving the rubble out of his way with the side of his foot, he knelt down on the floor.

The soldier, Horace, called out to him, "Is the treasure there, my lord?"

The king didn't answer. "Do you see how my hands are trembling?" he whispered to Gillian as he gently turned the knapsack over and let the contents pour out onto the floor. An old rusty, iron hinge spilled out first, and then stones of various shapes rolled out. A clump of dirt splattered, and a cracked wooden cup splintered in half when it struck the ground. The king shouted. A dirty piece of wool wrapped into a ball dropped onto his knees. As he unfolded the cloth, a man's tunic took shape, and when the last fold was turned over, the jewels atop the magnificent box glinted up at them.

Tears flooded John's eyes, and he was filled with memories of his sweet Arianna. Lost for the moment in the past, his head bowed, he mourned anew the death of his true love.

"My lord, is the treasure there?" Horace shouted again.

The king was too overwhelmed with emotion to notice the soldier's impertinence and insolent tone.

Brodick had noticed and was in the process of turning around so that his back was to his wife and the king when Horace gave the other soldiers a signal with his hand. His three cohorts quickly fanned out to form a half circle in front of Brodick. The only thing between them and the king of England was the Highlander, and fools that they were, they actually believed the odds were in their favor.

Brodick knew exactly what their plan was. His voice was low and filled with loathing when he said, "Your king is unarmed."

John, still down on his knees, looked up as the soldiers drew their swords. His eyes widened in disbelief, and for an instant he thought that the Highlander was in some way threatening him. Then he saw that Brodick's hands were still at his sides and his sword still sheathed. Where, then, lurked the threat that would make the soldiers draw their weapons?

Forgetting for the moment the treasure, John stood. "Where is the danger?" he demanded.

The soldiers remained silent.

"Gillian, tell your king his soldiers mean to kill him," Brodick said.

The leader of the soldiers smiled. "And we will be honored for our deed. Aye, we mean to kill you, John, and the Highlander and his wife as well." Nodding to Brodick, he added, "You'll be blamed of course."

John reached for his sword and only then realized he was defenseless.

"One shout from me and my men will come running."

Horace snickered. "You'll be dead before they get here."

Brodick shook his head. "I cannot allow you to kill your king because it would upset my wife, and you sure as hell aren't going to get near her. Have I made my intentions clear?"

They came at him all at once, and that error in judgment gave Brodick an added advantage. In their haste to get him, they stumbled into one another.

Moving with the speed of a predator, he became a blur to the men trying to kill him. They saw only the silver gleam of his sword and heard the whistling sound as the warrior swung it downward. His blade cut through two soldiers as he lashed out with his foot and broke the arm of another soldier, knocking him to the ground. He then arched back to avoid the last soldier's blade and, twisting, slammed his elbow into the man's face, shattering his jaw.

Gillian had grabbed hold of the king's arm and tried to pull him back out of harm's way, but John in a burst of true gallantry wouldn't retreat. He pushed her behind him and shielded her.

Before she could summon a good scream, two soldiers lay dead at Brodick's feet and the two others were doubled over in pain. Brodick wasn't even winded. He casually wiped his blade on one of the dead to rid it of English blood, then slipped the weapon back into the sheath and turned around. He couldn't hide his surprise at finding the king protecting his wife.

John was stunned. He stared at the traitors, then looked at Brodick. "Four against one," he hoarsely whispered. "Most impressive, Laird."

Brodick shrugged. "You've yet to see impressive."

A fire from a dropped torch crackled in the debris behind them as the king once again got down on his knees and gently lifted the treasure with both hands. Cautiously he pressed in sequence the hidden springs, and the box snapped open. For a long silent moment he simply stared down at what was inside.

And then a low guttural sound erupted from deep within his throat, a sound that grew into a tortured, monstrous roar that reverberated through the decay of years.

And the cry of anguish for what was lost became a howling fury.

The sound paralyzed Gillian, and it all became too much for her to bear, the heartache, the treachery, the deceit, the fear. She couldn't block the screams or the memories. And in her mind she was suddenly standing there at the top of those slippery steps in the dark passageway. The dragon was uncoiling from the wall with his long tail slashing out at her as she and Christen were hurled down into the black abyss. She was once again that terrified little girl, abandoned and all alone. She heard the anguished screams echoing around her and saw again her father looking up at her with such sorrow and regret in his eyes. He couldn't save her. She reached out...

And suddenly Brodick was there, standing in front of her, calling out to her.

"Gillian, look at me."

The tenderness in his voice and the touch of his hand against the side of her face cut through her terror, and with a sob, she fell into his arms.

"I want to go home," Gillian cried.

"Soon," he promised. "Now get behind me and stay there."

The harsh command jarred her, and she quickly did as he ordered, for she could hear the shouting soldiers running toward the stable. The smoke from the smoldering fire must have alerted them. The blaze behind her began to leap higher, and she knew that when the king's men raced inside and saw the dead soldiers, they would attack Brodick.

Turning to the king, she saw him wipe tears from his face and then snap the box closed. He wrapped the treasure in the tunic, stuffed it into the knapsack, and then staggered to his feet.

He, too, must have heard his soldiers coming because he moved to stand by Brodick. He raised his hand as his men closed in.

"Are these your men or his?" Brodick asked.

"Mine," the king answered.

His voice was deathly calm. "Come with me," he ordered Brodick, and then he left the stable.

Brodick dragged Gillian behind him, but when they reached the courtyard, he stopped and let out a shrill whistle. Dylan and Robert rode forward.

"Get her out of here," he ordered Dylan. "Robert, wait for Bridgid and take her with you."

She wasn't given time to argue. Dylan reached down, swept her up, and urged his stallion into a gallop.

"Let the Highlanders inside," John shouted to his soldiers, and then he motioned for Iain and Ramsey to follow Brodick and him inside.

Alford hadn't been idle while he had waited. He'd used the time to gather more of his soldiers, for there were at least a dozen standing together near the buttery. Brodick and Iain stood behind the king, but Ramsey spotted Bridgid sitting in the corner and immediately went to her. He grabbed her hand, jerked her to her feet, and without saying a word, pulled her along.

She was afraid to speak to him. She'd never seen Ramsey in such a fury before, and it scared her almost as much as the English barons did. He didn't say a word to Robert either, just motioned for him to take Bridgid away, and then he turned and, head down, went back inside.

The king was speaking in a low voice to Iain Maitland when Ramsey joined them. He didn't hear what John said until the king asked if it was Iain's son who was captured. Iain responded with a curt nod, and then the king put his hand out and requested the laird's sword.

"May I borrow it?"

Iain reluctantly let him have the weapon. John turned, and carrying the sword in one hand, he dangled the knapsack in the other as he slowly approached the table where Alford waited.

The baron started to stand, but John ordered him to stay seated. "This day has been filled with disappointments," he remarked, his voice as cold as a winter's eve.

"Then you didn't find the treasure after all?" Alford asked, and the smile was there in his eyes. When John didn't answer him, Alford assumed he'd been right. "Must the Highlanders be here, my lord?" he called out.

John noticed how agitated Hugh and Edwin were. They kept giving the lairds furtive glances, showing their obvious trepidation. The king glanced at Iain Maitland but the laird wasn't looking at him. Nay, his eyes seemed to glow with his hatred, and his gaze, like Laird Buchanan's, was locked on his prey.

"Do they frighten you, Alford?" John drawled as he tilted his head toward the Highlanders.

They did make Alford nervous, but he also was feeling quite smug because he knew they couldn't do him any harm. If one of them reached for his sword, his men and the king's guard would strike them down.

"No, they don't frighten me, but they are... uncivilized."

"Don't be inhospitable," John chided.

Gripping the knapsack in one hand and Iain's sword in the other, John began to slowly circle the table. "Today has brought back all the pain," he said then, and turning to the lairds, he offered an explanation. "I've only loved one woman, and her name was Arianna. My dearest friend, Alford, brought her to me and I fell instantly in love with her. I believe she loved me too," he added. "And I would have found a way to marry her."

He stopped pacing and dropped the knapsack on the table in front of Alford.

"Open it," he commanded.

Alford turned the knapsack upside down and watched the contents spill out on the table. The box rolled out of the tunic.

John told him what was inside. "My dagger is on the bottom. I sent it with the squire for Arianna to cut a lock of her golden hair. Do you remember, Alford?"

Before Alford could answer, John continued. "On top of my dagger is a lock of her hair. Tell me, Alford, what's on top of the hair?"

"I... I don't know," Alford stuttered.

"Yes you do. Your dagger."

"No, it's not mine," Alford shouted.

John slowly began to walk around the table. "No? Your crest is on the handle."

"Someone... stole my dagger... Gillian's father must have..."

John's voice lashed out like a whip. "Her father wasn't in court, but you were, Alford. You killed her."

"No, I didn't..."

John pounded the tabletop with his fist. "If you want to live, you will tell me the truth."

"If I want to live..."

"I won't kill you as long as you tell me the truth," John promised. "I want to know exactly what happened, but first you will admit it to me. You killed her, didn't you?"

"She was going to betray you," he stammered. "She wouldn't listen to my... counsel... and she was determined to come between you and your advisers. I sought only to protect my king. She had gone mad with power because she knew... yes, she knew she could control you."

"I want to know exactly what happened," the king demanded, his voice shaking with fury.

"I went to her chamber to reason with her, and she mocked me, my lord. Aye, she did. Your squire carried in the box and put it on the table. It was open and your dagger was inside. The squire didn't see me, and after he left, Arianna took your dagger and cut a lock of her hair. She put the dagger and the hair in the box—"

"And you continued to reason with her?" John demanded.

"Yes, but she wouldn't listen. She swore she wouldn't let anyone get in her way. She attacked me, and I had to defend myself."

"And so you cut her throat."

"It was an accident. I'll admit I panicked. Your squire had returned and was pounding on the door, and without thinking, I threw my dagger in the box and closed it. I was going to tell you. Yes, yes, I was," Alford cried out.

"And because you had a key to the chamber, your escape was so simple, wasn't it? You locked the door and took the box to your chamber. Is that right, Alford?"

"Yes."

"And then you consoled me when I found her body—good friend that you are."

"I was going to confess, but you were so distraught, I decided to wait."

"No, you decided to blame the Baron of Dunhanshire."

"Yes," Alford admitted, trying to sound contrite. "Gillian's father had come to my estate to discuss the common land we shared. He saw the box when he came into the hall unannounced but pretended he hadn't, and the second my back was turned, he stole it. He was going to keep it for himself," he ended.

"You didn't believe that," John muttered. "You knew he would bring it to me, didn't you, Alford? And so you lay siege to Dunhanshire and killed him to silence him."

"I had to kill Arianna," Alford repeated. "She would have destroyed you."

"Me?" the king shouted. He couldn't continue the game any longer. He stood behind Alford now and raised Iain's sword. "The Devil take you," he screamed as he thrust the blade through Alford's back.

The baron rigidly arched up and then slowly fell forward. John stepped back, his chest heaving with rage. The room was deathly quiet as John picked up the box and walked toward the door.

"Your son has been avenged," he told Iain Maitland as he motioned to his soldiers to follow him.

Hugh, who had been cowering behind the soldiers, called out to him. "My king, Edwin and I had no part in Alford's treachery."

John ignored his baron. As he was striding past the three lairds, he said, "They're all yours."

The door closed as Iain and Ramsey and Brodick slowly advanced.

CHAPTER THIRTY-NINE

Ramsey and Brodick weren't easily embarrassed or intimidated, but by the time Baron Morgan Chapman finished giving them a piece of his mind and a thorough tongue-lashing, the lairds were clearly mortified.

And men enough to admit it. Although they both wanted to argue with the crusty old man, they didn't dare because they had been taught to respect their elders, but Morgan was making it difficult for them with his wild accusations.

It seemed to take him forever to get to the heart of the matter. He stood facing the lairds with his arms folded and acted like a father who was chastising his boys. It was damned humiliating, but Ramsey and Brodick suffered through it.

"I've lived a peaceful life, but in the past two days I've heard enough wailing and carrying on by two very angry young ladies to last me a lifetime. You had the gall to dump them in my lap and send them home with me, and I swear to you my ears were ringing by the time we arrived. But did it end there?"

Ramsey made the mistake of guessing it didn't and shook his head, gaining him a scowl and a blasphemy from the cantankerous baron.

"Nay," he ranted. "The sweet lasses had only

just got started. I thought about taking to my bed, but I knew they'd follow me." Nodding to Brodick, he declared, "You've broken my Gillian's heart, and she wants never to see you again."

"Then she can keep her eyes closed, but I assure you she's going home with me."

"You married in haste."

"I knew what I wanted, and I took it."

"It? We're talking about my niece, aren't we?"

"Yes, sir, we are."

"She says you gave her your word, and then you broke it."

"Yes."

"She believes you used her."

"I did."

"Hell, man, you could at least explain why."

"You know why," Brodick countered. "I couldn't allow her to be in such danger. If anyone should be angry, it is I, for she recklessly followed me."

Morgan threaded his fingers through his white hair. "She doesn't believe you love her, and she insists she's going to live here with me."

Before Brodick could respond, the baron turned his hot temper on Ramsey. "Bridgid has also decided she wishes to stay with me. She insists she likes the English, God help me."

"She's going home with me," Ramsey announced.

"Why?"

Ramsey was surprised by the question. "Because she's a Sinclair."

"That isn't a sufficient reason. She says you keep trying to marry her off to get rid of her. She also says her mother tossed her out. Is that true?"

Ramsey sighed. "Yes, it's true."

"And aren't you doing the same thing?"

"No, I'm not," Ramsey insisted. "Bridgid told me she's in love, but she refuses to tell me who the man is."

Thoroughly exasperated, Morgan shook his head. "Did she tell you he was a stupid man?"

"As a matter of fact she did," he replied.

The baron's head dropped down, and he peered at Ramsey through his bushy eyebrows for a long, silent minute. Then he sighed. "Were you born yesterday, son? Who in God's name do you think she loves? Think hard and I'm sure it will come to you."

It wasn't what he said as much as how he said it that sparked the epiphany. The light dawned, and with it came a slow, easy smile.

Morgan nodded with relief. "So you finally figured it out, did you? And high time, if you ask me," he muttered. "If I have to suffer through another long-winded description of your charms, I swear I won't be able to keep my food in my belly. Are you going to forget this nonsense about marrying a lass named Meggan to keep peace with your clans?"

"She told you about Meggan?" Ramsey couldn't stop smiling.

"Son, I don't believe there's anything she hasn't told me about you. Have you stopped

608

being stupid then and come to your senses?"

Ramsey didn't take insult. "It seems I have," he agreed.

"She's a handful," he warned.

"Yes, sir, she is."

The baron straightened up. "Now then, I want both of you to listen carefully, because I'm going to give you my conditions."

"Your conditions, sir?" Brodick asked. He nudged Ramsey to get him to stop grinning like an idiot and pay attention. "I could use some help here," he muttered.

"My conditions," Morgan repeated. "Do you think I want to be saddled with two lovesick women?"

"Then let us take them," Brodick reasoned.

The suggestion earned him another glare. "I can see from the look in your eyes that you love Gillian. You might want to tell her so, son, and soon, because she's gotten it into her head that you don't care about her at all."

"She's my wife. Of course I care about her."

The baron snorted. "She's spirited."

"Yes, she is."

"And stubborn. I don't know where she comes by that flaw, but she is."

"Yes, sir."

"You won't be able to crush her spirit."

"I don't want to, sir."

"Good, because if there's any crushing to be done, she'll be doing it. I don't have to tell you to treat her well because knowing my

Gillian, she'll make sure that you do. She's a strong woman, but she's got tender feelings."

"Sir, you mentioned conditions?" Ramsey reminded him.

"Yes, I did," he replied. "I love my niece," he declared. "And I've taken a fancy to Bridgid as well. I won't have her thinking I'm tossing her out. I am," he hastily added, "but I won't have her thinking it. The way I see it..."

"Yes?" Ramsey asked when the baron hesitated.

"You've got to... encourage... them to leave. I won't have you threatening them," he added. "You broke their hearts; now you mend them."

After giving them the impossible command, Morgan left the hall to personally fetch the ladies. Ramsey and Brodick paced while they waited.

"The baron reminds me of someone, but I can't quite put my finger on who it is," Ramsey remarked.

"I swear my own father never talked to me the way Gillian's uncle just did."

"Your father died before you were old enough to know him."

"It was humiliating, damn it. He sure as certain wasn't what I expected. The way Gillian talked about him, I pictured a mild-mannered gentleman. She thinks he's... gentle. Is the woman blind? How in God's name can she love such a crotchety old..."

Ramsey's head snapped up, and he suddenly burst into laughter, breaking Brodick's train of thought. "It's you."

"What?"

"Morgan... he reminds me of you. My God, Gillian married a man just like her uncle. Look at the baron and you'll see yourself in twenty years."

"Are you suggesting I'm going to become a belligerent, foul-tempered old man?"

"Hell, you're already belligerent and foul-tempered. No wonder she fell in love with you," he drawled.

"I'm not in the mood to fight."

Ramsey slumped onto a chair laughing, then abruptly grew serious again.

"I cannot believe Bridgid thinks she's going to stay here."

"I expected my wife to welcome me with open arms, and she hasn't even come downstairs. If I have to drag her home, I will," Brodick said.

"You wished to see me, Laird?"

At the sound of Bridgid's voice, both Ramsey and Brodick turned. "Where's my wife?" Brodick demanded.

"Upstairs," she answered. "She should be down shortly."

"Could you give us some privacy?" Ramsey asked. "I was speaking to Brodick, not you, Bridgid. Come back here."

With a sigh she turned around and walked to Ramsey as Brodick left the room. He leaned against the table, folded his arms across his chest, and smiled at her. She didn't smile back. She bowed her head so she wouldn't be distracted by his adorable dimples.

She was acting shy and timid, and he wondered what game she was playing now because he knew Bridgid didn't have a timid bone in her beautiful body.

"Baron Morgan said you wanted to speak to me."

"Yes," he answered. "I have something important to say to you, but first, I want you to tell me how you managed it."

"Managed what, Laird?"

"Bridgid, look at me."

"Yes, Laird," she said, bracing herself. She looked up, and still her heart raced, and she got that familiar tingling feeling in her stomach. If he ever kissed her, she'd probably faint, she thought, and that ludicrous image made her calm down just a little.

"Have I said something amusing?"

"Yes... I mean, no, of course you haven't."

"Then why are you smiling?"

She lifted her shoulders. "Would you like me to stop?"

"For God's sakes, Bridgid," he said. "Pay attention."

"I am paying attention."

"I want to know how you managed to get all the way to England without being stopped or killed."

She thought about the question a long minute before answering. "I used trickery and deceit."

"I want a better explanation."

"All right," she agreed. "I tricked Proster into believing Gillian needed to see Annie

612

Drummond, and when we were on our way, I told him the truth. I hope you don't blame him or Ker or Alan. Gillian and I refused to go back."

"And because they're so young, they didn't know they should have dragged you back home no matter how much you argued with them."

"They shouldn't be punished."

"I have no intention of punishing them. They stayed by your side and did their best to protect you, and for that they'll be rewarded. You didn't make their duty easy."

"I hope you won't blame Gillian either," she implored. "She kept trying to get us to go home, but we wouldn't listen to her."

"Why did you sneak away from the soldiers and follow her inside Dunhanshire?"

"I thought I could help by pretending to be her sister, but as it turned out, I became a hindrance. Laird, may I ask you something?"

"What is it?"

"What happened to all of the soldiers and the servants at Alford's estate? Uncle Morgan's servants returned here, but what about the others?"

"I imagine they're back at the holding by now, waiting to serve a new baron. We don't kill the innocent."

"And the soldiers?"

"They weren't innocent."

He refused to elaborate and Bridgid didn't think she needed to know the gruesome particulars anyway. "Will you be going home soon?" she asked then.

"Yes."

She nodded. "Good journey to you, then." And with that she tried to leave.

"We aren't finished yet."

"What more do you want from me?"

"More? I haven't asked anything of you yet... have I?"

She shook her head.

"Come closer, Bridgid."

"I'm fine where I am."

"Come closer," he commanded, and there was a thread of steel in his voice now.

She wasn't going to miss his bossiness, she decided as she walked forward. She stopped directly in front of him. "Is this satisfactory?"

"Closer," he ordered.

She moved to stand between his outstretched legs. "Is this close enough for you?"

"For the moment."

He was obviously enjoying her discomfort, and she was thoroughly confused. Ramsey seemed to be toying with her, and that didn't make any sense at all. He couldn't possibly know what agony it was for her to be so close to him and not touch him. God, how she wished she didn't love him. It was misery. Just thinking about watching him leave made her want to weep, but she vowed she'd die before he saw one tear.

"Uncle Morgan said you wanted to tell me something. What is it?"

"Uncle Morgan? When did he become a relative?"

Her chin came up a notch. "I've become very close to him."

He rolled his eyes. "You aren't staying here. That's what I wanted to tell you."

"I've made up my mind to stay."

"Then unmake it. You're going home with me."

Bridgid was suddenly so angry with him for being such a stupid, obstinate man, her temper exploded.

"No, I'm not going back. I'm staying right here. Uncle Morgan said that I could. I like England, Laird. Yes, I do. You and all the other soldiers blatantly lied to me. You made England sound like purgatory, but I found out the truth. The land is as beautiful as ours, and the people are just like us. I'll admit they're a little difficult to understand because of the way they speak, but I'm getting used to it. Do you know how many Englishmen helped Gillian and me on our journey here? Hundreds," she exaggerated. "Families who could ill-afford to share insisted that we take their food and their blankets. They even offered us their beds. They looked out for us, and we were strangers to them. All those stories were just lies. I like this country, and I like Gillian's uncle. He's kind and sweet."

The last of her tirade made him laugh. "You think Morgan's kind and sweet?"

"Yes," she insisted. "And he likes me too."

"But you're a Sinclair."

"There's nothing for me there."

"What about the man you told me you loved?"

She took a step back, but Ramsey grabbed

her and pulled her close to him. She tried to look everywhere but at him so she could concentrate.

"I don't love him anymore," she declared.

"What the hell do you mean you don't love him anymore? Are your feelings so shallow, then, Bridgid?"

"No," she answered. "I loved him for the longest time, since I was a little girl, but now I realize he's completely unsuitable."

Ramsey didn't like hearing that. "What exactly is unsuitable about him?"

"Everything," she cried out. "He's obstinate and arrogant and very stupid. Yes, he is. He's a womanizer too, and the man I marry will be faithful to me. I'm not going to waste my time on him any longer. Besides, he can have any woman he wants. They throw themselves at his feet," she added with a nod. "And he's completely unaware of me."

"Ah, Bridgid, he's very aware of you."

"The man doesn't even care that I exist."

Ramsey smiled. "Of course he cares."

She pushed his hands away, but Ramsey caught her about her waist and began to slowly pull her up against him.

"What are you doing?"

"What I've wanted to do for a long time."

She couldn't move, couldn't think. She was lost in his dark eyes, and as he slowly lowered his head toward hers, she whispered, "Are you going to throttle me, then?"

He was laughing when he kissed her. Lord, she had the softest, sweetest lips, and he felt such incredible joy and peace holding her in his arms. His mouth opened over hers, taking absolute possession. His tongue swept inside to lazily mate with hers, and he was taking his time savoring her taste, believing he was in full control, until she began to kiss him back.

She shook him to the core. Ramsey had never experienced anything like it. His arrogance and his control vanished, and he was shaking with desire. It happened so swiftly, he had trouble catching his breath. His mouth slanted over hers again and again and passion ignited. He couldn't get close enough to her to satisfy him.

When he realized he was trying to justify tossing her on the table and making love to her then and there, he forced himself to stop. They were both panting for breath when he lifted his head.

She was having as much trouble regaining her senses as he was. She actually swayed when she took a step back. "Why did you kiss me?"

"I wanted to," he answered, his voice as smooth as velvet.

"Were you... Was it... a farewell kiss? Were you saying good-bye?"

He laughed. "No," he answered. "You're going home with me."

"I'm staying here. I'm going to marry an Englishman."

"The hell you are," he roared, and he was more stunned than she was by his burst of temper. No woman had ever been able to get that kind of reaction from him, but the thought of his Bridgid with any other man enraged him.

"You're a Sinclair, and you belong with us."

"Why do you want me to go back?"

For the first time in his life, Ramsey felt thoroughly vulnerable. It was a hell of a miserable feeling. "You want the truth, Bridgid?" he stalled.

"Yes."

Their gazes held while Ramsey got up the courage to tell her what was in his heart.

"You make the Sinclair land a joyful place. I cannot imagine life without you."

She shook her head. "No, you just want to marry me to some—"

He stood up and took a step toward her. "There has been a request for your hand in marriage."

"Is that why you kissed me? So you could take me home and then marry me to a man I don't love? Who is he?" she demanded, emotionally spent now and uncaring that tears were streaming down her face.

He started toward her.

"Don't you dare kiss me again," she ordered. "I can't think when you... Just don't," she stammered. "And as for the offer, I decline."

"You can't decline until you know who he is," he reasoned.

"All right. Tell me his name, and then I'll decline. You're going to praise him first though, aren't you? That's what you always do to try to get me to agree," she ended, and even she could hear the heartbreak in her voice.

"No, I'm not going to praise him. He's riddled with flaws."

She stopped trying to run away. "He is?"

He slowly nodded. "I have it on good authority that he's stupid and arrogant and obstinate, or at least he was until he realized what a fool he has been."

"But that's what I said about... you."

"I love you, Bridgid. Will you marry me?"

Brodick didn't know what the hell he was going to do. He felt as though his hands were tied behind his back because Morgan was his elder and he therefore couldn't browbeat him into ordering Gillian to go home with her husband, and he sure as certain couldn't tear the man's home apart searching for her. At the root of his frustration lurked the dark possibility that Gillian would never forgive him for breaking his word to her, but life without her at his side would be unbearable.

Ramsey might have been able to help him sway the baron—he was the diplomat, after all—but he was too busy wooing Bridgid to think about anything else. It had taken him a good hour to convince her he was sincere and determined to marry her, and after she had finally agreed to his proposal, they'd left for home. Iain hadn't stayed around to help either, as he was anxious to get back to his wife.

And that left Brodick to deal with the bad-tempered baron on his own.

Morgan was vastly amused when Brodick didn't eat any of his supper. Just as he finally made up his mind to help the poor, lovesick man, Morgan spotted Gillian coming down the stairs.

Brodick's back was to the entrance, and Morgan knew he hadn't spotted his wife.

"Son, you had to have known how stubborn Gillian was before you married her. Anyone who spends more than five minutes with the woman figures that out."

"I knew she was stubborn," Brodick agreed. "But I don't consider that a flaw."

"I think you should leave her here and go on home. You'll be better off."

Brodick was shocked by the obscene suggestion. "I don't have a home without her," he muttered. "How could you think I would leave her?"

"I would," Morgan replied cheerfully. "Tell me, why did you break your word to her?"

"I've already explained why," he snapped.

Morgan snapped back. "Explain it again."

"Because the thought of her in danger was unacceptable to me. I cannot lose her."

"Then don't ever lie to me again."

The sound of her voice made his heart feel as though it were about to burst with joy. He sighed, calm now, for his world suddenly made sense to him again. And then he turned around. "Don't you ever put me through this torment again," he ordered.

"Promise me that you will never lie to me again."

"Not until you promise me that you'll stop taking such foolish risks. When Proster told me you were inside with that bastard, I thought I was going to... damn it, you scared the hell out of me, Gillian, and I never want to go through that again."

"You hurt me."

"I know."

"That's all you have to say? You know you hurt me? Then I'm staying here. Go home, Brodick."

"Fine," he answered. Bowing to Baron Morgan, he walked out of the hall. She waited until the doors had closed behind him and then burst into tears.

"He's leaving me," she cried as she ran to her uncle.

"You just told him to leave," he pointed out.

"He's going home without me."

"But you just told him to," he argued. "I heard you plain and clear."

"But he never does what I tell him to do. Uncle, how am I going to live without him?"

He awkwardly patted her back, trying to console her. "You'll do just fine."

"I love him so much."

"But he lied to you, remember?"

"He was only trying to be noble. He wanted to protect me."

"Then why didn't you forgive him?"

"I was going to forgive him," she sobbed. "I don't want to live without him. How could he leave me?"

"You're giving me a pounding headache, lass.

Sit down and calm yourself," he suggested as he pulled a chair out and gently pushed her down. "Let me go look out the window and see if he's left yet."

"I cannot believe he would leave me," she whispered.

Morgan rolled his eyes heavenward and prayed for patience. Was his niece blind? Couldn't she see how much her husband loved her? He was too old and cranky to deal with a near hysterical woman, and he decided then that matters of the heart should be left to the young. They had more stamina.

He watched Brodick remove the saddle from his horse and toss it to one of his men. All of his soldiers had dismounted and were making themselves at home in his yard. When Brodick started back to the castle, Morgan decided to go upstairs. He'd had enough excitement for one day, and Gillian and her husband needed privacy.

"I'll be right back," he lied. "You stay where you are and wait for me," he hastily added so she wouldn't get the notion she could follow him the way she used to and drive him daft with her complaints until he gave in to whatever it was she wanted. He smiled when he realized she was more stubborn and strong-willed than he was.

Pausing at the entrance, he called out, "You know I love you, girl, don't you?"

"Yes, I know. I love you too, Uncle Morgan."

He started up the stairs then, but stopped when he heard the door open behind him. He didn't have to turn around to know who was there.

"You'll treat her well." It wasn't a question but a statement of fact.

"Yes, sir, I will."

"You don't deserve her."

"I know I don't, but I'm keeping her anyway."

"You know, son, you remind me of someone, but I can't think who it is." He shook his head in bewilderment and then suggested, "You'd best get on inside before she floods my hall with her tears. If anyone could do it, she could."

At the sound of her uncle's laughter, she glanced up and saw Brodick standing in the entrance, watching her. She stood up then and took a step toward him.

"You came back."

"I never left."

As though drawn by a magnet, they moved toward one another.

"You were angry with me. I saw it in your eyes."

"Yes, I was angry. I didn't know if I could keep you safe, and that scared the hell out of me."

He was close enough to take her into his arms, but he didn't dare touch her yet because he knew that once he started kissing her, he wouldn't stop, and he needed to mend the hurt he had caused her. Telling her what was in his heart seemed so easy to him now, and he couldn't understand why he'd been such a fool. Love didn't weaken a man; it strengthened him, made him feel invincible when he had a woman like Gillian at his side.

"I thought you went home."

"How could I go home without you? I've searched my entire life for you. I could never leave you. Home is wherever you are." His hand shook as he gently caressed the side of her face. "Don't you understand? I love you, and I want to wake up with you beside me every morning for the rest of my life. If that means I have to live in England to be with you, then that's what I'll do."

Tears of joy brimmed in her eyes. She was overwhelmed by the depth of his feelings for her and the tender, romantic way he'd told her how he felt.

She knew it was difficult for him. He hid his feelings behind his gruff exterior. She realized then she knew him better than he knew himself. It didn't matter that he'd broken out in a cold sweat or that he looked quite ill now; he'd given her what she needed. Aye, he'd said the words, and he couldn't take them back.

"Say it again," she whispered.

Gritting his teeth, he did as she asked. "I'll live in England."

She blinked. "What?"

"Ah, love, don't make me say it again. If it makes you happy, we'll live here."

She knew he meant it and was staggered by the sacrifice this dear, gentle man was willing to make for her. Lord, she needed to kiss him, but she decided to put him out of his misery first.